To
FRED

I've learned
alot from
you &
consider
your friendship
invaluable

A. Stolly

The New Adventures of

SHERLOCK HOLMES

Original Stories by Eminent Mystery Writers

Edited by Martin Harry Greenberg and
Carol-Lynn Rössel Waugh

Carroll & Graf Publishers, Inc.
New York

Carroll & Graf Publishers, Inc.
260 Fifth Avenue
New York, NY 10001

Library of Congress Cataloging-in-Publication Data

The New adventures of Sherlock Holmes.

1. Detective and mystery stories, American.
2. Detective and mystery stories, English. 3. Holmes,
Sherlock (Fictitious character)—Fiction. 4. Doyle,
Arthur Conan, Sir, 1859–1930—Parodies, imitations, etc.
I. Greenberg, Martin Harry. II. Waugh, Carol-Lynn
Rössel.
PS648.D4N47   1987   813'.0872'08351   87-15873
ISBN 0-88184-344-X

Manufactured in the United States of America

A STUDY IN SCARLET.

PART I.

(Being a reprint from the reminiscences of JOHN H. WATSON, M.D., *late of the Army Medical Department.)*

CHAPTER I.

MR. SHERLOCK HOLMES.

N the year 1878 I took my degree of Doctor of Medicine of the University of London, and proceeded to Netley to go through the course prescribed for surgeons in the army. Having completed my studies there, I was duly attached to the Fifth Northumberland Fusiliers as Assistant Surgeon. The regiment was stationed in India at the time, and before I could join it, the second Afghan war had broken out. On landing at Bombay, I learned that my corps had advanced through the passes, and was already deep in the enemy's country. I followed, however, with many other officers who were in the same situation as myself, and succeeded in reaching Candahar in safety, where I found my regiment, and at once entered upon my new duties.

The campaign brought honours and promotion to many, but for me it had nothing but misfortune and disaster. I was removed from my brigade and attached to the Berkshires, with whom I served at the fatal battle of Maiwand. There I was struck on the shoulder by a Jezail bullet, which shattered the bone and grazed the subclavian artery. I should have fallen into the hands of the murderous Ghazis had it not been for the devotion and courage shown by Murray, my orderly, who threw me across a pack-horse, and succeeded in bringing me safely to the British lines.

Worn with pain, and weak from the prolonged hardships which I

I

Facsimile of the first page of *A Study in Scarlet* published one hundred years ago in *Beeton's Christmas Annual*. (By courtesy of The Mary Kahler & Philip S. Hench Collection).

Publisher gratefully acknowledges the editorial assistance of Bluejay Books, Inc.
The Publisher wishes to thank Andrew Peck for his assistance in collecting the artwork reproduced in the work.

CONTENTS

FOREWORD

The late Sir Arthur Conan Doyle, the creator of Sherlock Holmes, wrote four novels and fifty-six short stories about the great detective, beginning with "*A Study in Scarlet*" first published one hundred years ago in *Beeton's Christmas Annual* for 1887. Taking the world by storm in the 1890s and the early years of the 20th century, Sherlock Holmes quickly became the point of departure for the vast volume of mystery fiction to come, and he remains the ultimate standard against which other detectives in literature are measured today. This collection of new Sherlock Holmes stories by well-known British and American mystery writers, an unprecedented form of homage by modern masters of Sir Arthur's craft, has been commissioned and compiled with the approval and consent of Dame Jean Conan Doyle, Sir Arthur's daughter and his surviving heir.

Jon Lellenberg,
on behalf of the estate
of Sir Arthur Conan Doyle.

221 B
(1887–1987)

Coin of ours can never ransom
Years now prisoner to Time:
Roars the bus, where once the hansom
Trotted on the trial of crime.
No more now a Stradivarius
Played by fingers long and fleet
Sounds the dirge of plans nefarious
Foiled by Him of Baker Street.

Could we, with an eye clairvoyant,
Find the dear remembered door,
Which, with trembling, many a client
(Fair or famous) stood before?
Here it was that Roylott forced an
Entry, like some savage bear;
Here, bright eyes of Mary Morstan
Fell to Watson's ardent stare.

Were a time-restoring charter
Granted by the grace of Heaven,
Who would not this tired age barter
For a night of 'eighty-seven,
When, as fog through pane and curtain
Softly grey comes creeping in,
Wise—immortal—strange and certain—
Sherlock plays his violin.

© MOLLIE HARDWICK
1987

The New Adventures of
SHERLOCK HOLMES

THE INFERNAL MACHINE

John Lutz

Illustration by Sidney Paget of a scene from *The Boscombe Valley Mystery* in "The Strand Magazine" 1891.

Not that, at times, my dear friend and associate Sherlock Holmes can't play the violin quite beautifully, but at the moment the melancholy, wavering tunelessness produced by the shrill instrument was getting on my nerves.

I put down my copy of the *Times*. "Holmes, must you be so repetitious in your choice of notes?"

"It's in the very repetition that I hope to find some semblance of order and meaning," he said. He held his hawkish profile high, tucked the violin tighter beneath his narrow chin, and the screeching continued— certainly more piercing than before.

"Holmes!"

"Very well, Watson." He smiled and placed the violin back in its case. Then he slumped into the wing chair opposite me, tamped tobacco into his clay pipe, and assumed the attitude of a spoiled child whose mince pie has been withheld for disciplinary purposes. I knew where he'd turn next, after finding no solace in the violin, and I must confess I felt guilty at having been harsh with him.

When he's acting the hunter in his capacity as consulting detective, no man is more vibrant with interest than Holmes. But when he's had no case for some weeks, and there's no prospect of one on the horizon, he becomes zombielike in his withdrawal into boredom. It had been nearly a month since the successful conclusion of the case of the twice-licked stamp.

Holmes suddenly cocked his head to the side, almost in the manner of a bird stalking a worm, at the clatter of footsteps on the stairs outside our door. From below, the cheerful voice of Mrs. Hudson wafted up, along with her light, measured footfalls. A man's voice answered her pleasantries. Neither voice was loud enough to be understood by us.

"Visitor, Watson." Even as Holmes spoke there was a firm knock on the door.

I rose, crossed the cluttered room, and opened it.

"A Mr. Edgewick to see Mr. Holmes," Mrs. Hudson said, and withdrew.

I ushered Edgewick in and bade him sit in the chair where I'd been perusing the *Times*. He was a large, handsome man in his mid-thirties, wearing a well-cut checked suit and polished boots that had reddish mud on their soles. He had straight blond hair and an even blonder brush-trimmed mustache. He looked up at me with a troubled expression and said, "Mr. Holmes?"

I smiled. "You've recently come from Northwood," I said. "You're unmarried and are concerned about the well-being of a woman."

Holmes, too, was smiling. "Amazing, Watson. Pray tell us how you did it."

"Certainly. The red clay on Mr. Edgewick's boots is found mainly in Northwood. He's not wearing a wedding ring, so he isn't married. And since he's a handsome chap and obviously in some personal distress, the odds are good there's a young woman involved."

Holmes's amused eyes darted to Edgewick, who seemed flustered by my incisiveness.

"Actually," he said, "I am married—my ring is at the jewelers being resized. The matter I came here about only indirectly concerns a woman. And I haven't been to Northwood in years."

"The hansom cab you arrived in apparently carried a recent passenger from Northwood," Holmes said. "The mud should dry on this warm day as the hansom sits downstairs awaiting your return."

I must admit my mouth fell open, as did Edgewick's. "How on earth did you know he'd instructed a hansom to wait, Holmes? You were nowhere near the window."

Holmes gave a backhand wave, trailing his long fingers. "If Mr. Edgewick hasn't been to Northwood, Watson, the most logical place for him to have picked up the red mud is from the floor of the hansom cab."

Edgewick was sitting forward, intrigued. "But how did you know I'd arrived in a hansom to begin with, and instructed the driver to wait downstairs?"

"Your walking stick."

I felt my eyebrows raise as I looked again where Edgewick sat. "What walking stick, Holmes?"

"The one whose tip left the circular indentation on the toe of Mr. Edgewick's right boot as he sat absently leaning on it in the cab, as is the habit of many men who carry a stick. The soft leather still maintains the impression. And since he hasn't the walking stick with him, and his footfalls on the stairs preclude him from having brought it up with him to leave outside in the hall, we can deduce that he left it in the hansom. Since he hardly seems a careless man, or the possessor of a limitless number of walking sticks, this would suggest that he ordered the cab to wait for him."

Edgewick looked delighted. "Why, that's superb! So much from a mere pair of boots!"

"A parlor game," Holmes snapped, "when not constructively applied." Again his slow smile as he made a tent with his lean fingers and peered over it. His eyes were unwavering and sharply focused now. "And I suspect you bring some serious matter that will allow proper application of my skills."

"Oh, I do indeed. Uh, my name is Wilson Edgewick, Mr. Holmes."

Holmes made a sweeping gesture with his arm in my direction. "My associate, Dr. Watson."

Edgewick nodded to me. "Yes, I've read his accounts of some of your adventures. Which is why I think you might be able to help me—rather help my brother Landen, actually."

Holmes settled back in his chair, his eyes half closed. I knew he wasn't drowsy when he took on such an appearance, but was in fact a receptacle for every bit of information that might flow his way, accepting this as pertinent, rejecting that as irrelevant— acutely alert.

"Do tell us about it, Mr. Edgewick," he said.

Edgewick glanced at me. I nodded encouragement.

"My brother Landen is engaged to Millicent Oldsbolt."

"Oldsbolt Munitions?" Holmes asked.

Edgewick nodded, not surprised that Holmes would recognize the Oldsbolt name. Oldsbolt Limited was a major supplier of small arms for the military. I had, in fact, fired Oldsbolt rounds through my army revolver while in the service of the Queen.

"The wedding was to be next spring," Edgewick went on. "When Landen, and myself, would be financially well-off."

"Well-off as a result of what?" Holmes asked.

"We're the English representatives of one Richard Gatling, the inventor of the Gatling gun."

I couldn't help but ask, "What on earth is that?"

"It's an infernal machine that employs many barrels and one firing chamber," Holmes said. "The cartridges are fed to the chamber by means of a long belt, while the barrels revolve and fire one after the other in rapid succession. The shooter need only aim generally and turn a crank with one hand while the other depresses the trigger. It's said the Gatling gun can fire almost a hundred rounds per minute. It was used in the Indian Wars in America, on the plains, with great effectiveness."

"Very good, Mr. Holmes!" Edgewick said. "I see you're well versed in military ordnance."

"It sounds a fiendish device," I said, imagining those revolving barrels spewing death to man and beast.

"As war itself is fiendish," Holmes said. "Not at all a game. But do continue, Mr. Edgewick."

"Landen and I were staying at the King's Knave Inn in the town of Alverston, north of London. To be near the Oldsbolt estate. You see, we were trying to sell the idea of the Gatling gun to Sir Clive Oldsbolt for manufacture for the British forces. The gun had passed all tests, and Sir Clive had offered a price I'm sure the American manufacturer would have accepted."

Holmes pursed his thin lips thoughtfully, then said, "You speak often in the past tense, Mr. Edgewick. As if your brother's wedding has been canceled. As if now Oldsbolt Limited is no longer interested in your deadly gun."

"Both those plans have been dealt the severest blow, Mr. Holmes. You see, last night Sir Clive was murdered."

I drew in my breath with shock. Holmes, however, leaned forward in his chair, keenly interested, almost pleased. "Ah! Murdered how?"

"He was returning home late from the King's Knave Inn, alone in his carriage, when he was shot. A villager found him this morning, after hearing the noise last night."

Holmes's nostrils actually quivered. "Noise?"

"Rapid gunfire, Mr. Holmes. Shots fired in quick, rhythmic succession."

"The Gatling gun."

"No, no. That's what the chief constable at Alverston says.

But the gun we used for demonstration purposes had been cleaned and not fired again. I swear it! Of course, the local constabulary and villagers all say that Landen cleaned it after killing Sir Clive.''

"Your brother has been arrested for his future father-in-law's murder?'' I asked in astonishment.

"Indeed!'' Edgewick said in great agitation. "That's why I rushed here after he was taken into custody. I thought only Mr. Holmes could make right of such a mistake.''

"Does your brother Landen have any motive for murdering his fiancée's father?''

"No! Quite the opposite! Sir Clive's death means the purchase of the Gatling gun manufacturing rights has been canceled. As well, of course, as Landen and Millicent's wedding. And yet . . .''

Holmes waited, his body perfectly still.

"Yet, Mr. Holmes, the sound the villagers in the inn described could be none other than the rattling, measured firing of the Gatling gun.''

"But you said you examined it and it hadn't been recently fired.''

"Oh, I'll swear to that, Mr. Holmes—for all the good it will do poor Landen.''

"Perhaps a different Gatling gun.''

"There is no other in England, Mr. Holmes. Of that you can be sure. We crossed the Atlantic just last week with this one, and Mr. Gatling knows the whereabouts of all his machines. Understand, sir, this is a formidable weapon that threatens the very existence of nations if in the wrong hands. It will change the nature of warfare and isn't to be taken lightly.''

"How many times was Sir Clive shot?'' Holmes asked.

"Seven. All through the chest with large-caliber bullets, like those fired by the Gatling gun. The village doctor removed the two bullets that didn't pass through Sir Clive, but they became misshapen when striking bone, so their precise caliber can't be determined.''

"I see. It's all very interesting.''

"Will you come at once to Alverston, Mr. Holmes, and determine what can be done for my brother?''

"You *did* say Sir Clive had been shot seven times, Mr. Edgewick?''

"I did.''

Holmes stood up from the wing chair as abruptly as if he'd

been stuck by a cushion spring. "Then Watson and I shall take the afternoon train to Alverston and meet you at the King's Knave Inn. Now, I suggest you return to your brother and his fiancée, where you're no doubt sorely needed."

Edgewick smiled broadly with relief and stood. "I intend to pay you well, Mr. Holmes. Landen and I are not without means."

"We'll discuss all that later," Holmes said, placing a hand on Edgewick's shoulder and guiding him to the door. "In the meantime, tell your brother that if he's innocent he need have no concern and might well outlive the hangman."

"I'll tell him that, Mr. Holmes. It will comfort him, I'm sure. Good day to both of you." He went out the door, burst back in momentarily, and added, "Thank you, Mr. Holmes! For me and for Landen!"

Holmes and I stood listening to his descending tread on the stairs.

Holmes parted the curtain and looked after our visitor as he emerged onto Baker Street. The shouts of vendors and the clattering of horses' hooves drifted into the room, along with the pungent smells of London. "An extremely distressed young man, Watson."

"Indeed, Holmes."

He rubbed his hands together with a glee and animation that would have been impossible to him fifteen minutes ago. "We must pack, Watson, if we're to catch the afternoon train to Alverston." His gaunt face grew momentarily grave. "And I suggest you bring along your service revolver."

I had fully intended to do that. Where a member of nobility is shot seven times on his way from inn to home, any act of the direst nature might be possible.

The King's Knave Inn was but a short distance from the Alverston train depot, just outside the town proper. It was a large tudor structure, bracketed by huge stone chimneys, one at each end of its steeply pitched slate roof.

Wilson Edgewick wasn't among the half-dozen local patrons seated at small wooden tables. A beefy, red-faced man, with a thinning crop of ginger hair slicked back on his wide head, was dispensing drinks, while a fragile blond woman with a limp was carrying them to the tables.

I made arrangements for satisfactory rooms while Holmes surveyed the place. There was a young man seated at a nearby table, looking disconsolate, as if he were too far into his cups. Two old-timers—one with a bulbous red nose, the other with a sharp gray hatchetlike face—sat at another table engrossed in a game of draughts. Three middle-aged men of the sort who work the land sat slumped about a third table, their conversation suspended as they mildly observed us.

"Now, you'd be Mr. Holmes, the famous detective," the red-faced pub owner, whose name was Beech, said to Holmes with a tinge of respect as he studied the guest register I'd signed; "or my guess'd be far wrong." Alcohol fumes wafted on his breath.

Holmes nodded. "I've enjoyed my share of successes."

"Look just like your pictures drawed in the *Daily Telegraph,* you do."

"I find them distinctly unflattering."

One of Beech's rheumy eyes was running, and he swiped at it with the back of his hand as he said, "Don't take a detective to know why you're here, though."

"Quite so," Holmes said. "A tragic affair."

"Weren't it so!" Beech's complexion got even ruddier, and a blue vein in his temple began a wild pulsation. A conspiratorial light entered his eyes. He sniffed and wiped again at the watery one. "We heard it all here, Mr. Holmes. Witnesses to murder, we was, here at the inn."

"How is that?" asked Holmes, much interested.

"We was standing here as we are now, sir, late last night, when we heard the infernal machine spitting its death."

"The Gatling gun?"

"That's what it was." He leaned forward, wiping his strong, square hands on his stained apron. "A sort of 'rat-a-tat-tat-tat,' it was." Spittle flew as he described the sound of the repeating-fire gun. "Well, we'd heard the gun fired before and knew the noise right off, sir. But not from that direction." He waved a hand toward the north. "In the morning, Ingraham Codder was on the north road to go and see Lord Clive at the house. Instead he sees one of the lord's gray geldings and the fine two-hitch carriage the lord comes to town in. The other gelding somehow got unhitched and was standing nearby. Lord Clive himself was slumped down in the carriage dead. Shot full of holes, Mr. Holmes. Seven of 'em, there was."

"So I've heard. Did anyone else here this 'rat-a-tat-tat' sound?" Holmes managed to describe the gunfire without expectorating.

"All three of us did," spoke up one of the farmers at the table. "It was just as Mr. Beech described."

"And what time was it?" Holmes asked.

"Half past eleven on the mark," Beech said. "Just about ten minutes after poor Sir Clive left here after downing his customary bit of stout." The patrons all agreed.

The young man alone at his table gazed up at us, and I was surprised to see that he wasn't as affected by drink as I'd assumed by his attitude. His gray eyes were quite clear in a well-set-up face; he had a firm jawline and a strong nose and cheekbones. "They've got Sir Clive's murderer under lock," he said. "Or so they say."

"And you are, sir?" Holmes asked.

"He's Robby Smythe," Beech cut in. "It's horseless carriages what's his folly. If you can imagine that."

"Really?" Holmes said.

"Yes, sir. I have two of them that I'm improving on and will soon manufacture and sell in great numbers, Mr. Holmes. In ten years everyone in England shall drive one."

I couldn't contain myself. "Everyone? Come now!"

Holmes laughed. "Not you, Watson, not you, I'd wager."

"Young Robby here's got a special interest in seeing justice done," Beech said. "He's engaged to Sir Clive's youngest daughter, Phoebe."

"Is he now?" Holmes said. "Then you know the Edgewick brothers, no doubt."

Smythe nodded. "I've met them both, sir."

"And would you say Landen Edgewick is capable of this act?"

Smythe seemed to look deep into himself for the answer. "I suppose, truth be told, under certain circumstances we're all capable of killing a man we hate. But no one had reason to hate Sir Clive. He was a kind and amiable man, even if stern."

"Point is," Beech said, "only the Edgewick brothers had knowledge and access to the Gatling gun. I say with the law that Landen Edgewick is the killer."

"It would seem so," Holmes acknowledged. "But why Landen Edgewick? Where was Wilson?"

Beech grinned and swiped again at the watery eye. "Up in his room at the top of them stairs, Mr. Holmes. He couldn't have had a fig to do with Sir Clive's murder. Had neither the time nor the opportunity. I came out from behind the serving counter and seen him step out of his room just after the shots was fired. He came down then and had himself a glass of stout. We told him we'd heard the gun, but he laughed and said that was impossible, it was locked away in the carriage house him and his brother had borrowed out near Sir Clive's estate." He snorted and propped his ruddy fists on his hips. "Locked away, my eye, Mr. Holmes!"

"Very good, Mr. Beech," Holmes said. "You remind me of my friend Inspector Lestrade of Scotland Yard."

Looking quite pleased, Beech instructed the waitress and maid, Annie, to show us to his best rooms.

Wilson Edgewick arrived shortly thereafter, seeming over-joyed to see us. He was, if anything, even more distraught over the plight of his brother. He had been to see Landen's fiancée Millicent Oldsbolt, the daughter of the man his brother had allegedly murdered, and the meeting had obviously upset him. A wedding was hardly in order under the circumstances.

Wilson explained to us that Landen had arrived here from London two days before he and had taken up lodgings at the inn. The brothers had declined an invitation to stay at the Oldsbolts' home, as they had final adjustments and technical decisions to make preparatory to demonstrating the Gatling gun to Sir Clive.

The night of the murder, from Wilson's point of view, was much as had been described by Beech and the inn's patrons, though Wilson himself had been in his room at the precise time of the shooting and hadn't heard the gun.

"The next morning, after Sir Clive's body was found," he said, "I hurried directly to the carriage house. The Gatling gun was there, mounted on its wagon, and it hadn't been fired since the last test and cleaning."

"And did you point this out to the local constable?" Holmes asked.

"I did, after Landen was taken in for the crime. Chief Constable Roberts told me there'd been plenty of time for him to have cleaned the Gatling gun after Sir Clive had been shot, then return on the sly to his room. No one saw Landen until the morning after the murder, during which he claimed to have been asleep."

Holmes paced slowly back and forth, cupping his chin in his hand.

"What, pray God, are we going to do?" Wilson blurted out, unable to stand the silence.

Holmes stood still and faced him. "Watson and I will un-pack," he said, "then you can take us to examine the scene of Sir Clive's murder, and to talk to the victim's family."

The rest of that afternoon was spent gathering large as well as minute pieces of information that might mean little to anyone other than Sherlock Holmes, but which I'd seen him time and again use to draw the noose snug around those who'd done evil. It was a laborious but unerringly effective process.

We were driven out the road toward Sir Clive's estate, but our first stop was where he'd been killed.

"See this, Watson," Holmes said, hopping down out of the carriage. "The road dips and bends here, so the horses would have to slow. And there is cover in that thick copse of trees. A perfect spot for an ambush."

He was right, of course, in general. The rest of the land around the murder scene was almost flat, however, and any hidden gunman would have had to run the risk that someone in the vicinity might see him fleeing after the deed was done.

I got down and stood in the road while Holmes wandered over and examined the trees. He returned walking slowly, his eyes fixed to the ground, pausing once to stoop and drag his fingers along the earth.

"What's he looking for?" Wilson Edgewick whispered.

"If we knew," I told him, "it wouldn't mean much to us."

"Were any spent cartridges found?" Holmes asked Edgewick, when he'd reached us. He was wiping a dark smudge from his fingers with his handkerchief.

"No, Mr. Holmes."

"And the spent shells stay in the ammunition belt of the Gatling gun rather than being ejected onto the ground after firing?"

"Exactly. The belts are later refitted with fresh ammunition."

"I see." Holmes bent down suddenly. "Hello. What have we here, Watson?" He'd withdrawn something small and white almost from beneath my boot.

I leaned close for a better look. "A feather, Holmes. Only a white feather."

He nodded, absently folding the feather in his handkerchief and slipping it into his waistcoat pocket. "And here is where the body was found?" He pointed to the sharp bend in the road.

"Actually down there about a hundred feet," Edgewick said. "The theory is that the horses trotted on a ways after Sir Clive was shot and the reins were dropped."

"And what of the horse that was found standing off to the side?"

Edgewick shrugged. "It had been improperly hitched, I suppose, and worked its way loose. It happens sometimes."

"Yes, I know," Holmes said. He walked around a while longer, peering at the ground. Edgewick glanced at me, eager to get on to the house. I raised a cautioning hand so he wouldn't interrupt Holmes' musings. In the distance a flock of wrens rose from the treetops, twisting as one dark form with the wind.

After examining the murder scene we drove to the carriage house and saw the Gatling gun itself. It was manufactured of blued steel and smelled of oil and was beautiful in a horrible way.

"This shouldn't be allowed in warfare," I heard myself say in an awed voice.

"It is so terrible," Edgewick said, "that perhaps eventually it will eliminate warfare as an alternative and become the great instrument of peace. That's our fervent hope."

"An interesting concept," Holmes said. He sniffed at the clustered barrels and firing chambers of the infernal machine. Then he wiped from his fingers some gun oil he'd gotten on his hand, smiled, and said, "I think we've seen quite enough here. Shall we go on to the house?"

"Let's," Edgewick said. He seemed upset as well as impatient. "It appears that progress will be slow and not so certain."

"Not at all," Holmes said, following him out the door and waiting while he set the lock. "Already I've established that your brother is innocent."

I heard my own intake of breath. "But Holmes—"

"No revelations yet," Holmes said, waving a languid hand. "I merely wanted to lessen our young friend's anguish for his brother. The explanation is still unfolding."

When we reached the house we were greeted by Eames the butler, a towering but cadaverously thin man, who ushered us into the drawing room. The room took up most of the east wing of the rambling, ivy-covered house, and was oak-paneled and well furnished with comfortable chairs, a game table, a Persian carpet, and a blazing fire in a ponderous stone fireplace. French doors opened out onto a wide lawn.

Wilson Edgewick introduced us around. The delicately beautiful but sad-eyed woman in the leather chair was Millicent, Landen's fiancée. Standing by the window was a small, dark-haired girl of pleasant demeanor: Phoebe Oldsbolt, Millicent's younger sister and Robby Smythe's romantic interest. Robby Smythe himself lounged near the stone fireplace. Standing erectly near a sideboard and sipping a glass of red wine was a sturdily built man in tweeds who was introduced as Major Ardmont of the Queen's Cavalry.

"Sir Clive was a retired officer of cavalry, was he not?" Holmes asked, after offering his condolences to the grieving daughters of the deceased.

"Indeed he was," Ardmont said. "I met Sir Clive in the service at Aldershot some years ago, and we served together in Afghanistan. Of course, that was when we were both much younger men. But when I cashiered out and returned from India, I heard the news that Sir Clive had been killed; I saw it as my duty to come and offer what support I could."

"Decent of you," I said.

"I understand you were a military man, Dr. Watson," Ardmont said. He had a tan skin and pure blue, marksman's eyes that were zeroed in on me. That look gave me a cold feeling, as if I were quarry.

"Yes," I said. "Saw some rough and tumble. Did my bit as a surgeon."

"Well," Ardmont said, turning away, "we all do what we can."

"You and Doctor Watson must move from the inn and stay here until this awful thing is settled!" Millicent said to Holmes.

"Please do!" her sister Phoebe chimed in. Their voices were similar, high and melodious.

"I'd feel better if you were here," Robby Smythe said. "You'd afford the girls some protection. I'd stay here myself, but it would hardly be proper."

"You live at the inn, do you not?" Holmes asked.

"Yes, but I don't know what it is those fools heard. I was in my shop working on my autocar when the shooting occurred."

Holmes stared at Major Ardmont, who looked back at him with those unrattled blue eyes. "Major, you hardly seem old enough to have just retired from service."

"It isn't age, Mr. Holmes. I've been undone by an old wound, I'm afraid, and can no longer sit a horse."

"Pity," I said.

"I understand," Holmes said, looking at Millicent, "that Eames overheard your father and Landen Edgewick arguing the evening of the murder."

"That's what Eames said, Mr. Holmes, and I'm sure he's telling the truth. At the same time, I know that no matter what their differences, Landen wouldn't kill my father—nor anyone else!" Her eyes danced with anger as she spoke. A spirited girl.

"You haven't answered us, Mr. Holmes," Phoebe Oldsbolt said. "Will you and Dr. Watson accept our hospitality?"

"Kind of you to offer," Holmes said, "but I assure you it won't be necessary." He smiled thinly and seemed lost for a moment in thought. Then he nodded, as if he'd made up his mind about something. "I'd like to talk with Eames the butler, and then spend a few hours in town."

Millicent appeared puzzled. "Certainly, Mr. Holmes. But you and Dr. Watson shall at least dine here tonight, I insist."

Holmes nodded with a slight bow. "It's a meal I anticipate with pleasure, Miss Oldsbolt."

"As do I," I added, and followed Holmes toward the door.

Outside, while waiting for the buggy to be brought around, Holmes drew me aside.

"I suggest you stay here, Watson. And see that no one leaves."

"But no one seems to have any intention of leaving, Holmes."

He gazed skyward for a moment. "Have you noticed any wild geese since we've been here, Watson?"

"Uh, of course not, Holmes. There are no wild geese in this part of England in October. I know; I've hunted in this region."

"Precisely, Watson."

"Holmes—"

But the coachman had brought round the buggy, and Holmes had cracked the whip and was gone. I watched the black, receding image of the buggy and the thin, erect figure on the seat. As they faded into the haze on the flat landscape I thought I saw Holmes lean forward, urging the mare to go faster.

When Holmes returned later that evening, and we were upstairs dressing for dinner, I asked him why he'd gone into town.

"To talk to Annie," he told me, craning his lean neck and fastening his collar button.

"Annie?"

"The maid at the King's Knave Inn, Watson."

"But what on earth for, Holmes?"

"It concerned her duties, Watson."

There was a knock on the door, and Eames summoned us for dinner. I knew any further explanation would have to wait for the moment when Holmes chose to divulge the facts of the case.

Everyone who had been in the drawing room when we'd first arrived was at the table in the long dining hall. The room was high-ceilinged and somewhat gloomy, with wide windows that looked out on a well-tended garden. Paintings of various past Oldsbolts hung on one wall. None of them looked particularly happy, perhaps because of the grim commerce the family had long engaged in.

The roast mutton and boiled vegetables were superb, though the polite dinner conversation was commonplace and understandably strained.

It was afterward, in the oak-paneled drawing room where we were enjoying our port, that Millicent Oldsbolt said, "Did you make any progress in your trip to town, Mr. Holmes?"

"Ah, yes," Major Aldmont said, "did you discover any clues as to the killer's identity? That's what you were looking for, was it not?"

"Not exactly," Holmes said. "I've known for a while who really killed Sir Clive; my trip into town was in the nature of a search for confirmation."

"Good Lord!" Ardmont said. "You've actually known?"

"And did you find such confirmation?" Robby Smythe asked, tilting forward in his chair.

"Indeed," Holmes said. "One might say I reconstructed the crime. The murderer lay in wait for Sir Clive in a nearby copse of trees, saw the carriage approach, and moved into sight so Sir Clive would stop. With very little warning, he shot Sir Clive, emptying his gun to be sure his prey was dead."

"Gatling gun, you mean," Major Ardmont said.

"Not at all. A German Army sidearm, actually, of the type that holds seven rounds in its cylinder."

"But the rapid-fire shots heard at the inn!" Robby Smythe exclaimed.

"I'll soon get to that," Holmes said. "The murderer then made his escape, but found he couldn't get far. He had to return almost a mile on foot, take one of Sir Clive's horses from the carriage hitch, and use it to pull him away from the scene of the crime."

Robby Smythe tilted his head curiously. "But why would Landen—"

"Not Landen," Holmes cut him off. "Someone else. The man Eames only assumed it was Landen when he heard a man arguing with Sir Clive earlier that evening. Landen was where he claimed to be during the time of the murder, asleep in his room at the inn. He did *not* later return unseen through his window as the chief constable so obstinately states."

"The constable's theory fits the facts," Major Ardmont said.

"But I'm telling you the facts," Holmes replied archly.

"Then what shooting did the folks at the inn hear?" Millicent asked.

"They heard no shooting," Holmes said. "They heard the

rapid-fire explosions of an internal combustion engine whose muffling device had blown off. The driver of the horseless carriage had to stop it immediately lest he awaken everyone in the area. He then returned to the scene of the murder and got the horse to pull the vehicle to where it could be hidden. Then he turned the animal loose, knowing it would go back to the carriage on the road, or all the way here to the house."

"But who—"

Phoebe Oldsbolt didn't get to finish her query. Robby Smythe was out of his chair like a tiger. He flung his half-filled glass of port at Holmes, who nimbly stepped aside. Smythe burst through the French doors and ran toward where he'd left his horseless carriage alongside the west wing of the house.

"Quick, Holmes!" I shouted, drawing my revolver. "He'll get away!"

"No need for haste, Watson. It seems that Mr. Smythe's tires are of the advanced pneumatic kind. I took the precaution of letting the air out of them before dinner."

"Pneumatic?" Major Ardmont said.

"Filled with atmosphere under pressure so they support the vehicle on a cushion of air," Holmes said, "as you well know, Major."

I hefted the revolver and ran for the French windows. I could hear footsteps behind me, but not in front. I prayed that Smythe hadn't made his escape.

But he was frantically wrestling with a crank on the front of a strange-looking vehicle. It's motor was coughing and wheezing but wouldn't supply power. When he saw me, he gave up on the horseless carriage and ran. I gave chase, realized I'd never be able to overtake a younger man in good condition, and fired a shot into the air. "Halt, Smythe!"

He turned and glared at me.

"I'll show you the mercy you gave Sir Clive!" I shouted.

He hesitated, shrugged, and trudged back toward the house.

"Luckily, the contraption wouldn't start," I said, as we waited in the drawing room for Wilson Edgewick to return with the Chief Constable.

"I was given to understand the horseless carriage can be driven slowly on deflated tires," Holmes said, "but not at all with this missing." He held up what looked like a length of stiff black cord. "It's called a spark wire, I believe. I call removing it an added precaution."

Everyone seemed in better spirits except for Robby Smythe and Phoebe. Smythe appealed with his eyes to the daughter of the man he'd killed and received not so much as a glance of charity.

"How could you possibly have known?" Millicent asked. She was staring in wonder at Holmes, her fine features aglow, now that her world had been put back partly right.

Holmes crossed his long arms and rocked back on his heels while I held my revolver on Smythe.

"This afternoon, when Watson and I examined the scene of the murder, I found a feather on the ground near where the body was discovered. I also found a black sticky substance on the road."

"Oil!" I said.

"And thicker than that used to lubricate the Gatling gun, as I later ascertained. I was reasonably sure then that a horseless carriage had been used for the murder, as the oil was quite fresh and little had been absorbed into the ground. The machine had to have been there recently. When Smythe here tried to make his escape after shooting Sir Clive, the muffling device that quiets the machine's motor came off or was blown from the pressure, and the hammering exhaust of the internal combustion made a noise much like the rapid-fire clatter of the Gatling gun. Which led inn patrons to suppose the gun was what they'd heard near the time of the murder. Smythe couldn't drive his machine back to its stall in such a state, and couldn't silence it, so he had one of Sir Clive's horses pull him back. If only the earth hadn't been so hard, this would all have been quite obvious, perhaps even to Chief Constable Roberts."

"Not at all likely," Millicent said.

"It was Smythe whom Eames overheard arguing with Sir Clive," Holmes continued. "And Major Ardmont, who is a member of the German military, knows why."

Ardmont nodded curtly. "When did you realize I wasn't one of your Cavalry?" he asked.

"I knew you were telling the truth about being in the cavalry, and serving in a sunny clime," Holmes said, "but the faint line of your helmet and chinstrap on your sunburned forehead and face doesn't conform to that of the Queen's Cavalry helmet. They do suggest shading of the helmet worn by the German horse soldier. I take it you received your sun-darkening not in India but in Africa, in the service of your country."

"Excellent, Mr. Holmes!" Ardmont said, with genuine admiration. "Mr. Smythe," he said, "had been trying to convince Sir Clive to get the British military interested in his horseless machine as a means to transport troops or artillery. A hopeless task, as it turned out, with an old horseman like Sir Clive. Smythe contacted us, and introduced me to Sir Clive. He told Sir Clive that if the British didn't show interest in his machines, he'd negotiate with us. And we were quite willing to negotiate, Mr. Holmes. We Germans do feel there's a future for the internal combustion engine in warfare."

I snorted. Much like a horse. I didn't care. The image of a thousand sabre-waving troops advancing on hordes of sputtering little machines seemed absurd.

"Sir Clive," Ardmont went on, "showed his temper, I'm afraid. He not only gave his final refusal to look into the idea of Smythe's machine, he absolutely refused to have as his son-in-law anyone who would negotiate terms with us. Possibly that's what the butler overheard in part, thinking Sir Clive was referring to Landen Edgewick and Millicent rather than to Mr. Smythe and Phoebe."

"Then you were with Sir Clive and Smythe when they clashed," I said, "yet you continued to let the police believe it was Landen Edgewick who'd had the argument."

"Exactly," Major Ardmont said. "To see Mr. Smythe off to the hangman wouldn't have given Germany first crack at a war machine, would it?"

"Contemptible!" I spat.

"But wouldn't you do the same for your country?" Ardmont asked, grinning a death's head grin.

I chose not to answer. "The feather?" I said. "Of what significance was the feather, Holmes?"

"It was a goose feather," Holmes said, "of the sort used to stuff pillows. I suspected when I found it that a pillow had been used to muffle the sound of the shots when Sir Clive was killed. Which explains why the actual shots weren't heard at the inn."

"Ah! And you went into town to talk to Annie, then."

"To find out if she'd missed a pillow from the inn lately. And indeed one had turned up missing—from Robby Smythe's room."

"An impressive bit of work, Mr. Holmes," Ardmont said. "I'll be leaving now." He tossed down the rest of his port and moved toward the door.

"He shouldn't be allowed to leave, Holmes!"

"The good major has committed no crime, Watson. English

law doesn't compel him to reveal such facts unless questioned directly, and what he knew about the argument had no exact bearing on the crime, I'm afraid.''

"Very good, Mr. Holmes," Ardmont said. "You should have been a barrister.''

"Lucky for you I'm not," Holmes said, "or be sure I'd find some way to see you swing alongside Mr. Smythe. Good evening, Major.''

Two days later, Wilson and Landen Edgewick appeared at our lodgings on Baker Street and expressed appreciation with a sizable check, a wedding invitation, and bone-breaking hand-shakes all around. They were off to Reading, they said, to demonstrate the Gatling gun to the staff of British Army Ordnance Procurement. We wished them luck, I with a chill of foreboding, and sent them on their way.

"I hope, somehow, that no one buys the rights to their weapon," I said.

"You hope in vain," Holmes told me, slouching deep in the wing chair and thoughtfully tamping his pipe. "I'm afraid, Watson, that we're poised on the edge of an era of science and mechanization that will profoundly change wartime as well as peacetime. It mightn't be long before we're experimenting with the very basis of matter itself and turning it to our own selfish means. We mustn't sit back and let it happen in the rest of the world, Watson. England must remain in the forefront of weap-onry, to discourage attack and retain peace through strength. Enough weapons like the Gatling gun, and perhaps war will become untenable and a subject of history only. Believe me, old friend, this can be a force for tranquillity among nations.''

Perhaps Holmes is right, as he almost invariably is. Yet as I lay in bed that night about to sleep, never had the soft glow of gaslight, and the clatter of horses' hooves on the cobblestones below in Baker Street, been so comforting.

THE FINAL TOAST

Stuart M. Kaminsky

Illustration by Frederic Dorr Steele of a scene from *The Adventure of the Golden Pince-Nez* in "Collier's" 1903.

Holmes was not himself that night.

Some time before dawn on a weekday morning in the winter of 189__, he burst through the door of our lodgings at 221B Baker Street, London West. Without removing his coat, he sat opposite me in a straight-backed wooden chair and looked about as if he were seeing the room for the first time. I must confess that I had been dozing in my armchair over an article in *The Lancet* on treatment of infection from saber wounds. It was not that the article had failed to hold my interest but that I had pondered over it beyond the moment when I could muster sufficient energy to rouse myself and prepare for bed. I remember telling myself that I would simply close my eyes for a few minutes and then, refreshed, awaken to prepare myself for a comfortable night's sleep.

When Holmes came through the door, my eyes shot open and I experienced a moment of confusion.

"Holmes," I said reaching down to retrieve *The Lancet* from the floor where it had fallen, "I thought you were on your way to Glasgow, thought you'd almost be there by now."

Holmes sat back in the shadows of the final embers of the fire, which I'd stoked halfway through the article that had been my undoing. With his fingers forming a temple before his face, he stared at me in a way that I found quite unnerving. In the half-light, his features looked a trifle too sharp, his voice sounded a bit too precise, as if he had been tightened by some Godlike puppet master. My face or manner must have betrayed me, for Holmes said,

"What is it, John? You look as if you've seen . . ."

"Nothing, Holmes. Nightmare. Surprise at seeing you, that's all."

Holmes rose suddenly, removed his coat and dropped it on the chair.

"A good cigar, John. Shall we smoke in the darkness while I tell you of the singular adventure that began this morning?"

"Well . . . yes," I agreed, as Holmes moved to the humidor. It was on the mantle next to his unanswered correspondence, which was secured to the dark wood by a jackknife. He opened the humidor and rattled the empty can.

"It seems," he said wearily, "that we will have to forgo the pleasure of tobacco."

"Pity," I said with a yawn, "but you have never been particularly dependent upon the weed in any case. I'd offer you some cigarettes, but since you never . . ."

"Quite true," he agreed returning to the chair as I rose rather languidly. "I'd like to get to the heart of my misadventure. As you know, I received a letter imploring me to come to Glasgow immediately, and in the letter . . ."

". . . was a ticket for the morning train and a sum in cash," I said rummaging around the room for something I urgently wanted to show him.

"Seventy pounds," he said. "A somewhat odd sum. But the letter was urgent."

"And," I added, finding what I was looking for in a drawer near the window, "the puzzle posed rather intriguing."

"Rather," he agreed watching my movements. "John. You appear a bit nervous. Would you like me to make some tea before I go on? This might well make one of your more interesting tales about my exploits."

"Sorry, Holmes," I said returning to my chair with my hands snugly in the pockets of my purple Randipur smoking jacket. "I'm sorry, there is nothing remaining from dinner for you to eat. I had no idea you were coming back. There are half a dozen eggs left on the sideboard, but I know how you dislike . . ."

A look of distinct distaste came over his sharp features, as if he had smelled something foul.

"I can do without the residue of barnyard fowl," he said.

"Shall I tell you of the case or not? I must say, John, you seem oddly preoccupied whereas I anticipated that you would be agog over this condundrum."

"You have no idea of how intrigued I am by your where-abouts this day," I said sitting up. "But may I first ask you what I believe to be a most important question?"

"Ask away, my dear fellow," he said brushing his hair back with his palm.

With that, I rose, removed the Webley handgun from my pocket, and aimed it squarely at his chest.

"Who are you?" I asked.

His face was lighted from below by the final embers of the fire. The last remnant of coal cracked and crackled, but I did not look away or flinch. I hoped I looked as unworldly to him as he did to me.

"Who am . . . Good Lord, John, how much have you had to drink? I'm Sherlock."

"Sherlock Holmes does not refer to himself as Sherlock," I said evenly. "Sherlock Holmes never calls me John. Sherlock Holmes knows full well that the cigars are kept, not in the humidor, but in the coal-scuttle. Sherlock Holmes has a passion for eggs. Sherlock Holmes would not refuse cigarettes when he was involved in a case. In fact he would accept any form of tobacco."

"Pray, continue," the man said, eyeing my weapon carefully and returning to the chair on which he had draped his coat.

"The light is poor, but your nose it a bit too sharp, your hair a bit too dark, your cheeks a jot too full and there's something . . ."

"About the way I walk and talk," he said.

"That also," I agreed, backing away. "You are a devilish approximation, I'll admit, but I know Holmes too well and I've seen through your sham. Now tell me what has become of the real Holmes or I shall fire upon you with no hesitation."

I expected many things, a lie, a confession, a warning, but I did not expect him to do what he did next. He laughed. The laugh was deep, quite natural. His hands clasped in front of him.

"You missed several things, Watson," he said. "For exam-ple, most people walk listing to one side or the other depending on which hand they favor. It is a slight thing in all save the elderly. We are often aware of it in others without consciously knowing that we are aware. I have made it my business to be consciously aware of such things. What others carelessly call instinct, I know to be unconscious observation. Thus, though you have not been consciously aware of it, you know that I normally walk without listing in either direction. That list, by the way, is what causes men lost in the desert to wander in circles. Actually, the diameter of the circle of a wandering man, judged by his footprints in the desert or on a moor, should be enough to tell you his approximate age and height. It can certainly tell you if he is right-handed or left-handed. General Kitchener . . ."

"Rubbish," I said, holding up my weapon. "You'll not get by on such rubbish. Where is Holmes?"

"I also put lifts in both my shoes to give me an extra quarter-inch over my normal height," he went on, walking to the Persian slipper on the table and filling the pipe he had removed from his pocket with tobacco stored in the slipper's toe. "The weapon you are holding is a 2 ½-inch barrel, .442 model 1872. It has no ejector rod. Spent cases are removed by removing the cylinder entirely, a rather cumbersome method which makes the weapon a chore to fire and clean. You don't wish the boredom of cleaning such a weapon and, as I know, you've never fired it and possibly are not even sure if a spent round now resides in each chamber. Are you satisfied, Watson?"

"Not in the least," I said. "But I am impatient and concerned about Holmes."

"Then let me put your final fears to rest, my friend," he said, and with that he removed something from the bridge of his nose, removed two small balls from his mouth, wiped his face with a handkerchief from his coat pocket and sat down to light his pipe.

"Holmes," I cried, "what is going on? What is the point of this bizarre charade?"

"Put away your gun, throw a few more coals on the fire, and pour some tea," he said comfortably. "And then I will explain."

Holmes, for I now knew him to be Holmes, began by removing a neatly folded sheet of paper from his vest pocket as I carefully placed the coals on the fire. When I had turned from the fire, which crackled suddenly to life again, I wiped my hands on the rag we kept near the mantle and took the sheet from his outstretched hand.

"It's a newspaper clipping," I said, folding it open with my back to the fire so I could read by the resurgent flame. I had moved to turn on the gas lamp but Holmes had stopped me.

Holmes puffed at his pipe and nodded before speaking.

"An advertisement from *The Thespian Chronicle*," he explained, looking not at me but into the fire. "Are you familiar with the publication, Watson?"

"Can't say that I am," I said, trying to read the fine print.

"It is a monthly publication, four sheets devoted primarily to advertisements for theatrical professionals, musical acts, touring players, stage hands, the like," he said. "I might have missed this piece, though I occassionally scan the publication, were it not for one of the Baker Street Irregulars, a rather clever lad named Chaplin whose parents are in the theater. Little Charlie has a sharp eye. Read what he directed to me."

The ad was simple:

"Wanted. For one morning's work. Excellent pay. Discrete actor who can impersonate a well known London consultant. Applicants should be slightly over six feet, quite lean, with sharp, piercing eyes and a thin, hawklike nose. Chin should be prominent and with a squareness which marks the man of determination. Appear at 13 Bellowdnes Road at 7 A.M. sharp, Monday."

When I looked up, Holmes was puffing away and staring at the fire.

"Well?" I said, handing him back the clipping which he took and replaced in his pocket without looking up.

"What do you make of the advert, Watson?"

"Make of it? Someone wants an actor for a sham of some kind and I suppose you want me to observe that the actor being sought bears a resemblance to you."

"Watson, that description is taken directly from your very first published tale chronicling my endeavors. Whoever wrote that hoped that those who answered it would know they were to engage in portraying Sherlock Holmes. The fact that my name is not mentioned, that the pay is to be high and that it is a singular job suggests . . ."

". . . a possible nefarious purpose," I supplied, "but it could also be some kind of a prank or even a promotion for some public house. It could be many things."

"It could be many things," Holmes agreed, "but when we combine the ad with the letter urging me to an intrigue in Glasgow—an intrigue which would have me on a train away from London at the moment my double was to be chosen, and the following morning when, I assume, he was to be used—and we have a very promising situation."

"Promising indeed," I agreed, sitting back in my chair to face him, "but promising of what?"

"That was what I determined to discover," Holmes said, his face covered by a soft gray puff of smoke. "I told you and Mrs. Hudson that I was on my way to Glasgow. I even went to the station, boarded the train and traveled one stop, on the chance that I was being watched. I then hurried back by coach to audition for the role of Sherlock Holmes. I might add that it was the most difficult deception of my career. I've been many things, a drunken groom, an aged Italian, a simple-minded clergyman, but to be myself was the ultimate challenge."

"I can't see why," I said. "You simply . . ."

"Nothing simple about it all all," he cut in. "I had to assume that whoever placed that ad knew what Sherlock Holmes looked like, had probably even seen me, watched me closely. So I had to resemble myself but not be myself. Imagine for a moment, Watson, that you had to masquerade as John Watson, M.D. What would you alter? Are you aware of how you walk? How you cock your head to the right when you are puzzled, as you are doing now?"

I straightened my head and nodded, seeing the problem he laid before me.

"Can you alter your speech slightly but not too much? And how do you alter it without losing the resemblance to yourself?"

"I find this all very confusing Holmes," I admitted. "Why not simply go to the address and confront whoever was there? I would gladly have joined you."

"And we would have discovered nothing," he sighed. "When we walked through the door, whoever was there would almost certainly have a covering story, a lame one perhaps, but no law has been broken. No, if I was to discover what this was about I would have to play the role. Besides, the suggestion of illegality in the ad, the fact that my name was not mentioned, and the fact that such steps had been taken to get me out of London convinced me that a crime was in the offing."

"And so you donned the disguise," I said.

"And so I did," Holmes agreed.

"I arrived at Bellowdnes Road just before seven," Holmes went on, looking into the fire as if he were seeing again the events of that morning. "There were two others seeking the role. The first was obviously ill-suited for the part, much too tall and not only thin but tuberculer. Of the three of us, judging by his cough and threadbare coat, he was most in need of employment. The other aspirant was closer to the mark, somewhat better dressed and about my height, but his nose would never do . . . too flat, obviously the result of several years of professional pugilism. We stomped in the cold early morning till the door opened and we were led in by a woman who kept her face covered with a shawl as if she were suffering from a cold."

"And she was not," I said.

"Decidedly not," Holmes agreed. "We were lead into a stark parlor where a man sat behind a table. The man and woman, who never identified themselves, questioned us, had us walk around, dismissed the emaciated actor after giving him a sovereign for his trouble and interrogated the former pugilist and I rather closely. For a few moments it seemed well within the realm of possibility that I would not be awarded the role of Sherlock Holmes. The other fellow was quite good, and I had to be careful not to betray myself."

"What finally got you the role?" I asked, assuming that Holmes did, indeed, receive the part.

"My thinly veiled zeal to do whatever had to be done, whether it be legal or not. When asked about our backgrounds, the pugilist erred in the direction of good citizenship. I, on the other hand, hinted at brushes with the law of which I preferred not to converse."

"And so," I said, urging him on. "You got the part."

"Let us say that I proved to be the most appropriate actor for the role," he said, and then paused to look at the bowl of his pipe. Outside, the clop-clop of a horse and coach some distance away punctuated our silence.

"All right, Holmes, for God's sake, what did they want of you, or of the impersonator of Sherlock Holmes?" I finally asked. My irritation had several causes, the tension of the situation, the late hour, a winter's twinge around the war wound in my leg. I threw the remnant of my cigar into the fire where the orange flames wrapped around it.

"Let me make you some tea, Watson. You seem particularly on edge this evening." Holmes began to rise but I waved him back.

"Just tell me what happened," I urged, "and then I'll go to bed."

"To bed," he said, looking first at me and then toward the

window beyond which the sound of the horse and cab were drawing closer. "I'm afraid not. I believe before the hour of seven I shall be in need of your able assistance. To answer your question, when the other thespian had departed, I was questioned further about my willingness to engage in less than legal acts and then informed that I was simply to dress like Holmes in clothes which would be provided—the very clothes I am now wearing."

"They do look like those you normally wear," I admitted.

"I was to go to Dartmoor Prison in the morning, just before seven, and deliver to prisoner Malcom Bell a small vial hidden in the cuff of my coat. The man and woman said that as Holmes I would certainly be admitted to see Bell and that Bell would be expecting me."

"But you are responsible for Bell's being in Dartmoor and his awaiting execution," I said.

"Precisely," Holmes went on. "The scheme is brilliant. Who better to make a delivery to a condemned man than the person who put him behind bars."

"Bell vowed to kill you," I reminded him.

"Yes," agreed Holmes. "I've grown devilishly hungry. I believe you do have something left from . . ."

I got up and hurried to the sideboard where some scones and a small brick of cheese sat covered by a white cloth. I carried the small platter to Holmes, who put aside his pipe and began to eat. Between bites he went on.

"I was told by the couple that my visit to Bell would be an act of mercy. Bell would be hanged on Tuesday morning, publicly hanged, and a man of his ego . . ."

"Who had been responsible for the deaths of six people," I put in.

". . . would prefer to thwart the hangman," Holmes continued. "The vial, they said, contained a strong, tasteless poison, which Bell would welcome. My pay was to be twenty-five pounds immediately and an additional twenty-five upon completion of the job. The final payment would be made at the same address where the audition took place."

"I see," I said.

"Do you, Watson? Capital. It took me a while to see."

With this Holmes popped a piece of cheese into his mouth and magically produced a small vial which he held between thumb and forefinger. By the light of the dancing flames, the vial seemed particularly menacing, as if the amber liquid within it were alive with virulence. Holmes eyed me momentarily and then flipped off the cork top of the small glass container. Before I could move, he put the vial to his lips and downed the contents.

I gasped and started out of the chair.

"Holmes, what kind of insanity is this?"

Holmes smiled up at me, replaced the cork and handed the vial to me.

"Watson, kindly refill this vial with claret. We may have some use for it."

"I must say, Holmes," I said, taking the vial. "That was a poor jest. You've obviously already removed the original contents and replaced them with some harmless concoction to stage this musical hall turn."

I looked at the vial and at my friend with what I hoped was the stern rebuke of an injured relative.

"No, Watson, I assure you. The liquid I just downed was the same as that given to me by the man and the woman this morning. I did, I confess, open the vial earlier to smell and taste the contents. It was claret with more than a touch of quinine."

It was then that I realized the room was growing brighter. The sun was coming up. I walked, vial in hand, to the table near the window, where a decanter of claret stood alongside an identical decanter of sherry.

"You have been hired for fifty pounds to deliver a harmless drink to a condemned man?" I asked as I carefully poured the claret.

"No, the total cost, including the train ticket to Glasgow and the retainer for the mystery I was supposed to solve there, is closer to one hundred pounds."

"To deliver . . ."

". . . Sherlock Holmes into the hands of the man who has vowed to kill him," he said. "Malcom Bell has studied me well. He used his two accomplices to lure me into the challenge of playing myself. He knew I could not resist. I'd have arrived here much earlier, but I first tracked down the boy, Chaplin, who readily admitted that, while he recognized me in the description in the advertisement, the ad had been brought to his attention by an actor, a tall, thin man with a flat nose, who had simply commented in Chaplin's presence that he was going to try for the role."

"The man who almost won the role, the pugilist," I cried. "What an extraordinary coincidence."

"Coincidence? Hardly. Charles Chaplin was chosen to bring the bait to me. I have no doubt that the pugilist followed him to our apartments to be sure he delivered the paper. Had he failed to do so, I am sure they would have found another, perhaps less subtle, means of bringing the ad to my attention. Remember, Watson, Bell has had nothing to do for the past three weeks while awaiting execution, other than to plan his revenge. Now, may I suggest that you load your Webley and come with me."

"To Dartmoor?" I said, moving to retrieve the pistol.

"To Bellowdnes Road," he corrected. "After we take care of the tall gentleman who is certainly lurking somewhere on the street to be sure that I appear at Dartmoor and that the show go on."

Less than fifteen minutes later, Holmes went out to the street and moved to the corner. I watched from the window in the growing light. Holmes was dressed warmly for the chill morning. As he turned the corner, a figure stepped from a passageway below and moved in his direction. I hurried to the door and down to the street to follow the man. We wandered the streets, a strange trio playing follow the leader, with Holmes in front. We met few on the streets, except for those slouching to early jobs and a handful of deliverymen. One drayman's cart, carrying coal, scuttled down the cobbled street as Holmes suddenly turned in a direction that was clearly not going to take him toward transportation to Dartmoor. The tall man following Holmes quickened his pace and I did the same. Somewhere near Old Surrey Lane, Holmes turned into an alleyway. The man following him hastened to catch up. I managed to reach the mouth of the shadowy dead-end alley just in time to see Holmes turn to face the man who appeared to have him trapped.

"What game are we playing here?" the man said in a voice that sounded scorched and dry. He advanced on Holmes menacingly, right hand thrust deeply into his right coat pocket.

"Trap the criminal," Holmes answered, his legs apart, his hands clenched at his sides.

The taller man laughed and kept advancing on my friend. From his right hand he drew something that looked like two bars of metal.

"Bell's going to be disappointed," the man said. "He wanted to do you in himself."

I stepped into the alley and raised my Webley, aiming squarely at the back of the man who now stood no more than four paces from Holmes. He was bigger than Holmes by several inches, heavier too, and not only did he have the experience of being a boxer, he also had what might be lethal weapons in both hands. In spite of Holmes's admonition, delivered before we left, that I should move temperately, I was prepared to fire before the man took another step. However, before he could take that step, or I could pull the trigger, Holmes bounded forward, ducked right, threw two punches to the man's middle section and then alternate punches with right and left hands to the man's face. The metal bars in the gnarled hands of the bigger man clanged to the alley stones as he fell back in a sitting position and turned his head in my direction with a look of complete astonishment.

Holmes lifted the startled man to his feet and produced a pair of cuffs, which he clasped around the man's wrists.

"Rather a dangerous move," I said, putting the gun away as I stepped toward them. "I've witnessed your boxing skill before, but it was lucky you . . ."

"Luck, Watson?" he said turning the the confused pugilist toward the opening to the street and pushing him forward. "Since when have you known me to rely on luck? This man's right hand is badly used and his left hand virtually normal, which made it evident that as a boxer he favored the right and would certainly punch with it first. I, therefore, moved to his left. His nose, as you can see, has been broken several times, indicating that he would not be particularly vulnerable to a single blow to the nose. Therefore, when I moved to his left, I threw a blow to his kidney and another to his solar plexus, directly at the point where his lungs would give up much of their supply of air. He was quite helpless when I delivered the next two blows to nerves in his cheek and neck."

"Forgive me, Holmes,' I said with some sarcasm as we returned to the street and began to search for a constable. "I should never have assumed that you might need my help."

"On the contrary, Watson, I had to determine what weapon he had with him, if any. Were we dealing with firearms I would have welcomed your shooting him squarely between the shoulders. I'm an observer of human nature, an amateur in the realm of human anatomy and a consulting detective, but I am certainly not a fool."

Finding a constable and explaining the situation proved to be a bit more difficult than Holmes would have liked, but find one we did, an older fellow nearing pension who recognized Holmes and was glad to be of service. Less than an hour from the time we had left 221B we were standing before the doorway on

Bellowdnes Road. Holmes, in spite of the fact that he had not slept for at least twenty-four hours, looked quite exuberant and awake.

"Won't they have cleared out?" I asked as he reached for the door.

"Why should they?" he said. "I'm not to make my appearance at Dartmoor for another hour. They believe they have fooled me and will be waiting for confirmation of my death at the hands of Malcom Bell from the gentleman we just turned over to the police. Ready your weapon, Watson. The end of this singular case is at hand."

He tried the handle of the door, which did not open, and then knocked loudly. The door was flung open almost immediately and Holmes reached forward, pushing it even further to reveal a heavy, dark woman in a black dress.

"What are you doing here?" she asked indignantly.

"Returning this," he said revealing the vial.

"This is not . . ." she began, but was interrupted by a man's voice from the shadows of the interior.

"Enough, Rose," the man said. "He knows."

"Kindly step forward," I said evenly, aiming my Webley into the darkness and trying to appear as if I could see him clearly. Fortunately, he limped forward into the dusty half-light of the small entranceway.

"I assume you are both relatives of Malcom Bell," Holmes said.

"I'm his sister Rose and this is my husband Nicholas," the woman said. Then, suddenly, she begun to sag and the man behind her moved forward to support her.

"I'm afraid," said Holmes, "Malcom Bell will have to take this final disappointment."

A cold slash of air chilled my neck and I followed Holmes into the house, closing the door with my shoulder while I kept the pistol at the ready.

"Not quite," the man said, leading his now-sobbing wife to a coarse wooden chair. "Rose isn't weeping because you caught us. Malcom thought you might be too clever. He has a vial of real poison hidden in his cell. Whether he had the chance to do you in or not, if you showed up at his cell he planned to switch the vials."

"So that I would be accused of having smuggled in poison," said Holmes. "If I survived or died, Malcom Bell would be credited with having bested me. And if I didn't show up?"

"If you don't show up before seven, Malcom, precisely at the hour, will take out that hidden vial and drink a toast to you and the hangman. He may not get his revenge, but he will avoid the noose and your justice."

"Quick, Watson," Holmes said. "The time."

I pulled my watch from my pocket and replied, "Seconds to seven, Holmes. I don't see what we can . . ."

Holmes pulled the vial of claret from his pocket, opened it and said, "Tell me when it is precisely seven."

The slumping woman, the man and I exchanged puzzled looks, but approximately ten seconds later I said, "Now. It's seven."

Holmes held up the vial and said, "To a formidable opponent who I will be both pleased and saddened to lose."

And with this he downed the amber liquid to the very last drop.

THE PHANTOM
CHAMBER

Gary Alan Ruse

Illustration by Frederic Dorr Steele of a scene from *The Adventure of the Dancing Men* in "Collier's" 1903.

A brilliant flash of lightning followed immediately by a sharp crack of thunder came close, startlingly close, outside the windows of our Baker Street flat, starkly illuminating the room and causing me to give an inadvertant jump. My friend, Sherlock Holmes, noticed my discomfort and allowed an amused twist of a smile to briefly intrude upon his solemn look. Then he returned his deceptively casual attention to the prospective client seated before us.

It was mid-morning on a gray and dismal spring day, with rain pelting down outside and seeming to enfold all of London, indeed perhaps all of England, in its damp shroud. Our gas lamps were lit and a small, cheery fire helped to dispel the gloom as well as the pervading humidity; and this warm glow was quite flattering to our visitor, a young woman whom I would guess to be in her mid-twenties. She was rather pretty in a quiet way, her manner warm and feminine despite her prim posture and frowning countenance. Holmes seemed intrigued by her, his alert eyes studying her with analytical curiosity, and also with what struck me as anticipation. I have no doubt that he hoped for the excitement of a case after several long weeks of boredom. But what dire events or dastardly deeds could he possibly perceive to be hovering about such a pleasant and ordinary young lady?

"Pray—" Holmes told her, "— do continue. You were about to tell us what brings you here in the midst of such foul weather. Watson, perhaps the lady would like a cup of tea."

"Yes, thank you," she replied as I rose and crossed to the table where a steaming pot stood waiting upon Mrs. Hudson's tray. She nodded her gratitude as she accepted the cup and took a sip, then seemed to draw herself up for what she was about to say. "It is kind of you to see me, Mr. Holmes, upon such short notice."

"Not at all. You have come at a good time."

"To begin with, my name is Grace Farrington, and I urgently need your advice. If I seem hesitant to speak, it is only because I fear that, when I *have* told you my story, you will at worst think me quite mad, or at best merely foolish."

"Then do not fear on that account. You may speak freely and be assured of our respectful attention."

"I want you to know I am a rational woman," she stressed, "not given to flights of fancy, or delusions. I do not believe in ghosts, or visions, or spiritualism. Yet I have seen something which defies explanation."

Holmes inclined his head slightly, bringing his steepled fingers to his lips. "Where and when did this event occur?"

"One week ago to-day, quite late at night, at the estate of my great-aunt, Lady Penelope, widow of the late Viscount of Thaxton," she replied. "The manor is in Surrey, near Woking. I should explain that I had only just returned to England the day before, after a long absence."

"Yes," said Holmes dryly. "I perceive that you have been in India of late, with your husband, who is an officer in Her Majesty's army."

Grace Farrington raised a delicate eyebrow in surprise. "My word, Mr. Holmes. How could you possibly know that?"

"Mere observation and simple deductive reasoning, nothing more. Your complexion, though fair, shows the vigor of a far more tropical clime than can be found in England, or the rest of northern Europe, especially after a long winter. Your wedding band is ample proof of your married status, and I noticed the umbrella you brought with you has a wooden handle inlaid with ivory in a pattern that is characteristic of India. The brass ferule of the grip also bears an engraved regimental crest. It has all the earmarks of a parting gift for an officer, or an officer's wife, and your manner, your bearing, your obvious breeding, all point in that direction."

"You are quite right," she replied, setting her cup down. "My husband, James, was indeed stationed in India, where he was a young captain with the 112th Artillery. We met there some fourteen months ago. My father, you see, is Colonel Edward Colebrook, a career soldier. He has been stationed in India for the past three years, and my mother and I accompanied him there as we did to many of his posts."

"And your parents are still there?" I asked.

The young woman gave a downcast look. "My father is, yes. We lost Mother during a cholera outbreak last summer."

"We are sorry to hear that," Holmes told her with genuine sympathy, but it was clear he was eager to press on. "Tell me, what precipitated your return to England? A new post for your husband?"

"No, Mr. Holmes. Quite the contrary. My husband was discharged from service after being seriously wounded in the leg in a rebel uprising. He saved a number of men's lives by his actions and is a legitimate hero, though he is sorely embarrassed by any fuss over the fact." Grace Farrington was nervously twisting at the corners of a lace handkerchief she held in her gloved hands, her troubled eyes shifting alternately from Holmes to myself. "At any rate, he was required to convalesce several months before being fit enough to travel. The journey back took more weeks, but at least we had the offer of a place to stay and the possibility of work."

"Arranged for by your great-aunt?" asked Holmes.

"Yes, quite so. I had never been very close to her, due to my father's far-flung duties. In fact, I can only recall seeing her once or twice when I was a small child. But as things would happen, we began to correspond a few years back and managed to develop quite a dear relationship, indirect though it was. So when she learned that we would be returning to England as soon as my husband was well enough to travel, she offered to let us stay at her estate; indeed she insisted upon it. And so we arrived there last week."

"Ah, good," Holmes said cheerily. "It must have been an eagerly awaited reunion."

"Eagerly awaited, yes. Yet not what we anticipated. For the strangeness of what took place there truly began from the moment of our arrival."

"How so?"

"Everything was wrong. Or so it seemed to me. The manor while not large, seemed even smaller than my childhood memories recalled. And the manor house, while quite a solid two-story structure, was so terribly grim and foreboding in aspect that the mere sight of it as our carriage pulled up on that gray day was enough to chill one's blood.''

"Perhaps," I could not resist suggesting, "you had merely grown used to life in more colorful lands. To return in such cheerless weather—"

"I know," she acknowledged. "I am sure there is some truth in what you say. But that cannot wholly account for it. The grounds were unkempt and in a state of disrepair. And when we knocked at the door, we were greeted with a cool reception. A young man in his thirties, whom I barely remembered as a distant cousin, admitted us. His name is Jeremy Wollcott, and his expression upon seeing us there at his doorstep, baggage in hand, was so piteously bewildered that I thought at first we might have come to the wrong place altogether.''

Holmes suddenly rose from his seat and strode to the stand beside his desk, there to rummage through a stack of newspapers, articles and foolscap notes he had allowed to accumulate. "Yes, go on, Mrs. Farrington.''

"Well, my husband and I introduced ourselves and explained why we were there. Jeremy *seemed* to know who I was, but for the longest moment he simply stared at us, speechless. Then at last he extended a hand to greet us.

" 'Forgive me,' he said to my husband and I. 'It is only that I was surprised to see you. Lady Penelope did not tell me to expect you, else I might have prepared things for your arrival.'

" 'Is there any problem?' I asked him. 'If it has become inconvenient for us to stay here we will gladly seek lodging elsewhere.'

"He hesitated a moment, then said, 'Well, no, there is certainly room here for you, and if Lady Penelope has invited you I can hardly turn you away. But sadly, things here are not as they once were. Lady Penelope is not at all well. Her health has been frail for some time now, and the advancing years have not been kind to her. I . . . I just want you to be prepared.'

"This was quite upsetting to me, Mr. Holmes, for my great-aunt's letters never mentioned poor health. Jeremy told me that she was too proud to complain about such things, and as he escorted James and me into the sitting room, he further told us that Lady Penelope's financial affairs were also declining. The servants had been let go, save for one woman who served as both cook and housekeeper. That explained the condition of the estate, I suppose.

"Jeremy said he would see that a room was made ready for us, and he went to tell Lady Penelope of our arrival. He was gone quite a long while. When he came back, he had Lady Penelope with him." Moisture welled up in Grace Farrington's eyes and she dabbed at it with her handkerchief. "She was such a pathetic sight, it . . . it tore at my heart. Lady Penelope was confined to a wheelchair. She looked horribly old, all gray and withered, barely able to hold her head up as Jeremy pushed her into the room. To have come to know her through her letters and to at last see her again under such circumstances—well, it was sad beyond measure.

"Only her eyes showed a spark of vitality and alertness. She was wrapped in a dressing gown and robe that were large upon her shrunken form, with a shawl clutched about her shoulders. Poor woman, she had a bit of thin veil half covering her face, in a feeble attempt to hide the many wrinkles and sallow complexion, but it did little good. Her voice, when she greeted us, cracked and wavered, barely above a whisper. Worse yet, though she *said* she was glad to see us, and her words were the essence of cordiality, she seemed insincere. And poor Jeremy, she constantly treated him in a cross and bullying manner, no matter how much he pattered about, attempting to satisfy her every whim. As much as I pity her, it troubled me to see her abuse such devotion from my cousin."

There came at that moment another great crash of lightning and thunder outside, this time a bit farther away. Holmes glanced briefly at one of the newspapers he had found in the stack, then he returned to his seat and focused his complete attention once more upon Grace Farrington.

"Tell me," said he, "how long had it been since your last letter from Lady Penelope?"

"About two months, I would say."

Sherlock Holmes let his gaze drift off into space. "Two months? Much can happen in two months."

"Indeed," said I. "And, I might add, it is not uncommon for someone of Lady Penelope's age and condition to become irascible with those close to her. I have seen it happen quite often among my elderly patients."

The young Mrs. Farrington nodded. "Yes, but now I wonder if her letters, which always seemed so sweet and dear, were merely like her cordial words, lacking any true feeling. I do not even know if she wrote them herself or only dictated them."

Holmes now leaned forward in his seat, his tone becoming a

bit impatient. "My dear Mrs. Farrington, I can certainly see that your reunion with your great-aunt was disillusioning, saddening, even bordering upon the tragic. But surely that in itself is not what brought you here?"

"My word, *no*, Mr. Holmes. It merely preceded the event which frightened me so. And now that you know the circumstances, I may explain the rest." She edged forward slightly upon her seat, her expression becoming both more earnest and more troubled. "It happened the very first night of our stay there. Dinner had been awkward for all of us, even though Jeremy attempted to make conversation. A friend of his who was visiting there, a Mr. Lester Thorn, asked quite a number of questions about India, which we obliged. But Lady Penelope asked to be taken to her room almost immediately after dinner, and my husband and I retired for the night an hour later ourselves.

"There was no storm that night. In fact, the weather appeared to be clearing. But I could not sleep at all. I don't know whether it was being in a strange house, or being overly tired from our journey. Perhaps it was just the unsettling state of things we found there. I tossed and turned for hours. My dear husband, bless him, was sound asleep, getting the rest he sorely needed, but I was wide awake.

"At last, at one in the morning, I could stand it no more. I arose, put on my dressing gown and slippers, and left our room as quietly as I could. I descended the stairs, taking a candle with me so that I might see the way, and made for the central corridor with the intention of going to the kitchen. I thought some warm milk might help. I did not plan to awaken the housekeeper, mind you. I would gladly have prepared it myself. But I never got that far."

"What happened?" demanded Holmes.

Grace Farrington visibly paled from the mere recollection. "The corridor was deserted, as one might expect at that hour. But one of the doors, about halfway down that long corridor, was standing open. A faint pool of light spilled out upon the floor, and as I drew near I was sure I could hear strange sounds from within.

"I continued walking, keeping very quiet, drawing ever nearer to the open door. As I reached it I became aware of two small objects lying upon the corridor floor, just inches beyond the doorway. I stooped to pick them up, and the light of my candle revealed them for what they were. One was a lady's glove, oddly stained, with small initials embroidered near the wrist.

The other was a baby's rattle. It made a small noise as I turned it in my hand. Frankly, Mr. Holmes, it puzzled me, since I knew that Lady Penelope was childless and had never told me in her letters of any children in the house.

"It was then that a sudden gust of air blew out my candle, startling me," the young woman continued. "As I jerked upright, I found myself looking straight into the chamber whose doorway stood before me. Though my candle had gone out I had no trouble seeing into that terrible room. There were no lamps lit, of that I am sure. But a strange light, cold and ghostly, seemed to fill the place. Not brightly, but with an eerie, unearthly glow.

"As I have told you before, I do not believe in ghosts. But I was ready to believe in them at that moment! Glowing eyes stared at me from literally dozens of places about the room, some quite high in the air. Demonlike shapes and great hulking monsters stood facing me in every direction, and a low moaning sound came from the chamber. As in a dream, ghostlike wraiths seemed to be shimmering and undulating in that chilling glow. And there was something else there as well. Something, whether human or not I could not guess, lay upon a chaise, clawing at some sort of netting which confined it. It was truly horrible!"

"My word!" I exclaimed, quite involuntarily, caught up as I was in Grace Farrington's vivid narrative. But I held my tongue as Holmes shot me an annoyed glance.

"Go on, dear lady," said he simply. "You have our rapt attention."

"I freely admit to you, Mr. Holmes, that never in my life have I been so frightened. I immediately dropped the rattle and glove, turned on my heel, and ran. I turned so swiftly that I lost one of my slippers by the doorway, but I dared not stop to retrieve it. I ran straight for the stair, stumbling more than once in the darkness, and found my way back to our room.

"I was quite out of breath as I reached our bed, and was uncertain of what to do. But I could not bear to be alone with the fear, so I awakened my husband. When I was sure he was clearheaded enough to understand, I told him what I had seen in the chamber. He held me closely and attempted to calm me.

" 'There, there,' he told me, 'don't tremble so. I'm sure there's nothing to be frightened of. It's just a bad dream you've had, nothing more.'

" 'But I was not even asleep, James!' I insisted, 'So how could I have been dreaming?' "

"I would not be dissuaded from my belief, so at last my husband threw on his own robe and got his cane. He lit a small lantern from the stand beside the bed and accompanied me back downstairs. Believe me, I did not wish to encounter that dreadful chamber again, even with my brave husband at my side, but I was determined to prove my sanity.

"The chamber door was still standing open when we reached the corridor, my slipper still lying upon the floor where I had lost it. You may believe that I stayed close behind my husband as we approached the doorway. James held the lantern well forward to light the way. To my surprise, the rattle and glove were gone. I am sure I dropped them in the corridor, but neither was there now.

"Even more amazing was what we found within the chamber itself! Our lantern lit it up quite well. The chamber was clearly a grand hall with a high ceiling, very spacious, with tables and chairs and fine paintings on the walls. In short, it was nothing like what I had seen just moments before. Gone were all the demons and staring eyes, the monsters, the unearthly glow. Furniture stood in all innocence where none had stood before. There were flowers in crystal vases and fine inlaid wooden cabinets. A lovely oriental carpet covered the floor.

"My astonishment gave way to chagrin, Mr. Holmes," Grace Farrington said. "What lay before my husband's skeptical eyes clearly made a liar of me. Nothing could be found to substantiate my story. Nothing! And to make matters worse, Jeremy's footsteps came on the stair, and he joined us in the corridor.

" 'I say, cousin, what's wrong?' Jeremy asked, rubbing at his eyes sleepily.

" 'Nothing, I'm sure," James told him. 'It seems my wife has had a bad dream. That's all.'

" 'Bad dream?' said Jeremy.

"I was quite bewildered, still staring into the chamber. 'But . . . but . . . I was sure I saw something terrible . . . horrible. I was *sure*. My slipper was here, after all. How do you account for that?'

" 'Sleepwalking, perhaps,' Jeremy suggested. 'I have a sister who frequently goes strolling about in the dead of night, and . . .'

" 'No!' I interrupted, my sense of certainty returning. 'No, I was not dreaming. Perhaps it was the next chamber.'

"Quite shamelessly, I ran to the next door down the corridor and threw it open. But it was only some sort of butler's pantry, a very small room. The next door down from that was the dining room. I checked all of the doors on that side of the hall, all to no avail. I have never felt more foolish.

"And then, as if James and my cousin were not already provoked enough with me, my commotion disturbed Lady Penelope's sleep. She called out to us from the small writing room on the other side of the corridor, which has been made over into a bedchamber for her as she can not climb the stairs. Jeremy looked in on her and I could tell she sounded very cross. I felt terrible. I apologized, and James and I returned to our bed. Near morning I dozed off for a few hours, but it was a troubled sleep at best."

Holmes nodded understandingly, his look very alert. "And did you inspect the chamber again in full daylight?"

"Most certainly," she replied. "And my husband accompanied me, but we had to be careful not to create too much of a stir after the previous night. Still, it was quite ordinary. The dreadful, ghostly chamber I had seen before had simply disappeared, without a trace. James still thinks I was dreaming. But I swear to you both—it *was* real! I did not imagine it."

Sherlock Holmes rose and began to pace, his lanky form stooped at bit, his hands clasped behind him. "And you are sure you could not be mistaken about the corridor?"

"Quite sure."

"Did you say anything to Lady Penelope about what you saw?"

"Why, no," replied Mrs. Farrington. "Under the circumstances, with her poor health and all, I thought it better not to."

"Did anything else unusual happen?"

"No, Mr. Holmes. Nothing at all like the first night. But a strange, oppressive atmosphere continues to hang over us. And I cannot shake the feeling that something is terribly wrong . . . that Lady Penelope has not told us everything. I cannot help wondering if she may have brought us here under false pretenses, though for what reason I cannot imagine. So when I learned that Jeremy was going to London on an errand for Lady Penelope, I asked him to take my husband and I along as well, on the pretext of doing some shopping. My intent was, of course, to consult with you. James is even now visiting some old army comrades, and I must leave to meet him shortly."

"What sort of errand?" said Holmes.

"What?"

"You said Jeremy had an errand to do for Lady Penelope. Do you know what that errand is?"

"Why, yes. Though I lack the precise details, I did hear her ask Jeremy to make arrangements for a solicitor to come to the manor later this afternoon. She was quite insistent about it." Grace Farrington now rose as my companion drew near in his pacing. "So what am I to do, sir? If I do not learn the truth, I fear I shall never have a moment's rest. Do you think me foolish?"

"On the contrary," said Holmes, "I would think you foolish if you did *not* seek the truth. Now listen, what you must do is this—return to your husband as you planned. Say nothing to him about our meeting, nor to anyone else. Nothing. Go back to Thaxton Manor with your cousin and go about your usual routine. But stay alert. My friend and I will call on you this afternoon, around three, and look into this."

The young woman pulled a folded slip of paper from her purse and handed it to Holmes. "I have taken the liberty of writing down directions to the manor, though I doubt you will have any trouble finding it."

"Excellent."

Holmes retrieved her cloak and umbrella from the hook where they had been drying by the fire, and held the cloak for her to don it. I moved to open the door.

"Thank you so much," Grace Farrington told us. "I feel better just having spoken to you."

"Until this afternoon, then," Holmes said with a gracious bow. "And you may have every confidence that we shall get to the truth behind this mystery."

She smiled for the first time since setting foot in our flat, calmed at last by my companion's assurances and charm. I am convinced that if Holmes were only less analytical in temperament and more romantic in nature, he could have his pick of ladies, in England or on the continent. But his professional facade faded as soon as Mrs. Farrington was out the door and down the hall.

"I say, Holmes, 'every confidence'?" I teased. "Quite a bold promise, even for you, considering the nature of the mystery. Ghosts and demons and monsters, indeed!"

My companion's look became very grave. "There are many kinds of monsters in this world, not all of them supernatural. Tell me, what is your opinion of Mrs. Farrington?"

"Quite a pleasant young woman, I should say. Intelligent and capable, if I am any judge. Medically speaking, she appears sound, unless there is some hidden problem."

"I agree. Her descriptions were detailed and clearheaded, and I think, not to be taken lightly."

I felt a faint chill as I recalled Grace Farrington's words. "Do you think she did see what she described?"

"I am sure she saw something," Holmes said. "But I am equally sure she misinterpreted its true nature."

"I certainly hope so. Have you a clue?"

"Several possibilities come to mind, from what I have already learned. But before I theorize further I shall need more data, some to be gathered here in London and the rest to be found at Thaxton Manor." Holmes grabbed up his travelling-cloak and cap, his lethargy of the past weeks gone in the twinkling of an eye. "What say you, my friend? May I count on your assistance in these inquiries?"

"It would be my very great pleasure!"

"Then let us be off, Watson! The game is afoot."

We were able to catch the 1:45 P.M. train out of Waterloo Station, with barely enough time for a hasty lunch before our departure. Sherlock Holmes and I had spent the several hours since our meeting with Mrs. Farrington by touring the West End, there visiting a number of the agencies devoted to securing employment for household servants with good credentials. My companion persisted in making his discreet inquiries until, at the fifth such establishment we tried, we found what Holmes was seeking. The agency, Atwater's, had represented the servants dismissed from Thaxton Manor, and at Holmes's skillful prodding, the gentleman in charge of the establishment well remembered them.

"Quite a sad turn of events, it was, if I may say so, sir," the manager, a Mr. Bryswicket, told us. "There they were, employed in the manorial household some fifteen years or more, thirty in the case of the butler. Why, they had all of them known Lord Henry, dead some dozen years now. Almost part of the family, they were. But with Lady Penelope's financial reverses, the lot of them were turned out with practically no notice whatsoever, and very little to tide them over."

"Yes," said Holmes with a sad shake of his head. "That was several months ago, was it not?"

"Nearly so," replied Bryswicket, flipping a page in one of his journal books. "Seven weeks, to be exact. I have found positions for two of the maids and for the gardener, but nothing yet for the butler and cook, nor the few other staff." Bryswicket rolled his hopeful gaze toward us. "Perhaps, gentlemen, if either of you have positions to fill, or know of anyone who has . . . ?"

"Sadly, not at the moment," Holmes said. "But if we should hear of anyone who does we shall most certainly put them in touch with you."

With that, we bid Mr. Bryswicket good day. We made but one other stop before heading for the station. While I waited outside to hold the carriage, Holmes entered a small shop specializing in used books and periodicals. He rejoined me in a few minutes and we were on our way.

And so it was that we now found ourselves aboard the train bound for Woking. The pleasant Surrey countryside was drenched, but, as the rain had at last let up, the weather was not nearly so forbidding as it had been that morning. Holmes busied himself for a time with some notes he had made and with several periodicals bought earlier, then turned his attention at last upon the passing scene beyond our window.

"Well, Holmes," I asked of him when I was sure I would not disturb his thoughts, "was the information we learned from Atwater's of any use?"

"Yes, I believe it shall prove very useful."

"It does confirm what Grace Farrington told us."

"So it would seem."

"Do you suppose these financial problems could have any bearing on the matter?"

"And how do you propose they might, Watson?"

"Well," said I, uncertain of my own theory now that the question was put to me, "it would seem to me that if Lady Penelope knew of her difficulties at the time she invited the Farringtons to live with her, and indeed, she surely must have known, then perhaps she expected them to assist her in some way."

"They seem in need of assistance themselves."

"Perhaps Lady Penelope meant for them to fulfill some of the duties of the servants she planned to dismiss. Or perhaps there is some inheritance due Grace Farrington, of which she is ignorant, but which would be of use to Lady Penelope. Not unlike our recent case of the speckled band."

"A possibility," said Holmes dryly, "but only one of many. I see that you share our client's mistrust of the good Lady Penelope."

"Yes, Holmes. I fancy I do."

"Well, such feelings are not unwarranted, my good fellow. And your theory as to the ghostly vision—?"

"I must confess, I have none," said I.

Sherlock Holmes folded his arms and leaned back in his seat, closing his eyes as if to nap. "Never fear, Watson. I am quite sure all the pieces of this puzzle will fit together quite nicely, once we've gathered them together. I only wish I could recall what it was I read about Lord Henry's death. I am sure there was some mention in the papers at the time, but after twelve years it simply eludes me. No matter. Tell me— did you remember to bring your revolver?"

"Yes, of course." I looked at my friend, whose expression had become quite grim. "Do you think it will come to that?"

"It remains to be seen. But of this you may be sure, there is treachery at work in Thaxton Manor, and it may well be murder we must prevent!"

The train took just under an hour, and upon our arrival at Woking, Holmes hired a trap to take us to the manor, which was a good five miles out from the station. Therefore, it was nearly three o'clock when the gray-walled manor house came into view ahead, rising tall and grim beyond a stand of fir trees.

"Driver!" Holmes called out abruptly. "This will do! Please let us out here. There is a parcel of property I must inspect, and it will save us a goodly walk if we disembark now."

Holmes paid the man, and as the carriage turned and headed back I started along the road. Holmes motioned me into the field instead.

"Come, Watson. Let us take a circuitous route and approach the house from the side, so that we are not seen. There is something I would inspect before we make our presence known, and it is most certainly not a parcel of land!"

We took advantage of the cover afforded by trees as far as we could, approaching Thaxton Manor from the east face. We were in the open only briefly as we crossed a field of heather, then a series of ornamental hedges shielded us from view the rest of the way to the house. I was, for once, grateful for the overcast sky. The flat gray light helped obscure our movements.

As we reached the wall, Holmes quickly surveyed the area, then grasped the trellis which rose the full height of the house. "Wait here," he whispered. "Stay out of sight."

"My word, Holmes!" I protested, but he was already scrambling up the trellis like some dapper circus performer. He reached the top easily and disappeared over the edge of the roof with scarcely a backward glance and no more sound than the rustling leaves.

All was silence, save for the sounds of the open countryside about me. I felt suddenly and terribly alone, huddled there against the wall of Thaxton Manor, hoping not to be seen and wondering what excuse I would offer should someone discover me. I half wished I had accompanied Holmes, but a glance up the trellis towering above me convinced me my friend had made the right decision in going it alone. Long, awkward minutes passed. I looked at my watch. It was now some five minutes past three. I had no doubt that Grace Farrington was anticipating our arrival at any moment. I only hoped her anxiety would not give her, and us, away.

A movement at the corner of my eye brought my attention to the road, even as the sound of a horse and carriage reached my ears. It was an expensive-looking rig, driven by a young man, with an older man as his passenger, and it was coming from the same direction in which we had just come. As I watched from my place of partial concealment I saw that the carriage was turning into the drive, its destination the very house beside whose wall I crouched. I was eager to impart this news to my friend, if only I could.

"Holmes!" I muttered to myself. "Where are you!"

"Nearer than you think, Watson," said he, making my head whip rapidly about in surprise, for Holmes was crouched just behind me, nearly at my shoulder. Yet I had not heard him approach. "Sorry to startle you, old friend. The view is better from up there, and I spotted the carriage coming while it was still a half mile off. But I feared they might see my descent upon the trellis as they approached, so I descended another on the other side, and came round the back of the house."

Calming myself, I said, "What did you find up there?"

"Something which confirms one of my suspicions and sheds a bit of light on this mystery," Holmes replied. With a quick gesture toward the arriving carriage, he added, "And that, I'll wager, is Jeremy Wollcott and the solicitor he has hired. I observed that carriage arriving at the station in Woking just as we were leaving in our own conveyance. The solicitor must have taken the same train as we, and Wollcott has met him."

"Awkward timing," I grumbled.

"On the contrary, it is fortuitous timing! Let us go take advantage of it."

Sherlock Holmes started forward, staying close to the wall. The carriage was, by now, out of sight at the front of the manor house, so it was unlikely we would be seen by its occupants. As we reached the corner at the northern face of the building we cautiously peered around. The horse and carriage could be seen standing by the entrance to Thaxton Manor, and the two men were just disappearing inside. The door closed behind them.

Holmes motioned me to follow, whispering, "Keep below the windows. They must not see us yet!"

By some great good fortune the horse was an even-tempered beast and was not spooked by the sight of two strangers skulking about in front of the place. As we neared the first window Holmes paused and ventured a cautious look inside. Then he motioned me onward. The same occurred at the next window. Next came the entrance with its solidly built door, and once past the few steps leading up to it, Holmes made for the third window in the building's northern face. He peered in at one corner, then motioned for me to join him. There was only a bit of shrubbery for concealment, but it would have to do.

"We are in luck, Watson," Holmes said in the lowest of voices. "The sitting room is just beyond, and the household appears to be gathering there."

I stole a glance through the window myself, as cautiously as Holmes had done, and saw the proof of his words. The solicitor and Jeremy Wollcott were standing with their backs to us, just beyond a settee by the window. Grace Farrington and a man I presumed to be her husband were just taking seats to the right, and a woman garbed in cook's whites stood off to the left. Framed in the doorway was another man, pushing a wheelchair-bound form into the room. Even in that swift glance I could see that Grace Farrington's description of Lady Penelope was no exaggeration. The woman looked horribly old and frail, her gaze agitated and peevish.

The window was open a bit to admit fresh air, and it also allowed the voices of those within to reach our ears. We heard Jeremy Wollcott introduce Lady Penelope and the others in the room to the solicitor, one Mr. Joshua Trenton. The man pushing the wheelchair proved to be Lester Thorn, the friend of Wollcott's, of whom Mrs. Farrington had spoken earlier.

"I appreciate your promptness," Lady Penelope said, her voice weak and quaking. "Did you bring the papers?"

"Most assuredly, I have, Madam," came the solicitor's reply. "It is a standard document. All that remains for me to do is to fill in the specifics as you wish, have you verify its accuracy, and obtain your signature; then all will be in order. We are fortunate to have more than enough witnesses present.''

I cast a look at Holmes that surely must have conveyed my curiosity and suspicions about what this document might be. He merely brought a finger to his lips to signal silence, then listened all the more intently.

''This is against my own advice,'' Jeremy Wollcott's voice came next. It was a young man's voice, clear and strong, yet showing a certain timidity. ''I really do not see—''

''Hush, Jeremy!'' snapped Lady Penelope, her voice harsh despite its weakness. ''This must be done. I . . .'' she paused, seemingly for breath ''. . . I entertain no delusions about my health. Neither should you. Now then—Mr. Trenton, is it? —have you set to-day's date to the document?''

''Indeed, Your Ladyship.''

''Very well,'' Lady Penelope replied. ''The rest of you, I want you to know . . .'' another pause for breath ''. . . that the document which Mr. Trenton is drawing up is my last will and testament.''

There was a small gasp from Grace Farrington, a tiny sound of surprise and sadness. I suspect her reaction might have been less, were her nerves not already on the edge.

''My dear child,'' Lady Penelope addressed her. ''Your concern is touching, but reserve your sympathy for others. I have . . . I have led a full life, and it does not trouble me greatly that I do not expect to see many more days on this earth.'' She paused, making several quiet, hacking coughs. ''Now, Mr. Trenton, I wish you to set down the following: Upon my death, Thaxton Manor and its grounds, and such few monies as I have remaining in my accounts, and whatever belongings as I may have, I wish to leave to one person.''

The room was so silent I could literally hear the scratch of the solicitor's pen as he added to the document. When he had caught up, Trenton said, ''and the beneficiary is to be—?''

Lady Penelope gave another small cough. ''My husband and I were never blessed with children. Therefore, I have decided to leave everything to my grand-nephew, Jeremy Wollcott.''

''It is a kind gesture,'' Jeremy protested weakly, ''but I really wish you would reconsider.''

The old woman shook a trembling finger in the air. ''Nonsense! I have made up my mind, Jeremy. Your parents, while they were alive, were very dear to me, and I promised them I would look after you. As it turned out, you have looked after me, and it is time you were rewarded for the indignities you have suffered.''

Jeremy Wollcott made no reply to that, and I wondered if he had told the ailing woman just how poor her finances were, and how limited a reward he would be reaping. I dared another look through the window and saw that Grace Farrington looked solemn, but not unhappy with the terms of the will.

"There," said the solicitor at last. "It is complete. Now, Mr. Wollcott, if you would be so good as to have your great-aunt review the document and sign it, we shall be ready for the witnesses."

Jeremy Wollcott rose and, with some reluctance, took the completed will to Lady Penelope. The woman produced a lorgnette from her robe and peered through the lenses at the will. It took only a moment for her to be satisfied with it and, as the solicitor hastily brought her his pen, she signed the document with a shaky hand. Jeremy motioned for Grace Farrington and her husband to witness the will, and the cook and Lester Thorn followed behind them toward the table.

"I think we have seen and heard quite enough," Sherlock Holmes said abruptly, pushing me in the direction of the door. "Hurry, Watson! There is not a moment to lose!"

"Wait, Holmes," I sputtered, but my companion was already pounding on the door with the fervor of a madman, setting up a horrid din. "Surely we cannot just barge in this way!"

"There is a time for caution, and a time for bold action. There is more at stake here than you guess. Now follow my lead!"

Holmes had barely uttered those words when a flurry of footsteps approached us from within. The door was unlatched and swung open to reveal Jeremy Wollcott, his face blanched and uncertain. The solicitor and Lester Thorn stood a short distance behind him.

"What the devil, sir!" Wollcott cried. "Just what do you think you're doing?"

"Preventing a great injustice, if we are in time!" Holmes pushed past the young man without waiting for an invitation to enter, and I quickly followed him into the building's entrance hall. Spying Grace Farrington's astonished look from the open door of the sitting room, Holmes asked, "Have you signed that document, Mrs. Farrington?"

"Why, no!" said she.

"Excellent. Make sure you do not."

"Now see here!" Jeremy Wollcott protested, still standing by the open front door. "How dare you burst in upon us in this fashion. You have no right!"

James Farrington pressed past his wife, and limping with his cane for support, came forward to join the others. Though his wounds had affected his strength, it was clear his military spirit was undiminished. With a commanding voice he said, "I quite agree. I demand to know who you are, and what business you have with us!"

"Fair enough, sir. I am Sherlock Holmes. My friend here is Dr. Watson. And I assure you that we have your own best interests at heart. In addition, I intend to serve the interests of Lady Penelope as well."

The old woman was just now entering the hall, pushed in her wheelchair by the cook. She fixed Holmes with her sharp gaze. "But I have not asked for your help, sir!"

"Be that as it may, I am here and I shall not leave until I have stated my case." Holmes's tall, gaunt figure was a commanding presence, his expression steely and resolute. "You are all here, now. Good! I would make of you witnesses of quite a different matter. Now follow me, all of you, if you wish to learn my business here. Mrs. Farrington—I trust this is the way to the corridor in question?"

Holmes was already striding off purposefully as the young woman nodded in agreement. Grace Farrington and her husband followed him, with the others close at their heels. I followed last, to keep an eye on them and insure that no one left the group unnoticed. I thought I observed Jeremy Wollcott and Lester Thorn exchange worried looks, but whether it was due to some unspoken concern or merely to Holmes's brusque intrusion I could not guess.

My companion led us through the connecting hall at a brisk pace and, with Grace Farrington's further direction, brought us into a long, central corridor dotted with doorways. A carpet runner of rich oriental pattern formed a path down the middle of the corridor, while the inlaid wood floor was exposed along the sides. Randomly placed along the walls were stands with china vases or bits of sculpture, as well as several tall bookcases.

"Now we may begin," said Sherlock Holmes as we neared the corridor's mid-point. "Mrs. Farrington has called my attention to something unusual which occurred here last week."

"Really, Mr. Holmes," Grace Farrington said, obviously ill

at ease. "I did not expect this. I thought a more discreet investigation possible."

"My apologies, dear lady. That was my wish, but the situation now demands something more."

Lady Penelope's high and trembling voice came next, "What are they speaking of? Jeremy, I was not told of anything."

"There was nothing to tell," came Wollcott's irritable reply. "Nothing of consequence. Grace merely had a bad dream. I thought we had resolved that, but I see now she has been brooding about it. Really, Grace—to have brought an outsider here over something so trivial!"

"Have a care, sir," James Farrington shot back. "My wife would never do anything she did not feel was necessary."

"But there is nothing extraordinary here! See for yourselves!" With that, Jeremy threw open the chamber door.

The grand hall revealed within was exactly as Grace Farrington had described it to us in our flat that morning: spacious, well decorated with tables and chairs and fine cabinets, with an oriental carpet on the floor and flowers in crystal vases. It was quite a pleasant room, with nothing to suggest frightening visions.

Holmes glanced in, his gaze quickly encompassing the room. "Quite right," he said as his narrowing eyes returned to the group before him. "Nothing extraordinary, *here*. Think back, Mrs. Farrington. You told me you came downstairs, found the chamber door standing open, the baby's rattle and the glove on the floor. Your candle was extinguished by a gust of wind, you looked into the chamber, you saw a horrifying scene before you. You ran back upstairs to get your husband, then returned."

"Yes," said she. "That is correct, Mr. Holmes."

"And how long were you gone from this spot?"

"Only a few moments, I'm sure."

'It may have seemed that, in the excitement of the moment, dear lady," Holmes told her gently. "But in truth, you were, by your own description, stumbling in the dark on the way back. You had to awaken your husband, tell him your story, then convince him. He could not, with his present injury, walk very fast, especially upon the stairs. All of that took time. It is therefore my contention that you did not return for a good ten minutes after your first encounter. Plenty of time for the deed to be done."

"Deed?" James Farrington asked. "What deed? And by whom?"

"The disappearance of a chamber of ghosts," replied Sherlock Holmes.

"This is absurd!" cried Jeremy Wollcott.

"Not at all. I never doubted there was a rational explanation for what Mrs. Farrington saw. And the date of the occurrence, taken together with several seemingly unrelated facts, led me to suspect a reason for it all. My inquiries earlier, and what I found upon your roof, confirm those suspicions."

Grace Farrington had a bewildered look. "The roof?"

"Skylights, my dear lady," Holmes told her. "There are two of them above this portion of the manor, placed approximately thirty feet apart. One you can see up there in the high ceiling of this chamber, for there is no second floor above it. But where is the other skylight? It is not to be found here. The butler's pantry? I think not! The dining room? Too far away from this room. Where then is the chamber which corresponds to the second skylight? Where is the chamber into which I peered from the roof must minutes ago, and whose contents made me remember the manner of Lord Henry's death some twelve years back."

"Then I was not mistaken? The room I saw exists?"

"You may be sure of that, Mrs. Farrington." Holmes stepped along the corridor, stooping to study the floor as he moved. Passing a bookcase, he scraped his thumbnail across the wooden flooring next to it, raising a thin rill of some white substance. "Soap," he announced. "And the wall here is not as faded as the rest. Here, Watson—I shall need your help with this."

I moved to where he indicated, across from him on the other side of the bookcase. I was reluctant to take my eyes off the others even for a moment, but I was also eager to learn the truth.

"Push, Watson!" cried Holmes.

Sherlock Holmes tugged backward upon the tall bookcase even as I pressed forward. There was a brief low groan at first, then the case slid silently across the soaped wooden flooring. Despite its weight, the bookcase moved with relative ease. We pushed it a distance of roughly five feet along the wall. No more was needed.

"Look!" cried Grace Farrington.

She pointed at it with vindication as much as surprise. For a closed door, which had been hidden behind the bookcase, now stood revealed. Holmes strode quickly toward it, reaching out a hand for the latch.

"Stop!" The angry shout had come from Lady Penelope, and

with unexpected strength. Whirling to face her, I saw the old woman produce a good-sized pistol from the folds of her robe and level it at Holmes. She rose from her chair and took a step forward, then in a voice remarkably unlike her own she said, "This has gone far enough, Jeremy. They know too much!"

"You fool!" Wollcott cried.

Then with a swiftness that surprised us all, James Farrington brought his cane down sharply across Lady Penelope's gun-hand. The weapon clattered to the floor, where Holmes scooped it up. In a flash the old woman darted forward, attempting to escape, but she tripped over the edge of her long robe and fell, virtually at my feet. I drew my own revolver and held it ready.

Attempting to take advantage of the momentary confusion, Jeremy Wollcott and the man I presumed to be Lester Thorn turned to flee in the opposite direction. They had not taken more than two steps when Holmes leveled the captured pistol at them and his commanding voice rang out.

"Halt! Halt, or I shall shoot!"

The two men stopped in their tracks, for there was no doubting the sincerity in Holmes's words. They grudgingly turned back, beaten men.

Holmes handed the pistol to James Farrington, instructing him, "Keep watch over them, Captain, and the cook as well, until we are certain of her innocence. I doubt Mr. Trenton, here, is a part of it, though."

The solicitor blanched and mopped at his forehead with his handkerchief. "Most assuredly not," he ejaculated. "Before today, I had not even met this Wollcott, or Lady Penelope!"

"As far as the latter is concerned," replied Holmes, "you still have not."

Holmes crossed to where the old woman, or what purported to be one, still struggled to rise from the floor. Roughly hauling the person up to face the others, Holmes grasped the sheer veil and also the gray hair beneath it. A yank brought both off, and elicited a startled gasp from Grace Farrington. Close-cropped hair, dark brown in hue, was beneath the wig, and as Holmes quickly peeled off skillfully-applied layers of gutta-percha and pale makeup, the face of a slightly built young man was revealed.

"This, unless I miss my guess, is a fledgling character actor known as Anthony Cleason," announced Holmes. "I have in my pocket a playbill from a recent theatrical production called 'Widow's Dilemma,' in which Mr. Cleason played the part of an elderly woman. Lester Thorn's name also appears there. The producer of that play was none other than Jeremy Wollcott. His name struck me as familiar, Mrs. Farrington, when you mentioned it this morning. I still had a copy of a *Daily Telegraph* article describing a string of Mr. Wollcott's plays, all of which failed to make money; and that, taken together with your description of Lady Penelope's unexpected behavior, set me to wondering if your cousin might not be staging a much more menacing sort of drama here at Thaxton Manor.''

"The servants!" I said abruptly.

"Precisely, Watson. They *had* to be dismissed, and not because of money problems. They knew Lady Penelope too well not to see through the personation. But while Wollcott had told Mrs. Farrington that the cook had been kept on, it is clear from what we learned at the agency that the cook was fired as well, and replaced with another. That struck me as highly suspicious."

"But Lady Penelope—the real one—what has become of her?" Grace Farrington said with anguish.

"I think the answer to that my be found here," Holmes replied, rushing to the previously hidden door. He tried the latch and found it unlocked. Swinging it boldly open, he said, "Here, Mrs. Farrington, is your phantom chamber!"

The young woman drew in her breath sharply as the chamber's interior came into view, then she frowned in curiosity and stepped closer to the door for a better look. Awestruck revelation supplanted her curiosity as her eyes swept the room.

Sherlock Holmes stepped inside ahead of her, his keen eyes alert to danger. "Watson!" he called. "Give me your revolver. Quickly, man! Your professional attentions are needed here."

I joined him in the chamber, turning over my weapon to him as I passed. Holmes indicated a chaise along one wall where lay a human form, bound in place and partially sheltered by a hanging curtain of rope netting. I rushed over and found it to be an elderly woman. "You are right, Holmes. This must be the real Lady Penelope."

Grace Farrington drew closer, her hand to her mouth. "Is she—?"

"Alive, yes!" I cried. "There is a pulse, but she appears drugged."

"Do what you can for her, Watson," said Holmes.

"There is little I can do at the moment," I replied, loosening the ropes which held her to the chaise. "But she needs fresh air."

Holmes crossed to where a second door stood in the side wall, and though it was locked he succeeded in forcing it open. Shelves at the rear of the butler's pantry could be seen beyond, and with both doors open, air began to move through the room.

The chamber was smaller than the grand hall next door to it, but this one also reached up through both floors of the manor. The skylight Holmes described could be seen above, and the light which entered through it illuminated a horridly neglected room. Dust lay everywhere, and it was apparent the chamber had been left unused for many years.

The high walls of dark wood paneling were lined with hunting trophies. Peering down from a variety of heights were the stuffed heads of antelope and gazelle, wild boar and buffalo, their glass eyes glimmering brightly. Cobwebs that hung in thick gray masses from the heads swayed in the air currents in a way that could easily suggest ghostly forms. Tables bore other trophies—a lion here, a leopard there—also cobwebbed and dusty. Sheets were draped over chairs and cabinets, and in one corner a stuffed polar bear stood upon its hind legs, its forepaws extended menacingly.

"I understand now," said Grace Farrington as she knelt beside Lady Penelope. "Even by daylight this place is strange and frightening. But what of the ghostly glow I saw?"

"The date is the clue," replied Holmes. "One week ago to-day there was a full moon, and by one o'clock in the morning it would have been directly overhead. Its cold glare through the skylight is what made this room so eerie. Clouds may have obscured the moon later, when you looked into the other chamber. Overall, the timing was crucial. Had you not been sleepless and come downstairs that night, you would never have found the door open and seen all this."

"But, why was the door left open?"

"I am sure that your cousin thought it safe enough at that hour," replied Holmes. "He must have been here, in this very room, at the time."

Grace Farrington gently stroked Lady Penelope's forehead. "You mean, drugging her?"

"Perhaps, but more likely he was looking for something." Holmes approached the cabinets standing close together by the door. "Remember, you found that rattle and glove on the floor just beyond the doorway. That suggested a hasty search."

"But I did not see him, and there was no lamp lit."

Holmes was pulling open drawers, now, and inspecting their

contents. "He must have heard you coming and extinguished his lamp, if he had one lit. It was too late to close the door. All he could do was hide and wait to see who it was. When you stooped to pick up the things on the floor he seized the opportunity and blew out your candle, hoping not to be seen. It was merely a happy accident for him that you were frightened by the strange look of the place, and by Lady Penelope's moans."

"Indeed I was!" said Mrs. Farrington.

"Faced with the knowledge that you might return with help at any moment, and not wanting to risk further investigation and possible discovery of his hostage, he sought to discredit your story. He tossed the rattle and glove inside the chamber to deal with later, closed the door behind him and roused his actor friend, who was asleep in the writing room. A simple bar of soap rubbed upon the floor enabled them to move the large bookcase easily and quietly. They then opened the door to the grand hall and moved your slipper there to further the illusion that that was the room you had seen. Anthony Cleason returned to the writing room, and your cousin hid somewhere beyond the staircase until you and your husband passed. Then your cousin pretended to come down the stairs and made innocent conversation. It seems he is quite an actor himself."

Grace Farrington shook her head in dismay. "And I did not even notice it was a different door!"

"Most people would not," said Sherlock Holmes. "In an unfamiliar, darkened house, after a frightening experience, it is small wonder your cousin's trick worked. He still had access through the door connecting with the butler's pantry, so he merely left Lady Penelope hidden away where she was, and continued with his plan to steal her wealth by means of the false will."

"But, Holmes," said I, "what of the signature? If someone were to check it against an earlier document or letter—"

"They would find, what? The shaky handwriting of an ailing woman? Even a mediocre forger could get away with it! The key to the plan was to establish her failing health, and to have her personator sign the will in front of a solicitor and witnesses. As a relative not mentioned in the will, Mrs. Farrington's witnessing of the document would have made it all the more convincing, all the more binding. It would have also made her seem an accessory to the crime, which is why I had to stop her. I am sure they planned Lady Penelope's death, by one means or another, to shortly follow. Then Mr. Cleason could quit his disguise and share in the ill-gotten inheritance.''

"Mr. Holmes,'' said Grace Farrington suddenly, "you mentioned Lord Henry's death. Do you suspect foul play there as well?''

"Not at all, dear lady. Lord Henry died in a hunting accident, crushed by a rogue elephant in Africa. I had quite forgotten, until I looked through the skylight and saw these trophies. I suspect that is why Lady Penelope, grief-stricken over the manner of his death, ordered his trophy room closed up years ago, and why it remained neglected. Except for storage, it is apparent the room has been unused until your cousin exploited it for his evil purpose. Halloa! What have we here?''

Holmes had been searching through the bottom drawer of the cabinet closest to the door, and he now brought forth the fruits of his labor. He held up the objects for us to see.

"The baby's rattle, Mrs. Farrington,'' he announced, "quite old, from the look of it. And the lady's glove as well. The stains you mentioned are only mildew and discoloration from age. These are what you found that night, I trust? But there is something else here you did not see. Perhaps it is the object of your cousin's late-night search.''

Holmes brought over a framed boudoir-size photograph for us to see. It was of two women, quite young, standing side by side in a well-tended garden. The one on the right held an infant in her arms.

"Do you know these women?'' asked Holmes.

"Why, yes!'' answered Grace Farrington. "I am certain the woman on the right is my late grandmother. How young she looks in this! That babe she holds must surely be my own mother, for the child's garments are feminine, and my grandmother's other two children were sons.''

"The other woman could well be Lady Penelope, herself, Holmes,'' I ventured, looking from the photo to the drugged woman and back again. "The resemblance is strong, despite the intervening years.''

"I quite agree, Watson.''

"Yes,'' Mrs. Farrington concurred. "But, I do not understand. What could there be about this photo that would hold such fascination for my cousin? Such that he would ransack these cabinets for it upon the very first night of my arrival?''

Holmes studied the photo a long moment more, then his serious gaze fell upon Grace Farrington's delicate features. At last he said, "There would be no point in guessing. I suggest, instead, that the facts must come from Lady Penelope herself, when she is capable. Doctor—do you think it safe to move her now?"

I reexamined her quickly and was encouraged by what I found. "Yes, her pulse is strengthening. I think she will be up to it."

"Excellent," said Holmes. He started toward the corridor. "We shall see these brigands well secured first, and then make a litter to transport Lady Penelope to more favorable quarters. Once that is done I shall go and bring the constable. Mr. Trenton—I shall need your testimony to be given to the authorities."

"Gladly, sir," came the solicitor's reply.

"Ah, good fellow. Captain—let us tend to your prisoners."

It was some two weeks later, with the weather much improved, that Grace Farrington again called upon us, this time accompanied by her husband. She extended to Sherlock Holmes an envelope thick with bank notes.

"From Lady Penelope," she said, "for consideration of your extraordinary services."

Holmes took the offered fee graciously. "She is most kind. Tell me—how is she feeling?"

"Fully recovered, now. Thankfully, her constitution is strong, and not at all like the impression my cousin gave us. She is also just as dear and sweet as her letter had led me to believe."

"Wonderful news!"

"There are no money problems, of course, so we have rehired the servants, and my husband is doing what he can to help restore the grounds. Lady Penelope insists that it is our home as well, now."

"Then all has worked out well," Holmes replied. "And did you put to her the question of the photo?"

"Indeed. She has told me all—it was quite a revelation." Grace Farrington averted her eyes briefly, her face colouring. "Here, Mr. Holmes. She has explained it in a letter she asked me to give you. Thank you. Thank you both, so very much!"

With that she gave us each a hug, much to Holmes's consternation. Then she and her husband bid us a fond good day and departed our Baker Street flat.

Holmes settled with a sigh into his chair, opening the letter and reading it silently for a long while despite my obvious interest. Then he smiled.

"Ah," said he. "It is even as I suspected."

"What, Holmes? Do not keep me in suspense."

"You remarked to me at Thaxton Manor that the unidentified woman in the old photo bore a resemblance to Lady Penelope, whom in fact it was. But you seemingly did not notice that it also bore a remarkable resemblance to our client, Grace Farrington."

"Mrs. Farrington?" I said. "Why, yes. I suppose you are right."

"With good reason. It seems that Lady Penelope, some years before she married Lord Henry, had a brief and unfortunate liaison with another man. A child resulted, and as she was young and unmarried, and of high-born family, it was arranged for her sister to adopt the child and raise it as her own."

"Then, Lady Penelope is not Mrs. Farrington's great-aunt, but her grandmother?"

"Quite so," replied Holmes. "Apparently Jeremy Wollcott had found the photo when exploring the trophy chamber, and was so struck by Mrs. Farrington's resemblance to the young Lady Penelope that he had to look at it again. Ironically, it was his undoing." My companion now fixed me with a sympathetic look. "There is one other thing. Due to the nature of this information, Lady Penelope requests that we keep the entire matter to ourselves, at least for the forseeable future."

"But, Holmes!" I cried, "I have already set down the events on paper."

"There, there, my friend. We can but do as the lady wishes."

I sighed heavily. "Very well. You are right, of course. I shall lock the account away, with those other cases of a delicate nature, and merely hope they see publication at some later date." I fell silent a long moment, then added, "Something still troubles me, though. What colossal nerve Wollcott and the others had, to continue with their deception even after the Farringtons' arrival, and even after *we* appeared on the scene."

"They had no choice," said Sherlock Holmes. "They were already committed to their scheme by then. Besides, my dear Watson," he added with a twinkle in his eyes, "when have you ever seen an actor, good or bad, who did not relish a larger audience!"

THE RETURN OF
THE SPECKLED
BAND

Edward D. Hoch

Illustration by Sidney Paget of a scene from *A Case of Identity* in "The Strand Magazine" 1891.

A pril of '83 will always be remembered as the time when my good friend Mr. Sherlock Holmes and I journeyed to Stoke Moran, in Surrey, for that most singular and frightening case which I have recorded elsewhere as *The Adventure of the Speckled Band*. Until now, I have not written of the even stranger events that formed a sequel of sorts to that remarkable affair. They were to involve us with a particularly clever and despicable murderer, and a situation fully as dangerous as that memorable night when Holmes and I waited in Helen Stoner's bedroom at Stoke Moran.

But I am getting ahead of myself. The case really began in September of '83, some five months after the conclusion of the speckled band affair. It was a quiet time for us on Baker Street, and Holmes was taking advantage of the lull to begin work on his proposed monograph on human ears. I was reading the morning's *Times* when there was a knock from Mrs. Hudson announcing the arrival of a visitor.

"A man or a woman?" Holmes asked, glancing up from his writing.

"A man, sir. Tall man with coal black hair and dark eyes. He says it's very important."

"Show him up, then, Mrs. Hudson."

She returned in a moment with a man who was as she had

described him. He gave his name as Henry Dade and accepted the seat Holmes indicated. "I thank you for seeing me at once," he began. There was a trace of an accent in his voice, but I could not place it. "It is most important."

"Ah, Mr. Dade," said Holmes, stepping forward with a smile, "I see you have given up the wandering life of a gypsy and have settled for the noble trade of blacksmithing."

The black-haired man jerked back in alarm. "Who told you I was a gypsy? Has Sarah been here before me?"

"No, no. I only observed the nearly-healed hole in each earlobe where earrings have been worn. And your scorched shirt from an infamiliarity with the operation of the bellows: the scorched area stops abruptly at the point where a blacksmith's apron would cover it."

"You are a wizard, Mr. Holmes. Everything I heard about you is true."

"Sit down and let me get you a cup of hot coffee. These September mornings bring a certain chill to the air. And pray tell me what mission has brought you to my lodging."

Henry Dade cast an uncertain eye in my direction. "It is of a confidential nature—"

"Watson is my good right arm. I would be lost without him."

"Very well." Dade accepted the comment and settled down to tell his story. "As you already know, I recently gave up the wandering life of a gypsy to become a blacksmith, in the western Surrey village of Stoke Moran—"

The words brought an immediate reaction from Sherlock Holmes. "Stoke Moran! Were you the blacksmith there in April of this year?"

"I was, sir. I know of your dealings with Dr. Roylott. You may have heard that we had a dispute in the final week of March, shortly before your visit. Roylott hurled me over a parapet into a stream. I wanted to have the man arrested, but his step-daughter, Helen Stoner, paid me a goodly sum to hush it up."

Holmes had rung for Mrs. Hudson, and when she appeared he asked that a pot of coffee be brought up. Then he said, "Tell me, how is Miss Stoner since the unfortunate events of last April?"

"She has been on holiday in the south of France, fully recovered from her ordeal."

"Good, good! Now continue."

"Grimesby Roylott was always a friend to the wandering gypsies and allowed them to camp on his land. In fact, that is what we argued about the day he hurled me into the stream. My brother Ramon had remained with the gypsy band on the Roylott property, and he wanted me back with them. He objected to my marriage to Sarah Tinsdale, a young woman from the village. He said I had betrayed the gypsy way of life. That day I accused Roylott of poisoning Ramon's mind against me, and he threw me into the water.

"As you know, Roylott owned a cheetah and a baboon which wandered freely on his grounds. After his death this past April, Miss Stoner wanted to dispose of them. My brother Ramon made her an offer, which she accepted. The animals went to him, together with any other wildlife he might find on the property. Miss Stoner only wanted to be rid of it."

"Go on."

"One of the things my brother found on the grounds following Roylott's death was a mate to the dreaded speckled band— the deadly swamp adder that caused the tragic events of last April."

"That's impossible!" I exclaimed. "There was only one snake, and I saw Holmes throw it into the iron safe himself. The police later disposed of it."

"Roylott kept a second snake in a wire cage in one of his outbuildings. My brother found it and took it along with the baboon and cheetah. I fear now that he means to use it as Roylott did, to bring harm to myself or my wife."

"Has he threatened you?"

"Worse than that—he threatened Sarah. She encountered him in the village two days ago. He had the snake with him on his wagon, and he showed it to her. She was frightened half to death."

Holmes took up his pipe and filled it with tobacco. "It seems to me, sir, that your problem is one for the local police rather than a consulting detective here in London. There is no mystery to be solved, and I am not in the habit of furnishing bodyguard service."

"I came to you because of the previous incident, Mr. Holmes. They say the swamp adder is the deadliest snake in India. You have faced one, and bested it. I beg you to protect Sarah and me from my brother's wrath."

I could almost see the indecision written on Holmes's face.

Mrs. Hudson entered at that moment with a steaming pot of coffee and the expression was replaced with a familiar smile. "Certainly I could speak to him. Preventing a crime in advance is preferable to solving it after the deed is done."

"Then you'll come down to Stoke Moran?"

"We'll take the morning train tomorrow," Holmes promised. "You might arrange a room for us at the Crown Inn. I remember it as a pleasant enough lodging."

After coffee our visitor departed, and Holmes stared out the window after him. "What is it?" I asked. "You seem uneasy, Holmes."

"The entire story seems far fetched in the extreme, Watson. This tale of a second snake may be nothing more than a gypsy ruse of some sort."

"Then why are we going?"

Holmes smiled and replied, "If it is a ruse, I wish to learn the purpose of it, and whether it presents any danger to Miss Stoner when she returns from her travels."

Remembering our previous excursion to Stoke Moran, I slipped my revolver into the pocket of my coat when we departed in the morning. It was a dank autumn day, one of the first we'd had following an unusually pleasant summer. The train from Waterloo Station was on time, and we took it as far as Leatherhead, hiring a trap at the station inn just as we had done on the previous journey, nearly six months earlier.

"The weather is not so pleasant this time," Sherlock Holmes remarked. "But then, spring always holds more promise than autumn. Look, Watson! There is the gypsy camp!"

We were passing the gray gables and high, pointed roof of the late Grimesby Roylott's mansion, and off in the distance, almost as far as the woods, we could see the wispy smoke of a campfire. "So it is, Holmes. I believe I can see one of those animals—the cheetah—prowling around."

"Driver," Holmes called out, "please leave us off here!"

The black-hatted driver turned to us. "It's a mile walk into the village."

"That's all right. We'll make it on foot."

"Straight ahead down this road."

Holmes paid him, and we scrambled out of the trap, watching while it turned in the road for the journey back to Leatherhead. Then we set out across country, through the wayside hedge and up the gently rising hill toward the gypsy camp. As we approached, the cheetah caught our scent and moved into a crouch. For a tense moment my hand felt for the revolver in my coat pocket, but then a young gypsy, wearing a colorful shirt, ran up and grabbed the animal's collar.

"I am looking for Ramon Dade," Holmes said. "I am told he is the owner of this animal."

The dark face relaxed just a bit. "I am Ramon. Who sends you here?"

"My name is Sherlock Holmes. I have come out from London at the behest of your brother Henry."

"Henry!" He almost spat the word. "He is no longer my brother. He deserts his tribe to live in the village."

"He is married and a blacksmith now."

"We have horses. He could be a blacksmith to us, but that woman took him away."

"His wife, Sarah?"

"I will not speak of her."

"He says you threatened her with a snake and frightened her half to death."

"Those are all lies."

"But you do have a snake—the mate to the swamp adder that killed Dr. Roylott."

"I bought the animals from Miss Stoner. A cheetah and a baboon."

"And a swamp adder."

"She told me I could have any other animals I found on the property. Her stepfather had the second snake in a cage in an old potting shed."

"Take me to it," Holmes said.

The gypsy hesitated. Some of the others in the camp had paused in their activities to watch our confrontation, and once again I was glad I had brought the revolver with me. However, no one produced a knife or any other weapon. A small boy appeared with the baboon in tow, and the mood lightened at once. Perhaps I was wrong to feel threatened by these people.

"You can see the snake if you want," Ramon Dade decided with some reluctance. "Come this way."

We followed him to a potting shed that stood on the edge of the formal gardens, now grown over with weeds and wildflowers. "Will Miss Stoner keep this house?" Holmes asked.

"No. It has too many bad memories for her. She has already offered it for sale. The new owner will want us out, and we will move on to another county."

"That is why you are urging your brother to come along, so you will not be parted?"

"He must choose between that woman and his people." He lifted the hasp on the wooden door and we followed him inside. The place was thick with cobwebs, and in the dim filtered light I imagined it to be alive with spiders. The thought so unnerved me that I forgot we had entered this place to view the deadliest snake in India, a creature far more dangerous than any spider.

Ramon felt on one of the shelves for a dark lantern, which he lit. Then he announced in a hushed voice, "Behold the speckled band!"

A gasp escaped my lips as the lantern light fell upon the wire cage. At first I saw only a rock, slightly larger than a man's head, and the branch of a tree. Then my eyes focused on the peculiar band, the speckled band, coiled around the top of the rock. Even as Holmes and I watched, it started to move. "My God, Holmes!"

"Steady, Watson."

It was my first really good look at the creature whose mate had claimed two lives. "The swamp adder," I breathed.

"A little known offshoot of the krait family." Holmes turned to the gypsy. "This creature must be destroyed, or at least confined to a zoo. Its bite causes death within ten seconds. All your lives are in danger."

"I have been milking it of its venom," Ramon Dade answered. "We will be moving soon and the snake will travel with us." Even as he spoke, the creature reared up, its squat head weaving slightly as it faced us. I took a step backward, fearing it might try to strike through the wire mesh.

We stepped outside the potting shed, where Holmes offered a final word of advice. "Let your brother and his wife live in peace," he cautioned. "Stop frightening her with the snake."

"I have no brother, and I do not frighten that woman."

As Holmes and I walked back to the road, we observed one of the other gypsies watching us. I wondered who he was, and if he had any special interest in our visit. "What now, Holmes?"

"I have one other person to see who may shed some light on the matter—Sarah Dade, Henry's new wife."

Our lodgings at the Crown Inn, consisting of a bedroom and sitting room, were fully as good as on our first visit, although this time the view faced the village instead of looking out on the Roylott manor house. We ate a light lunch in the downstairs dining room where Holmes asked directions to the blacksmith's shop. It proved to be in the next block, near the little creek that bisected the village.

"No doubt that is the very parapet where Dr. Roylott and Henry Dade fought," Holmes remarked as we passed it. He led the way into the shop, where we could see Dade at work forming horseshoes on the anvil.

He stopped work when he saw us, plunging the steaming metal into a trough of cold water. "Mr. Holmes, Dr. Watson! Welcome again to our little village. Did you have a pleasant journey?"

"Very pleasant," Holmes said. "On the way we stopped at the gypsy camp to speak with your brother Ramon."

Henry Dade's body went rigid. "What did he have to say? Did he admit to keeping the other snake?"

"Oh, yes! In fact he showed it to us."

"The man is brazen if nothing else."

"I would like to speak with your wife, if I may."

"Certainly. I will call her."

Their living quarters were upstairs over the blacksmith shop, and she quickly came down in answer to his summons. Sarah Dade was a thin woman with a pretty face and nervous hands, her dark hair drawn back from her face and arranged in a bun. She wore a knitted shawl wrapped around her shoulders, over a dark brown dress that reached to the floor. "You are Mr. Sherlock Holmes?" she asked. "My husband has told me about his visit to you."

"I thought I might speak to you about your encounter with your brother-in-law."

"Help them in any way you can," Henry Dade told his wife. "I will be upstairs relaxing for a few minutes. Hammering horseshoes is tiring work."

Sarah Dade smiled after his retreating figure. "He likes his naps. The life of a blacksmith is for a younger man."

"How old is your husband?"

"He will be forty-five in a few months. His brother Ramon is ten years younger. The family had some gold, which went to the eldest son, and Henry used it to buy this shop. Ramon resents the fact that he abandoned the life of a gypsy. More than anything, he resents Henry marrying me and using the gold for this shop."

"He has threatened you?"

"On more than one occasion. He showed me that damned

creature—yes, damned by God since the beginning of time—and told me the speckled band could come for us anywhere. He reminded me of Aaron's staff in the Bible, the one that turned into a serpent.''

"Holmes!" I said, pointing out to the street where a figure scurried along on the opposite side.

"What is it, Watson?"

"That gypsy we saw at the camp! I think he followed us here.''

"It is Manuel," Sarah Dade said. "He is feeble-minded but harmless. He runs errands for us. You see, all of the gypsies are not our enemies. Only Ramon would cause us trouble.''

"Let us hope our visit today has deterred him," Holmes said. "We will remain overnight at the Crown Inn before returning to London by the morning train. If anything unusual transpires, we are close at hand.''

"Come up to see Henry before you leave.''

"Very well.''

We followed her up the narrow staircase to the second floor living quarters. She opened the door to a comfortable parlor, and I could see her husband seated in a large armchair, his head down, apparently dozing. She walked over to him, clutching the shawl about her shoulders as if to ward off a sudden chill. She bent, shook him, and uttered his name. "Henry! Mr. Holmes and Dr. Watson are leaving now.''

"Is he all right?" Holmes asked, sudden alarm in his voice.

"Oh my God!" Sarah backed away, one hand to her mouth. "He's—''

She collapsed in a faint before I could reach her. Holmes hurried to the man in the chair. "Careful, Watson!" he warned. "We are not alone in this room.''

My revolver was in my hand as I searched the corners with my eyes. "Holmes, do you mean—?''

"Henry Dade is dead. There are the twin punctures of a serpent's fangs on his neck. It is the speckled band again.''

I helped Sarah recover, with the aid of some smelling salts, and she insisted on going for the constable while Holmes and I searched the room for the deadly swamp adder. "It's fangs may be empty but it is still dangerous," Holmes warned. "Keep your weapon in hand.''

"The window is close, Holmes. How did that terrible creature gain access to the room?''

'When we find him we may know the answer to that.''

But we did not find the swamp adder or any other snake in the room with Henry Dade's body. Every inch of the room was searched without result. I was especially careful of the umbrella stand, expecting one of the canes to come alive in my hand as it had for Aaron, but they remained merely wood. "It is not here," I said at last, after a half-hour search.

"I quite agree, Watson."

Sarah had returned with a Constable Richards, a stout young man who'd had little experience with violent death. "I will have to summon Scotland Yard," he told us. "We have no facilities here for investigating a murder by snakebite."

"Dr. Roylott—" I began.

"The official inquiry concluded that Dr. Roylott died accidentally while playing with a dangerous pet. But you say this is murder."

"The victim's wife says it is," Holmes corrected. "I have not completed my investigation of the facts."

"His brother killed him," Sarah Dade insisted. "There is no other explanation."

"There seems none," Holmes agreed, "but pray tell me how the deadly serpent was introduced into the room."

"I left that window slightly ajar when I came downstairs. Henry must have closed it when he came up here to nap. The serpent had entered through the window and hidden itself somewhere."

"But there is no snake here now," my friend pointed out. "Your husband was hardly in a position to open the door or window for the serpent after he'd been bitten. Dr. Roylott lived only ten seconds, you remember."

"That is true," she agreed. "My God, is it possible Ramon has the power to change staffs into serpents?"

"Whatever his power, we need to speak with him," Holmes decided. "And with that other gypsy, Manuel, too. He was across the street at about the time the deed was done."

There was no doctor in the village itself, so I pronounced Henry Dade officially dead. Though I'd had little experience with death from snakebite, the symptoms seemed to bear it out. While snakebite death was rarely this instantaneous, we knew from the case of Dr. Roylott that it was certainly possible.

When Ramon Dade arrived, in the company of Constable Richards, he went at once to the body of his brother. There were tears in his eyes as he turned and told us, ''I did not do this thing. The snake has been in its cage in the potting shed this whole day.''

Sherlock Holmes stepped forward. ''Do you deny threatening your brother's wife with the snake?''

''I threatened her, yes,'' he admitted. ''She lured Henry away from the family for the gold he had. He belonged to us, not to her.''

Holmes turned to the constable. ''What of the snake?''

''I have it in its cage, in my trap.''

''And the other gypsy, Manuel?''

''He is downstairs, but you will not get any information out of him.''

''We'll see,'' Holmes said.

I followed him downstairs to speak with the gypsy named Manuel. When I saw him close up, I was struck by the ugly deformity of the man. The poor devil had suffered some childhood injury which had left the working of his brain impaired. His few words of speech were mere noise, hardly recognizable to my ears.

''Manuel,'' Holmes said, ''you came here earlier this afternoon.''

''Yes—''

''Did you like Henry and Sarah?''

''Yes, like.''

''Did you do errands for them?''

He nodded his head, smiling with comprehension.

''And did you bring them a snake today, the gypsy snake?''

This required a little more thought, but finally he shook his head. ''No, no snake.''

''Did you ever touch the snake in its cage?''

''No, no! Snake bad.''

Holmes sighed in exasperation and tried a different approach. ''Did Ramon take the snake today? Did you see him with the snake?''

He shook his head, looking frightened.

''All right,'' Holmes decided. ''There is nothing more to be learned here. Let us go look at the villain in its cage. Perhaps it will tell us how the crime was committed.''

To me, the swamp adder looked much as it had a few hours earlier. Its brownish speckles seemed almost pretty at times, and I had to remind myself that it was a deadly killer. ''It's close to three feet long, Holmes,'' I observed.

''About the length of a walking stick.''

"Are you back to that again? We examined the ones in the umbrella stand."

"So we did. And did it not strike you as odd that a gypsy turned blacksmith, a reasonably vigorous man in his forties, would possess those walking sticks? Certainly he did not need them for support, and he had no walking stick with him yesterday in London. What were they doing in his parlor? What purpose did they serve?"

"Holmes, you can't believe the snake was hidden in one of those canes! Even if it had been, how did Ramon manage to retrieve it?"

"Let us speak to Sarah Dade about this most interesting question of the superfluous walking sticks."

Sarah seemed surprised at Holmes's question, but answered it immediately. "They belonged to the previous blacksmith's father, who died last year. When the blacksmith moved out, he said he had no use for the canes, and he left them for us. I decided they looked nice in the umbrella stand."

"As simple as that," Holmes said with a laugh. "Watson, you must remind me of this the next time I seem too pompous and self-assured with my deductions."

It was decided that Sarah Dade should spend the night at the Crown Inn, too, on the slim chance there might be two snakes, one of them still loose and undiscovered in her flat above the blacksmith shop. The constable had promised a more thorough search of the furniture and closets in the morning, when the Scotland Yard people would arrive to join in the investigation.

We dined with Sarah on the main floor of the inn, but she was still understandably distraught at her husband's death. "I was the one who insisted he come to you," she told Holmes. "I was so fearful something like this might happen. Now he is gone, and I have nothing but the memory of our brief time together."

"His killer will be brought to justice," Holmes promised her.

I had assumed we would retire early and spend a peaceful night, but once we were alone in our room, my friend paced the floor like a caged animal, deep in thought. Finally he seemed to reach a decision. "There are things to be done tonight, Watson. Come along now, and bring your revolver."

"Holmes—"

But he would say no more, and before I knew it we had left the inn under cover of darkness, carefully slipping out the back door. He headed through the alleys, approaching the blacksmith shop from the rear, and quietly opened the back door. "I took the liberty of unbolting this earlier," he explained in whispered tones. "Move very softly, now. We're going upstairs to the living quarters."

"You think the serpent is still there?"

"We shall see."

I followed him through the darkness, barely able to make out his form as he moved up the steps, testing each one first for possible squeaks. "Step over this one, Watson," he whispered, halfway up. "Not a sound, now!"

We entered the living room where Henry Dade had been killed, and he motioned me to take up a position behind the sofa. "My revolver, Holmes," I said, offering it to him.

He waved it away. "Keep it ready, Watson, but don't use it unless I tell you to."

It was like the night we spent in Miss Stoner's bedroom, a dreadful vigil in the dark, and I half expected to hear again the low, clear whistle with which Roylott had summoned the speckled band. The ticking of the mantle clock was the only sound for a long time. My leg was cramped beneath me, and at last I tried shifting to a more comfortable position.

At that instant we heard a squeak on the stairs. Someone, something, was approaching. I gripped the revolver more tightly as the door to the room opened slowly inward. The figure that entered could barely be discerned in the darkness. It crossed the room quickly and seemed to kneel by one of the chairs.

That was when Holmes moved.

He struck a match and yelled, "Don't move! There are two of us!"

The figure gasped and Holmes sprang forward, his right arm raised as if to ward off a blow. The burning match fell to the floor and went out, plunging us into darkness again. I heard the struggle, the panting breath, and hurried forward with my weapon. "Holmes! Are you all right?"

"I think so, Watson, though it was a close call. Strike another match, will you?"

I did so, and by its glow I saw that he had pinned Sarah Dade to the floor. In her right hand, carefully held in Holmes's powerful grip, was a pair of hypodermic needles tied together with string, side by side.

"Here, Watson," Holmes gasped as she struggled to free herself. "Here are the fangs of the speckled band, and no less deadly than the real thing!"

*   *   *

After Constable Richards had been summoned, and Sarah Dade was placed in custody, Sherlock Holmes explained. "I felt certain she'd come tonight to retrieve those needles. The Scotland Yard people would be searching the place in the morning, and she couldn't risk their being found."

"I still don't understand, Holmes," I admitted. "Henry Dade showed every symptom of having been killed by snakebite."

"It was a clever plan to dispose of a husband she'd married only for his gold. Dr. Roylott's crime was well known in the village, of course, despite the verdict of accidental death, and my part in the investigation was known, too. When Henry's brother, Ramon, showed Sarah the snake and made some ambiguous comments, she chose to interpret them as threats. She even went further, persuading her husband to summon me here to protect them. With us on the scene when Henry Dade was killed, it was sure to be seen as another crime like the earlier ones involving that deadly snake. She arranged the crime in such a way that it seemed impossible for her to have committed it."

"It was impossible, Holmes!" I insisted. "Sarah Dade was with us in the blacksmith shop when her husband was killed."

"So it seemed at the time, Watson. Remember, though, that Henry went upstairs to rest a bit, and he even seemed to be dozing when we entered the room. That is exactly what he was doing, sleeping in his chair, until Sarah ended his life by injecting the poison into his neck in our presence."

"You mean we saw the murder committed?"

"I fear so, Watson. Remember how she clutched the shawl around her, hiding the twin needles she'd prepared earlier. She even shook him, to cover his involuntary jerk as she injected the poison. He was dead almost instantly, and she shielded his face from us in those crucial few seconds. Then she had only to dispose of the needles. She pretended to faint, and while on the floor, pushed them into the bottom of the chair. She was attempting to retrieve them tonight when we surprised her."

"What was in those needles, Holmes?"

"The poison Ramon Dade had milked from the fangs of the swamp adder. Remember he told us he did that for safety's sake, and no doubt he told Sarah, as well, when he showed her the snake. I feel certain she paid the dim-witted Manuel to steal the venom and bring it to her. He often did errands for them, and he would not have realized the full import of his task."

"How did you know she was guilty, Holmes?"

"It was more a matter of knowing the snake must be innocent. She relied on the window being left open a bit, but Henry must have closed it when he came up for his nap. There was no way the snake could have escaped, and it was not in the room when we searched it. The twin punctures in his neck were also most suggestive to me. They were right where Sarah had stood, bending over the sleeping man. But, to be certain, I still needed to catch her in the act of retrieving those hypodermic needles."

"She might have killed you, Holmes!"

"So might the speckled band on our last visit."

"The next time we come to Stoke Moran—"

Sherlock Holmes interrupted me with a laugh. "I hope, Watson, that we have had our last visit here. Let us return by the earliest train to the peace and quiet of London!"

THE ADVENTURE
OF THE UNIQUE
HOLMES

Jon L. Breen

Illustration by Sidney Paget of a scene from *The Red-Headed League* in "The Strand Magazine" 1891.

It is difficult to estimate on how many occasions I have been handed a letter or a calling card, or some other object or message, by my friend Sherlock Holmes and been asked to interpret it. Although I could never glean as much information from such items as he could, I rather enjoyed the game and flatter myself that occasionally I may have been able to pass along some bit of insight helpful to my gifted companion. During one of my periodic visits to the old rooms in Baker Street, shortly after the dawn of the present century, I was handed two messages for inspection; and they were singular indeed.

In each case, the plain white paper seemed ordinary enough, the hand cultured. One seemed clearly masculine, the other feminine, but I was robbed of any chance to gloat over this perception by the fact that the notes' contents made all questions of gender obvious. The first read,

"Mr. Holmes: I am desperate for your help, for I am greatly worried about my husband, who has been acting in an exceedingly strange manner of late. He goes about in full makeup in the daytime, even on Mondays. Please advise me as to when it would be convenient for me to call on you.—(signed) Mrs. Albert Fenner"

And the second,

> "Mr. Holmes: I beg leave to consult you on a most
> mysterious matter, one which could greatly profit me
> if it is brought to a successful conclusion. I must say
> at the outset that your participation in my problem
> would have to be contingent upon receiving a fee at its
> satisfactory conclusion. I am unemployed at present
> (simply because the next turn clumsily slipped on the
> water and glycerine) and cannot pay you unless the
> mystery is solved.—Yours, very truly, Anthony
> Croydon"

"What do you make of them, Watson?" my old friend asked.

"Very cryptic indeed," I confessed. "I can make little of
them, but both seem to offer interesting features, the second
perhaps more than the first. Which case are you more inclined
to take?"

"I may take both cases, my dear fellow. In fact, both poten-
tial clients will be visiting us this morning. You will have
perceived that the two matters are connected."

"Truthfully, I can't say I have."

"Well, come then, Watson, what *can* you deduce from the
two letters? You know my methods well enough."

"I feel great compassion for the writer of the first letter, but I
hardly think a consulting detective is the person to help her. An
alienist might be more to the point. Her husband is obviously
suffering from a form of sexual perversion rather embarrassing
to discuss. I have, in my practice, seen men who affect wom-
en's clothing, and the wearing of powder and paint, such as
even a *lady* of culture would disdain, is surely a similar type of
deviance."

"Have you no idea, Watson, of the husband's profession?"

"I see no clue whatever, Holmes. For what profession is
safe? 'There, but for the grace of God . . .' and all that sort of
thing."

"Why does the writer say 'full makeup in the daytime'?"

"Perhaps, if he practices his particular fetish in the evening,
in the privacy of their home, she does not mind, but now that it
is infringing on the daylight hours and possibly being revealed
to others, she feels matters are getting slightly out of hand."

"A much less circuitous explanation presents itself, Watson.
That it is not surprising for him to wear full makeup in the

evening, or perhaps even in the daytime on days other than Monday: that he is by profession an actor.''

"Oh, I see. Yes, of course, quite obvious, isn't it? And he would wear makeup for matinees, but the London theatres do not have such on Mondays. Of course. But why, then, is he wearing makeup on Mondays and not telling his wife?''

"I can offer a quite probable hypothesis, Watson. He is spending his days making extra money posing for cinemato-graph pictures, an occupation any legitimate actor would want to keep secret, perhaps even from his wife. And now you doubtless perceive the connection between the first note and the second.''

"The second, Holmes, is intriguing, but most unenlightning. I cannot imagine what it can be about—the 'next turn clumsily slipped on the water and glycerine.' Pure gibberish, as far as I can see.''

" 'Turn', Watson, is a term used in the music halls for a performer's particular specialty. Mr. Croydon's performance left a residue of water and glycerine on the floor for the next performer to slip on, and the next performer was both angry and influential enough to lose him his employment in the halls.''

"I see. Some knockabout comedy act, I daresay.''

"I think not, Watson. Cinematographs have become a staple of the music hall programs, and they are projected from the rear on a fine calico screen damped down with water and glycerine. I believe Mr. Croydon's 'turn' was showing cinematograph pictures, and on the occasion in question he was careless in the damping process. That is the connection between the two letters.''

"A common element, yes, but hardly a connection, if you ask me, Holmes.''

"Consider, then, the coincidence of their both arriving the same day, Watson.''

I grumbled a bit at that. I don't like coincidences. They do not make for a neat story, as my literary agent so often reminds me. Magazine editors scorn them, and often truth is not a sufficient defense.

"It would be my hope, my dear fellow," I said, "that it is not a coincidence at all.''

"Very good, Watson. You are more perceptive every day, I swear it. No, I do not believe it is a coincidence.''

Holmes stepped to the window and looked down on Baker Street. "Our visitor, I think, Watson," he said, indicating a comely young woman alighting from a cab. "I told her eleven would be convenient, and she is scrupulously prompt."

"Admirable in a woman, Holmes."

"It speaks of a well-planned plot, Watson."

My friend's cynicism nettled me, particularly when the woman had taken a seat among the clutter of my friend's sitting room, which was even more disorderly than it had been in the days when we shared quarters. I had seen enough treachery in the fair sex through the years of following my friend's activities to have shed the greater portion of my gentlemanly credulousness, but surely this magnificent creature, red of hair, blue of eye, fair of feature, and matchless of form, could not have any part in an underhanded scheme or plot.

"Mrs. Fenner, is your husband having difficulty pursuing his acting career?"

She gasped. "Mr. Holmes, what they say of you is true. You are surely clairvoyant."

"Is it true, then, that he finds roles with difficulty?"

"Quite true. He has been most despondent about it. He spends all day seeking work."

"And wears his makeup?"

"It is not usual for actors to go about in the daytime in their makeup, Mr. Holmes. It is almost as if his mind has gone unhinged, though he seems his old self in other ways."

"Why do you consult me in this regard, rather than a Harley Street physician? Is there some reason to connect his behavior with a crime?"

"No, of course not."

It seemed to me that Holmes was being unnecessarily cryptic, cruel even. Why did he not reveal his brilliant deduction about the cinematograph posing? I felt sorry for the lovely lady but held my tongue, knowing my friend usually had a reason for his bizarre behavior.

For several minutes he went on, asking questions far afield from what we had discussed before the lady's arrival. Even when she mentioned that friends had seen her husband walking the streets of Brighton, that hub of cinematograph production, Holmes kept silent. If I had not known he had put his finger on the answer almost at once, I should have been convinced he was baffled.

"Is there, then, no help you can give me, Mr. Holmes?" she cried out at last.

"It is possible a medical man is your best answer, Mrs. Fenner. Perhaps Dr. Watson can recommend a specialist who . . ."

"Really, Holmes!" I cried, unable to contain myself any longer.

Holmes threw back his head and laughed. Mrs. Fenner reddened and rose to go. My friend's behavior was both inexplicable and damnably rude. I conveyed apologies on his behalf to the woman and showed her to the door, but something told me I should not say anything of the deduction of the cinematograph.

"Holmes, what is the meaning of this outrage?" I cried when the lady had left.

"My dear fellow," he replied, barely controlling his mirth, "you are a trouper indeed. You always remember your lines and deliver them with conviction. While I, amateur that I am, refuse to deliver mine when they come from an inferior script."

"I cannot share your amusement, Holmes. The poor woman . . ."

"Further discussion must wait, my dear fellow. I hear the step, on the stair, of our second visitor."

Anthony Croydon proved to be a small, weasel-featured man who affected the dress and demeanor of a racecourse tout. Continuing his pattern of perversity, Holmes dealt with Croydon very openly, immediately repeating his deduction of the glycerine and water, to Croydon's amazement, and asking for details of the matter on which Croydon wished to consult him.

3   "Mr. Holmes, I have been fiddling about with cinematographic apparatus since the game started back around '96. I saw R. W. Paul's remarkable exhibition in March of that year at Olympia, and I was immediately struck by the possibilities of the medium both for entertainment and enlightenment. Along with a friend of mine who had a mechanical bent, I started my own business.

"We did it all. We were in business in time to do a film of Persimmons's Derby of '96, and we showed our film of that in music halls, in tents and at fairs all over the country. We did the Henley Regatta and the Boat Race and Her Majesty's Diamond Jubilee—deuced bad vantage point for that, however.

"We even filmed the Boer War," he added with a chuckle.

"I hardly think that tragic event is a matter for levity," I said with some severity, unable to keep silent any longer. Croydon's lecture had the suggestion of a prepared speech for fairground delivery, but Holmes was listening with rapt and apparently respectful attention.

"No offense intended, Doctor," Croydon said. "But we

didn't really film the war, you see. We recreated it in our studios, with actors taking the parts of the soldiers. Very realistic, though, I must say, what with exploding shells and falling bodies and all.

"Well, like any business, this one has its ups and downs, and for me they've been only downs for some little time. After that little incident that left us out of the halls, the business went three-quarters down the drain, and I foolishly allowed my partner to buy me out for a fraction of what the business is worth. He has a fine studio of his own in Brighton now and has moved from actualities and topicals into 'made-up' films, employing the finest London actors. And I, sad to say, am out in the cold."

"Your discourse on the cinematograph business is most interesting and instructive, Mr. Croydon," Holmes said. "But you have not explained how I may be of service. Perhaps it has something to do with regaining your share of the business?"

"No, it's bigger than that, Mr. Holmes. Much bigger. It so happens I am the heir to a fabulous fortune in America, left to me by an eccentric gold-prospecting uncle. He left me a map, do you see, showing the location of his strike in Colorado. But half the map has disappeared, and I am convinced that my former partner has absconded with it."

"Then you desire me to retrieve the other half?" My friend said, his features totally serious as he gazed keenly at the visitor.

I believe I snorted, but both ignored me. Surely, here was a far more fruitful field for mirth than the plight of poor Mrs. Fenner. Abscond with half the map, indeed! An absurdly unlikely story. I wanted to ask why not the whole map, but Holmes passed this obvious point right over.

"And where are your ex-partner's lodgings?" Holmes asked.

"He has rooms just behind his studio. Surely you must come there, Mr. Holmes. In some disguise, perhaps. I have heard you have a genius for disguise."

"You flatter me. No, your former partner's studio is the last place I should look. There are some things that are too obvious to be fruitful. Tell me, Watson, can you join me for a journey northward? I daresay we can be in a first-class carriage for Doncaster within two hours."

"Doncaster!" exclaimed Croydon. "How does Doncaster come into it?"

"You have been there in the course of your employment, have you not?"

"Why, yes, numerous times, to take pictures of the St. Leger. But . . ."

"And was it not in Doncaster that your partner snatched half the map?"

"No, sir, we were never in Doncaster together."

"Exactly as I expected," said Holmes. "Then Doncaster it must be. And now, if you will excuse me Mr. Croydon, we have work to do. Rest assured you shall have your map."

He showed the baffled and flustered Mr. Croydon out. When the weasellike man had left, Holmes roared with long-suppressed laughter. I had never seen him so amused, nor felt myself less able to share the joke.

"Are we off to Yorkshire, then?" I asked rather snappishly when the torrent of mirth had subsided.

"No, no, surely not, Watson. And even more surely, we shall give a wide berth to Brighton in the days to come. Unless it is your secret longing to have your figure projected upon a screen."

He saw my confusion and at last took pity on me. "My dear fellow, the deductions I made initially about the two messages were precisely the deductions they wanted me to make. It's obvious the lady and the gentleman are in it together. Indeed they may be husband and wife."

"Unthinkable!" I remonstrated.

"Harder to believe than the Colorado treasure map?" he asked, and seemed almost on the verge of dissolving in merriment again. But he controlled himself and continued. "Of course, it was incredible that the actor's wife should not have realized the possibility of her husband's appearing in cinematographs. Especially when her husband was supposedly sighted in full makeup in the vicinity of one of them. And also, do you imagine that cinema performers, any more than stage performers, go about in the streets with their makeup on? Surely they apply it and remove it at the scene of their . . . of their crimes?" He chuckled. "No, it was all a sham. That, along with the question of the half-a-treasure-map, was supposed to lure me to the Brighton studio where, either openly or clandestinely, they planned to immortalize me on celluloid. Chasing some robber, perhaps, through the streets. But surely, Watson, that is no suitable way to display my talents, small though they may be, to the public. And besides, I have neither the need nor the desire for more publicity.''

''I have not known you to shun it in the past.''

''No, but retirement may not be far away. I hope for a quiet life of writing and bee-farming, and continued sensational depictions of my exploits, either through your rather highly-colored magazine accounts or through, may God forbid, cinematographs, will not be welcome.

''I daresay we have not heard the last of these resourceful camera-crankers, Watson. Perhaps getting away from London for a few days would be in order. But not to Doncaster—a cinematographic crew may await us at the station before many hours have passed.''

Once Sherlock Holmes had retired to his Sussex Downs bee-farming, his visits to London were few. As a rule, he travelled incognito, and I was visited by him, during that period, in a variety of diverse and remarkable disguises. His aversion to publicity and his insistence that his days as a consulting detective were over were expressed to me so strongly that he often made me think of the lady who protested too much. Perhaps, I speculated, he really longed for the pleasures of the hunt and was simply unwilling to admit it. Certainly I missed the old days—my wife seemed aware of it, even when I was in the dark about the cause of my chronic restlessness.

It was during one of these restless periods, several years after the appearance in Baker Street of Mrs. Fenner and Mr. Croydon, that my wife induced me to visit a cinema theatre not far from our house to see a picture called *Sherlock Holmes Triumphs*.

I must confess, I did a good deal of muttering on the way to the ''electric palace,'' as we used to call them. ''Probably confounded rubbish,'' I said. ''Why, if Holmes knew, he'd haul the lot who made it into the law courts, I have no doubt.''

''It's merely harmless entertainment, John,'' she retorted. ''You must relax and enjoy it. I'm sure Mr. Holmes would, too.''

''Very likely,'' I replied, with a muted guffaw.

Sitting there in the dark as the film began, I considered the possibilities of a quick nap during its course. I had seen cinematographs before, and once the wonder of seeing a train coming straight toward you had passed, the severe limitations of this threadbare novelty were all too clear.

The initial scene of the silent drama placed before us had three characters. A comely ingenue with a sweet and open expression, a gentleman in a black cape and topper who seemed rather too smooth and obsequious and immediately roused my suspicions as to his motives, and a bent elderly lady who sold flowers on the street corner. The most realistic street scene exacted more of my interest than the actors before it, until my wife leaned over to whisper something in my ear.

"Does one of those persons look familiar to you at all?" she asked.

"Why, yes," I said, as it suddenly dawned on me. The helpless and winsome young girl was the woman I had known as Mrs. Albert Fenner. But how would my wife know her? I was sure they had never met.

This recognition caused me to take a more personal interest in the action. It was obvious that the gentleman in the cape, appearing to be her protector, was actually luring her into a trap. He had in his pocket a copy of her father's will, which he examined when she turned to speak with the flower-seller, cleverly allowing the camera to read over his shoulder that he, her uncle, would be the heir to her father's fortune should she die before reaching twenty-one.

The scene changed miraculously—these camera chaps were clever, I had to admit—to a small room where the uncle confronted his unsuspecting niece with a revolver. He brandished it at her. I had an urge to rush down the aisle toward the screen to come to her aid, but, of course, I realized it was all a play. Through the window of the room came a handsome young man, evidently the young lady's gentleman friend, who struggled with the villain for the gun for a few moments. Gradually, the larger man overpowered the youngster, and in the next scene the boy was bound to a chair in the room, the girl cowering in the corner, the villain still brandishing his gun.

Now the young man spoke, and a representation of his speech appeared on the screen: "You shall not escape, for I have secured the services of Mr. Sherlock Holmes."

The villainous uncle found this an occasion for boisterous mirth. I stirred in my chair. "I'd love to biff him one," I said to my wife, but she stayed my arm. Other spectators around us had begun to cast annoyed looks in my direction. I reminded myself it was only a film and subsided.

In the next scene, the wicked uncle was prodding his niece along the street again, in the vicinity of the elderly flower-seller.

"Do you see no one else you recognize?" My wife asked me.

So I did! The wicked uncle was the man who had called himself Anthony Croydon. I should have realized it before. But my wife had never met him either. For an instant, I pried my eyes from the screen and looked at her lovely, enigmatic profile. The ladies hold more puzzles for us than ever Professor Moriarty spun.

The uncle's next ploy was to drag his unwilling ward to the entrance of an Underground station. I feared I knew what his plan was: to throw her in front of a train in a simulated accident. Just when there seemed no hope she could be saved, assistance came from a most unexpected quarter. The elderly flower-seller came sprinting toward the uncle. In panic, the wicked uncle dropped the now-fainting girl on the pavement and ran. The chase through the streets of London was thrilling indeed—so thrilling that I completely forgot my amazement at the unexpected athletic prowess of this elderly woman.

At last the wicked uncle was cornered, and the chase ended in a most remarkable display of fisticuffs. By now, the hat and wig of the flower-seller had been lost in the chase, and she was revealed to be a man, which explained much. The flower-seller was obviously a trained boxer, an attainment, thank God, of few of the gentle sex.

When, at last, the flower-seller turned his face to the camera, I received a shock that cause me to roar aloud, to the annoyance of those around me, "It is Holmes!"

I believe my wife knew it all along. Surely she, who knew Holmes much less well than I, would not be quicker to see through one of his disguises. It was only on the way home that the inadequacy of the film as an account of one of his exploits struck me. The lack of speech obviated any possibility of displaying his remarkable deductive reasoning. And it rather nettled me that the filmmakers offered, with Holmes's collaboration, the impression that he worked alone, without the aid of an associate.

At last I realized that the disguises Holmes affected when he visited me were not connected with either practicing or avoiding the profession of detective, but rather with a lucrative sideline of acting in the cinema. Either through monetary promises too handsome to ignore or through the chance of playing roles other than that of himself, Holmes had finally given in to the celluloid entrepreneurs. I believe they must have tried to lure him many times prior to the day I have described here, explaining the laughable and rather desperate elaborateness of their effort on that occasion. Indeed the very extent to which they were willing to go may have softened Holmes's resolve.

In any case, this late-blooming and pleasant second career must have helped keep Holmes going in the years after Baker Street. I had often wondered how bee-farming in Sussex, or even writing a textbook on crime detection, could be sufficient diversion for a man of his far-ranging intellect and undoubted flair for the dramatic.

SHERLOCK HOLMES AND "*THE* WOMAN": AN EXPLANATORY MEMOIR BY DR. JOHN H. WATSON, MD.

Michael Harrison

Illustration by Sidney Paget of a scene from *The Adventure of "Gloria Scott"* in "The Strand Magazine" 1893.

The death of Lady de Bathe during the year just passed has reminded me that certain facts, though intended either for posthumous publication or (which is the more likely) no publication at all, ought to be committed to permanent record for those who, in years to come, may wish to know the full truth of my friend Mr. Sherlock Holmes's singular and lifelong infatuation.

Of course, many persons, well acquainted with what went on outside of the reporting (though not by any means outside of the cognizance) of the newspapers and journals, were long ago aware that the lady (whom I called "Irene Adler" in "A Scandal in Bohemia") was the well-known—perhaps too well-known—intimate friend of every young-to-middle-aged male member of the contemporary Royal Family—from His Royal Highness the Prince of Wales downwards . . . though His Highness was not the first member of the Royal Family to cultivate the friendship of the lady, who was at that time the wife of Mr. Edward Langtry.

Inevitably, as the identity of "Irene Adler" was known to Mr. Holmes, the identity of her denouncer—the person whom I somewhat facetiously sought to disguise as "Wilhelm Gottsreich Sigismond von Ormstein, Grand Duke of Cassel-Felstein, and hereditary King of Bohemia"—was equally and instantly recognizable as that of the still very young former Sovereign Prince of Bulgaria, His Serene Highness Prince Alexander of Battenberg. I make no secret of, nor am I in the least excusing the fact that, in preparing a supposedly fictional narrative for a popular monthly magazine, I made every effort to disguise the true identities of the persons concerned. Looking back, I realize now, with something of amusement, how almost certainly I was influenced to concoct for the real Prince Alexander—known as "Sandro" to our own Royal Family, with whom he was a great favourite—so preposterously orotund an imaginary name as "Von Ormstein," and the rest.

I imagine that, reflecting on the success, as an adventuress, of Mrs. Edward Langtry, *née* Emilie Charlotte Le Breton, daughter of the dean of Jersey, I found myself considering the even more dazzling success of yet another of that Frail Sisterhood who were, to the Victorian world, what the overpaid Hollywood "film star" is to the present generation: not indeed "a byword and a hissing," but rather objects of admiration, envy and—as far as possible—emulation. The lady whom I must have had in mind was that daughter of a Cologne tailor and his French wife: the sometime flower-girl from Bordeaux, Hortense Schneider.

How well I recall a time when, after she had achieved Europe-wide success as La Grande Duchesse de Gérolstein, in the play of that name, her portrait was to be seen everywhere, side-by-side with those of the crowned heads of Europe. Of her numerous lovers, the Prince of Wales was one—and I remember well, on an early visit to Paris just after the defeat of the French by the Germans, how this (as I thought) somewhat plain woman enjoyed almost royal honours, and certainly expected to be—as indeed she always was—treated with the deference due to one, as an English historian has since remarked, "whose sovereignty, unlike that of some other rulers, was really based upon · the love of her people."

Yes . . . now that I come to reflect, it must have been Madame Hortense Schneider's tremendous *coup de théâtre* which gave me the "echo," as it were, of "Gerolstein"—"Ormstein" —for I recollect clearly that it was in the year that I first made Mr. Holmes's acquaintance—1881—that I read in *The Times* of Madame Hortense Schneider's retirement from the stage and of her subsequent marriage to Count Emile de Bionne. (So much for the career of the tailor's daughter from Bordeaux . . . and, for the regrettable confounding of the moralists, for the Wages of Sin!)

As for that reference, in my invented title for Prince "Sandro," to "Bohemia," the name—or rather the *concept*—of "Bohemia," of "Bohème" and of "La vie de Bohème" had long since become familiar to the more educated of our people through Henri Murger's *Scènes de la vie de Bohème*—very popular in its English translation, and more recently, through Du Maurier's perhaps too-romantic novel of Parisian artistic life, *Trilby*. I cannot now recall, without reference to the record, whether or not Puccini had yet given us his splendid opera by the time that I came to prepare *A Scandal in Bohemia* for publication in *The Strand Magazine,* but, as I have said, the concept of "Bohemia," with its overtones of romantic freedom-from-discipline and fairly innocent loose-living, had become pretty well fixed in the average British mind. So, it must have seemed not unreasonable to the young man that I then was —hardly forty, I recall—to call a self-indulgent foreign nobleman, calling on us to complain of the "base" conduct of his light-o'-love, the imaginary but not, I think, ill-fitting title of "King of Bohemia."

I shall explain the true nature of his complaint later. . . .

The British newspapers, I must say, not only gave the late Lady de Bathe ample mention in their obituary columns, but, as is traditional with the better class of journalism, refrained discreetly from explaining the sources of her wealth, merely contenting themselves with explaining that, in her younger days, she *and her husband, Mr. Edward Langtry,* had enjoyed the friendship of Their Royal Highnesses the Prince and Princess of Wales and of some lesser, but by no means, unexalted, persons of consequence. All quoted a remark of the septuagenarian lady, made to a reporter in a recent interview: that she would dearly have liked to return to the stage, *"if only in a walking-on part in* Bulldog Drummond." The obituaries did *not* mention the daughter—still most charmingly with us*—whom, if all accounts be true, she bore to a member of a German noble family, *à la main gauche,*† but it did mention that her widower, Sir Hugo de Bathe, baronet, was commissioning an eminent sculptor to execute a bust in "the purest white Carrara marble" for her tomb in St. Saviour's, Jersey. One needs to be a journalist

*Later Lady Malcolm, organizer of the annual "Servants' Ball."
†Prince Louis of Battenberg, father of the late Lord Mountbatten.

to know how important—and unimportant—are facts, and which are safe to mention. Thus, all the papers remarked that "only a week or two since, Lady de Bathe, seemingly in the best of health, played several rounds of golf with her friend, Lady Dudley, on the links at Hythe"—Lady Dudley, a musical-comedy singer had early in her career gained the friendship of England's wealthiest duke, and so had never needed, as had Lady de Bathe, when Mrs. Edward Langtry, to cast her net so widely abroad.

In the highly modified version of our encounter with Prince "Sandro" of Battenberg, which I prepared for *The Strand Magazine* under the title of *A Scandal in Bohemia,* I made it appear that my friend, Mr. Holmes, possessed quite considerable knowledge of the lady whom I called "Irene Adler"—but knowledge recorded in his files, and not gained in personal acquaintance.

In fact, however, Mr. Holmes had already met the lady. I had better give her right name from this point and never refer to her other than as Mrs. Edward—"Lillie"—Langtry.

He had not only met her; he had had professional dealings with her, and had "acted" (as the solicitors say) on her behalf.

And now, I think, it is time to make clear exactly what Prince "Sandro," who had been recommended to Mr. Holmes's care by His Royal Highness the Prince of Wales (and had arrived at Baker Street most preposterously "disguised," in one of the spanking Marlborough House broughams) wished my friend to do for him. In the fictional account that I prepared for *The Strand,* I said that the Prince wished to marry—and this is true: the lady in question not being an imaginary "Princess Clotilde Lothman von Saxe-Meningen" (a name of my own fabrication), but the very real Princess Victoria, daughter of Their Imperial Highnesses the Crown Prince and Princess of Germany—the Princess being the daughter of our own Queen. The proposed match was eagerly urged by our entire Royal Family, but bitterly opposed by the Crown Prince's heir, Wilhelm (afterwards Emperor Wilhelm II, now, if we may believe the journalists, relieving the tedium of his exile at Doorn, Holland, in chopping down trees). I wrote that "Count von Kramm . . . etc." wished to regain possession of a compromising photograph before it could be—or might be—shewn to the straight-laced "Princess Clotilde." In truth, it was something far less intrinsically dangerous, and far more intrinsically valuable, than a compromising photograph. It was a most valuable collection of jewels, and it was not miserliness on the Prince's part which made him so desperate to recover the gems; it was the *very* awkward fact that the jewels, which included a magnificent *parure* of diamonds of the finest water, had never been the Prince's to give, since they were entailed, and might never, legally, be permitted to pass out the Family's possession, either by sale or by gift.

"A very tricky little situation," Holmes commented after the Prince, his predicament described, had left us; "but a pretty—a *very* pretty little problem, none the less."

"Are you confident," I asked, "that you may be able to persuade Mrs. Langtry to return them? After all, as the Prince assured us, money is no object here. . . ."

Holmes put the tips of his fingers together, and smiled in that enigmatic fashion which told me that he had withheld some fact of importance from me, and was now prepared to divulge it.

And so it turned out.

"Mrs. Langtry," he observed, "would no doubt be willing to take cash for the return of the jewels . . . *if they were still in her possession.* . . . Alas! They are no longer hers to return.

"Great heavens, Holmes!" I cried. "She has sold them . . . ?"

"Worse . . . far worse. Had she sold them, I could have negotiated with the buyer . . . or buyers. No: She has not sold them. They have been stolen . . . and" here he laughed "by as pretty and simple a trick as ever graced the annals of Grand Larceny."

"How . . ." I began, but Holmes continued.

"What it boils down to, Doctor, is a matter of one common but almost invariably dangerous indulgence. However complicated any affair may seem—may actually become— even the most complicated affair *always* originates in one simple cause. That is one of Life's truly invariable rules. In this case, the origin of what has surely become an important, if not exactly a complicated business, is the lady's most human and perfectly understandable vanity. The matter is easily explained . . ."

"I should be interested to hear it."

"And so you shall. Well, in the first place, the lady—in common with many others of the class known as 'the professional beauties,' and whose photographic portraits are in hundreds of shop-windows—was asked by the makers of Pears' Soap if (for a fee, of course: The lady rarely offers *any* service, save for the appropriate fee!) she would consent to give her testimonial to the excellence of this soap. Here, let me shew you . . ."

He rose from his basket chair and crossed the room to his rolltop desk, from every pigeonhole of which papers of every size were jutting and cascading. But only a moment's riffling through the apparent chaos let him find what he sought. He returned to his chair, handing me, at the same time, what was obviously a piece cut from a newspaper. It was the very Pears' Soap advertisement that he had mentioned as having been at the start of all this troublesome business.

"Go on; read it," Holmes invited, loading the new bulldog briar that he had only that afternoon bought at Fribourg & Treyer in the Haymarket.

I did so. There was quite a lot of what the journalists call "copy" in the relatively small space: references to the opinion of Professor Sir Erasmus Wilson, FRS, "the Greatest English Authority on the Skin;" "15 International Awards;" "Specially Prepared for the Delicate Skin of Ladies and Children;" and much, much more of the same. And at the bottom of the advertisement, in bold, flowing script: "For the hands and complexion I prefer it to any other." There was a cut of the lady—not a very attractive one, it seemed to me—and in the bottom right-hand corner the affectedly "individual" signature: "Lillie Langtry."

Observing me closely, Holmes, seeing that I had read the whole effusion, reached across and gently took the slip from my fingers.

"You saw that it is signed . . . ? Yes," he added drily, "so did the thief." He laughed. "No three-pipe problem here, Doctor. Mrs. Langtry had deposited what she estimated as forty thousand pounds worth of jewels with the Union Bank—the branch at the corner of Pont Street and Sloane Street. You know it . . . ? Of course: next to the Cadogan Hotel.*

"Well, a 'person of respectable appearance'—and, between ourselves, of consummate impudence—called on the Bank almost immediately after the first appearance of this advertisement in print and presented an order, signed apparently by Mrs. Langtry, requiring the Bank to hand over the jewels to the bearer of the note. They, unfortunately, did so."

"Without their having checked the note's validity with Mrs. Langtry! Why, Holmes, such carelessness is quite impermissible!"

"So Mrs. Langtry indignantly maintains. But, Doctor, I'm not so sure. In any successful forgery, the forgery itself is

---

*In a private room of which, in 1895, Oscar Wilde was arrested.

carefully designed to—if I may so put it—provide its own undeniable authority. Add to this the obviously persuasive bearing of the man who presented the note—he may or may not have been the actual forger—and, what would you have? Of *course* the Bank officials accepted the note at its face value. But Mrs. Langtry is determined to sue—and herein lies a difficulty of the utmost delicacy."

"You have been retained by Mrs. Langtry . . . ?"

"I have agreed to render what assistance lies in my power. The lady was recommended to me by two persons who are acquainted with my methods: the more important, an Illustrious Client, with whom Mrs. Langtry is—or has been recently—on terms of intimacy far beyond the limits of a conventional friendship; the other, the so-called 'Society' solicitor, George Lewis, to whom go all of Mrs. Langtry's circumstances when in trouble. I must say," Holmes added, with something of contempt, "the man has a remarkable faculty for whitening dirty linen in private.

"But to return to the matter of the stolen jewels. . . ."

"You think that Mr. Lewis will force the Bank to pay over the value of the gems?"

"I'm afraid: not more than a quarter of the value. . . ."

"A quarter! But *why,* Holmes?"

"Because," he answered drily, "the Bank asked an appraiser to estimate their value, when the Bank accepted them for safe-keeping. And the appraiser, who evidently knew a great deal about the more famous jewels, recognized three-quarters of the total as jewels which could only have been *lent* to Mrs. Langtry, seeing that they were entailed. The Bank refuses to admit liability for jewels which, so they maintain, were never Mrs. Langtry's legal property at all. They conceded a claim on them for roughly a quarter of the total—say, ten thousand pounds, and I'm afraid that Lewis will have to settle at that. So it is that Mrs. Langtry has appealed to me; the gems *must* be recovered, though rather for the sake of her Prince than for her own. Well, you saw for yourself that he is at his wit's end to know, if he's called upon to explain their loss, *how* he can account for their having left his possession."

"Have you any idea who the thief might be?"

"I can think of several likely rogues who could have done this. The means here are not important: a simple matter of forgery, that any nimble-fingered penman could have effected. The paper on which the note was written tells me nothing, save that it was on writing-paper bearing the name and address of the Savoy Hotel—paper that any casual visitor might have taken. There are, however, two possible sources of identification: the knowledge that the jewels were deposited with the Union Bank; and, of course, the admirable *sang-froid* of the man who presented the note. His description counts for nothing: 'respectably dressed' simply means starched linen, a morning coat or frock coat and a well-brushed top hat. Gray hair, gray moustache . . . nothing there. My hope for the recovery of the jewels is this: If the thief knew so much, he will have known more—that he might gain considerably more by ransom than in any breaking-up of the jewels.''

Well, the Bank, as is well known, paid no more than a quarter, which, after all, was the full extent of Mrs. Langtry's loss; and—having by his own methods identified the thief as among those who, from an expert knowledge of gems and, even more important to a thief, the means of disposing of them—my friend returned to the Bank and sought to identify his jewel-robber from what little, and it was not much, that the Bank-official remembered of his caller.

As Holmes remarked when he returned from what, on first impressions, had been a futile journey, "Again and again we have the frustrating experience of examining witnesses who see but do not observe. However, I think that the man at the Bank, however unobservant, may have provided me with some evidence of value. He told me that the caller seemed to have had a noticeable accent—slight, but most certainly to be heard; and that it occured to the Bank-man that the caller might have been an American. If that is so, then it narrows down the field considerably: the hunt would not be on only for a thief within the very limited field of experts in the jewellery-robbing line.

"But there is one thing further of—at least, so I think—evidential value. I pressed the man at the Bank to try to remember any unusual use of words or syntax which gave him—apart from the slight accent—the impression of the caller's being foreign. The man, searching his memory, remembered only one unusual expression. When he brought out the jewel-box containing Mrs. Langtry's gems, the caller asked: 'Worth here . . . what would you say?' This abrupt mode of expression certainly surprised the man at the Bank. He told me that he would have expected some enquiry such as 'Have these been expertly appraised . . . valued?'—something like that. But the abrupt 'Worth here . . . what would you say?' struck him as odd indeed, and in its blunt, vulgar way, rather out of keeping with the caller's most respectable appearance.''

"Yet he was not suspicious? He handed the gems over? A pity that the strange expression didn't arouse his suspicions!''

"Well, the fact is that it did not. But here, I imagine, we have a valuable clue. I said that the thief was a man of the coolest nerve. I think—since to that nerve, as the saying goes, we add a challenging impudence—that the gentleman left, not his visiting-card, but . . . his name.''

"His name!''

"Do you remember, some twelve years ago''—all this happened in early 1888—"the theft of Gainsborough's portrait of the Duchess of Devonshire from Messrs. Agnew's art-gallery in Bond Street . . . and, even more to the point, the daring simplicity with which the actual theft was carried out? Agnew's had paid ten thousand guineas for that portrait at Christie's, and on the theft's discovery, offered one thousand guineas for its return. It has never been been returned.''

"Destroyed—as being too dangerous to keep?''

"No. The danger would be in the thief's trying to sell it. No, Doctor: this is a thief who is sufficiently patient, and sufficiently rich, to hold for ransom. I am *almost* convinced that his coup—the coup, I should say—at the Union Bank is his work: Certainly it bears all the signs of his peculiar skill. He specializes in jewel-robbery; nothing could have exceeded, both in careful planning and sheer impudence, the theft of the 'diamond mail' from Hatton-garden post office on a foggy night of Nevember, 1881, the year in which we met. Do you not remember the details? Ah well: After having 'cased' the post office, the thief entered it at about five o'clock in the evening, when two registered mailbags, consigned to various diamond merchants on the Continent, were hanging, sealed, on iron hooks behind the counter. A well-dressed man, followed by a telegraph messenger with—it was remembered—yellow curls peeping out from beneath his uniform cap, asked for a shillingsworth of stamps. As the thief stood at the counter, waiting for his stamps, the pretended messenger—actually a young girl confederate—slipped past him, ran down the steps leading to the basement, and turned the gas off at the main. As soon as the lights blinked out, the thief vaulted the counter, seized the two mailbags of diamonds, and, followed by his girl-partner, ran out into St. Martin's-le-Grand, where a cab that he had hired stood awaiting them. They were never caught.

"Even more daring and profitable—he netted between seventy and eighty thousand on this particular venture—was his robbing the Kimberley 'diamond mail' whilst the bags were on their way to Cape Town—the robbery not being noticed until the bags were opened at journey's end."

"Have they ever caught him . . . ?"

"No. He has not even been arrested."

"But they know that all these crimes may be attributed to one man . . . ?"

"Because all these crimes are 'signed' by him as surely as a book by its author or a painting by the artist—and an artist he is indeed."

"Do they know his identity?"

"Not truly. Only the name by which he is known to the admiring world of crime It may be his true name, but in all likelihood not. Some say that he is an Austrian Jew, settled in New York; but only he might tell us who he really is."

"And the name," I asked, "by which the criminals . . . and the police . . . know him?"

Holmes smiled—a little ruefully, I thought.

"It is the name that he left with the Bank official."

"Did he give a name? I don't seem to remember . . ."

"When he puzzled the Bank official by using the word, the phrase, 'worth,' rather than 'valuation' or some such more usual term. Yes, Doctor, the name by which he is known in criminal and police circles is . . . Adam Worth. If any man ever deserved the title of 'Napoleon of the Criminal World' it is he. Yes . . . he must have thought it at least possible that I should be called in on the Union Bank affair: It was for me that he 'signed,' as it were, this latest exploit. Well, we shall see.

"But how hard it is, Doctor, to withhold admiration for a man who, to unload the Kimberley diamonds on the market, actually set one of his gang up as a Hatton-garden diamond merchant and sold back diamonds to some of the men whom he had robbed!"*

As I have pointed out, that call upon us by Prince Alexander

*This is true. Worth set up his criminal associate, Wynert, in "legitimate" business as a diamond-merchant in Hatton-garden, then, as now, the centre of Britain's diamond trade. Within eighteen months, Wynert had unloaded all the Kimberley haul, much of it on its legitimate owner, also a Hatton-garden diamond merchant! — Editor

of Battenberg, whom I have somewhat facetiously presented to the reader as the preposterous "Count von Kramm, Grand Duke of Cassel-Felstein," etc., was by no means the first time that Mrs. "Lillie" Langtry, *alias* (in my *doctored* tale) "Irene Adler" had entered Holmes's affairs—and here, I feel, is the proper place in this memoir, not to be published until after the death of both Mr. Holmes and myself (Prince Alexander died many years ago; Mrs. Langtry—Lady de Bathe—in the past year) to marvel, as I still marvel, at the all-powerful infatuation with which this woman of so many commercially based *liaisons* inspired my friend.

Austere, reserved, even almost physically withdrawn—though always, of course, with that deferential courtesy which is so far above the conventions of formal politeness—my friend's "reaction" (as the newer phrase has it) to a necessary encounter with a lady of the easiest virtue would have been, in the ordinary way, to have called that austerity, that reserve, that— yes, I must say this—near-prudishness into an obviousness impossible for any to overlook.

Of course, even I, with the image of my lost Mary so present in my memory that all women, compared with her, seemed— their beauty, I mean—of no account, could not deny Mrs. Langtry my tribute to her charm. I saw, as she sat in that creaking basket chair by the glowing fire (it was cold in that March of 1888, I recall) how, not so much her physical charms as her physical and mental *presence* could dominate and subtly attract and—inevitably, I must admit—seduce.

It was curious, but though my mind told me that she was a harlot, and a shameless one at that; and though my mind toyed with the description of her by a shorter but still Biblical word; my heart could not accept this cruel but honest valuation.

As she talked to my friend, I studied her, both as a medical man and as—well, let me admit it to the privacy of this very private memoir—as a mere man. I conceded her physical beauty: the violet eyes, the splendid copper-coloured hair; the flawless complexion (owing nothing, I could reflect later, to Pears' Soap!). But, as I gazed at her covertly, studying each element of that body, that personality, which had enslaved so many men, I found myself startled by the inescapable conclusion that—yes, this is true—there was, if not more masculine than feminine in her composition, then there was surely far too much of the masculine that she might lay claim to a complete femininity. Her shoulders, too wide for femininity; hands which were large and (one felt) strong; a jaw too firm for female beauty—and with all these physical paradoxes, an assurance stopping only a shade this side arrogance; a near–arrogance stopping only a shade this side impudence. . . . (No: Unlike my friend, I never, I am happy to say, fell under this very soiled dove's spell; never disloyal, not merely to the memory of my Mary, but, more, never disloyal to the wonderful standard of normal womanliness of which my beloved Wife was so shining an example.) In the forty years since we first had dealings with Mrs. Langtry, a new word, a most expressive word—I think it has come to us from America—has appeared. This word is "hooked"; and, looking back, I may find no better way of expressing my friend's enthrallment than by saying that he was, in every way, "hooked." I cannot explain why this should have been so. The French have a word, too, which describes my friend's surrender better even than does our phrase, "absolutely bowled over." The French call this condition of quite abject surrender to overwhelming emotional shock: *bouleversement* —but even as I give the palm for the *mot juste* to the French, an even better phrase comes to mind, a phrase that I have heard used by the servants when they believed themselves to be talking privately: " 'E was knocked all of a 'eap" Alas! I may record only, though with the deepest regret, that my poor friend was indeed knocked all of a heap. . . .

As I write for my own most personal record, ten years after "the War to end all wars" (Can we ever have been so blind!) I feel like Sir Bedivere, at least in the sense that I am "revolving many memories"—and memories crowding in upon me, as it were jostling the others for precedence, so that I am bewildered by a dozen conflicting and confusing recollections.

Forgotten or half-remembered phrases press into my consciousness . . . so many and so very different; yet all springing from the different emotions of a long, long experience. Why, for instance, should the Duchess of Orleans's—that Duchess who was married to the effeminate Monsieur: the coarsely-spoken German princess—why should her description of Madame de Maintenon come into my mind: "A woman with lovely eyes"—I think that is what she wrote—"seemingly modest, but with a rebellious bosom." She certainly mentioned the "rebellious bosom"—and I know now that I am thinking of the fair (oh, never let her be called "frail"!) "Lillie," of the far too well-developed chest. . . . And is it the memory of my womanly

Mary which brings to mind some words written by a poet* who died in the War: ". . . Gentleness, in hearts of peace, under an English heaven . . ." Yes: The memories of rebellious bosom and gentleness in hearts of peace strive for precedence in my mind . . . but it is of gentleness, rather than rebelliousness, that I am thinking, as I close this part of my record and move on to what Mr. Phillips Oppenheim, Mr. Louis Tracy and all the other "sensational" novelists like to call the *dénouement* of my tale.

Some time—I think that it cannot have been more than a fortnight—after the very widely reported theft of Mrs. Langtry's jewels from the Union Bank, I was standing one misty April evening by a window overlooking Baker Street, when the clopping of hooves, and rattle and jingle of harness and traces informed me that a smart brougham had pulled up outside our modest residence.

"Hello!" I exclaimed. "One of the Marlborough House carriages again. Has the Prince returned to consult you once again?"

"Marlborough House—yes," said Holmes, quietly. "But not, I think, the Prince. I think that now we have a different visitor."

And so it proved. It was a lady whom Billy, our "buttons," introduced into our sitting room.

"Mrs. Langtry!" my friend greeted her with an undisguised warmth, hurrying to move the basket chair to a more convenient position. "Dr. Watson, of course, you have already met . . ."

The lady's small bow acknowledged my unimportant presence.

"I was reading an advertisement in *Beeton's Annual*," she said, with apparent irrelevance, "about some of the improvements recently introduced for the home. The one which caught my fancy, Mr. Holmes—and might well have caught yours—is a non-creaking basket chair. All the comfort of the old type, you know, but, my goodness! what an aid to quiet conversation!"

"Dr. Watson has contributed to that magazine, madam," said my friennd imperturbably; "I have no doubt that he shall be able to put his finger on the advertisement that you mention and communicate with the manufacturers, should he think that desirable. And now, Madam, how may we be of service to you?"

Such ladies, in those days, as I have said, were known

---

*Rupert Brooke, who died on the Greek Island of Skyros, while on military duty, in 1915. All references to "the War," are, of course, references to what was, until 1939, called "the Great War;" that is, World War One. — Editor

collectively as "the professional beauties," membership of that
somewhat ill-defined group being generally accorded to those
whose photographic "portraits" were to be seen, silver-framed,
in the shop-windows. (Many, even now, will remember the
curious libel action, in which Mr. and Mrs. Langtry joined,
brought by Colonel and Mrs. Cornwallis West, much of the
gravamen of the action concerning itself with such photographs
of Mrs. West, yet another of the Prince of Wales's handsome
female intimates.)

With quite indescribable assurance, this lady now composed
herself to tell us what it was that she had come to say. My
friend's patent (and to me, most regrettable) admiration she
accepted as no more than her due, whilst my obvious—for I
could hardly conceal my feelings—disapproval she treated with
a half-amused contempt. (If the Prince of Wales and so many
other male members of our Royal Family had sought—and paid
for—her favours, how might she be interested in, let alone
affronted by, the opinion of a half-pay military medico?)

"I have come," she began, when Holmes raised a hand to
interrupt.

"Forgive me, madam—but I think that I can guess what
brings you here . . ."

"Can you really, Mr. Sherlock Holmes?"

This was asked with a by-no-means timid smile; but it was an
unsmiling Holmes who answered.

"Yes, Madam; I am *sure* that I can. You have come in
connexion with the jewels abstracted from your *coffre-fort* at
the Union Bank . . ."

" 'Abstracted,' Mr. Holmes? A curious expression, surely . . . ?"

"You think so? And what expression, pray, would you have
had me use?"

" 'Stolen' is a shorter and more accurate description, one
would think?"

"One might, indeed, were that the word to use. But no
matter. I would suggest that you have called upon us to return
the trinkets that Prince Alexander had no right to give you. Am
I not correct . . . ?"

"Yes, Mr. Holmes, you are correct. I have them with me"
—and here she tapped the unusually large morocco reticule that
she carried. "I return them on conditions, Mr. Holmes . . ."

"Naturally. I would have expected no less. And the conditions are financial ones, doubtless?"

"You gentlemen are men of honour. I am satisfied that you

would not seek to possess yourself of what I am carrying by main force? Of course not. Well, then: they are for sale. The Bank, as you may have heard, is refusing to recompense me for what, in their insolence, they claim was never my property— nor Prince Alexander's either. I had thought of retaining Mr. George Lewis to bring an action against the Bank . . . but, I don't know. One must consider a possible scandal . . .'' (Good lord! I thought: Can impudence go further!?)

"Quite so,'' Holmes commented gravely, putting the finger-tips of one hand against those of the other. "I believe that you estimated the value—or should I say, the *worth?*—of all the gems at forty thousand; and that the Bank declines to settle at more than a quarter of that sum: say, ten thousand? A decision, on the part of the Bank, which leaves you the loser by some thirty thousand pounds?''

The lady said quietly, "*Sixty* thousand, Mr. Holmes . . .''

My friend rubbed his chin; then his eyes lit up.

"Ah! I think that we are now coming to what the American thieves call 'the cut'!''

"Mr. Holmes! You are insulting!''

"To whom, Madam? To you or to Mr. Adam Worth?''

"He approached me, Mr. Holmes, and offered to sell me the Hesse jewels for thirty thousand. Naturally, I leapt at the chance of getting the jewels back . . .''

"Quite setting aside the fact that, in treating with a self-confessed thief, you were guilty not only of misprision of felony, but also of compounding that felony . . . ?''

"Pooh! Fiddle-faddle, Mr. Holmes. You sound like Mr. Lewis with his petty legal quibbles. We need realism here, Mr. Holmes, a facing of the facts, not some hair-splitting over purely theoretical questions of guilt or innocence. Do you agree?''

Holmes nodded.

"Yes, I'm afraid that I do. So Mr. Worth asks thirty thousand for the jewels? Oh . . . did you pay him, by the way . . . ?''

The lady's fair skin coloured a little.

"No . . . well, you see, Mr. Holmes, he trusts me . . .''

My friend leaned back, slapping his knees with both hands. He laughed as loudly as I had ever heard him laugh.

"Forgive me, Madam, but that is priceless! That really is rich''—and once again he was off in a burst of uncontrolled mirth. (I have remarked elsewhere how loudly my friend could laugh when, as the novelists of the last century liked to say, "his risible faculties were provoked.'')

But, composed once again, he added: "You will not contradict me, I feel, when I suggest that you have not called on me merely to arrange a payment to Mr. Adam Worth? That would be carrying altruism a little too far for—what did you call it, Madam: Realism?—realism, then. I take it that something is to be added to recompense *you* . . . ? Ah! I see! And what is this additional sum? What the Bank refused to pay you? Of course. Thirty for Mr. Worth, and—thirty?—yes, thirty for yourself. Sixty thousand. And who—or rather, *how,* is this money to be paid? Have you any suggestions?"

The lady said impatiently, "All the Royal Family, from the Queen down, are very fond of Sandro—of Prince Alexander. They all wish that he should marry this simpering Miss of a Princess Victoria of Prussia . . ."

"A very charming young lady, Madam."

"No doubt. But we are talking of money. Why, they'd *all* subscribe, if you made it clear to them that I shall stand no nonsense. The Prince of Wales . . ."

"May I remind you, Madam, that I, too, have the privilege of His Royal Highness's acquaintance—and that, from my own observation, I have concluded that His Royal Highness has always considered it more blessed to receive than to give."

"That's true enough," said the lady grudgingly. "But why are we wasting time talking? You can get the money, Mr. Holmes. I trust you," she said, rising from that creaking basket chair of ours, and gathering up her reticule. She opened that big morocco purse and took out a chamois bag, which she emptied onto the top of a small walnut occasional table. "You smiled, Mr. Holmes, when I once again mentioned trust. But here is the proof. Here are all the Hesse jewels that I ever received. Take them, Mr. Holmes. I look forward to my receiving your cheque—in the not too distant future," she added pulling on her gloves.

The details of how that sixty thousand pounds' worth of blackmail was raised are unnecessary to be recounted here. Suffice that my friend collected the money from what the lawyers call "interested parties," and Mrs. Langtry received her check.

"I wonder," Holmes smiled, sealing the envelope containing his draft on Goslings, "if Mr. Worth will receive *his* cheque so promptly? And now Billy may post this, and I shall be pleased to give you my thoughts on this remarkable case.

"Do you recall that, some years ago, I called your attention to a story in an American magazine—*The Century, Harper's Bazaar, The Atlantic Monthly*—I forget which exactly; but an American journal, at any rate. A most memorable story. It was called "The Lady or the Tiger," by a writer named Stockton. You recall it? Good. The unique point about Stockton's tale is this: Most other tales end by explaining, for the benefit of the reader, exactly what happened. Stockton, in his admirable little tale, completely reverses the common practice, and not only fails to tell us what happened, but deliberately refrains from telling us. We are left to guess what choice the lady made.

"Well now: Here we have something of the same sort. We have seen the lady; we have listened to her tale; we have accepted her impudent conditions, and here is her cheque, ready to be posted. In the ordinary way, I should say that that ends the affair. But I am left with a feeling most uncomfortable—and most unusual with me: the feeling that I do not know what truly happened. Oh, I can make a fair guess—"

"I should be most interested to have your theories—"

"You shall have them, Doctor. But the real puzzle in this case—the centre, as it were, of the puzzlement—is the written order to the Bank to hand over the jewels to the bearer of that order."

"The forged order, with the signature copied from the Pears' Soap advertisement."

Holmes stroked his chin; always, with him, a sign of deep thought.

"Hm. Well . . . *forged,* you say? I wonder . . ." He sat down and rubbed his thin hands together. "Let us consider this order, around which the whole case revolves. A forged order. Yes. So the story goes. And, if the newspapers do not know this, the man known to the police of several nations as 'Adam Worth' (whatever his true name be) is a man of infinite re-source, of daring and cunning. He is known as a forger of consummate skill. He is an expert in the knowledge of stones—apart from the knowledge of their ownership and present place of so-called safety.

"All this agreed. But let us bend our minds a little to what we know—*or ought to know*—of banks and their methods.

"Banks keep careful record of the specimen signatures of all their customers; and all the staff who have dealings with those customers take the greatest care to familiarize themselves with each signature. They are not easily deceived . . ."

"In this case, it seems that they were . . . ?''

"Please bear with me, Doctor. And, yes, tell me what could—I mean: which order to hand over goods to the bearer—what could be more persuasive, more convincing, more 'official,' shall we say, than . . . (Yes, Doctor, I see that you are beginning to understand my train of thought) . . . than a *genuine* order? No forgery, but a *genuine* order, written out and signed, not by a skilled 'penman,' but by the person from whom the order is purported to have come. An order which, if disputed, challenged, is completely verifiable by the signatory. You follow me . . . ?''

"Only with . . . well, Holmes, only with . . . well, not so much astonishment as . . . well: consternation. Can I really be following your train of thought?''

"Pretty well, I should say. And now let me attempt what my friend of the Sûreté, Monsieur Dubuque, would call a reconstruction of the crime.

"A few facts: this Adam Worth is an expert in the valuation, as well as in the most adroit stealing, of jewels. He can value them; and he knows where all the most valuable jewels are to be found. Be sure that he knows where Mrs. Langtry's jewels are; what they are worth; and—here is the most important thing: that, sooner or later, she *must* be made to return what Prince Alexander had no moral or legal right to give her. In that certain knowledge we have the whole motive for this most impudent conspiracy; but a conspiracy which, I feel sure, was of this 'Adam Worth's' ingenious plotting.''

"Holmes . . . surely! You cannot mean a conspiracy between . . .''

"Of course. What else? Mrs. Langtry and this man Worth. But, as I see it, the plan was of Worth's concocting—and based on, inspired by, some knowledge which had conveniently come his way. He knew that the lady was short—very short—of money. It is true that she could have raised money on the jewels to which she could lay a positive legal claim—but she could not sell the others; even her boldness was not equal to that. So this very persuasive Mr. Worth suggests a scheme whereby both she and he could make money, even (and this, Doctor, must have seemed to the lady like the beauty of the scheme) she could raise money, yes!, even on the jewels which did not belong to her. All that was needed was a note from her—authenticity, of course, to be denied later, to make the abstraction of the jewels from the Bank look like robbery—and that was all. You know the rest, Doctor . . ."

"And not," I asked, "what happens?"

"I don't understand you, Doctor. Why should anything 'happen'? What is there to happen? The case is closed. The lady and her accomplice have their well-earned money, and her Prince—her 'Sandro,' I mean—has recovered the jewellery that only a love-besotted clown would have given her. No," he said, rubbing his hands together with every sign of high self-approval, "I think that the matter turned out well—very well indeed. And now: What do you say to a small dinner at Goldini's; the manager tells me that they have a new, and even better chef."

"But Holmes!" I cried; "you are . . . but this is a criminal conspiracy! You can't, Holmes; you simply can't . . ."

"That's tautology, Doctor: All conspiracy is criminal—at least under our Law. And what good will it do to pursue the matter? Do I shock you? I can't see why. Even *you* know that I have compounded many a graver felony . . . if," he added, musingly, "a felony has actually been committed. But yes or no, that, as I have said, concludes the matter.

"But, oh, Doctor," he rhapsodized, his eyes shining, "what a *woman*, eh! *What* a woman . . . !"

THE SHADOWS ON THE LAWN:

AN ADVENTURE OF SHERLOCK HOLMES

Barry Jones

Illustration by Sidney Paget of Holmes and Moriarty locked in what
Watson supposed was their final mortal combat.

Of all the cases presented to my friend Mr. Sherlock Holmes during the lengthy years of our association, few presented such sinister features of interest as that connected with the little Berkshire village of Buckley-on-Thames. I refer, of course, to the mysterious death of young Peter Wainwright and the singular shadows on the vicarage lawn. Even now, after the passing of so many years, I fully recognise that the greatest delicacy and discretion must be exercised in placing the facts before the public.

It was on 23 April 1884, that our attention was first drawn to the affair. Holmes and I had spent the afternoon strolling through Regent's Park. The immense exertions of my friend on behalf of Major Prendergast of the Tankerville Club scandal had left his iron constitution flaccid and drained. It was heartening to see the colour return to his cheeks and the old spring to his stride. His keen eyes surveyed the crowds of people who were, like us, enjoying the first real sunshine of the year.

"And yet, my dear Watson," he remarked, leaning on his cane, "I can never contemplate such a scene without the gravest misgivings."

"Surely not?"

"Consider. Amid this vast shoal of humanity, there must be countless individuals bearing the most unspeakable sorrow locked tight within their breasts. For such as they, there is a shadow amid the sunlight.''

"That is surely taking misanthropic pessimism a little too far, Holmes,'' I protested, warmly. "You remind me of a remark attributed to Mr. Thomas Hardy: that he could never contemplate the multitudes of London without imagining them a hundred years hence stiff in their coffins.''

"Well. I trust you will acquit me of such crass morbidity, Watson. But I am something of a disciple of Aurelius. I believe it was he who affirmed that the source of all wisdom resides in a daily acknowledgement of life's rending contrasts. Take that poor fellow, for example.''

He indicated an unfortunate beggar with a hideously scarred face, who was attempting to sell matches at the Chester Gate end of the park.

"A victim of the Zulu War, as you will doubtless have noticed,'' he went on. "That assegai scar on his cheek and the ribbon of the South Wales Borderers on his breast pocket proclaim as much. Who knows what personal drama lies there, Watson? Not merely the outward tragedy of his penniless state, but the deeper grief, the shattered self-esteem, perhaps the loss of a wife, the destruction of those sweet, homely ties that even I, who am not a family man, can appreciate. Now behold that guardsman, in all his splendour of blue and gold, with his girl on his arm. Recently betrothed, see how she continually fingers that exquisite sapphire. The haves and have-nots, Watson, since time immemorial, one of the eternal verities. On such a day as this, I never feel that truth more intensely.''

Dusk was beginning to fall when we arrived back at Baker Street. The lamplighter was already making his rounds from Oxford Street end. I chanced to glance up at our window and was astonished to see a yellow square of light, before which a dark figure was restlessly pacing to and fro.

"A client, Holmes!'' I exclaimed.

"And a general practitioner, I see.'' I followed the direction of his gaze and observed a doctor's gig drawn up outside. A couple of lamps attached to either side of the vehicle shed a warm, red glow over the kerbstone.

Mrs. Hudson was waiting for us at the open front door. "An old gentleman to see you, Mr. Holmes,'' she cried. "He's been up there for two hours, and in such a state, too, stamping up and down with his stick and muttering to himself—wouldn't take tea—and refused to leave until he'd seen you. I'm relieved you've come, Mr. Holmes, and no mistake.''

Sherlock Holmes chuckled. "I think I recognise the symptoms, Mrs. Hudson," said he. "Come, Watson. Let's see what your fellow practitioner has to say for himself.''

As we entered our room, we were confronted by a pair of singularly bright, gray eyes, twinkling at us from behind a pair of gold-rimmed spectacles. The rest of our portly visitor's countenance was framed in a tangle of fluffy white hair, save for the top of his head, which sported a flaming red bald patch. He was arrayed in russet tweed with a corduroy waistcoat across which dangled a heavy gold watch and chain. He was in the act of replacing the latter as we entered. There was something of Mr. Pickwick in his earnest air of old-world courtesy as he bobbed and bowed before us, clutching a thick-knobbed walking stick of the kind known as a penang-lawyer.

"This is indeed an honour, Mr. Holmes," said he, in a slightly high-pitched voice. "To meet so illustrious a man, an honour which . . .'' Our visitor reddened to the ears and bowed again.

"My dear sir, since you evidently enjoy the honour, rest assured I have no intention of depriving you of it," my friend replied curtly. "Pray be seated. May I ask whom I have the pleasure of addressing?''

"I am Dr. Moore Agar," the old gentleman said. "And I must beg pardon for descending on you without prior notice. I have come on the most urgent business—the most inexplicable business, sir, which will necessitate your presence at Buckley-on-Thames this very night.''

Sherlock Holmes, having donned his dressing gown, lit a cigarette and eyed Dr. Agar with amused interest.

"Such a beautiful rural retreat must come as a blessed relief after your early years in Australia, Dr. Agar, where I believe you practised as a schoolmaster.''

Our visitor gaped. "How could you possibly know such things, Mr. Holmes?''

"Surely I need not insult your intelligence, my dear sir, by drawing attention to the yellow parchment colour of your complexion, which is peculiar to the southern continent. Though a man may have left that country for many years, I have invariably noticed that the fierce Antipodean sun has left its mark. If any further proof were needed, note that miniature silver boomerang, Watson, attached to Dr. Agar's watch-chain.''

"But what of the school-mastering, Mr. Holmes?" Dr. Agar scratched his crimson bald patch in obvious bewilderment. "It's true I was at Wallangooba School in Victoria for ten years, but how you could surmise it is beyond me."

"Observe the thumb and forefinger of your right hand. They exhibit the deep, silvery indentation which is the result of several years clasping a chalk stick. Your right shoulder is higher than your left for a similar reason—that you have exercised it more often in stretching up to write upon a blackboard. As for your teaching and Australasian experience having occurred at the same time, I thought it more than likely that this occupation was associated with your earlier life, since it takes many years to establish a medical practice in this country."

Dr. Moore Agar mopped his brow.

"My goodness, that was smart," he declared. "It quite brings the sweat out on one. Yet how absurdly simple it is. At first, I thought you had done something really clever."

Sherlock Holmes yawned and crushed his cigarette into a tea cup. "Perhaps you would be kind enough to let us know in what way we can be of help to you, Dr. Agar," he said, with a weary glance in my direction.

By way of answer, Dr. Agar unfolded an ordnance map and spread it out upon his ample knees.

"This, gentlemen, is a detailed map of Berkshire, and here is the little village of Buckley, some ten miles from Maidenhead, with which our story is most intimately concerned. It is a quiet and picturesque place, and has been my home for the past twenty years. But virtue of the nature of the locality, most of my patients are farming folk. A singular exception is the Reverend Joseph Wainwright, who arrived in Buckley some five years ago."

Dr. Agar bit the end off a cigar and proceeded to light up. "Father Wainwright, as he is parochially referred to, is, I must confess, a dour, brooding personage, who has laboured in vain to gain the popularity of his parishioners. He is distinctly High Church and his sermons, in particular, are a chilling illustration, not only of his ecclesiastical attitudes, but of his own formidable personality. Hellfire and damnation pour from his lips on a weekly basis. I have myself seen, on two occasions, people faint in the pews on account of his fearful oratory. And yet, perhaps, he may be pardoned his sombre nature, for life has dealt him a particularly bitter blow."

To my astonishment, our client turned in my direction. "Dr.

Watson, here, will understand when I refer to a condition of acute and rapid muscular deterioration.''

I eyed Dr. Agar in horror. ''But, surely,'' I protested, ''this man cannot conduct his parochial affairs in such a condition.''

''It is not to Father Wainwright that I refer, Dr. Watson.''

Dr. Moore Agar brushed the cigar ash from the map that still covered his knees. ''It is to his son, ten-year-old Peter, who has been bed-ridden these past four years.''

''How dreadful!'' I exclaimed.

''Yes, it is a very sad case, and as you know, there is very little we can do to alleviate it. There is an incipient paralysis that inevitably leads to a total breakdown of the body's resources, and to ultimate death. I give poor Peter, who is a bright enough lad in himself, but another two years of life. At present, he can still use his hands and walk some distance, but he swiftly tires and is, as I say, confined to his bed for most of the time.

''He is Father Wainwright's youngest son. The eldest, Jack, is now sixteen, a tall, well-built lad—you couldn't find a greater contrast. He attends Hereward School in Reading and it is his mother's intention that he obtain a scholarship and study law.

''Mrs. Wainwright, herself, is an interesting study. The daughter of a don, she met Wainwright while he was a rector near Oxford. She has tremendous will-power and is certainly the driving-force behind Master Jack's ambitions. She it is who has several times raised the question of her husband becoming a canon—a matter about which he remains supremely indifferent. He appears totally committed to the life of a parish priest. This, then, is the household at Buckley Vicarage—a great, gloomy mansion of a place, all covered in lichen, on the edge of Quarry Wood.''

''A singular household, indeed,'' my friend observed, quietly.

''I have ringed the spot for you,'' our client explained, handing the map to Holmes who proceeded to examine it carefully.

''I now come to the beginning of that odd, even sinister, sequence of events that has brought me here this evening.

''You must know that it is my habit to visit young Peter a couple of evenings a week. Though there is little I can do, I feel it incumbent upon me to call upon him and to bring him a few books—he is very fond of reading—and in general, to spend a little time chatting to him and attempting to raise his spirits. The boy lies at the top of the house in a small attic immediately facing a latticed window. He has been moved there on my orders, since I regarded the downstairs room, in which he had

been confined since the onset of his illness, as totally inade-
quate, tucked away at the back of the house with but the
smallest of windows, affording him little light and air.

"I remember the evening well when he first began to describe
his strange experiences. I had been reading *Treasure Island* to
him, but it was clear, on this occasion, that his attention was
wandering. Outside, the twilight was gathering fast. The window was still half open and through it wafted the damp fra-
grance of the distant meadow. Suddenly, I was aware of the boy
gripping my arm and staring intently into my face with his
large, dark eyes. 'Dr. Agar,' he said, breathlessly, 'do you
know of a tall man with a huge beaked nose and a tall stovepipe
hat?'

"I was about to chuckle at the earnestness of this question,
but something in his face and voice deterred me.

" 'Why do you ask, Peter?' I said.

" 'Because he stands on that lawn every afternoon and watches
my room.'

"I must confess a chill went through me at those words, Mr.
Holmes, but I attempted to smile jocularly.

" 'Now then, Peter,' I said, 'You lie here all day with your
books and no doubt you've read something in them—'

" 'You think I'm imagining it, Dr. Agar,' he interjected
sharply. 'But I'm not. He's been there for the past three days.'

"I asked him at what time he had seen this person. He
informed me that, without fail, he appeared about midafternoon.
Yet, it transpired, it was not the actual man himself he had
seen, but his shadow, stretched out across the lawn in the
vincinity of the summerhouse. I naturally dismissed the boy's
talk as begotten of his solitary existence. But, on my next visit,
he referred to the matter again, this time in the strongest terms.
He had again seen the stranger, he said, two days ago, and this
time could describe him more accurately. 'Well,' I said, somewhat impatiently, 'describe him.'

" 'He is very tall and wears a long overcoat with a raised
collar. His hands are thrust in his pockets. He has a tall stovepipe hat on his head, a sharp chin and a hooked nose. The sun
was shining brightly and I could see his shadow quite distinctly.'

" 'And in what direction was he looking?'

" 'His face was in profile, but at an angle that suggested he
was contemplating my window. There was something so awful
about him, Dr. Agar, so sinister, that I could bear to look no
more. I crept back to bed and buried my head under the

blankets. When I dared to look again, later that afternoon, he had vanished.'

"I sat for a while patting the boy's hand, attempting to reassure him in what feeble way I could, when suddenly the door opened and Father Wainwright appeared. His dark, stern features darkened the more as he beheld us. 'So,' he said in a menacing voice, 'this is what your visits amount to. Listening to a foolish boy's daydreams. Yes, I have heard all about it, and I can tell you now, if this tomfoolery continues, my lad, you'll return downstairs.'

" 'But, father!' the poor boy protested. 'If you'd only come here one afternoon and see for yourself. I swear to you—'

" 'Swear?' The clergyman stared loftily at his son. 'Do you dare to refer to so solemn an act as that in connexion with so trivial a matter as this?' He strode to the window and shut it firmly. 'I think it would be advisable if you left us, Dr. Agar,' said he. 'And, while you are here, perhaps it would be as well for you to know that my wife and I would prefer that you limit your visits to once a week only.'

" 'My dear sir—!' I protested.

" 'Once a week, sir. And consider yourself very leniently dealt with. If, in the ensuing weeks, this nonsense still prevails, I shall hold you personally responsible and shall look elsewhere for a physician.'

"I was about to reply to this dreadful and unnjust indictment of my moral standing, when suddenly the boy buried his face in the pillows and began to sob convulsively.

" 'There, there, my son,' The clergyman laid a hand on the child's head and stroked it affectionately—for it is clear, despite everything, Mr. Holmes, that he is very fond of Peter. 'Let's try and forget the whole business.'

"It was then that the boy turned his pale face upon us, the huge, feverish eyes filled with the utmost fear. 'But you don't understand, father!' he cried, 'I have not told you everything. I have also seen *her*—and the *children*—' The last words were almost shrieked at us.

"It was now Wainwright's turn to display emotion. He turned a deathly white, bit his lip, and passed a hand across his brow. 'What . . . what do you mean?' he stammered.

" 'I saw the shadow of the man standing there yesterday,' the boy went on. 'As I have so often seen him before, silent and terrible. And then I saw *them*. Immediately opposite to him, and turned toward him, were the shadows of a woman and two children.'

" 'Describe her,' I said.

" 'She was stout, with a kind of heavy coat on. She was clutching the children in the folds of her coat, and all three appeared to be staring intently across at the man.'

"I saw Wainwright turn away and stagger to the window. He leant on the ledge, and I saw that the sweat was trickling down his cheeks. I offered to help him, but he waved me aside. 'Go now, Agar—in God's name. Leave me to myself.'

"I therefore departed with as much dignity as the circumstances would permit.

"As I walked back down the drive, however, I was suddenly seized by the feeling that I was being watched. I glanced back at the drawing-room windows and there, clearly visible against the glass, was Father Wainwright himself, watching me with the utmost intensity. A shudder went through me as I beheld him. There was something terrible in those saturnine features, fixed immovably upon me.

"I was relieved to get home and to attempt to shake off the whole ghastly affair. Then, curiously enough, at about eleven o'clock that night, I was summoned to a patient at Dean Farm.

"I was returning home about midnight when I decided to take, for no other reason than that it was a fine, warm night with a bright moon shining, the old rutted lane that runs past Buckley Vicarage. As I passed the gates, you can imagine my mind reflecting once more on the strange business that was being enacted therein. I suddenly became aware of a strong smell of burning, emanating from the vicarage garden. I pulled up the gig and crept along by the garden wall, which runs in a horseshoe shape around the grounds, with wrought-iron gates in the centre of it. I found myself clambering up a tree stump and peering over. Fortunately, I had selected a spot that commanded a very clear view of the lawn at the back of the house. The whole lawn, and the great cedar that overlooks it, were bathed in moonlight. And there, by the French windows, I beheld the Reverend Joseph Wainwright himself. Mr. Holmes, he looked completely mad. His hair was standing on end and he was gibbering to himself. He looked to all the world like some great ape, lumbering about and gathering fuel, which he was throwing onto a small heap of burning logs, the firelight throwing a garish illumination on his features. And I saw that he was actually grinning diabolically, muttering at the same time, 'That'll do it. That'll do it.' At length, he slunk away and I heard the closing of a door.

"I stood for some time in an indecisive state, much alarmed by what I had just seen, the thick smoke from the conflagration pouring across the lawn into my eyes, causing them to water. Then, for no other reason than my overpowering curiosity—for I am no hero, Mr. Holmes—I climbed stealthily over the wall and crept toward the blaze. Imagine my sensations when I saw, clearly placed on the top of the fire, *a tall, stovepipe hat* and the *smouldering remains of a greatcoat.''*

I saw Holmes start up, his eyes glittering with excitement.

"Without further ado," our client continued, "I turned and fled. Somehow, don't ask me how, I managed to scramble back over the wall, praying desperately that the terrifying figure of the clergyman would not suddenly reappear. Mercifully, it didn't. Today, I could bear no more of it. I decided to call upon the one man in England who might be able to throw some light on the matter."

"And very glad am I that you have done so," said Holmes, lightinng his pipe and stretching his legs out to the hearth. "Tell me, is there anyone of your acquaintance who resembles the figure seen by the boy?"

"There can be no possible doubt that, Father Wainwright himself, if he wished to pose as the figure, could capably do so. He has the height, for example, and that undeniable air of mystery and terror that his figure evidently inspires. Yet there are difficulties. You see, Wainwright does not wear a stovepipe hat, which, in any case, is not distinctly unfashionable. His nose, too, though sharp enough, has not the prominence that this stranger's clearly has. Of course, one can do wonders with theatrical disguise."

"Quite. But for what purpose would the Reverend Joseph Wainwright choose to exhibit himself in this manner? You say he is fond of the boy? Then I cannot see a fond father wishing to persecute his son, particularly a son who is also a chronic invalid. You say that the boy was moved to this room on your instructions? How long has he now been there?"

"Six weeks."

"And he has never spoken of any similar incident until his removal to this room?"

"That is so."

"You say there is a summerhouse near the spot where the boy saw the man's shadow? Is it kept locked?"

"As far as I know, yes."

"Is there a side-gate to the garden?"

"Yes."

"Can it be reached from the main drive?"

"You merely turn along a terraced walk and into it."

"Is it locked?"

"No."

"Ah! Of course!" my friend shrugged. "In view of your own athletic prowess in scaling the wall, what an elderly gentleman can do, another man can surely emulate. Of course, we must establish Wainwright's whereabouts at the time this figure was seen. If it can be proved that he was at the vicarage or within its immediate vicinity at the time, then this, to some degree, strengthens the case against him, however imponderable his motives."

"And what do you propose to do now, Mr. Holmes?"

"To smoke on it."

"You will not come back with me tonight?"

"No, I rather think that this is a three-pipe problem. Besides, our presence in your company might seriously jeopardize your own position with the Wainwrights—a position already threatened enough."

My friend rose and shook our client's hand. "Rest assured, Dr. Watson and I will come down tomorrow and look into this little matter for ourselves. In the meantime, keep watch and ward, Dr. Agar, for I very much fear that matters may come to a head sooner than we think. Goodnight to you."

A gray, sunless morning found us, in due course, at Buckley village. Holmes wasted no time in hastening to the vicarage. This proved to be a rambling, Gothic edifice, half hidden from the lane by a fortress of elm and sycamore.

A gaunt, forbidding atmosphere hung over the lichen-covered building as we made our way up the main drive. The mullioned windows on either side of the front door were thickly shaded by an overhanging oak and, as we were ushered into the drawing-room by a demure maidservant, I was aware of an oppressive stillness, heightened the more by the remorseless ticking of a grandfather clock.

In a room whose walls were hung with grim Old Testament texts and Doré's frightful illustrations of Dante's *Inferno,* we found ourselves confronted by a tall, heavily bearded man, with something of the Romany in his dark, swarthy features. He eyed us imperiously, twirling my friend's card in his hand. "Well, Mr. Holmes?"

"I have come, Father Wainwright, at the direct bidding of Dr. Moore Agar, on a matter which he believes of the most pressing urgency concerning your son Peter."

Father Wainwright sniffed with sardonic disdain.

"You are perhaps unaware, Mr. Holmes, that I have already expressed my resentment of what I believe to be Agar's unwarranted intrusion into our family affairs. My son's medical adviser he may be, but his function ceases there. It is highly reprehensible on his part to attempt to trespass further by openly encouraging my son's pathetic fantasies, which are clearly begotten of the boy's lamentable illness and the solitude arising therefrom. Under the circumstances, I consider your presence here totally without justification and I must ask you to leave."

Sherlock Holmes's response was to take a seat by the window. "You may rest assured, Father Wainwright, that I am aware of your present antipathy toward the worthy doctor. On the other hand, from what he has told me, I understand your son believes himself to be under some form of persecution."

"Imaginary persecution, Mr. Holmes, would be the more appropriate phrase."

"Well, a form of persecution, anyhow, which is occasioning him considerable distress. It is my duty, at least, to ascertain whether there is any foundation for his fears."

Father Wainwright took a stride toward the bell.

"By all means ring for your maidservant," my friend murmured, closing his eyes and placing his fingertips together.

"It was the police I had in mind, Mr. Holmes."

"I do not doubt it. My feeble excuse on their arrival will be merely one of attempting to help a chronic invalid who believes a certain group of strangers is watching his room. As the handcuffs are produced, I shall hopelessly direct the worthy constables' attention to the fact that the boy's father is totally opposed to any such assistance. As Dr. Watson and I are carried to the Black Maria, my last beseeching cry will be a mere humdrum reference to the selfsame father having been seen at dead of night, burning the possible clothing of at least one of these mysterious intruders."

Wainwright's hand shrank back from the bellpull. His dark features paled significantly, and he fell back into an armchair.

"I don't know who's been talking, Mr. Holmes," he said in

a trembling voice, "But what I do in my own garden is my business."

"In the light of recent events, I think not. Still, if you are content to let the matter pass into other hands—"

"Mr. Holmes." The voice of Father Wainwright now sounded half-strangled as he rose and commenced pacing the room, to and fro, biting his lip. "You are a man of discretion, I have no doubt. My actions in the garden, I can assure you, were not borne of any criminal intention on my part. They are the result of a private matter which I am not prepared to discuss. I have, of course, heard of your wonderful gift, for which, I trust, you daily thank your Maker. I believe you to be a man of strong principles. If I were to let you speak with my son—?"

"Providing there is no factual evidence of any intended crime, you may rely on my discretion, Father Wainwright."

"Then come this way, sir."

We were about to follow the clergyman from the room, when the door suddenly opened and a woman entered, accompanied by a tall youth of about sixteen, who eyed us in a suspicious and slightly hostile manner.

"What is the meaning of this, Joseph?" Mrs. Wainwright cried. She was a strikingly handsome woman, middle-aged, and yet, with her luxuriant blond hair, clear violet eyes and shapely figure, retaining much of what must have been a considerable beauty in her earlier years. "The boy is sick," she continued, her bosom rising and falling rapidly in her evident distress. "And I believe his mind is sick, too. Why," she exclaimed, turning upon my friend, "Why can't you leave us in peace? Have we not suffered enough already without having to endure these impertinent and heartless questions? It is enough that our child will shortly die—we have to live with that realization every moment of every day. I ask you politely, could *you* bear it?"

Sherlock Holmes bowed. "I have every sympathy with your feelings in this unfortunate affair, Mrs. Wainwright," said he. "But it is my responsibility to ascertain the validity, or otherwise, of your son's story. If I find it to be well substantiated, then the whole matter could prove to be very serious indeed."

The youth who was dressed in a smock and mud-stained farm boots, broke into a jeering laugh. "If you are the famous Sherlock Holmes, sir," he declared, "I wouldn't have thought you'd waste your time on a mere fairy tale."

"Be silent, Jack," Father Wainwright interposed.

"I shan't be silent." Jack Wainwright exchanged a glance with his mother, who placed her arms around him.

"Jack has been studying so hard of late, Mr. Holmes—he intends to study law once he's matriculated, you see—that you must forgive his temper. The whole matter is seriously affecting his concentration. It would be a terrible blow to us all if this silly nonsense of Peter's should jeopardise my Jack's future."

"It's just a fairy tale," repeated the youth with a sneer. "I know my brother. He lies up there all day and reads these adventure yarns of his, and it all goes to his head. I know he's ill, but he doesn't seem to realize other people"—here he smote his chest—"have important things to do. He *is* selfish, isn't he, Mother?"

Mrs. Wainwright planted a kiss on her son's cheek and hugged him. "You must try to be patient, Jack," said she. "I'm sure this will all pass quickly—it's just a phase. The important thing is to see you get that scholarship."

"Nothing will stop me getting that, Mother," asserted the son, gazing ardently into his mother's eyes.

Sherlock Holmes threw the lad one of his keen, penetrating glances. "I perceive you have been working on some local farm, Jack," said he.

"That's right. I clean out the stables and look after the horses on Lord Oxley's estate. He lets me work there during the hols."

"But don't think, Mr. Holmes," Mrs. Wainwright interjected sharply, "that my Jack will remain content with such menial employment. I assure you that, in ten years' time, he will be the talk of Lincoln's Inn. You mark my words." She concluded this assertion with yet another vehement embrace of her son, who blushed and smiled at her, with another look of the utmost devotion.

"Well, Mr. Holmes," came the incisive voice of Father Wainwright, who appeared embarrassed by this display, "If you and Dr. Watson care to follow me—"

We found ourselves mounting a narrow, winding staircase. The same gloomy pictures and texts accompanied us till we reached a little arched door of polished oak which the clergyman promptly flung open.

Peter Wainright, supported by a couple of huge pillows, was sitting up in bed with a book in his hands. I have seen many sick people in my time, but few whose faces so pitifully illustrated their condition. Peter Wainwright's hideous pallor was rendered the more terrible by the deep, sunken eyes, feverishly brilliant as he surveyed us. "Mr. Sherlock Holmes," he gasped, on being introduced to my illustrious friend. He straightaway bombarded him with so many breathless questions that Holmes was compelled to lay a restraining hand on his arm.

"It is my intention, young Peter, to sort out your own little mystery," he remarked, gently. "So perhaps my own tedious exploits of the past can wait for a while. Tell me all that has happened."

With glowing admiration in his eyes, the boy recited all that Dr. Agar had previously divulged. Holmes listened intently, as if he were hearing it all for the first time. The boy leaned forward and clutched my friend's arm. "There's something else, Mr. Holmes. Something you don't know—no one knows. It only happened last night."

"Come, my son. Mr. Holmes is a busy man," interrupted the clergyman sharply. "What nonsense is this?"

Peter Wainwright stared long and penetratingly into Holmes's face. "The man on the lawn," he whispered. "He was in this room last night."

We all stared at the boy with the same chilling sense of incomprehension and expectancy.

"What time was this?" inquired Holmes.

"I don't know—it was well past midnight. I believe I heard the church clock chiming one. I kept on tossing and turning, unable to sleep. Suddenly, I heard the handle of my door being turned. I was terrified. I could hear this low, heavy breathing. Then, slowly the door creaked open. I dived under the bed clothes. The breathing grew louder and nearer. I could feel whoever it was, standing over me. Slowly, I removed the blanket. The moon was shining brightly through the window. On the wall immediately opposite to me, I saw the thing that I most dreaded—I saw the shadow of a tall man in a tall hat with a greatcoat pulled up above his ears. So terrified was I, I could hear my teeth chattering in my head. And then I heard a voice close to me—I was so frightened, I dared not turn and look. But I heard this voice." He paused, clutching and unclutching the sheet, his eyes searching each of our faces, as if craving support.

"And what did the voice say?" asked Holmes, at length.

"It said, 'Peter Wainwright, I am Death. And I shall be coming to take you soon.'" As he uttered these words, the unfortunate boy turned and buried his face in the pillows.

"There, there," murmured Holmes, patting his shoulder. "You must not fear. I shall do all I can to clear this matter up for you.'' He turned to Father Wainwright who was clutching a corner of the brass bedstead, his head sunk upon his breast. ''I must inform you now that I have not the slightest doubt that your son's story is true.''

''You mean someone broke into this house last night, totally unobserved, came up those stairs, equally unobserved, and entered this room?''

''What other explanation is there? Tell me, Peter, do you recall the sound of this man's voice?''

''I can never forget it. It was deep and rough, and had a kind of burr to it, like the village folk have.''

The effect of this statement upon Father Wainwright was devastating. He went as pale as if he had seen a ghost. With a tremendous effort, he mastered himself, but the sweat glistened on his brow. His reaction was not lost upon my friend, who eyed him with the utmost curiosity.

''I would be obliged if I might take a stroll upon the lawn, Father Wainwright,'' he remarked. ''If you have no objection.''

The clergyman waved a hand toward the door.

''Do what you must, Mr. Holmes,'' he said gravely.

As soon as we were outside, Holmes commenced a meticulous examination of the lawn. He lay full-length upon the grass. He scampered to and fro, his coattails billowing behind him, so that he resembled some strange, predatory animal. At length, he drew himself up, indicated the old summerhouse, remarked that it had clearly been locked up for at least a year judging by the state of the lock, and then drew my attention to a gate at the end of the garden. ''It is, in coloquial parlance, a kissing-gate, Watson. Let us see what secrets it can divulge.''

A glance at the lock was sufficient for him to start up, his eyes gleaming. ''Recently placed here, Watson,'' said he, ''and beyond, lies the meadow. And, ah, that interesting spot of fresh brown earth nearby. I rather think our business is completed for the day. Since the sun declines to shine, it is hardly worth our while hunting for shadows.''

He returned with a grim face to the vicarage, made his apologies to the clergyman for his intrusion and confessed that the case was proving ''difficult.''

Later that evening, however, in the comfortable parlour room of the village inn, he divulged his plan for the forthcoming night. ''We must return in the early hours, Watson,'' he said. ''The map suggests that we can reach the meadow at the back of the vicarage by a footpath. I have borrowed a torch from Mine

Host." His eyes twinkled. "I foresee an interesting end to our nocturnal expedition. Are you armed?"

"I have my old service revolver."

"Then do keep it to hand. The Reverend Joseph Wainwright is not a man whose temper I would trust should it be put to the test."

The church clock was striking midnight when we at last made our way across the lane and onto a well-worn footpath. Overhead, the sky was a mass of fleecy clouds rushing aross the face of the moon. The Quarry Wood, dark and menacing, lay to our right, whilst in the far distance, I could just glimpse the gloomy façade of the vicarage, looming through the trees. Not a light was visible, and there was about that Gothic edifice an ominous stillness, vibrant with the mystery and terror that lurked within its lichened walls.

"Father Wainwright is an interesting specimen, is he not?" my friend remarked, as we reached the kissing-gate, keeping close to the dense shade of a sycamore. "Did anything strike you as curious about his behaviour?"

"Holmes," I whispered, "he *knows* the identity of that man? I swear it."

"Yes, so his reaction to the boy's story would suggest. I have seldom seen such fear on a man's face. And yet, my dear Watson, there is surely something more than fear."

"What do you mean?"

"Guilt. The man is harbouring some painful secret, that is obvious. And within that secret is both guilt and, I would say, remorse. But here we are. Hand me that torch." He knelt down, flashing the torch over the earth. "Someone has been digging here, as I suspected."

He started to scrape away at the loose earth with his bare hands. "Keep your eyes on the vicarage, Watson, as you value your life," he muttered, intent on his labours.

At length, he uttered a loud exclamation of triumph.

In the glare of the torch, I saw that he held something shiny and metallic. Drawing closer, I saw that it was a gold watch and chain. On the earth below lay the remains of a waistcoat. "Look at this, Watson." He pointed to a faint inscription on the watch. "To A.H.W. from J.W. 1864."

"In heaven's name!" I ejaculated. "What does it all mean?"

"Devilry, Watson," he replied, gravely, placing the watch in his pocket and gathering up the waistcoat. "Come. There is nothing more to be learned here."

And yet there was something more. As we retraced our steps, I chanced to glance back at the vicarage. It may have been the merest fancy, but I could have sworn that, for a brief moment, a light had flashed on in some upper room, and clearly silhouetted against it was the figure of a man in a tall hat, who appeared to be staring fixedly out into the night. The next moment, the vision had vanished. I drew Holmes's attention to it. For a few minutes we stood waiting. But not a light now showed; all was as dark and silent as the grave.

We arose rather late, and it was early afternoon by the time we sat down to lunch in the inn parlour. Holmes appeared rapt in the deepest thought. He sat by the window, the very picture of despondency. "I have a strange premonition, Watson," he said, "that something is about to happen. However, so bizarre is this affair, compounded of such diverse threads, that it is impossible at this stage to ascertain in what sudden direction events might turn."

"You feel the boy is in danger?"

"Very great danger. But if we could pinpoint that danger, this case would cease to be the connoisseur's problem that it undoubtedly is. Indeed, it is one of the most memorable of my career. Its subtleties run deeper than the mere glimpse of shadowy figures on a vicarage lawn, and yet—"

He ceased abruptly, his fingers drumming excitedly on the table.

"What is it, Holmes?"

I saw that he was staring intently through the window at the cobbled yard. The sun was shining brightly, and I could hear the birds singing, yet the beauty of the afternoon was evidently lost upon my friend.

"The stones," he muttered. "Great heaven, how blind I have been!" He clapped his hand to his head. "Come, Watson. Our place is at the Wainwrights'."

We hurried across the yard. Within minutes we were descending the winding lane that led to the vicarage. Suddenly, the sound of a horse and carriage, furiously driven, fell on our ears. The next moment, round a sharp bend, Dr. Moore Agar came hurtling into view, a raised whip in his hand, his face distorted with horror. As he saw us he uttered a fearful cry, the whip fell from his hand, and he himself, in pulling up the reins, toppled from his seat, landing among the hedgerows. The panic-stricken horse, with its riderless carriage, clattered past us.

"My dear sir, what on earth has happened?" Holmes helped the unfortunate doctor to his feet.

"A most terrible thing, Mr. Holmes, a most appalling tragedy!"

Sherlock Holmes turned a ghastly face upon me. "What, then, Dr. Agar?"

"Young Peter Wainwright is dead. His body was found barely an hour ago. He had flung himself from his bedroom window."

This frightful news stunned us both into silence for a moment or two. I saw Holmes cover his face and stamp upon the ground. "Fool that I have been!" he exclaimed bitterly. "Yet how was I to know the exact time, the hour—you are going for the police, of course? Then, by all means, hurry. Watson and I will go on up to the vicarage."

"He was driven to it, Mr. Holmes, if ever a boy was. He was still alive, you understand, when I arrived. He spoke to me."

Holmes pricked up his ears. "And what was it he said?"

"He said—very faintly, for he was in a great deal of pain and very near his end—'*It was him, Dr. Agar. He came for me!*' They were the last words he uttered."

Holmes grabbed my arm. "Come, Watson. There's not a moment to lose. Though we cannot save him, we can at least avenge him!"

Before long, we found ourselves once more in that dark parlour room. Father Wainwright was sitting with his face buried in his hands. He broke into sobs as he attempted to describe what had happened. It was Jack Wainwright who supplied the terrible details.

"Peter had seemed all right when I looked in about lunch-time, Mr. Holmes," said he. "He was sketching and talked quite excitedly about entering one of his pictures for the Reading Festival. About two o'clock we were all in this room having some tea. Father was discussing the arrangements for the Garden Fête next week, when suddenly we heard this shriek from upstairs. We all rushed up. The window was wide open. . . . Anne, our maidservant, who had just taken up Peter's tea, was standing there, near hysterical, pointing below. We all looked down into the garden. On the terrace we saw Peter lying. We carried him in and summoned Dr. Agar but he passed away shortly after the doctor arrived."

Mrs. Wainwright, a handkerchief to her red, swollen eyes, waved a hand toward the door. "If you wish to see my son, Mr. Holmes, he's lying in the next room. Oh, what he must have been going through to have done this! Tiresome he may have been at times—perhaps he had a right to be—but I should have shown more patience and understanding.''

Master Jack placed an arm around her. ''There, Mother, you mustn't blame yourself. You did all you possibly could for him,'' said he.

All the while, Father Wainwright continued to sit with his head in his hands, the tears streaming down his face, such an abject picture of paternal grief that it wrung my heart to behold him.

In a small adjoining room, with the blinds half drawn, we looked upon the body of the unfortunate boy. Even in the stillness of death, the upturned face exhibited a look of the utmost terror, the lips parted and the eyes staring.

A cursory examination on my part revealed that death had resulted from a combined fracture of the skull and spine. I could not but reflect upon the overwhelming pathos of the death. That such a life—fraught as it had already been with a mortal illness—should end in this fashion, struck me as being a singularly cruel fate.

Sherlock Holmes examined the victim's shirt, which was speckled with russet stains. We then went outside where he examined the terrace, Mrs. Wainwright indicating the exact spot where Peter had been discovered. Finally, we went upstairs, where Holmes commenced a meticulous examination of the boy's room. I noticed he picked up something from the floor, scrutinized it through his lens for some minutes, and then placed it in his pocket book.

''What is it, Holmes?''

''A piece of straw, Watson. You see its significance, I trust? Those curious russet stains on the boy's shirt are of equal importance.''

At that moment, I chanced to glance out of the window.

''Holmes!'' I grasped his arm. ''Look!''

Clearly outlined upon the lawn was the shadow of a man. He wore a stovepipe hat and an ulster, and standing perfectly motionless, appeared to be staring intently in the direction of Peter Wainwright's room. I could see quite clearly the great hooked nose and sharp chin that the unfortunate child had described. There was something so spine-chilling and arresting about this gaunt, spectral shape, that I found myself staring mindlessly at it, lost to my friend's voice as he tugged at my sleeve.

"The gentleman has company," he pointed out. Glancing to the extreme right of the lawn, immediately opposite the man, I beheld the shadow of a woman. She was of medium height, with a kind of shawl drawn about her shoulders. Clutching at her skirt-folds were a couple of children, of indeterminate sex, since their shadows afforded but the barest outline of their presence. The next moment the sun had vanished, and the people on the lawn had melted away as silently as they had come.

My friend turned to the door. "Come, Watson. The shadows on the lawn shall trouble us no more!"

I followed him outside. Save for a couple of blackbirds, the lawn was deserted. I glanced keenly about me, but not a sign of those mysterious intruders was to be discerned.

"Holmes!" I exclaimed. "This is absurd. They *must* be somewhere. In heaven's name, where are they?"

His answer was unforgettable.

Stretching forth his sinewy arm, he pointed up toward the rooftop of Buckley Vicarage, to the motley collection of tall, crooked chimney stacks. "There," he said quietly.

The police still had not arrived when we found ourselves confronting the Reverend Joseph Wainwright in the gloomy parlour room of that ill-omened house. The clergyman had recovered his composure enough to eye us with a certain severity.

"My son is dead, Mr. Holmes. Is that not sufficient for you? Have you no compassion? I believed you to be a man of some sensibility, yet to continue to pester us at such a time as this is a rebuke to all common decency."

Holmes raised a protesting hand. "I fully sympathise with your grief. But the interests of justice must still be served."

"I fail to understand you. What possible good can come of any further investigation? Let my poor boy rest in peace."

"Amen to that," murmured Mrs. Wainwright, whilst her eldest son grasped her hand and patted it reassuringly.

"I can assure you that Dr. Watson and I have no wish to trouble the spirit of the departed. In which case, perhaps we should speedily clear up what little of this mystery remains." He took from his pocket the gold watch and chain that we had unearthed the previous night and placed it on the table. Wainwright stared open-mouthed at this revelation.

"Albert Henry Wainwright," my friend said in sombre tones. "Hanged at Sheffield in 1868 for the murder of his wife and children. This is the guilty secret that you and your family have shared for so long. When I discovered the watch— evidently a gift from yourself, Father Wainwright, to your unhappy brother—I recognised the initials as conceivably referring to the Park Road Murderer, as he was so described. You will note the watchmaker's Sheffield address on the back here."

Father Wainwright staggered to a chair and sat there, thumping his head in a gesture of uncontrollable anguish.

"What purpose lies in further deception, Mr. Holmes?" he broke forth at last. "You appear to know so much."

"No, Joseph—let us not speak of *him*—I beg you," Mrs. Wainwright had leapt up, but her husband's arm restrained her.

"We must face it, Sarah," he said. "Who knows, if we had been honest from the start, my son might still be alive. Yes, Mr. Holmes, I am the brother of Albert Wainwright, and though I loved him dearly, the knowledge of his crime has hung about my neck like a great millstone these sixteen years. We were devoted to each other, and he, with his Oxford scholarship and career at the Bar opening before him, was the dazzling star of the family. But arduous hours over his law books had left its mark upon him. While he was still at Oxford, he began to drink heavily and to spend his evenings in various low taverns. It was in one of these places that he met his wife, an Irish barmaid.

"I shall never forget that hot summer night, shortly before his examinations, when he came to me and told me all—that she was carrying his child and that, in all honour, ill-bred and illiterate as she was, he would have to marry her. The news was like a bullet through my father's heart. He died a few months afterward. Albert had already left Oxford without a degree or a penny to his name. He became an usher at a grammar school in Sheffield. There, in a hovel of a place, in one of the most disreputable regions of the town, he attempted to live with a woman whose foul tongue and intemperate habits goaded him beyond endurance. One night, in a fit of unbridled rage, when she had returned home in a drunken state with a local cobbler, he strangled her and those two lovely children, a boy and a girl. It was an unspeakable thing to do and the horror of it has never left me, indeed it haunts my every hour.

"Albert's own explanation, with regard to the children, was that he could not bear the thought of leaving them to the Parish—he envisaged the horrendous poverty, the appalling suffering, that awaited them. But on the night before he was hanged, he sat with a Bible open on his knee and confessed to me the indescribable remorse he felt. 'I have thought less about

Kathleen lately,' said he, 'poor creature that she was, than about John and Rose. I see their little faces yet, looking up at me. Joseph,' he begged me, 'be always loving to your children—cherish them all your days—and that will be of some comfort to my soul—wherever it may be in the world beyond.' Father Wainwright lifted his head and surveyed Holmes searchingly. 'You may rest assured, Albert,' I told him, 'on that account.' And so, I have attempted to be true to my word, Mr. Holmes. Even when Peter—poor Peter—was born and the evidence of mortal sickness began unmistakably to declare itself.

"But consider. After we had settled here and attempted to put the past behind us, imagine what I felt when Peter began to talk of those shadows on the lawn. Conceive with what horror it began to dawn upon me that the figures closely resembled those of my lamented brother and his wife and children. It was as if the whole terrible drama were being reenacted before my child's eyes.

"You now know that he had been judiciously kept in ignorance of the past. Only Sarah and Jack shared my knowledge. I felt increasingly that I was cursed. That soon the whole ghastly truth would be exposed. I was like a madman. I scarcely knew what I was doing. I gathered together what relics of Albert we still retained—the stovepipe hat he invariably wore, a greatcoat and some other items, and burnt them in the garden. So as not to arouse suspicions with yet another blaze, I buried his waistcoat and watch by the meadow. Perhaps I entertained hopes that, by these acts, I could exorcise his memory—that the terrible imagery upon the lawn would haunt us no more.

"Then Peter began to speak of visitations in the early hours of the morning. Even the rustic burr that he detected in the voice of his sinister visitor recalled my brother, whose East Anglian accent was always stronger than mine. I began to believe that he was actually being haunted—that perhaps my brother had become a restless, earthbound spirit whose sole satisfaction was to become a torment to us—may God forgive me for thinking so!"

He sank his head in his hands and continued to sit thus, whilst Sherlock Holmes walked to the window, drew the heavy curtains back and gazed out across the garden.

"Of course, it should have been obvious to me from the start that these shadows could only have been cast from a great height," he explained. "The room to which young Peter had been moved faced east, which meant that, by midafternoon, the sun, having passed its meridian, would be in just the most appropriate position, high above the back of the house, to cast those sinister shadows of the chimney stacks. Of course, the supposed shadows of the woman and children were always there; the fact that they were overlooked at first was a result of the boy's terror. His eyes were fixed on the first figure he saw, that of the man. The fact that they only appeared at a certain time, and that their manifestation only arose on the boy's removal to this particular part of the house, should have alerted me at once to their probable origin. I was, however, distracted by the distinct physiognomy attributed to these figures. It was only when I detected similar shapes on the cobbled yard of the inn that I realised my error.

"You will recall, Watson, that on one side of the roof there is a single stack, surmounted by a tall funnel with a circular base . . . and that on the other side there is a dumpier stack, with a group of two smaller stacks clustered about it. The shadows cast by these stacks are extraordinary in their human likeness. Yet I venture to assert that such phenomena invariably pass unnoticed unless viewed under those peculiar conditions of solitude and imaginative speculation that characterised young Peter's daily hours."

"Yes, of course, it is all true, Mr. Holmes," muttered Father Wainwright. "I saw only what my boy saw, I believed only what he believed. But, oh, that he should have taken his own life because of it!"

Holmes placed a small, dirt-encrusted piece of straw upon the table. "I must beg to disagree with you, Father Wainwright," said he. "Your son did not take his own life."

The clergyman leapt up, his eyes staring wildly.

"What are you saying, Mr. Holmes?"

"I repeat. Peter Wainwright did not die by his own hand." He lowered his voice. "Another hand was responsible."

A tense silence followed these words.

I saw Mrs. Wainwright clap her hand to her bosom, her face white to the lips. Young Jack Wainwright eyed the floor, whilst Father Wainwright continued to tug nervously at his beard.

"The murderer was well acquainted with the house," Holmes pursued, "Sufficiently well acquainted to dress up in a stovepipe hat and ulster and to terrorise the boy in the early hours. You, Watson, on our expedition of last night, were not deceived by your vision. You did indeed catch a glimpse of this personage as he stared from an upper window. When I discovered, on the shirt of the deceased, the faint evidence of finger-marks of a russet hue, the result of hands having been in recent contact with Wilkins' Solution, which is used in the treatment of worn leather saddles—and, moreover, when I discovered a piece of mud-covered straw on which were traces of horse dung—it did not take me long to surmise that the person intimately involved in the death of Peter Wainwright had recently been working in a stable.'' He paused, then dramatically pointed towards Master Jack Wainwright. ''There stands the murderer of your son, Father Wainwright, and it is a grievous thing for me to have to reveal that fact.''

To my astonishment, the youth ventured no protest. Instead, he eyed my friend almost haughtily.

''Yes, I killed him. He was a blight on our lives.''

''Jack!'' Mrs. Wainwright stared uncomprehendingly at her son.

''I did it for you, Mother—don't you realise that?''

He attempted to place his arm around her and kiss her, but she averted her face.

''But, Mother!'' he protested. ''Your life was a misery with him—and him—'' he spat out the last word and flung a savage glance at his father. ''I wanted you to be free, Mother, and to be happy. How could that be unless he died? He was going to die anyway, so did it matter?''

Only the relentless ticking of the clock answered him in that dark, oppressive room.

''After he started to talk of the shadows on the lawn, I suddenly saw how I could silence him forever, and in a way that would baffle even the most brilliant mind. Or so I thought,'' he sneered, glancing at Holmes. ''I bought a secondhand hat and I borrowed one of your ulsters, dear Father—I had heard you speak of uncle, of how he looked and how he spoke. Peter would divulge this, and you yourself would then believe the house was indeed haunted. You see, I wanted to hit you hard, as well as Peter. He was always your favourite, you never cared tuppence for me. Only Mother has stood by me. Dear Mother.''

Mrs. Wainwright, however, her face like death, seemed to be in a trance. Her husband shook his head. ''I tried to be fair to both of you, Jack,'' he said.

''Fair!'' Jack Wainwright threw his head back and laughed bitterly. ''Anyway, my time came this afternoon. I donned my hat and coat and went to his room. Hadn't I told him my name was Death and that I would come for him? He almost fainted when he saw me at the door in the clear daylight. I thought he was going to scream, so I placed my hand over his mouth. I carried him to the window and I slid him through it. All the time, his eyes were begging me to help him. I enjoyed that. I wanted him to suffer. Hadn't I suffered enough? Hadn't he made all our lives a misery with his cursed illness? I really believe his crippled limbs were a curse on us for the evil deeds of the past. He had to die. So I let him slip from me, gently—I watched him fall. It was all so simple.''

Suddenly, Jack Wainwright broke into a fit of hysterical giggling. As he did so, the door opened and the burly figure of Inspector Wylie of the Berkshire Constabulary filled the aperture.

Later, in the golden evening sunshine as we strolled upon the lawn of Buckley Vicarage for the last time, Holmes outlined to me his final impressions of the case.

"On my arrival here, Watson," he observed, "it struck me as highly improbable that the Reverend Joseph Wainwright himself could be parading theatrically on his own lawn. If, as I surmised, the initials on the watch referred to the murderer Albert Wainwright, then clearly this was a family secret that the worthy clergyman might attempt to conceal. All his behaviour— his reaction to his son's description of the people on the lawn, the bonfire in the garden and his subsequent burial of the watch and waistcoat—supported this supposition. Furthermore, he clearly loved the boy, and a doting father does not persecute his offspring in this manner. A conclusive fact, however, which I gleaned from Dr. Agar, was that Wainwright was at a parish meeting on the afternoon when both the man and his supposed family were seen."

"What made you suspect the elder son?"

"You must surely recall his obsessive behaviour with his mother, and hers with him. It was possessive love of a most violent kind. Both seemed at odds with the father, and it struck me that, if the lad were to vent his animosity toward his father, he could not have stumbled upon a more devastating method than to strike at his most vulnerable spot: the man's deep-rooted guilt about his dead brother. Young Peter's talk of the shadowy figures provided him with that opportunity. You perceive the diabolical cunninng of it, Watson. For, having himself ascertained from whence the shadows were appearing, he began to play upon the poor boy's imagination with the aid of his own macabre embellishments. Indeed, his notion of dressing up as he did was a positive stroke of genius.''

"And evil genius, surely?"

"Well, art in the blood can take the strangest forms, Watson, as I have remarked before. It is not for nothing that the Wainwrights are distantly related to Daniel Wainwright, the eighteenth century painter and debauchee. In Master Jack's case, the creative inheritance was directed toward some more malevolent end."

"But surely it supposes some gross gullibility on the part of the clergyman to be so taken in by those shadows, whose origin must surely have occurred to him, since he had lived here for so long?"

"Not necessarily, Watson. How often have you remarked upon the strange configuration engendered by the Baker Street chimney-pots? Besides, people *are* so gullible."

"One thing still troubles me. How was it that the shadow of the man exhibited the sharply-etched hook nose, which apparently perfectly resembled that of the dead brother?"

"The masonry on one side of the tall chimney stack is broken, and a jagged piece of stone protrudes."

My friend turned and surveyed the broad front of the house, where the pigeons were gathering along the rooftop, basking in the mellow warmth and stillness of the spring evening. "There is a curious irony here, Watson. To think that such shadows should so pointedly represent a dark family secret. It is a lesson to us all—to face the truth we fear, rather than to attempt to repress it. The whole basis of the case, however, resides in the curious personality of Mrs. Sarah Wainwright."

"Why so?"

"Because Master Jack was really acting unconsciously under her pervasive influence. He felt that the removal of young Peter would gain her love totally and completely, since there would then be no second party to distract her attention. Her possessive love for Master Jack, on whom she lavished all the passion engendered by her own marital bitterness, was really the motivating force behind the elder son's actions. Yes, my dear Watson, you who are so ardent a connoisseur of the sex, should remember in future that, if you wish to study a woman's character, look to her children. It is an axiom that has seldom failed me. And now, if you are willing, we will take a stroll by the river. I have a strong inclination to savour the local ale, for which I have heard the most extravagant claims. There is a delightful public house, I noticed, overlooking the creek, so I shall be more than happy to put the matter to the test."

Author's note:

from: *His Last Bow.*

". . . Dr. Moore Agar . . . whose dramatic introduction to Holmes I may one day recount . . ."

—"The Adventure of The Devil's Foot"

THE ADVENTURE OF THE GOWANUS ABDUCTION

Joyce Harrington

Cover portrait for the 1903 issue of "Collier's" by Frederic Dorr Steele.

It was on a dreary afternoon in January of a recent year, as I was attempting without much success to relieve the symptoms of a fresh head cold, that the house telephone rang and the doorman announced the arrival of a bicycle messenger with a package for me. My first instinct was to instruct Carlos to sign for the package. I would pick it up later in the day when I descended from my penthouse aerie to lay in a supply of nose drops, tissues, and fresh lemons. But the turgid antics of television soap operas had palled, and curiosity got the better of me. I ordered him to send the messenger up.

Moments later, the doorbell rang. Attired as I was, in an ancient woolen dressing gown with a scarf tied Sikh-fashion around my head to ward off drafts, I answered the summons.

The personage who stood before me in the open doorway was an astonishing sight. He was tall, well over six feet, and dressed entirely in black Spandex with the exception of a black bicycle helmet upon his head and a multicolored knitted ski mask covering his face—revealing only a pair of large and luminous dark eyes, which gazed impassively down into mine, and a wide, fleshy mouth, which uttered not a word. Over his shoulder was slung a bulging black canvas satchel, and his hands were covered by close-fitting black leather gloves. In one of those hands, he carried a brown manila envelope, which he

163

thrust toward me along with a slip of paper and a ballpoint pen. A gloved finger pointed to the line on which, clearly, he desired me to sign.

I did so, at the same time groping in the pocket of my dressing gown for a dollar bill with which to reward his labors. He snatched pen, paper, and bill from me and, still without a word, loped away to the elevator, where he vigorously punched the call button and waited, impatiently jogging from foot to foot while the heavy satchel jounced upon his back like a malignant dwarf rider urging a recalcitrant steed to greater effort.

I had, of course, seen many of these two-wheeled Mercuries speeding about the streets of the city, and indeed, more than once had narrowly escaped collision with one or another of his brethren; but this was the first time that anyone had chosen this means to communicate with me.

As I stood there in the open doorway, rather more befuddled than usual, due, no doubt, to the congestion of my sinuses, he turned to face me, and in a gravelly voice uttered a single word. "Irregular."

Irregular, indeed! I realized that I cut a far from dashing figure with my red nose and head wrap, but what right had the fellow to comment upon my infirmity, especially after receiving such a generous gratuity? I was about to protest vehemently when a sneeze of such magnitude erupted from my clogged nasal passages that I was quite incapable of speech for several seconds. When, after the use of a half-dozen or so tissues, my faculties had cleared, the hallway was deserted, the elevator doors were closing, and my visitor was gone.

Retreating back into my apartment, I turned my attention to the envelope in my hand. It was addressed to me in a heavy black scrawl that almost defied deciphering, and there was no return address. The envelope itself showed signs of much wear, being wrinkled and creased, with smudges of dirt ground into the creases. I turned it over and found that the flap had been sealed with several layers of transparent tape upon which two or three clear fingerprints had impressed themselves. I stared at them for a while but they told me nothing, and I longed for the keen sight and quick mind of the one-time companion of my life.

But the many-talented and moody Diana—actress, artist, musician, poet of some renown, chef of cordon bleu stature, huntress of wild beasts as befits her name (but with a Nikon instead of an elephant gun), and these are but a few of her many accomplishments—had long since left our mutual establishment on a quest, as she put it, "Of the secret of my existence."

Two years had gone by since the New Year's Day in 19— when she had packed a small rucksack with essentials and departed, saying only, "Keep the apartment ready, Watson, my love. I'll be back."

I had, of course, pleaded with her to allow me to accompany her on her journey, but she remained adamant in her refusal. "Too dangerous, dear friend, and you enjoy your civilized comforts too well," was the only reason she gave me.

Another man might have been insulted by such a commentary upon his courage and stamina, but not I. Diana could be irritating, but she was always right. My health had been impaired by youthful indiscretions committed during the Age of Aquarius when I dropped out of medical school and led the life of a flower child. I was now content to remain at home, recording on my word processor the adventures of my dearest friend, as she had related them to me (and in some of which I had taken a modest share) on lazy summer evenings while we reclined on our terrace overlooking the great metropolis.

It had been two years, as I say, since she had set forth, and in all that time, no word had come of her whereabouts. Is it any wonder, then, that I gazed upon the enigmatic envelope in my hands with a mixture of hope, dread, and insatiable curiosity? Open it and quickly satisfy that curiosity? Yes. My hand went out to the ivory letter opener, a souvenir of *The Adventure of the Promiscuous Pachyderm,* upon my desk. But dread stayed my hand. What unwelcome news might this packet contain? Would it not be better to fortify myself against despondency with a tot of brandy in the freshly brewed cup of tea that was still steaming beside my easy chair?

To the sideboard, then, I went for the curiously crafted decanter, a relic of Diana's narrow escape from death in what I call *The Glassblower's Last Gasp,* and measured a careful half-ounce into my teacup. Thus armed against disaster, I settled into my chair, wrapped myself cozily into my afghan, and allowed hope to surge paramount in my breast.

From the size and weight of the envelope, I was sure it must contain a considerable amount of reading material. Once again I examined the black scrawl of the address, but it bore no resemblance to any hand familiar to me. Diana writes in a clear, firm script, almost Spencerian in its exactitude, and scorns the modern usage of felt-tipped markers in favor of an antique fountain

pen, much given to blots and leakages. At last, with trembling
fingers, I slit the envelope open and reached within.

If I had expected a written account, in Diana's own hand, of
her adventures of the past two years, along with notification of
her imminent arrival, I was doomed to disappointment. The
envelope contained nothing but a magazine of the sort said to
appeal to prurient youth and unclean old age. With a sigh and a
slight cough, (Heavens! Was the head cold threatening to invade
my thoracic cavity?) I dropped the loathsome publication onto
the floor and gazed out the window. Sleety rain had begun to
fall, producing a chill grayness outdoors the equal of that under
which my spirits faltered.

A practical joke. That's all it could be. But who would go to
the trouble and expense of contriving such a poor stratagem,
which contained not even the dubious pleasure of seeing the
effect upon the intended victim (me)? It made no sense.

And yet, there it was. I glanced down. The face and remarkable upper torso of a young woman beamed glossily up at me,
inviting me to sample further fleshy delights within the pages of
the publication. But even when in the best of health and spirits,
it has never been my custom to assuage my loneliness with
photographic representations of the divine form of womankind.
I love them all too dearly for that, and Diana far too well to
sully mind or eye with any further commerce with the thing
other than to pitch it into the open fireplace—where the low pile
of glowing embers reminded me it was time to lay on another
artificial log.

With this chore in mind, I crumpled into a ball the manila
envelope which had been lying athwart my thighs. To my
surprise, I felt inside the folds of paper something small and
hard. Quickly, I flattened out the envelope and plunged my
hand within. The object I drew out was as familiar to me as the
palm of the hand on which it rested. It was a ring, old, but of no
great value except to the wearer, who, in all the years of our
acquaintance, had never let it off her finger. It was Diana's, and
although she had never told me its history, I knew it was more
precious to her than all the gold and jewels in Harry Winston's
stronghold.

In dull amazement, I gazed from the ring to the magazine on
the floor to the envelope upon my lap. How came the three
together? What meaning was there in this message, for such I
now perceived it was? I slipped the ring onto my little finger for
safekeeping (and, if the truth were known, to gain what spiritual

vibrations I could from its last association) and rent the envelope in two. Alas, there was nothing else within, and I put it aside.

To the magazine then, with fingers that both shook and recoiled, I went. Page by page, I examined it, forcing myself to the most minute scrutiny of every photograph, scanning each line of print for some microscopic alteration that would reveal itself to be a message from Diana. I even availed myself of the magnifying glass which she had used to such astonishing effect in *The Adventure of the Spinster's Dream,* but the hours I spent thus occupied were wasted. There was no message that I could discern.

As I closed the magazine, more mystified than when it first came into my hands, the ring upon my little finger caught on the mailing label affixed to its cover and almost tore it off. The name on the label was unknown to me, the address somewhere deep in the bowels of Brooklyn. Who was Alfred J. O'Brien of Union Street, and how had he come by Diana's ring?

I quickly saw that I must go there at once. I took a Hagstrom Street Guide from the shelf and located the street in question, which ran through Brooklyn from the waterfront to Grand Army Plaza at the entrance to Prospect Park. My mind offered up a dim recollection of a monumental arch, glimpsed but briefly some years ago as Diana and I were speeding to the Brooklyn Museum to assist in the search of a fabled article, which I am forbidden to name and which had gone missing from their Egyptian collection. I can only say that Diana found the missing article within fifteen minutes of entering the museum and saved its director untold embarrassment.

The address in question, however, lay nowhere near park or museum but adjacent to a narrow body of water identified on the map as the Gowanus Canal. It is certain that in this most favored of all cities one is perpetually discovering new delights. I had no idea that New York City harbored such a thing as a canal, and as I dressed for the journey my mind filled with images of gondolas, or at the very least small pleasure craft piloted by smiling boatmen. Perhaps Diana had returned from her adventures, and this was her way of summoning me to a romantic rendezvous in an idyllic spot, little known to the fashionable trendsetters who swarm about Manhattan in search of novelty.

I did reflect that the weather was hardly conducive to pleasure boating, but Diana was remarkably impervious to such considerations once she was determined upon a course of action. Consequently, I wrapped myself in several layers of warm clothing topped off with a waterproof coat that had seen much service in the days long past, when I had drifted alone and homeless across the vast expanses of the North American continent. My outfit was completed by a pair of army boots, much in vogue among the young and rebellious. Thus attired, I and my head cold would safely weather any tempest the day might hurl at us. I telephoned down to the faithful Carlos to summon a cab for me.

The cabbie, a mahogany-hued lascar with the unlikely name of Rameshwar Das emblazoned on his hack registration, grumbled wrathfully upon learning our destination, but quickly changed his tune when a ten dollar bill appeared, reflected in his rear view mirror, from which dangled a garish image of Kali the Destroyer. We set off into the pelting sleet.

After an hour or so of slithering through the slippery streets, we seemed no nearer our destination than when we had left the familiar environs of Central Park South. Within moments, however, the surly driver pulled up in front of a windowless, derelict edifice, whose grimy yellow-ocher face was heavily decorated with that peculiar urban art form known as graffiti. The building seemed to be a warehouse, or perhaps had once been the home of some light industry or other, but on this cheerless day, with a corrugated steel shutter blocking entry to its double garage-type doors, it appeared to be abandoned.

"Is this the place?" I queried.

The driver merely shrugged and pointed significantly to the meter which read $22.50. A small enough price to pay, I reflected, if the journey brought me news of Diana.

"But where is the canal?" I asked, gazing out the side windows at a landscape of broken pavements, overturned trash cans, and cannibalized automobiles. My dream of secret Venetian delights evaporated into an uneasy sense of dangers lurking behind every door that faced upon this misbegotten street.

The driver waved vaguely in the direction the cab was facing. I peered through the streaked windshield and saw, rising into the gloom before us, the gray iron tracery of a small bridge. The low yellow building, which was apparently my destination, extended northward to the banks of the canal, if canal there was.

I paid the driver, adding to the fare the promised ten dollars, and clambered out of the cab and into the icy sleet, which, on this deserted thoroughfare, was driven by a fierce wind that threatened to sweep me off my feet. No sooner had I slammed the door than the driver gunned the engine, and the cab hurtled away, over the bridge and out of sight. I was alone, with no notion of how to gain entrance to the building or what I would find behind those sickly walls.

Close examination of the entry revealed to me two things. The steel shutter was secured with a heavy padlock, and in the wall beside it was embedded an ordinary doorbell. I was about to press finger to bell when a sudden cautionary thought occurred. If there were someone inside the building, he or she (Dare I hope that Diana was within, perhaps held prisoner and waiting for me to rescue her?) would not be able to open the shutter, but would be apprised of my presence and could, through some other means of exit, escape the building and even creep up behind me to thwart my mission.

I glanced up and down the desolate street. In the distance, a bus labored toward me. A few feet away, a bedraggled cat suddenly streaked across the street to huddle under the wreckage of an automobile, of which little more remained than its twisted chassis. I saw no human on the street, not surprising in view of the weather, but a slight frisson warned me that I was being observed. Imagination, perhaps, but I have learned to trust to these sensations of alarm. It could be nothing more than an idle housewife in one of the nearby tenements, gazing out the window. Or it could be something more inimical. What, I wondered, would Diana do?

As I hesitated, wishing that I had not been so precipitate in dismissing Rameshwar Das and his taxi, a bicycle whipped around the near corner and skidded to halt at the curb. Its rider dismounted and quickly secured his machine, with a great U-shaped locking device, to a steel pole on top of which a sign advised motorists "Don't Even Think Of Parking Here."

"What took you so long, turkey?" the bicyclist snarled at me.

Although his costume resembled that of the messenger who had delivered the envelope to my door, and his face was obscured by a similar ski mask to which was added a pair of Plexiglas goggles, I could tell he was not the same individual. This person was small and wiry, and his voice high-pitched, almost girlish in its intonations. I began to fear that I had fallen into some kind of trap or a conspiracy of bicycle thugs.

He grasped my hand and began dragging me toward the banks of the canal. I held back, demanding an explanation.

"No time," he piped. "Got to get inside before it's too late."

"Too late for what?" I queried.

But I was fated to remain ignorant. With amazing strength for one so slender, he constrained me to follow him around the corner of the yellow building and along the muddy bank of the canal. Although we moved swiftly, I could not fail to notice that the waters lapping at the concrete retaining walls of the canal were of a vile greenish hue, and that a peculiar stench permeated the chilly air. An icy crust underfoot made our rapid progress perilous in the extreme, and I entertained a fleeting image of plunging into the poisonous stream. So much for gondolas.

As we rounded the side of the building and approached its rear, my guide let go of my hand and, from somewhere on his person, produced a formidable key of the sort known as a Fichet. He quickly inserted it into an equally formidable lock in a steel-plated door set into a niche in the otherwise featureless wall. The door creaked open, and I gazed over his shoulder into total darkness.

"Inside!" the bicyclist hissed, while extracting from the satchel on his back a powerful flashlight, which he proceeded to beam into the interior.

Intrigued, I followed him, peering into the path of the light in an attempt to discover the reason for my presence here. Inside my glove, the ring upon my little finger seemed to emit a degree of warmth, which, in a superstitious soul, might bespeak a message from its owner. But I pride myself on being a practical fellow, albeit well aware that there are forces at large in the universe of which we, with all our amazing technology, have no knowledge. I reminded myself that this was the hand the young fellow had gripped so strenuously in our traverse of the muddy canal bank; the heat I felt was probably nothing more than a bruise left by that grip. I put it out of my mind and concentrated instead upon our surroundings.

The little fellow led the way on tiptoe, flashing his light hither and yon. In its beam, I caught glimpses of luxurious appointments; here a glimmer of a mirrored bar where ranks of bottles, glasses, and nargilehs awaited a celebratory moment, there the dull sheen of red velvet upholstery brightened by pillows of an intricate Oriental design. Although I, too, walked on tiptoe in unconscious emulation of my guide, there was no need for such a precaution. A thick carpet muffled whatever sound our progress made.

"What is this place?" I ventured to ask.

"Be silent," came the whispered response. "There may be someone left on guard."

Somthing about the voice had changed. It was still high-pitched and impatient, still retained its irritating note of command, but the choice of words was no longer that of an uneducated street urchin.

"Who are you?" I demanded. "Not a step further until I know."

Whereupon the flashlight was extinguished and total darkness descended. But even in that Stygian gloom, my senses were fully alert. I heard an unmistakable click and felt against my throat the cold thin edge of a blade.

"You will know in due course," my companion whispered. "I had hoped not to use force. It's against my principles. But you leave me no choice. Come willingly or come at knifepoint, it's all the same to me. But come you will or never see your friend again."

"Diana!" I groaned. "You fiend! What have you done with her?" The finger that her ring encircled throbbed painfully, as if echoing her distress.

"Calm yourself. She's not far away. Was it not the message from her that brought you here?"

"Yes. The ring. But how do I know it came from her?" And then the dread thought came to me. "For all I know, it was cut from her dead hand."

"It was not," he assured me, and then as if in explanation, "I am one of the Irregulars."

"That means nothing to me."

"The Irregular Messenger Service. One of our riders delivered the envelope to you."

"Yes. But what has that to do with Diana?"

"She helped us once, in *The Case of the Exploding Bicycle.* We are forever in her debt. Has she not told you of it?"

"No," I muttered, somewhat offended that this raw youth possessed a portion of Diana's history that was denied to me. "But where is she, and why are we prowling this Godforsaken structure?"

"We're wasting time. Are you with me? Your medical talents may be needed."

"But I'm not a doctor," I protested. "I never completed my studies."

"You know enough to be useful. Will you follow?"

I sighed. It seemed I had no choice. It was either follow or be propelled along at knifepoint. Or worse. And since Diana was somehow involved in this adventure, I was loath to shame myself in her eyes. "I'll follow," I vouchsafed.

A click told me the switchblade had been sheathed. The light resumed its powerful beam, and we proceeded through several rooms of the sprawling building, each one more gaudily appointed than the one before. At last, we came to a wooden door and behind it a narrow staircase that plunged downward into an even deeper blackness than we had thus far encountered. These stairs were uncarpeted and their treads creaked loudly as we descended. At the bottom, an iron gate blocked our passage, but once again my guide produced a key, and we quickly passed through and into the basement regions of the building.

Here, all was quite different from the floor above. Gone was all luxury and comfort. The floor, concrete by the look and feel of it, was filthy with decades of grit and grease. The very walls oozed moisture, and the scent of the putrid canal hung heavy in the air. Wherever the flashlight beam penetrated, legions of cockroaches scurried to escape its glare. Cobwebs brushed my face and clung, stifling, to my mouth and nose. God help Diana if she were imprisoned in this moldering catacomb!

Onward we marched into the vast underground cavern, seeking I knew not what. Suddenly, my guide gave a muffled exclamation and began to run. I followed him as swiftly as I could, keeping my eyes always on the wildly swinging beam of his light. That proved to be a mistake. I missed my footing and stumbled over some object in my path. Down I went, face forward into the filth. Hot blood gushed from my nose, but hotter still was my mortification. I rose to my knees and groped in my pocket for a handkerchief to stanch the flow. It was then that I heard the clear, bell-like tones of the voice for which I'd yearned these two years past.

"Watson! Come quickly! I need you!"

"Diana!" I shouted. "Where are you?"

At the same moment, a sound like muffled thunder reverberated throughout the building.

"Over here!" came the beloved voice. "Hurry!" And the flashlight beam described an agitated arc against the ceiling on the far side of the immense basement.

Unsteadily, I gained my footing and tottered toward the light, expecting to find my dearest friend in dire need of medical attention, which was, perhaps, beyond my meager abilities. I had but small knowledge, dimly remembered, and not even the most elementary of first aid equipment upon my person. If I should fail her now, I would never forgive myself.

But the figure lying on the noisome floor was not Diana. It was that of a child, a boy of no more than ten or twelve years, who lay as still as death. I knelt beside him and touched his brow. He was warm, indeed, feverishly hot to the touch. In perplexity, I looked up at my guide for answers to all the questions that were racing through my brain.

Shock drove all questions away. The bicyclist had removed both helmet and ski mask and held the light so that I might see, fully illuminated, the hitherto concealed features. The golden hair, the wide-space, intelligent gray eyes, the delicate yet aquiline nose, the purposeful mouth now smiling tenderly down at me. "Sorry to play such a trick on you, old friend. It was necessary, but I can't explain it to you now. There isn't time. We've got to get this boy out of here before they discover our presence."

"Diana!" I gasped. "But he's sick and there seems to be a bad storm brewing. I just heard thunder."

"That was not thunder. Someone has just raised the steel shutter at the front of this den of kidnappers. These are desperate men. If they find us, this child is doomed. Can you get him loose while I guard our escape route?" Whereupon she handed me both switchblade and flashlight and disappeared into the darkness.

As her footsteps dwindled, I examined the thick ropes, which bound the unfortunate lad hand and foot and were secured to an iron ring set firmly into the wall. I propped the flashlight against the boy's feverish body and sawed away at the rope. As I cut through the last strand, Diana was back at my side.

"Good work, Watson," she whispered. "Now pick him up and let's be off."

"I wish you wouldn't call me Watson," I complained, even as I did her bidding. "You know how it annoys me." My name truly is Watson, John Conan Watson to be exact. Both my parents were avid fans of the storied detective and his faithful chronicler. But years ago, weary of the constant jokes of the "elementary, my dear Watson" variety, I had my name legally changed to Moriarty.

"Moriarty's a mouthful," she retorted, "and Watson suits you. But we have not time for pointless argument. A half-dozen ruthless fanatics are upstairs celebrating the ransom they have

received for the safe return of the child. But they have no
intention of returning him. They have carried him here all the
way from New Delhi, and his fate is nothing less than the
bottom of that vile canal outside. As soon as they have fortified
themselves with drink and dope, they'll be down here to carry
out their evil plans.''

Once again, she led the way across the cavernous underground space until we reached a small window, set high in the
wall, its panes obscured by generations of grime. As she struggled to released the rusted latch, I heard the door at the top of
the stairs creak open and stealthy footsteps begin to descend. I
tapped Diana on the shoulder to alert her to the danger. At that
moment, the latch gave way and the window, hinged at the
bottom, fell open with a crash.

Diana scaled the wall with the agility of a mountain goat and
disappeared through the opening. She reached back to receive
the unconscious boy from my arms. The effluvium from the
canal wafted into my face, causing me to sneeze. The footsteps,
no longer stealthy, approached at a run, and a hoarse voice
uttered a stifled cry. "Please be waiting! I am coming with
you!''

I glanced over my shoulder. Looming up out of the basement
gloom, illuminated by the fading light from the open window,
was the agitated face of Rameshwar Das. He flourished a plastic
shopping bag.

"I have retrieved the dollars," he panted. "They will kill me
if I am not escaping.''

"Good work, Das," said Diana. "I was beginning to worry
about you. Give him a boost, Watson.''

As I lifted the lascar through the open window, I heard once
again the thunderous sound of the steel shutter at the front of the
building. It had been rolled open and now it was being rolled
shut. I had no idea what it meant, but I lost no time in gripping
the window frame and hoisting myself through and out onto the
ice-encrusted mud at the side of the building. As I rose to my
knees, I saw the tall, black-clad form of the messenger who had
initiated this adventure lope around the corner of the building
with his arms upraised in a victory salute.

"The door be locked!" he shouted. "They can't get out that
way.''

Diana nodded her approval and pointed toward the open
window. The messenger reached into his canvas bag and with-

drew an object I recognized from my ardent days in the peace movement: a tear gas canister.

"Wait until they're all in the basement. Then toss it in," Diana instructed him. "Then get on your bike and ride for the police."

We left him and headed for the rear of the building. There, at the rear door, a short, rotund gentleman of florid complexion had just finished constructing a barricade consisting of several old mattresses and a rusted bedspring.

As we ran past, the unconscious boy once again in my arms, Diana shouted, "It won't hold, O'Brien. They'll have it down in a trice."

"Ah, don't fear, lady," O'Brien twinkled back at her. "I'm driving me old truck up against it. It'll not budge."

"Be quick about it, then," Diana warned him. "We want them bottled up in there when the police arrive."

"And I want to be long gone from here when that happens," said O'Brien. "The blue boys have no love for me."

He dashed off toward a dilapidated pickup truck parked at the curb, while we followed Rameshwar Das to his taxi.

All this while, the boy had remained limp and senseless in my arms, but as we settled down in the backseat and Das started up the engine, his eyes flickered and he uttered a soft moan.

He lay across our laps, his head resting on Diana's bosom. She stroked his brow and soothed him with astonishingly maternal care. "There, there, now. You're safe," she crooned. "You'll soon be back home. Your father is waiting for you at the Plaza Hotel."

The taxi driver turned full around to beam at us. "You will be telling Sri Purandar Krishnamurthi of my part in this amazing rescue? He will be giving me perhaps a reward?" His eyes fell longingly on the plastic bag, now resting safely on the seat beside me.

"We're not safe yet," Diana told him sternly, "and we won't be if you don't keep your eyes on the road." Then her tone softened. "Sri Krishnamurthi is a generous man. He will not let you go unrewarded. I will tell him of the great danger you have faced to help us free his son."

"And I will be praying that Kali turn her dark face from your path, and that Parvati grant you many fine sons." With that, Rameshwar Das gave his full attention to finding our way out of Brooklyn, all the while emitting a high-pitched repetitive melody, not unpleasant to the ear but certainly no top of the pops.

*   *   *

An hour later, we were gathered around a tea table in an elegant suite in the Plaza Hotel. Our host, an ascetic-looking middle-aged gentleman with only a distinguished hint of gray threading his jet black hair, smiled as his much-younger wife, clad in a gorgeous green and gold sari, wept for joy.

"If you cry now, Anjali," he chided her gently, "what would you have done if these brave souls had not returned our son to us?"

"I would have died," she said simply. "He is our only child and there can be no others." She turned to Diana. "You have performed a miracle," she said. "Please don't think me rude if I leave you and go to sit with my son. I know the doctor says he'll recover, but I wish to be there the moment he opens his eyes, so that he will recognize his mother's face."

She hurried away, into the bedroom where the boy lay, surrounded with all the care and comfort his father's resources could provide.

"She doesn't yet realize," said Purandar Krishnamurthi, "and I hope she never will, that this plot was directed against her. It was not merely to gain the ransom money, but to distract her from her crusade against wife murder. In our unfortunate country, thousands of young brides are killed by their husbands each year for the sake of their pitiful dowries. The dowries are small and life is hard. If the husband or his family are greedy, they will arrange a kitchen 'accident.' The young wife is burned to death, and the husband is free to marry again and collect yet another dowry. The police profess themselves powerless to stop it. Anjali has decried this practice publicly and is a leader in the movement to protect these poor women. Her cause is so just, she finds it hard to believe that she has made many enemies. They learned that she is scheduled to make a television appearance here in the United States and hoped, by this means, to put a stop to her plans."

"I think there's a little more to it than that," said Diana. "You are influential in your country's politics. I have heard you spoken of as a man on the rise. You have enemies, too. If they had succeeded in killing your son, Anjali would have been their next victim. Her death would have been made to seem another of those wife murders. They would have said you killed her because she can give you no more sons. The scandal would have ruined your career. The police, by now, will have arrested the kidnappers, but they are merely a fragment of the forces ranged against you. Be very careful, during your visit here and when you return home.''

''I cannot thank you enough, Miss Diana Adler,'' said Krishnamurthi, adopting a somewhat ceremonial tone. ''If you had not chanced to be in the audience on that dreadful day, only a week ago, when Anjali was handed the ransom note, we might never have seen our boy again. I would like to reward you for your resourcefulness and courage.'' His hand fell upon the shopping bag full of money.

Diana smiled and shook her golden head. Across the table, Rameshwar Das was happily sipping tea and nibbling petits fours. Diana said, ''If there is to be a reward, it should go to the brave lads who have served us well in this adventure. To the masked rider of the Irregular Messenger Service, to Alfred J. O'Brien, custodian of the premises where your son was held, and to Rameshwar Das who infiltrated the gang and retrieved the ransom.''

''So be it,'' said Krishnamurthi.

''Oh, immense good fortune!'' cried the taxi driver, swallowing an entire petit four in one gulp. ''I will open a restaurant immediately. My wife will cook. My sons will be waiters. My daughters will wash dishes. We will all become rich.''

It wasn't far from the Plaza Hotel to our apartment building on Central Park South. Although Rameshwar Das offered to drive us in his taxi at no charge, we chose to walk. The sleet had slackened off, leaving the early evening clear but still cold. There were so many questions whirling in my brain, I hardly knew where to start.

''What on earth were you doing in India?'' was my first.

''I have been around the world,'' Diana replied. ''India was merely my last stop. It was time to come home, and I would have come anyway even if I had not found this adventure to bring me here.''

''And what did you discover?'' I inquired next.

''Ah, that, Watson. That is a topic for another day. A day when the sun is shining on our terrace and we are in the mood for stories. For the moment, I can only say that what I long suspected is true. My middle name is Irene, as you know, and my great-grandmother was an opera singer. She died young, but not before leaving a child. Who the father of that child was has always been a family mystery. He was known not to have been Irene Adler's husband, nor, as sometimes rumored, was he the King of Bohemia. I think I have solved the mystery.''

"But who . . . ?"

We had reached the entrance to our apartment building. Faithful Carlos flung open the door and welcomed us effusively. "Miss Adler!" he exclaimed. "Thought I'd never see you again. A policeman came by and left a message for you and I've been waiting for you ever since. Welcome home!" Whereupon, he handed her a sealed envelope with her name scrawled upon it.

"Thank you, Carlos," she said, pocketing the envelope. "When my luggage arrives, there's something in it for you. A memento from your homeland."

"You've been to Ecuador, too?" I exclaimed.

"Around the world," she repeated wearily. "And now I must rest." We entered the elevator and she slumped against the wall.

"But what about the message from the police?" I asked.

"It can wait," she murmured. "It's either to tell me what I already know, that the gang of kidnappers has been captured and put behind bars, or it is to summon me to a case they cannot solve. I'll read it in the morning. But tonight, Watson, my love, tonight we shall become reacquainted."

And with that, I had to be content.

DR. AND MRS. WATSON AT HOME: A COMEDY IN ONE UNNATURAL ACT

Loren D. Estleman

Cover illustration by Frederic Dorr Steele for the edition of "Collier's"
containing *The Adventure of Black Peter*.

TIME: 1890-ish

SCENE: The sitting room of JOHN H. and MARY MORSTAN
WATSON's London home. MARY is busy knitting.

MARY.   Knit one, purl two. Or is it purl two, knit one?
What's the difference anyway? Ever since those
buffoons lost the Agra treasure, the closest I've
come to real pearls is an occasional oyster at
Simpson's. (Knits some more in silence.) What
an elaborate waste of a Victorian lady's time. It
wouldn't be so bad if I knew how to knit something besides mufflers. I'll bet if you laid all the
mufflers I've made end to end they'd reach
twice around London. Or once around Mycroft
Holmes's neck. Boring. There's only one thing
I can think of that's more tedious than a muffler.

WATSON.   (calling from outside) Mary? I'm home.

MARY.   Zowie.

WATSON enters, pecks MARY on the cheek.)

WATSON.   Hello, lambchop.

181

MARY.   (without enthusiasm) Hello, James.
WATSON.   John. My name's John.
MARY.   Oh, yes; I keep forgetting.
WATSON.   Why is it that after three years of marriage you still call me James?
MARY.   Can I help it if I get mixed up? Everyone you do business with is names James: James Phillimore, James Mortimer, James Lancaster, all three Moriarty brothers—
WATSON.   (looking around quickly) Moriarty? Where? Where?
MARY.   Oh, calm down. He's not here. I swear, you've a fixation about that poor man every bit as bad as your friend Sherlock Holmes's.
WATSON.   Poor? Professor Moriarty? The Napoleon of Crime? The most dangerous man in London? The organizer of half that is criminal and of nearly all that is undetected in this city?
MARY.   That's exactly what I mean. How's the fellow to make anything of himself if all everyone does is criticize?
WATSON.   (massaging his temples) Don't start, Mary. I've had a trying day. It's murder being around sick people all the time.
MARY.   Why'd you become a doctor then?
WATSON.   The ceramics class was full. What's for supper?
MARY.   Woodcock.
WATSON.   Damn.
MARY.   What's wrong with woodcock?
WATSON.   I had it for lunch.
MARY.   You've been eating with Sherlock Holmes again, haven't you?
WATSON.   How did you know?
MARY.   Elementary, my dear dum-dum. Woodcock is the only thing Holmes eats.
WATSON.   That's not true. Just last Christmas Peterson, the commissionaire, gave him a goose.
MARY.   I always wondered about him.
WATSON.   (thoughtfully) He does fuss a lot with his uniform.
MARY.   I'm talking about Holmes, not Peterson.
WATSON.   Holmes! How can you say that about the best and wisest man I've ever known? Are you for-

	getting that if it weren't for him you and I would never have met?
MARY.	(dryly) That's hardly a point in his favor.
WATSON.	If you're bored with me, I suggest you get a job. I understand there's an opening at the Copper Beeches.
MARY.	Funny. What's the Great Detective up to this time, counting orange pips?
WATSON.	He was deciphering a palimpsest, whatever that is. And staring at a lot of dancing men.
MARY.	(smugly) What'd I tell you?
WATSON.	No, no. It's a cipher of some kind. Has to do with a fellow and his wife out in Norfolk. I must say it's too deep for me.
MARY.	*McGuffy's Reader* would be too deep for you.
WATSON.	(impatient) Isn't it time you visited your mother?
MARY.	My mother's dead. Now who's forgetting? You talk like you write.
WATSON.	Let my writing alone. It pays the bills, doesn't it?
MARY.	*Something* has to.
WATSON.	What is that supposed to mean?
MARY.	Let's face it, James—
WATSON.	John. My name's John.
MARY.	Whatever. The Speckled Band couldn't live on what you make off that crummy practice of yours.
WATSON.	You knew what I was when you married me. Whoever heard of a rich doctor?
MARY.	Anstruther does all right. He bought his wife a fur coat for her birthday. And you know why he can afford it, don't you?
WATSON.	Don't start, Mary.
MARY.	He can afford it because you keep turning over your patients to him so you can run off and do God-knows-what with your friend Sherlock Holmes.
WATSON.	You're starting.
MARY.	And how does Holmes show his appreciation? By treating you like a servant. Has he ever once offered to share with you his reward for solving a mystery?
WATSON.	What about that gift he gave us last Christmas?

MARY.	Hallelujah! A six-karat gold snuff box with an amethyst in the lid. Talk about your bad taste!
WATSON.	I happen to think it's beautiful. Anyway, Holmes wouldn't insult me by offering me money.
MARY.	He could be discourteous now and then.

(There is a knock at the door.)

WATSON.	I'll get it. (exits)
MARY.	(knitting) I hope it's Jack the Ripper making a house call.
WATSON.	(reentering, carrying a fold of paper) It was a messenger.
MARY.	Did you tip him?
WATSON.	I couldn't. There's no cash in the house and I left my cheque-book in Holmes's desk.
MARY.	That's what you told the last messenger. Pretty soon they'll catch on.
WATSON.	(unfolding the paper). It's from Holmes.
MARY.	Just as I thought. Junk mail.
WATSON.	He needs me, Mary. He's on something.
MARY.	When isn't he?
WATSON.	I must go to him. Where is my trusty service revolver?
MARY.	In the top drawer of the bureau, under your faithful socks.
WATSON.	Forget it. No time. I'll borrow Holmes's hair-trigger.
MARY.	Don't tell me that mangy animal has started up again out at the Baskervilles'. Why can't they call the dogcatcher like everyone else?
WATSON.	I'll explain later. (pecks her on the cheek) Don't wait up for me. I may be late.
MARY.	(coldly) Who is it this time, Violet Hunter or that hot-blooded Ferguson vamp?
WATSON.	What are you talking about?
MARY.	You know very well what. Holmes, ha! The last time you said he needed you, you came back with a long brown hair on your coat.
WATSON.	I *told* you that hair belonged to an ichneumon!
MARY.	I don't care what her nationality was. If you

	don't stop seeing other women, I'll leave you. Put *that* in your cherrywood and smoke it!
WATSON.	We'll talk about this later.
MARY.	We most certainly will, James.
WATSON.	John. My name's John.
MARY.	Whatever.

(WATSON exits. MARY continues knitting a moment longer, then straightens in the attitude of listening. Satisfied her husband has left, she picks up the telephone, rattles the fork.)

MARY.	Professor Moriarty, please. (waits) Hello, Jimmy? Mary. He's gone. No, he won't be home until late. Are you free tonight? Wonderful. What? (pause) New monograph? Yes, bring it along, by all means. (coquettishly) Yes, I'd love to discuss the dynamics of your asteroid. I'm counting the minutes. Good-bye, love. (She hangs up. CURTAIN.)

THE TWO
FOOTMEN

Michael Gilbert

Illustration by Frederic Dorr Steele of a scene from *Wisteria Lodge* in
"Collier's" 1908.

In the autumn of 1894, as you will find recorded in my account of the case of the Norwood Builder, I sold my slender medical practice and rejoined Holmes in our old quarters in Baker Street. His sensational return from supposed death, followed by the trial of Colonel Sebastian Moran for the murder of the Honourable Ronald Adair, had revived and, indeed, increased his practice to such an extent that he was more often away than at home, and I found myself spending long hours in front of the fire in our sitting room.

I did not resent this. On that particular evening the wind was driving the rain in icy spears down the street outside. The wound I had suffered at Maiwand fourteen years before was, of course, fully healed, but when the wind was in a certain quarter I still felt twinges. To pass the time, I had taken down one of the long row of ledgers and books of cuttings that lined the wall beside the fireplace. It turned out to be a hollow case rather than a book and to contain a number of miscellaneous objects. They were not arranged in any methodical way, although no doubt each one of them meant something to Holmes.

A pearl-handled buttonhook, a paper knife broken across the blade, a pack of cards, which proved, on inspection, to be missing the ace of spades, but to have two aces of clubs. None of them meant anything to me until I picked up a small white cardboard box which must, from the dusty crumbs in it, have contained, at one time, a portion of wedding cake. I was able to read, on the outside—"Mary Macalister and Sergeant Jacob Pearce. The Baptist Chapel, Friary Lane. December 10th 1886."

I was thinking, "Good heavens. Was that wedding really eight years ago? It seems like yesterday," when I heard Holmes's footsteps on the stairs and he burst into the room, seemingly in high spirits. It looked as though his investigation into the papers of ex-President Murillo was going well. He glanced at the box I was holding and said, "You are savouring, I see, one of your earliest successes."

"Yours, Holmes. Not mine."

"On the contrary, my dear fellow. You did all the spadework—Mrs. Pearce appreciates that, I'm sure. Has she not appointed you godfather of her eldest boy and named him John in your honour?"

It was on a November day, in 1882, that Mary Macalister had come to our rooms in Baker Street. I said "had come." It would have been more accurate if I had said that she had been propelled in, for it was only the support of Mrs. Hudson behind her that got her up the stairs and through the door. She was a pretty girl, with a fresh look in her rosy cheeks. I did not need Holmes's deductive powers to see that she came from the country and was of comparatively humble stock. Also that she had been crying.

Holmes ushered her, with every courtesy, to a seat, and since she seemed overcome by the occasion, it was Mrs. Hudson who spoke for her.

"Miss Macalister," she explained, "is my niece. She works at Corby Manor."

"The seat of Sir Rigby Bellairs?" said Holmes.

The girl nodded.

"And what has Sir Rigby done to cause you such distress?"

"Oh no, sir. It wasn't Sir Rigby. It was Terence."

"Terence Black?"

"Yes, sir."

"I see," said Holmes. "He was a friend of yours perhaps?"

The girl, who seemed to be on the point of bursting into tears again, gulped out, "We were engaged. The marriage was to have been at the end of the month."

"Then indeed," said Holmes, "I am very sorry for you."

"I told her," said Mrs. Hudson, "that if anyone could do anything for her it would be you."

I could read the indecision in Holmes's face. Though considered by some people to be a misogynist and devoid of human feeling, the sight of beauty in distress naturally moved him. At the same time he was, as I knew, engaged in a complex investigation in the City of London. It was not a type of case which he greatly favoured, but at that early point in his career he could not afford to be too selective and this matter, involving as it did a number of members of the peerage and one of the leading City financial firms, could hardly be neglected for the troubles of a servant girl, however appealing.

All these thoughts must have been passing through his mind while the girl and Mrs. Hudson watched him anxiously. In the end he said, "We will help you if we can. I can promise nothing personally. But my colleague, Dr. Watson, will make a preliminary investigation to unearth any facts that the national press omitted, and he will keep me informed of everything."

Before the girl could speak Mrs. Hudson said, "That's very kind of you, sir. And more than we could have hoped for," and she gently, but firmly, steered her niece to the door and we heard them going downstairs.

I said, "Our landlady is becoming a tactician. I'm sure Miss Macalister would have preferred your personal attention."

"You underrate yourself," said Holmes. He was busy among his press cuttings. "The Globe has the best account of the Corby affair. We'll discuss it this evening and make up our minds whether any action is possible. Meanwhile, I must get back to the City."

"Tragedy at Corby Manor" was the heading of the extract. It started with a brief summary of the career of Sir Rigby Bellairs and a description of the find old manor house at Corby. I could not avoid the reflection that these details were considered more important than the fate of the comparatively unimportant victim of the crime. It seemed that Sir Rigby and his wife had been awakened, shortly after one o'clock in the morning of October 7th, by the sound of a pistol shot. Warning his wife not to follow him, he had run out into the long southern corridor which contained a number of guest bedrooms. His house at that time was full for the shooting: his estate was famous for both its partridge and its pheasant drive.

Outside the bedroom door, three along from his own room, he had almost fallen over the body of Terence Black, one of a number of footmen who had been taken on to supplement the regular staff for the occasion. Black had been shot through the heart and must have died instantly.

The room outside which he had fallen was occupied by Mrs. Ruyslander, the widow of Jacob Ruyslander and the owner of the famous Ruyslander diamonds. Hearing no sound from inside the room, Sir Rigby had tried the door and found, somewhat to his surprise, that it did not seem to be locked. The first thing he saw when he ventured in was that the window was wide open and that a long ladder had been propped against it. He could see the top of it projecting over the sill. By this time a number of male guests had come into the corridor, together with the butler, an ex-soldier called Peterson. Lady Bellairs was with them. He signalled her in and said, "See if you can wake Mrs. Ruyslander."

She went over to the bed and found Mrs. Ruyslander so deeply asleep that it needed a considerable effort to awaken her. And when, at last, she did sit up, she seemed too dazed to take in what had happened. Sir Rigby acted with commendable decision. Leaving his wife to look after their guest he went out into the corridor, ordered Peterson to guard the bedroom door, cleared the others back to their rooms and sent an outdoor servant hotfoot to Lewes for the police.

The paper then adverted to the Inquest, which had taken place three days later. A number of facts had been elicited, all of which seemed to point in the same direction.

The first question which had to be answered was, what was Black doing in the corridor at all? The indoor staff were segregated in the two wings of the house; the male staff in the west wing, under the surveillance of Peterson, who slept there himself; the female staff in the east wing, under the equally watchful eye of the head housekeeper, Mrs. Barnby. To get from his bedroom to the south corridor, Black would have had to go by the back stairs to the ground floor and climb the main staircase. A considerable and, for him, a totally unauthorised journey.

A second point which came out was that the lock on Mrs. Ruyslander's bedroom door had been rendered inoperative by the removal of the retaining latch. In other words, though the key had been turned, the door could still be opened.

Finally, the medical evidence showed that a strong sedative must have been administered to Mrs. Ruyslander. It was recollected that she had complained of feeling sleepy almost immediately after taking a cup of coffee after dinner. Lady Bellairs gave evidence on this point. She said, "I do not approve of the habit of gentlemen sitting for a long time over their port. They know that coffee will not be served until they emerge from the dining room, and on this occasion they had joined the ladies within twenty minutes of our retiring from the table. I then gave the signal to the three footmen in attendance to hand round the coffee."

The Coroner: "Do you recollect who handed coffee to Mrs. Ruyslander?"

Answer: "I remember very clearly. It was Terence Black."

The theory which was now very clearly emerging was that Terance Black, assisted by an unidentified accomplice, had planned to steal Mrs. Ruyslander's diamonds. He had fixed the lock of the bedroom and slipped a sedative into her coffee. At the last moment there had been some dispute. The accomplice had shot Black, made his way down the ladder and taken himself off.

The jury accordingly found a verdit of murder against some person, or persons unknown. The Lewes police had called in Scotland Yard and their enquiries were continuing under Chief Inspector Leavenworth of the Uniformed Branch and Inspector Blunt of the Criminal Investigation Division.

At the foot of the cutting Holmes had scribbled—"Leavenworth is a pompous ass. Blunt is quite a good man."

Twenty-four hours later, at Holmes's suggestion, I was installed at the Kings Arms, a small, but comfortable, hostelry in the main street of Corby. My instructions were to make contact inside the Manor, to see whether I could locate any suspicious character inside or outside the house and to have a further word with Mary Macalister. "I am sure," said Holmes, "that she has not told us everything. If we are to help her to clear the name of her fiancé, she must be frank with us."

Such suggestions were easy to make, but not so easy to carry out, and I must confess that first fortnight I was there I made very little progress.

I knew from the papers that many of the guests who had been at the original house party in October for the partridge shooting were back now for the first of a series of pheasant battues, which had been planned for the second week in December. It was an even larger assemblage than last time, some forty gentlemen and ladies with their own servants; and I surmised that the house staff would have increased proportionately. I noted that Mrs. Ruyslander was still among the guests. Evidently her earlier experience had not alarmed her too much.

The size and importance of the gathering, coupled with his previous alarming experience had led Sir Rigby to take certain precautions. The manor house and park were surrounded by a formidable wall, through which there were only two entrances, the south and the west lodge. By day these were guarded by the lodge keeper and by night the gates were shut and chained. However, if I could not get in, information could get out. The indoor servants might be kept hard at work in the house, but the stable and garden hands had more liberty, and their favourite port of call was the saloon bar of the Kings Arms. As a resident it was quite natural for me to drop in during the evening and listen to their talk, or even to join in. I prided myself that my time in the army had made me at home with all types of men, but with most of them I found it difficult to extract more than a few civil and noncommital answers.

The one exception was a rat-faced individual, addressed by the others as Len, who had, I gathered, acquired a temporary job in the stables. He did not seem to be over-popular with the permanent hands and was therefore very willing to accept pints of beer from me and give me his views on life in general and Corby Manor in particular.

"A stuck-up lot," he said, "who've never done a hand's turn of honest work in their lives. A pal of mine who's got a job as a footman says the women come down in the evening covered with diamonds and pearls enough to keep ten poor families for a lifetime."

I supplied more beer and agreed that the wealth of this country was very unevenly divided. I don't attempt to reproduce his accent, which was a sort of cockney whine.

"And what do they come down here for? To shoot a lot of birds which never done them any harm. If they want to shoot, they'd be better off in the army."

I agreed, perhaps over heartily, because he said, "Would you be an army man yourself, then?"

"I had some army experience," I agreed, "but I was a doctor."

"And what would you be doing down here, if you don't mind me asking?"

I minded very much, but ordered another pint for both of us, which seemed to satisfy him. I was then forced to listen to a stream of socialist clap-trap, but after half an hour I'd had enough and retired to my room. I had considered writing a report to Holmes, but in fact I realised that, as yet, I had nothing to report and went to bed instead.

The next morning, I was sitting on a bench outside the inn smoking my after-breakfast pipe when I heard a clattering of hooves coming down the cobbled street. There was something alarming about the sound, and as I put down my pipe and rose to my feet, a horse came into view. Two things were immediately apparent. The horse was out of control and its rider, a girl of about eleven or twelve, was incapable of doing anything about it.

As the horse came level with me I jumped forward and managed to seize the cheek strap with one hand and the girl with the other. The sudden checking of the horse, who swivelled round, bucking wildly, threw the rider off. The grip I had on her arm broke her fall, but I could not prevent her hitting her head on the railing which ran along the front of the inn. Fortunately, one of the tapsters came running and grabbed the horse, who had quietened down as soon as he was firmly handled, and I was able to attend to the girl. She seemed to have fainted and there was a lot of blood, but I had had enough experience of scalp wounds to be sure that the situation was not serious. I carried her into the inn parlour, put her on the sofa and started, with the help of the landlady, to bandage her and clean her up. Sure enough, after a few minutes, she opened her eyes and tried to sit up. The landlady told her to lie still. "I've sent a boy for your father," she said. "He'll be here soon."

Almost as she said the words the rattle of a trap being driven at speed announced his arrival. A grizzled man, of about my age, burst into the room. Like all parents, as soon as he saw his daughter was not in danger, he proceeded to give her a piece of his mind.

"Let the poor lamb be, Mr. Pearce," said the landlady. "This is the gentleman you have to thank that things were not a great deal worse."

Mr. Pearce looked at me for the first time. The frown on his face was replaced by a smile. "Why, doctor," he said, "if that doesn't beat everything."

"Sergeant Pearce," I said, "I've been hoping for years to see you again."

Sam Pearce had been my medical orderly, and when General Burrows's force had been routed at Maiwand and I had been severely wounded, he had put me across a horse and led me through the night to Kandahar. I had been so dazed at the time and in the hospital for so long afterwards, that I had lost touch with Sam, who had left the army and gone to Canada. I had not even had an address to write to and, in the end, had given up trying to find him and thank him.

"What are you doing here?" I said. "Why did you come back?"

"Canada's a fine country for a young man. When you're as old as I am, you feel your own country calling. I've got a nice cottage and a fine job at the Manor. Head gardener, with six men under me. My wife will be longing to meet you."

During all this, his daughter's plight seemed to have taken second place. After a final scolding for taking out a horse she couldn't manage, we were both packed into the trap and soon bowling along towards the South Lodge.

"This is an old friend of mine," said Pearce to the lodge keeper. "Remember his face and don't try to keep him out." The lodge keeper promised that I should enjoy the freedom of the park. Ten minutes later we were sitting in front of a fire of logs in Sam Pearce's very pleasant abode.

The fortress had fallen.

One thing I decided on at once. I would take Pearce into my confidence. I had total confidence in my one-time medical orderly. I was only afraid that he might be upset at the idea of me playing the spy. I need not have worried. His reaction was indignation, not against me, but against Chief Inspector Leavenworth.

"The man's a fool," he said, thus echoing Holmes's opinion. "He can't see farther than the nose on his face. Because there was a ladder propped up against the window—it came from the grape house by the way—he jumped to the conclusion that one of my gardeners must have been involved. I've known them all for years and I told him I'd trust them as far as I'd trust his own policemen—or further."

"Nor did he like that," said Mrs. Pearce with a smile.

"I said, if these thieves have got the bedroom door fixed, like we've been told, what do they need a ladder for? All they've got to do is walk downstairs and use the back door. It was a blind, of course. The people he ought to be questioning are the house staff. More particularly the ones who've come in during the last week or so. No one knows anything about them. They come with a reference, but that can be forged."

"Peterson's supposed to keep an eye on them," said his wife.

"Peterson's a loudmouth and a bully."

"He's not popular," agreed his wife. "Mrs. Barnby—she's the housekeeper and a particular friend of mine—had often talked about him."

"And here's one thing that wasn't mentioned at the Inquest," said her husband. "He's got a revolver. Brought it with him when he left the army, I expect."

"Has he indeed," I said. New possibilities were opening up every moment. "Is it your idea, then, that Terence Black's accomplice was one of the other temporary footmen?"

"Speaking for myself," said Mrs. Pearce, "I never could bring myself to believe that Terence had anything to do with it. As nice a boy as you could meet. It nearly broke poor Mary Macalister's heart."

"You're friendly with the housekeeper," I said. "Do you think you could prevail on her to let Mary come over here to have a talk. I'm sure there are things she hasn't told us."

"I'll have her here for tea tomorrow," Mrs. Pearce promised.

Before I left, Mr. Pearce took me for a conducted tour of the gardens, of which he was justifiably proud. At that time of year there was not much to show in the beds themselves, but there were three hothouses and row upon row of cloches and cold frames. Finally we reached the grape house, which must have been one of the finest in the country, with its own heating system and an amazing framework of vines trained in espalier. Coming out at the far end we were behind the stable block, and I saw a figure I recognised. It was my socialist acquaintance, Len. He was in earnest conversation with a tall, thin footman. Both had their back so us, and it occurred to me that they had stationed themselves in such a way that they could not be seen from the stable yard.

Hearing our footsteps, Len swung round, recognised me and said with a sly grin, "Inspecting the high and mighty in their native surroundings, doctor?"

"I'm inspecting the gardens," I said shortly.

The footman had slipped off. When I was saying goodbye to Pearce I commented, "There seems to be one footman who isn't confined to barracks."

"That tall streak," said Pearce. "He's a recent acquisition here. I think I've seen him round the stables before. Maybe he was getting Len to lay a few bets for him at Ludlow this afternoon."

"Very likely," I said.

That evening I sat down to start my first report to Holmes. It was not, I hope, an unduly immodest document, but I could not help feeling a little pleased with the progress I had made.

*   *   *

The morning papers reached Corby at eight o'clock, and over a leisurely breakfast I was able to read that outsiders had won the principal race at the Plumpton and the Ludlow meetings, and I wondered if the tall footman had made a killing at one of these. I also studied a report, on the financial pages, of the matter that was occupying Holmes's attention at that time. It was written with the calculated reserve that journalists employ when they sense that a scandal is imminent, but are afraid, as yet, to attach actual names to it. Reading between the lines I deduced that Mayhews Bank, a small, but respectable banking institution, was in trouble. A consortium of three eminent depositors (no names) owed the bank a considerable sum of money. The loan was a joint one and could not be called in without the consent of all three men. One of them was standing out against the others. The difficulty the bank was in was clear. The last thing it would wish to do was to take action against three important clients. On the other hand, it had to consider the interest, of its other depositors. A decision would have to be taken soon, said the financial editor.

The more that I studied it, the less did it seem to me to be a matter which would engage Holmes's talents. Nor could I spare much sympathy for any of the parties to the dispute. The financiers of the City of London seemed to me to be as irresponsible and as ruthless as the Pathans I had known on the North West Frontier. I switched my mind back to my own problem. Would Mary Macalister be able to throw any light on it when we met?

Mrs. Pearce was as good as her word and Mary was there when I arrived. At first I was disappointed. She was ready to talk in a general way about life in the Manor—the kindness of Mrs. Barnby, the rudeness of Peterson, the great shoot which was to take place on the following Monday—but this was not what I was after. In the end, I guessed that it was the presence of the Pearces that was inhibiting her. I think they saw this, too, and when tea was cleared they tactfully removed themselves.

As soon as they were out of the room, Miss Macalister turned to me and said, "If I tell you something—something which may shock you—will you solemnly promise to tell no one else?"

"Except Holmes."

"Yes," she agreed, though regretfully I thought, "you may tell Mr. Holmes if you must. My sister, Alice, who also works at the Manor, shares a bedroom with me. Terence and I had much to discuss about our coming wedding. There was no opportunity to talk by day. So he came up to our room that night.''

"I don't find that very shocking," I said. "When did he come and, incidentally, how did he get there?''

"He had to wait until midnight, when most people were in their own rooms. Then he crept down from his quarters in the west wing, crossed by main bedroom corridor and up to our room at the top of the east wing. We must have been talking for an hour, because I heard the stable clock strike one as he left.''

"And he would have planned to return by the way he came?''

"I imagine so.''

"Tell me," I said. "Did you hear the sound of a shot?''

"No. It's a rambling old house and the walls are very thick. I don't think anyone up in the wings could hear anything much from the main part of the house.''

It was this answer which convinced me that the girl was speaking the truth. Before setting out, I had read up all that I could about Corby Manor, and a book which I had extracted from Holmes's considerable library of reference works had informed me of one important point. The wings had been added at a later date. This would mean that there were, in effect, two walls separating them from the main body of the house. If Miss Macalister had pretended that she *had* heard the shot, a few minutes after her fiancé had left her, in an attempt to absolve him from participation in the robbery, then I should have suspected that she was lying.

At the same time, it did not clear her fiancé. At the Inquest, Sir Rigby had been woken by the shot "shortly after one o'clock.'' That might mean anything up to ten or fifteen minutes. If Black had made his preparations beforehand there was still time for him to have met his accomplice and proceeded with the robbery.

Miss Macalister was clearly distressed. There was not much else she could tell me, and I soon took my leave. I had several paragraphs to add to my report and the last post left Corby at seven o'clock. I therefore accepted Sam Pearce's offer of a lift back to the village and sat down to work.

That same evening my enquiry took a decided step forward. It fell out in this way.

My report was finished and sealed by a quarter to seven, and I hurried out into the main street to post it. It was a clear and frosty night. To reach the pillar box I had to pass the front of an ale house called "The Fox and Hens.'' It was not a very attractive hostelry and I had never been inside it. As I approached, the door of the public bar swung open, and a man stepped out and went off down the street at a swinging stride. I had only seen his back view before, but I recognised the tall footman I had seen in conversation with Len the ostler two days before. I had had a feeling, too, that I had encountered the man before. Now, noting his lean, supple figure and his way of walking, which was almost a prance, I was suddenly able to put a name to him.

Jim the Fly.

When I had been helping Holmes in one of his earliest cases, which resulted in the breaking up of the Camden Town gang, the only member of that unsavory fraternity who had escaped prison, on a technicality, had been the actual operator of their thefts, the man who climbed into the house and abstracted the diamonds or other precious stones which were their objectives.

As these thoughts were passing through my mind I was, as you may imagine, in hot pursuit. My quarry was moving so fast that I had almost to trot to keep up, and it was a relief when he stopped outside the twelve-foot-high park wall. To my astonishment, he seemed to climb the face of the wall like the fly he was named after. When he reached the top, he pulled himself over, and I heard him drop down on the other side.

When I came up to the place, some of the mystery was solved. I found that three short iron spikes had been driven into the brickwork, one at knee height, one at shoulder height and a third one above. I should have had great difficulty in using this unofficial ladder myself, but to a man like Jim it was as good as an open door.

As I walked thoughtfully back to my hotel, fate dealt me a second card. Glancing through the bar window of "The Fox and Hens," I saw Len. No doubt he had been meeting his accomplice there, but at the moment he was engaged in earnest conversation with a florid man, a Central European I guessed, whose London style garb seemed curiously out of place in an ale house.

The plot was thickening, but the outlines were becoming somewhat clearer. I was sorry that I had posted my first report to Holmes. Now I should have to sit down and write a second one as speedily as possible.

When I reached the hotel I found that there was a letter for me in the rack. I recognised Holmes's angular handwriting, but the envelope was unstamped. It was marked: "By Hand. Urgent." Before opening it, I asked the hall porter who had brought it. "A young boy," he said. He could give me no further description. Evidently, he was a man to whom all small boys looked alike.

I took it up to my room. It contained a single half-sheet of paper on which Holmes had written, "I advise you to study Peterson's ears." That was all.

Well, if he had no further news for me, I had plenty for him.

"From observations I have made," I wrote, "and deductions from those observations, I have been able to arrive at a firm conclusion as to what took place at Corby Manor in October, and more importantly, as to what is planned to take place there in the near future, unless steps are taken to prevent it. The key in both cases is a temporary stable hand known as Len. He has the foxy face and shifty appearance which immediately suggest that he is a member of the criminal classes. When his real name comes to light it will, I am sure, be discovered that he has a record. His objective was, and is, to purloin Mrs. Ruyslander's diamonds. On the first occasion it is possible that his accomplice inside the house was Terence Black. On this occasion there is strong evidence that his new accomplice is one of the temporary footmen. Having seen the latter in action, both moving fast and climbing a wall, I conclude that he is none other than Jim the Fly, a name which will, I am sure, be familiar to you."

I felt a little malicious when I wrote this. Jim's escape from the net of the law on the previous occasion was a matter which had rankled Holmes.

"A second possible accomplice is a foreign gentleman I observed talking to Len. His function will, no doubt, be to dispose of the diamonds once they have been abstracted. The timing of the attempt is also clear. On Monday occurs the first great pheasant battue. All the men will be taking part, and the ladies traditionally accompany them to a sumptuous open-air luncheon at one of the butts. Apart from the fact that many of the house staff will be assisting at this function, I understand that stable and garden hands are invited to act as beaters, being no doubt well paid for their services. In short, the house and grounds will be practically deserted. Your connections with Scotland Yard will, I am sure, enable you to devise a suitable reception committee."

With my mind on the shooting, I added, "In this matter I am acting as beater. You and the police are the guns."

You will appreciate that I felt justifiably proud of this report, and in order that there should be no delay, I got one of the boys from the hotel to take it into Lewes next morning, which was Friday, to catch the early post. Holmes would receive it on Friday evening, which would give him plenty of time to make his preparations. Also, incidentally, time to write to me. On this occasion, I thought, I should certainly get something less terse and unhelpful than his previous communication.

The weekend passed slowly. On Monday morning I was down early. The post had arrived and the letters had been placed in the rack, but there was nothing for me. As I was turning away, the hall porter said, "This is for you, doctor. I was just going to put it in the rack."

"How did it get here?"

"By hand, sir. Same boy as before."

To say that I was surprised would be an understatement. However, I assumed that the letter would clear up the mystery. Instead, it deepened it.

"Most important," Holmes had written, "You are to be at the outside door which leads to the kitchen quarters at half past one this afternoon. Please persuade your friend Pearce to come with you. You should both be armed. You, I know, have your service revolver. Pearce will, no doubt, have a sporting gun. Both should be loaded. We are dealing with very dangerous animals. When you arrive at the door, please follow precisely the instructions you will be given."

Being, by now, totally confused, I thought that the only course open to me was to do what I was told. When I got to the cottage I found the Pearce's sitting down to lunch. I showed Sam Pearce the letter. He read it slowly and then said, "I take it this would be from that friend of yours, Mr. Sherlock Holmes?"

"No doubt about that," I said. "I don't believe there's a man alive who could imitate his handwriting well enough to deceive me."

"He seems to know what he wants. We'd better follow our instructions. Will you join us for lunch? It's only a matter of laying an extra plate." He added, with that grin of his which always appeared when any excitement was in prospect, "If we're going tiger shooting, we may as well go on a full stomach."

I found Pearce's confidence in Holmes a comfort and did justice to an excellent pheasant stew prepared by his wife. At half past one he led me, by a back path, to the kitchen door. He had put on a light coat to conceal the shotgun he was carrying.

My trusty revolver was in my jacket pocket, as it had been at other times when I had set out with Holmes at the crisis of one of his cases; though I could remember no occasion on which I had no less idea why I was carrying it, or whom it was to be used on.

During the morning, we had heard the sound of distant shooting. That had now stopped, and I assumed that the guests, beaters and servants were together engaged in one of the Lucullan open air repasts which were a feature of these battues. The garden and grounds were deserted, and I could hear no one moving inside the house. We reached the door, and I was about to knock on it when it was opened. I had speculated a number of times as to who might appear to give me instructions. All such speculations proved to be wide of the mark. Standing inside the door, with a finger to his lips enjoining silence, was the stable hand, Len. He said, speaking very softly, "I hope you are both armed. Then follow me." Had he not, by saying this, indicated that he knew the contents of Holmes's letter, I must confess that I should have hesitated. As it was, I did what he said.

We traveled a long basement passage, climbed two flights of stairs, and emerged through a green baize-covered door into what I took to be the main bedroom corridor. There were a number of doors on each side, and I could see, halfway along on the left, a door which might have been the one in front of which the body of Terence Black had fallen. The silence was absolute.

Len opened a door at our end of the passage and motioned us through. It was evidently a gentleman's bedroom. When the door was safely shut I turned, rather angrily, to him and said, "Now, perhaps, you will be good enough to explain."

He put his finger up again and said, very softly, "I beg that you will keep silent, doctor. I promise you that it will not be for long."

For the first time I noticed, in his face, an air of shrewdness and purpose, which had certainly not been there before. I said, "Very well. Since we seem to be involved in melodrama, let us play it out to the end." After that silence fell again.

The corridor was carpeted and it was difficult to be certain, but after about ten minutes I thought I heard footsteps—two lots of footsteps—passing our door. Then the sound of a door opening farther down the passage. After that, silence again.

Len now had our door open a fraction and was peering

through. Standing over him, I could see down the passage. The door to the room which I had already, tentatively, noted as being Mrs. Ruyslander's bedroom swung open and Peterson came out, followed by Sir Rigby Bellairs, who was carrying a small case. I saw them staring in our direction and thought they had noticed our partly open door. However, it was not at us that they were looking, but at the tall footman, who was advancing toward them, at a stately pace, down the corridor.

Sir Rigby said, in tones in which astonishment and fury were mixed, "What the devil are you doing here, Simpson?"

"I was keeping an eye on Mrs. Ruyslander's diamonds," said the footman. "I take it that they are in that case?"

It was only when he spoke that I knew for certain who it was.

"I assume," the footman went on, "that on the previous occasion when you attempted this theft, you were interrupted by Terence Black. Of course you had to silence him. Yes, I can see that you are both armed. I am only uncertain which of you used your gun on the poor fellow."

"Does it matter?" said Sir Rigby thickly. "It seems that history has repeated itself. We find you here, with the diamonds in your possession—"

"No, no," said Holmes. "I'm afraid that on this occasion that scenario won't work. You are out-gunned. Allow me to make the introductions. My name is Sherlock Holmes. This is my colleague, Dr. Watson. The gentleman with the shotgun you will, of course, recognise as your own head gardener. Finally, this is Detective Inspector Leonard Blunt of the Criminal Investigation Department, Scotland Yard."

"I am charging you both with robbery," said Blunt, stepping forward. "And there will be a further charge against one of you for murder."

Peterson had already dropped his pistol. Sir Rigby, after one furious glance, first at his accomplice and then at us, reluctantly followed suit.

In the event, Peterson, who was a coward as well as a bully, gave evidence for the Crown against his employer. His insistence that it was Sir Rigby who had shot Black was supported by forensic evidence which matched the bullet in his gun with the one in the murdered footman. Peterson received a short, but salutary sentence of imprisonment. Sir Rigby was hanged.

"It was an interesting case," said Holmes. "I had, it is true, one more item of information than you, yet I knew from the very first who the villains were. What I knew, but you did not, was that Sir Rigby was one of the three recalcitrant depositors at Mayhews Bank. I therefore knew that he was desperately short of money and would go to any lengths to obtain it. Really, the rest of the truth was in that newspaper report. It contained three glaring improbabilities. I, like you, had studied the excellent account of Corby Manor in Gillespies 'English Manor Houses,' and once I had done so I realised how unlikely it was that a single shot—which, incidentally, Miss Macalister, who was wide awake, admits she did not hear—would have woken Peterson, who was sleeping just as far away in the other wing. And if it had woken him, how could he have arrived in the bedroom corridor—a considerable journey—at the same time as the gentlemen who were sleeping there? No, no. I was sure from that moment that he was in the plot. As soon as I encountered him, this suspicion became a certainty. I recognised him from the curious shape of his ears as George Peters, a man with a long criminal record. And if he was involved, surely his employer was as well. The second point was the fixing of the door lock. For a footman, supervised and busy about his duties, it would have been almost impossible. For Sir Rigby and his head butler, very easy. Finally, there was the sleeping draught in the coffee. This totally exculpated Black. There were three footmen handing round, how could he be sure that he was going to be the one to hand the cup to Mrs. Ruyslander? Apart from which, have you considered *how*, in the course of taking it to her, the drug was to be added. This was surely done by Lady Bellairs, before the cup was despatched. I fancy, though it will never be proved, that she was involved in the plot. However, justice was served without looking for a third victim. I fancy that clears up the main points.''

I had a number of unanswered questions in my mind, but the only thing I could think of immediately was to say, ''You were surely very fortunate to obtain the job.''

''Not in the least. I offered my services at under the going rate and was able to supply references from a High Court Judge and a Bishop. Blunt followed a similar course. We were both welcomed with open arms.''

''And why did you take the risk of visiting 'The Fox and Hens' in Corby village? Surely you could have held any necessary discussions more safely in the grounds.''

''A risk, but a necessary one. I had to identify the foreign gentleman for Blunt. You were quite right. He was a notorious middle man in illicit diamond dealing, named Bernstorff. We would have liked to have included him in the charge, but the evidence against him was too slight."

I had one final question, and in putting it I tried to keep the reproach out of my voice. I said, "Could you not have taken me somewhat sooner into your confidence?"

"My dear fellow," said Holmes, "your conviction that the villains were a particular footman and a stable hand—a conviction which soon reached Peterson, through Mrs. Pearce and her friend Mrs. Barnby—was invaluable. It meant that the real criminals could pursue their plans with confidence. Which they did, to their undoing. Incidentally," he added with a twinkle in his eye, "I read both of your reports when I got back to Baker Street. I found them most illuminating."

"Good God," I said, remembering my description of "Len," "I hope you haven't shown them to Inspector Blunt."

"They shall remain entirely confidential to the two of us," said Holmes.

There is not much more to record. A cousin inherited Corby Manor and kept on most of the permanent staff, including the Pearces and Mary Macalister. Jacob, the Pearce's eldest son, returning from the wars, wasted no time in seeking Mary's hand, and their marriage was solemnised on a cold December day in 1886. Eight years later, as I have recorded, I was sitting in our Baker Street room looking at the few crumbs of wedding cake in the small white box, when Holmes burst in and found me doing so.

I have a suspicion that he still felt a twinge of regret for the deception he had practised on me in that early case. Maybe at that stage in our collaboration he had not acquired the full confidence which developed through the years. Whether for this reason, or some other, he took the unusual course of explaining to me the background of the relics in that box. They were all fascinating stories, none more so than the case of the pearl-handled buttonhook, which I hope to relate someday.

SHERLOCK HOLMES
AND THE MUFFIN

Dorothy B. Hughes

Illustration by Sidney Paget of a scene from *A Scandal in Bohemia* in "The Strand Magazine" 1891, in which Holmes is disguised as a drunken-looking groom.

I

The icicles did indeed hang by the wall on that early December morning; quite as Sherlock Holmes was caroling as he came from his bedroom into our sitting room:

> "When icicles hang by the wall,
> "And Dick the shepherd blows his nail,
> "And Tom bears logs . . ."

A bump on the corridor door interrupted. It was half after six and our early morning tea had arrived. As he was nearby, Holmes opened the door. Lustily, he resumed his song:
> "And greasy Joan doth keel the pot . . ."

The tweeny entered, balancing the heavy silver tray, with its two brown china pots of Jackson's best English Breakfast blend, a large container of steaming water, two cups and saucers of Wedgewood china, a sugar bowl and milk pitcher also of Wedgewood, and two silver spoons. She managed with care to put down the tray without spilling anything. She then faced up to Holmes. "My name is not Joan," she stated, "and I am not greasy. I wash myself every morning and every night, and on Saturday I take a full bath in m'Mum's washtub." She emphasized, "Every Saturday."

She was a little thing, of no more than ten or eleven years by the looks of her. Over her dress she wore an overall, evidently one of Mrs. Hudson's in the way it hung almost to her ankles. Her mousy brown hair was cut as a small boy's, a straight fringe to the eyebrows and square below the ears. Her eyes were as gray as this wintry morning.

Tweenies came and went at Mrs. Hudson's. Our exemplary landlady was not so goodhearted to underservants as to her tenants. I had frequently heard her berating one or another tearful child. Tweenies being on the lowest rung of domestics, and hence lowest paid, none remained long in Mrs. Hudson's employ.

But this one had spunk. And Sherlock himself was in fine fettle, by which I assumed a new case had come his way. As he so often said, "Give me problems, give me work. I abhor stagnation." Without a problem, he took to his mournful Stradivari violin and his pipe of 7½% solution.

Although his eyes were laughing now, his face remained grave as did his voice. "If you are not Greasy Joan," he said, "What name are you called?"

"My name is Muffin."

"Muffin?"

"Muffin," she repeated firmly, daring him to disdain it.

"Well, Mistress Muffin," he bowed slightly, "You may pour me a cup of your excellent tea. First a spill of milk, then the tea, and lastly two lumps of sugar."

She hesitated, as if it were not her job, as indeed it wasn't, to pour the tea. I had already serviced my cup, with a generous pour of the milk, and with one lump of sugar, and stir and stir, as we were taught in boarding school. But she followed his instructions, quite as if she were accustomed to this extra duty. She knew how, I must say. She probably played Mother for her Mum of an evening.

"And where did you get that fine name, Mistress Muffin?" Sherlock inquired politely as he ventured a sip of his scalding tea.

"M'Mum named me that," she replied. "Ever before I was born, she once saved a ha'penny from her wages, and she bought for herself a muffin from the Muffin Man. She says it was the best thing she had ever in her life. And when I came to her, she named me Muffin." As she was concluding, she had edged her way to the door. "Excuse me, sirs, but she'll be accusing me of twattling if I don't get backstairs. I will return for the tray later on."

With that she was gone like a streak.

When she was well away, Sherlock burst into laughter. "Muffin. Because it was the best thing she ever had." Then his face became serious. "Poor woman. Waiting—how long?—until she could spare a ha'penny for her special treat. I daresay the child has not ever tasted one."

"Not on a tweeny's wages," I agreed. I poured myself more tea. "You are up early. A new case?"

"It would seem so. A chest of jewels shipped from India on *The Prince of Poona* is missing. This morning I meet with the ship's captain and representatives of the viceroy. After I learn more of the details, I shall decide whether or not I wish to undertake this case."

"Not the Gaekwar of Baroda's gems!" I had read of their worth this past week in the dallies.

"Indeed, yes. From your service in India, Watson, I daresay you know that the Gaekwar receives each year from his subjects his weight in gold and jewels. Doubtless this is why he emulates a Strasbourg goose at table." We could exchange a smile, having seen news photographs of the present Gaekwar. Holmes continued, "It seems he has decided to have some of his treasure set in pieces—breastplates, coronets, rings and things, possibly as gifts to his ladies and to favored courtiers."

"But why London?" The East Indians were noted for their skills as lapidaries.

"Why indeed? Because the best stone-cutters are now in London, it seems. At least the Gaekwar considers this to be so. And he will have no one else cut these gems."

Beneath his dressing gown, Holmes was dressed save for his coat jacket. Briefly, he returned to his room, only to emerge in his stout boots, his Inverness topcoat, several woolen mufflers wrapped about his neck, and carrying his fur-lined winter gloves. On his head was a fur hat he had bought in Russia. He had lowered the ear flaps.

Because of the weather, I suggested he take a hansom cab to his meeting place. He scoffed at that. "Cold fresh air is what my lungs have needed." And he was off. I envied him. I was still more or less housebound, nursing the wounds of my services in Afghanistan. I gathered by the fire, settling in an easy chair with my briar and the morning *London Times*. Sherlock claimed that the *Times* was read only by intellectuals, of which ilk I make no claim. But for me, the *Times* was the only paper which gave proper news.

I'd forgotten about Muffin until she thumped the door later and reappeared. In one breath she said, "Miz Hudson says your breakfast will be ready in one hour is that too late and will you be down?"

Holmes and I usually took our breakfast in the downstairs dining room, it being difficult, if not impossible, to keep toast and eggs and bacon properly warm when a tray has to be loaded and carried two flights from the kitchen to the first floor front, where we had our quarters.

"Yes, I will be down." I told her. "And eight o'clock will suit me properly. And please to inform Mrs. Hudson that Mr. Holmes will not be coming to breakfast as he has already gone out." This was not unusual when he was on a case. There were times when he actually left before early morning tea!

"Yessir," said Muffin. She had been stacking the tray with the remains of this early morning's. She made as if to take it up now, but I halted her. "I want you to know," I said, "that Mr. Holmes was not speaking of you when he spoke of greasy Joan. He was just singing one of Mr. Will Shakespeare's songs."

Her face lighted. "Oh. I have heard some of them before. When I was little, m'Mum took me to see some of his plays at the Lyceum. There was one where a father's ghost appears to a prince named Hamlet. Ever so scary. And another one called *Twelfth Night* where a girl pretends to be a boy and where there are two old gentlemen who sing and dance. Very comical they are."

I wondered, "Your mother is in theatre?"

"Oh, no, Dr. Watson, sir. It was when she was charing at the Lyceum. It is not far from the docks, just off the Strand. The usher let her bring me in if I would sit quiet on the steps." She tossed her head. "I can tell you, young as I was, I was much more quiet than the folks in the stalls or the balcony." She hoisted the tray, it was not so heavy with the teapots empty. "I'd best hurry before Miz Hudson gets crotchety again." And off she went.

That evening by the fireplace I regaled Holmes with the further revelations of Muffin. He was as impressed as I at her knowing of Shakespeare. "I wonder can she read and write," he reflected.

Education for females was still scarce to nonexistent, although the National Education Act was initiated by Parliament some years before. To a goodly extent, Parliament had acted because of John Stuart Mill's movement for the improvement of schools for females, to which Miss Florence Nightingale had added her influence. Both Holmes and I were staunch supporters of education for all.

That night Holmes did not talk of his new case, save to say he had accepted it and would be leaving early in the morning for the docks. Possibly the docks were somewhat improved now, in the late 19th century, but they were still unsavoury at best and dangerous below that. Not that Holmes was ever fearful walking even the meanest alleys. His lean frame gave no hint of the muscular power beneath. Holmes was as fine a boxer as any professional, and with exercise and proper diet, he kept himself fit. Nevertheless, he did not rely on brute strength alone. The stick he carried was weighted, as more than one malefactor could testify.

He did remark, "It is to be hoped that the cache is not in the hands of a dredger. It might be somewhat difficult to retrieve."

For the most part dredgermen were steady, hardworking men of the lowest class, searching among the flotsam for objects of possible value. They also had the duty of recovering drowned bodies from the river. For this latter they were paid "inquest money." Unfortunately, smugglers larded themselves among the decent dredgers. These were most active when East Indian ships rode at anchor in the river.

Holmes puffed placidly on his after dinner shag. "Certainly, with diamonds the stakes, time is of the essence."

"Diamonds!" I could not help but exclaim.

"The cache contains diamonds, in weight near 500 stone."

"And you are to recover it?"

"I intend to try." His lips were unsmiling. "I do not intend to fail."

II

The following morning Muffin did not linger after bringing our early morning tea. I daresay Mrs. Hudson had dressed her down for yesterday's lapses. Holmes had his tea with his customary before-breakfast pipe, filled, as always, with the day-before dottle, which he dried on his bureau overnight. With it he had his usual two cups with two sugars, but he did not linger over them. He was off to his room in no time to dress, eager to get himself down to the docks.

I lighted my briar and poured myself a third cup. Without warning, without even her customary thump, Muffin burst into the room. In each hand she held a man's walking boot. "Is not Mr. Holmes here?" she demanded.

"He is here. In his room, dressing," I replied.

She gasped, "Someone put his boots in the dustbin. I went to empty the kitchen baskets into the bin and saw them atop the leavings. The dust cart comes this afternoon, and they would have been taken to the dust yard." She tossed her head. "If the dustman did not keep them to sell."

From his doorway, Holmes called out, "What is this you say?"

Muffin spun around, and the boots fell from her fingers. In a moment, she gulped, "Gor, Mr. Holmes. You gave me such a start." She let out a deep breath. "I took you for a lascar."

Holmes was now concealed in the guise of one of those fierce East Indian sailors. An angry scar slanted down his entire left cheek. His face was colored as brown as coffee. Even to me, a medical man, and in these close quarters, it appeared to be an actual scar.

"You are familiar with the lascars?" Holmes asked her.

"Oh yes, m'Mum and I live near the docks. My Da was a seafaring man until his ship was lost in the Indian Ocean, all hands aboard. I never knew him; I was just a babe." She shook off memories and returned to the present. "Lascars are mean. They'd as leave knife you as give you the time of day."

Holmes now turned to me. "And do I pass inspection with you, Doctor Watson?"

"You've passed a stiffer test," I informed him. "It is more difficult to deceive children than it is their elders." I then explained to him, "Muffin rescued your boots from the dustbin."

Having recovered them from the floor, she held them out to him.

"How good of you to look out for me, Mistress Muffin. However, these are boots I have discarded."

"But Mr. Holmes," she protested. "The leather is not broken. Look. And the soles! Yet strong—"

"I no longer need them," he told her. "My Jermyn Street

bootmaker delivered my new ones this week. These you may consign again to the dustheap.''

"If you say.'' Reluctantly she turned to depart, still rubbing her thumb on the smooth leather. And then she turned back to him again, asking in a small voice, "Would you mind if instead of the dustbin, I kept them myself?''

He was taken aback for a moment. "Not at all. But I fear they would be rather too big for you, Mistress Muffin.''

"Oh, not for me, sir. For m'Mum. Her feet are that cold when she comes home late at night from her charing, like sticks of ice they are. When it's damp out her shoes are wet clean through to her skin. Her soles are paper cardboard.''

"Won't they be too big for her?'' I put in dubiously. "A woman's foot is different from a man's.''

"Not with new-old stockings. Maybe two pair to fill the chinks.''

"New-old stockings?'' It was an expression I had not heard.

She told me, "All the Mums make them. They cut off the worn foot and sew together what's left. And then they cut a top piece off another old stocking and sew that to the top to make them long enough. And you have a new-old stocking.''

A peremptory knock on the door silenced her. It was Mrs. Hudson knock. I noted only then that Sherlock had made an unobtrusive exit while Muffin and I were engaged.

I opened the door to our landlady. She bade me good-morning, then directed her gaze to Muffin. "You are needed below.''

"Yes'm,'' the child said meekly and scuttled away.

"I am sorry I kept her this long helping me,'' I assumed the blame, hoping it would be of some help to Muffin. I noted that she had managed to conceal the boots under her overall before her quick exit.

"Any time you need help, Dr. Watson,'' Mrs. Hudson said graciously, "just inform me. I will spare one of the maids.''

With that, she rustled away. From the fullness of her skirts she must always wear several petticoats and at least one of taffety. I had no doubt that, by now, Muffin would have the boots well secreted below until she departed that evening.

It was after dark before Holmes returned. From his morose visage, his day had not gone well, and I asked no questions. Not until he had scrubbed away all vestiges of the lascar, and was comfortably by the fire, wrapped in his purple dressing gown, did he discuss the venture.

"The docks were teeming with lascars, Watson. Although I speak several of their dialects, none were willing to talk with me. Otherwise the area was near deserted of its denizens. Whether for fear of them or on orders from one Jick Tar, I was unable to ascertain."

"Jick Tar?" I repeated. The name had no meaning to me.

"Or Jicky Tar. He has a chandler's shop down there and seems to rule the neighborhood as absolutely as an Oriental potentate."

I continued to puzzle. "Not Jack Tar? Jick Tar."

"Possibly once he was a Jack Tar and changed the name when he left the Royal Navy. For good and sufficient reasons, I have no doubt. I did discover him to have been a dredger, or to have used that cover for his operations. I understand he lost a leg in one such and could no longer work in the water, and therefore opened the shop. I made to enter it but was thrust away roughly by one of the bullies at his door."

"You will not need to return?" I hoped.

"I must if I am to discover the jewels. But I shall vary my guise."

Our dinner arrived at that point. I had ordered it sent up when I realized he would not return in time to dress for the dining room. I was pleased to see that far from retreating into the doldrums, he had good appetite. After the sweet, he opened a bottle of claret, and I brought out the Havana cigars. The day's setback obviously only added to the challenge of solving the case.

He was by the fire in our sitting room before I was up, next day. For all of my knowledge he may have sat there through the night. But he was far from disheartened, which I took as an indication he had thought of one or more other plans of procedure.

At promptly six thirty, Muffin arrived with the morning tea tray. She looked worried. After setting it down, she approached Holmes. "I have done you a wrong," she quavered. "It was the boots. When I was carrying them home last evening, I met up with Jacky and Little Jemmy and they said I had stole them and I said Indeed I had not and that Mr. Sherlock Holmes had given me them."

Holmes was endeavoring not to laugh at her childish agitation. "Not so fast," he pleaded.

She gulped a breath. "They said they were going to tell Jicky Tar, but when I spoke your name they took off like rabbits. Only—" she took breath again, "they followed me this morning. I fear they mean harm to you. And m'Mum was so grateful for the boots, she even cried tears.''

Holmes asked, ''Where are these boys?''

''Across the roadway.'' She led us to the broad front windows and pointed down and across. ''There, by the second dun house.'' In the morning darkness we could just make out the shapes of two small figures huddled together on the cold kerb.

''They are Jicky Tar's boys?'' Holmes inquired.

''Oh no, they are Mud Larks.'' This was the name given to those miserable children who scavenged the muddy verges on the banks of the river for bottles or lumps of coal or whatever lost articles they might sell for a few pence. In spite of modern reforms, there were still too many street children in London, those whose parents, unable to care for them, had turned them out to beg or otherwise do for themselves. ''But Jicky Tar buys some of their findings,'' she said. ''And they fear his displeasure.''

''I will see them,'' Holmes stated. ''Go tell Mrs. Hudson to send up the fireboy to do an errand for me.''

The fireboy turned out to be a dour old man whom I had never seen before, as he came to build our fire before I was awake. He stumped up the stairs and Holmes met him at our door. ''There are two boys across the road. I want you to bring them along to me. I would speak with them.''

With neither aye nor nay, the man stumped off again, down the stairs.

Holmes left the door ajar and came to the table. ''Today greasy Joan has indeed keeled the pot.''

''I'll ring for more hot water,'' I said.

''This will do. There isn't time to be particular.'' Even as he spoke we could hear voices below, and shortly thereafter the door opened wider and an urchin, bundled in all manner of mufflers and mittens, peered in. He was about the size of Muffin, but better fed, with a round nose and round blue eyes in a round face. His cheeks were red from the cold.

Holmes said, ''Come in, boy. You are—''

''Jacky, sir.'' His voice was hoarse with cold.

''And where is Jemmy?''

''M'brother's over there,'' he gestured. ''Minding the box.''

Holmes contained his excitement. ''The box—''

''It's too heavy to carry far.''

''What is in the box?'' Holmes queried.

''Rocks,'' the boy said. ''Nuffin but rocks.''

''Then why did you bring it here?''

The boy looked about the room suspiciously, particularly at me.

"Why?" Holmes repeated.

"I want you should see it. I want you to see it's nuffin but rocks. I don't want Jicky Tar to be saying I stole from it."

"Fetch it," Holmes directed. "Can you carry it up the staircase?"

"Me and Little Jemmy together can. Like we carried it all the way to Baker Street."

Holmes waited at the head of the stairs, just in case Mrs. Hudson should not allow Jacky to return with Jemmy. Not that she was unused to the queer company which Holmes often kept. I moved to the doorway and watched as the two boys appeared, hoisting a wooden box step by step until Holmes took it from them up top. Little Jemmy scarcely reached to Jacky's shoulder. He could not have been more than seven or eight years. Like Jacky, he was bundled, but his thin face seemed parched white from the bitter weather. All of us entered the sitting room and Holmes directed the boys to the hearth by the fire. He set the box before them on the floor. "Will you open it?" he asked.

The box or chest seemed to be made of fine heavy teak, although much abused from having been immersed in river water. It was perhaps half the size of a child's traveling trunk. Jacky lifted the latch and raised the lid.

It contained rocks. Nothing but dirty rocks. Some were small as a cherry but most were large as plums.

"What do you want me to do with these?" Holmes inquired of the boys.

"Do what you like," Jacky told him. "But don't tell Jicky Tar we brought them to you."

Little Jemmy cautioned fearfully, "He give you a clout with that stick of his to knock you down, and he stomp you like a bug."

Holmes assured them, "I shall have none of him."

After the boys had departed, each clutching a new sixpence within his mitten, Holmes turned to me. "Come, Watson. We must dress and be off at once. If these rocks are what I surmise them to be, I need you for a witness."

"And our breakfast?" I reminded him.

"We will breakfast later."

I did not dispute him. In record time both of us were ready to depart. I went ahead, carrying his stick, while he carried the chest down. I was fortunate in procuring a hansom cab for us almost immediately. Holmes directed the driver, "To Ironmonger's Lane."

When we were underway, Holmes explained, "I am taking the chest to a certain Signor Antonelli, who is, I have been informed, the finest lapidary in London. For centuries the East Indians were the only lapidaries in the civilized world. As you doubtless learned in your years in India, that country was the only known source of diamonds until the early 18th century and the discovery of them in Brazil."

"Indeed yes," I recalled. "The best and most famous stones have come from the Golconda area near Hyderabad. The Kūh-a-Nūr, which was a gift from India to our royal crown, is the longest diamond known. The Daryā-i-Nur, another of the great stones, is in Persia. It was taken there along with all those now known as the Persian Crown Jewels, by the Nadir Shah when he sacked Delhi in 1739. They say the Persian jewels surpass all others in vastness of number, size, and quality, although our own crown jewels contain some of the most precious gems, particularly in diamonds." The toe of my boot nudged the chest. "You believe these rocks are diamonds?"

"I do," replied Holmes. "Both in India and Brazil, diamonds were found only in gravel deposits. As sedimentary rocks come from some deeper deposit, obviously this was not the original source. But only with the discovery of diamonds in South Africa, less than twenty years ago, have we learned that they come from within deep pipes of igneous rocks. In its uncut form, the diamond cannot be distinguished from any sizable rock."

When Holmes investigated a subject, he did it with thoroughness. "Diamonds are pure carbon. True, some poorer stones have small crystals of other minerals embedded, but these are not used as gem stones, only for diamond dust and other mean purposes." He mused. "The history of diamonds is fascinating, Watson. They are known to have been worn as precious stones as far back as 300 B.C. In ancient documents it is recorded that Alexander, the Macedonian Greek who conquered Persia, and added 'The Great' to his title as he proceeded to take over all the mid-east, decked himself in diamonds. The very name is from the Greek, *adamas* or 'invincible'."

Holmes had evidently found time, along with all else he was engaged in, to visit the reading room of the British Museum. He continued, "The diamond is the hardest of gemstones, therefore the most difficult to cut. It alone ranks ten, the highest point, on

Mohs' recently tabulated scale. Of special interest to me are the differences in judging the beauty of a diamond. In the East the beauty is primarily in its weight, whereas in the West it is in color and form. The Indian lapidaries devised the rose cut, which best preserved the weight. But they found it next to impossible to polish this cut to bring out its fire.

"It was the Venetian lapidary, Vincenti Peruzzi, who in the late seventeenth century began experimenting with adding facets to the table cut. The result was the first brilliant cut. Cutting is a science. Peruzzi had studied with East Indian lapidaries. As has Signor Antonelli. And that is why we are here," he concluded as the cab drew up before a very old shop on Ironmonger's Lane.

Holmes alighted. While he was paying off the driver, I pushed the chest over to where he could lift it out more easily. I then stepped down to the walk and started across to the shop door. At that instant I saw a man who was approaching at a rapid pace, despite the hindrance of a peg leg.

"Holmes!" I warned quickly.

At the alarm in my voice, he turned, and he too recognized who this person must be. None other than Jicky Tar. He was large although not tall, and his seaman's knit jumper could not conceal his bulging muscles. His visage was a malevolent mask. He brandished a cudgel, knobby as are those heavy clubs which come from the village of Shillelagh.

One glance, and Holmes thrust the box at me. He extricated his stick from under my arm, then advanced a few paces and stood waiting. Only then did I see the two bully boys who had come round the corner in Jicky Tar's wake. One had Jacky immobilized in an arm lock, the other had a viselike fist around Jemmy's small arm.

Holmes saw them as I did, and he thundered, "Release those boys! At once!"

"Not until you return my property," Jicky snarled. He had advanced to a distance of several yards from Holmes before taking his stance. It was obvious that he was accustomed to street fighting, where striking distance was needed in order to swing a cudgel for the fullest impact.

"What property of yours do you claim I have?" Holmes asked.

"The box." Jicky gave a quick glance to where I was standing. "The box those picaroons stole from me and gave to you."

The boy Jacky shouted atop his words. "He's lying, Mr. Holmes! He's lying! It wasn't his, it was ours. We found it. Not him."

Jacky was twisting and straining to release himself from his captor, aiming his kicks to where they would do the most good. One found its mark. The bully howled, and for a moment his grip on the boy was loosed. Jacky wrenched away and darted at high speed up the lane.

The bully shouted, "Jicky, he's got away! The bloody little wretch got away! I'll go after him."

"No," Jicky ordered. "Stay! We'll get him later. He won't go far. Not without his sniveling little brother." He then turned his full attention to Holmes. "Will you give me the box or do I take it?"

Holmes stated with authority, "The property belongs to the Gaekwar of Baroda and I shall return it to him."

Without warning "on guard," Jicky Tar swung his cudgel, while the unencumbered bully came under it toward Holmes. Holmes's well-aimed feint at Jicky became a blow to the bully's head, felling him. It was then just the two men, both experts, in this tit for tat, manoeuvering as swordsmen, one to disarm the other. The bully came to his feet too soon and moved in to join the fray. I feared for Holmes with two against one, but I need not have. With enviable deftness, Holmes's stick struck and dropped the bully again. Holmes stick was then raised to disarm Jicky Tar when a police whistle sounded.

"It's Jacky," Jemmy cried out. "He's brought the Peelers."

It was indeed Jacky, running ahead of one bobby while another followed, blasting his whistle. The police quickly took charge of Tar and his henchman. The one who had mishandled Jemmy had faded away during the rumpus, releasing the boy, who ran to his brother's side.

Holmes told the policemen, "Take these men to Inspector Lestrade. I will be there shortly to inform him as to their misdeeds. And take the boys with you."

"Gor blimey," Jacky cried, while Jemmy clung to him. "He's shopped us!"

"Not at all," Holmes told them. "It isn't safe for you to return to your old haunts. Just stay with the police until I come, and I will then find a better place for you to live."

While he was speaking, the police wagon, summoned by the whistle-blasts, came down the alley. The villains were quickly locked inside. With great reluctance the boys were boosted beside the driver and the wagon clip-clopped back up the road. Holmes brushed off his coat and straightened his cap. He then took the box from me and we proceeded to enter Signor Antonelli's shop.

It was dim and dingy inside. There was just the one room, a counter separating the front from the larger rear. There, shelves were laden with all manner of rocks, and on a long table were more, in various stages of grinding. The diamond dust recovered from grinding is the only substance hard enough to produce the necessary high polish for fine stones.

At this table, bent to his work, was a wizened old man, his face scarred doubtless from rogue bits of gemstone. His scant yellow-white hair fell below his ears and he wore spectacles with lenses of heavy magnification. If he was aware of the recent commotion outside his shop, he gave no indication. He ignored our entrance.

After a moment, Holmes spoke. "You are Signor Antonelli?" The question was ignored. Holmes continued, "I am Sherlock Holmes, and this is my friend, Dr. Watson."

The old man did not respond.

As the awkward silence continued, Holmes hoisted the chest to the counter and unhasped it. He took one of the rocks and held it out to Signor Antonelli. "Will you tell me what this is?"

Antonelli ceased work and shuffled over to us. He took the rock from Holmes. "I will see," he muttered.

We watched as he carried the rock back to his worktable. With instruments which had no meaning to either Holmes or myself, he began grinding a bit at the edge. Shortly he brought it back to the counter. "It is a diamond," he stated.

"From the *Prince of Poona* cargo," Holmes told him.

The Signor muttered, "I have been waiting for these. I was told you might bring them here."

"Then I may leave the chest with you?" Again there was no response. But Holmes continued as if there had been. "I shall so advise the viceroy. He will inform you about what is wanted by the Gaekwar."

The ancient nodded once. Without a word of farewell to us, he lifted the chest as if it were no heavier than a dog's bone, carrying it back to his working area. Holmes and I, exchanging amused glances, took our own departure.

It was necessary to walk to a more traveled thoroughfare before finding a hansom cab. "I will drop you off," Holmes told me. "It may be that Mrs. Hudson will serve you a late breakfast. At least she will fetch something to tide you to the lunch hour."

"And you will eat. . . ?"

"Later," he said. "First I must go to Scotland Yard to confer with Lestrade. From now on I am certain that he will keep a wary eye on Jicky Tar. I must also arrange a place where the boys can be safe. Thanks to Muffin they came to me with their find. If they had gone to that villain, I daresay by now the 'rocks' would all have been flung into the river."

III

It was nearing the dinner hour before Holmes returned.

"And will ye be wanting your breakfast now?" I jested him in the cook's broad Scots. "Or will ye be waiting for the dinner?"

"Lestrade and I had lunch after we reported to the viceroy," Holmes replied. "I may just pass our dinner tonight. After the cuisine prepared by the chef of the Savoy, Mrs. Hudson's cook does not tempt my appetite."

"Although she does prepare a bountiful Scotch breakfast."

"True," he agreed as he laid off his coat and cap.

"What of the boys?" I inquired.

He answered with enthusiasm. "I have turned them over to a pair of my Irregulars. Stalwart young chaps who will not only arrange a place for Jacky and Jemmy to live but will initiate them into the ways of the Irregulars. We will be seeing them again, I have no doubt."

"Nor I," I nodded.

"In case you puzzled, as I, how Jicky Tar knew of Signor Antonelli's shop; he had an informer from the *Poona* who advised him that the chest would find its way there. Once he learned that I was on the case, Jicky had me watched. Hence our being followed. All's well that ends well," he quoted, and suggested, "Perhaps a small glass of amontillado would not go amiss?" He walked to our sideboard, fetched two wine glasses and the bottle. After he poured, I lifted my glass. "To yet another success."

He dismissed the tribute. "Pure happenstance this time."

"But based upon accumulated knowledge," I amended.

"And a tweeny." He now raised his glass. "To our Mistress Muffin," he toasted. "You know, John," he said as he seated himself, "I am not accustomed to accepting remuneration for help I give to those in need of solutions to their problems. But now and again, I do make a settlement. This was a time when I did. The Gaekwar can well afford it."

He sipped his sherry. "I have in mind to send Muffin to a school—a good school for females. But how to arrange it? It is quite obvious that both she and her Mum are independent personages who would not accept charity, or anything that hinted of it." He shook his head. "Yet for their living they find it necessary for both to go out to work."

"With the cost of living these days, it seems to be essential," I commented.

"I have been pondering this problem." He refilled our glasses. "I have thought of some kind of scholarship. Not to cover fees alone, but with enough over to at least pay for their lodgings. This way her mother could afford to have Muffin take advantage of schooling. The child has such a bright mind and unusual spirit, it would be wasteful not to allow her to better herself. Perhaps become a teacher."

"Or perhaps a scientist," I suggested.

"Or a doctor of medicine," he countered.

"That day will come for women," I agreed. "And before too long."

"But how to devise a scholarship? And how to make sure that Muffin will make use of it? This is as knotty a problem as yet I have encountered."

"You will solve it," I spoke with certainty.

"I must," he responded. "It is, if I may invent a phrase, a 'finder's fee'."

The first bell sounded from below. We began to gather ourselves together, to be ready to descend the stairs before the second. Holmes smiled as he put down his wineglass. "I have a notion to play Father Christmas to our young friends. A warm coat and winter cap for Muffin, and the same for the boys. Perhaps even a new pair of stout boots for each of them."

The second bell sounded.

"Do you not think I could pass muster, even to wise children, in a long white beard and a long red coat and a red bonnet on my head?''

I made no reply. To the boys, yes, I believed he could. But not to our Muffin.

THE CURIOUS COMPUTER

Peter Lovesey

Illustration by Sidney Paget of a scene from *A Case of Identity* in ''The Strand Magazine'' 1891.

It was already four A.M.

George Harmer, better known as "Grievous," was having a sleepless night in his penthouse suite in Belgravia. His brain had been working like a teleprinter for the last two hours. He was in despair.

So he tossed and turned: tossed caution to the winds and turned to the naked blonde who lay beside him. She was Silicon Lil, a stripper of manifest charms who performed nightly in his chain of nightclubs and afterwards by special arrangement.

"Lil."

She barely stirred.

"Lil."

She stirred barely.

"Lil, are you awake?"

"Tie a knot in it, Grievous."

"I want to talk to you. I've got something . . ."

"What?" She snatched at the light switch and sat up. "What did you say?"

". . . something on my mind. I can't think of anything else."

"Don't you ever give up?" Lil flicked off the light and resumed the attitude of slumber. "What you want is a cold shower."

If anyone had spoken to Grievous like that in daylight they wouldn't have lasted long enough to complete the sentence. He was the undisputed boss of organized crime in Britain. Undisputed and unforgiving. But at four in the morning he was pathetic. He said in a voice like a choked-up waste disposal unit, "Lil, I just want to bend your ear."

She sighed, rolled over and said, "You must be desperate. What's bugging you, then?"

"Holmes."

There was a pause.

"What sort of homes? Stately or mental?"

"Holmes with an 'l,' Lil."

"As in Sherlock?"

"Right."

Lil smiled to herself in the dark. "Him with the deerstalker, Grievous?"

"Not him exactly." Grievous flicked on the light again, hopped out of bed, switched on the TV and slammed a cassette into the video.

"Give me a break, Grievous," Lil protested. "I'm not watching some old detective movie at four in the morning."

"Shut your mouth, bint!" said Grievous savagely. He was becoming his normal, psychotic self. "This ain't Peter Cushing. This is a top secret video that was smuggled out of Scotland Yard for me. It's being shown to every chief constable in the country."

The TV screen flickered. A countdown of numbers appeared, then a famous head in profile, with pipe and deerstalker.

"That's no secret. That's in the tube at Baker Street," Lil commented.

Grievous silenced her with a growl.

The title of the video was superimposed.

Introducing Holmes . . .

A voice-over spoke in the ponderous tones peculiar to documentary films: "Everyone has heard of Mr. Sherlock Holmes, the world's greatest consulting detective. In his day, if Sir Arthur Conan Doyle is to be believed, this celebrated sleuth consistently outwitted everyone, including the police. He was streets ahead of the best brains at Scotland Yard."

Stills of wooden-faced Victorian policemen were superimposed over Old Scotland Yard. A hansom cab stood waiting.

"In the modern police, it's another story."

A clip of New Scotland Yard, with buses and cars cruising past.

"Holmes is working for the police. Holmes is a computer system for use in large-scale enquiries. Home Office Large Major Enquiry System."

The words appeared on the screen with the initials blown up to triple size.

"They've got to be joking," said Lil.

The commentary continued, "Holmes is the most valuable aid to the detection of crime since fingerprints were classified. Holmes will range beyond the boundaries of the police forces, providing instant information on suspicious persons and vehicles. Through free text retrieval, it will provide data on, say, all bald-headed men on record over forty owning *D* registration Rolls-Royces."

"My God, that's you," said Lil.

Grievous fumbled for a cigar.

The screen was filled by a close-up of the computer's interior.

"Holmes is more powerful and more flexible than the Police National Computer," the commentary continued as the camera panned over crowded logic boards. "It is a means of linking different forces engaged on similar investigations. Holmes can issue descriptions of persons interviewed or noticed, listing their previous convictions, addresses, telephone numbers and vehicles. It can collect information received from any source, whether it amounts to a verifiable fact or a mere opinion. No member of the criminal fraternity can sleep easily now that Holmes is working for the Yard. The game's afoot!"

The screen went blank. Grievous had pressed the "stop" button.

He said in a voice laden with doom, "This is the end of crime as we know it."

"Come off it!" piped up Lil. "It's only a computer, for crying out loud. You wouldn't let a piece of hardware get you down, would you?"

"It isn't just me," moaned Grievous. "It's the movement I represent. It's employment for thousands of skilled professionals. It's generations of experience and hard graft. It's major industries like prostitution and drugs and pornography. Nothing's sacred no more, Lil. We're all under threat."

"Strippers?" enquired Lil, betraying some concern.

"With Holmes on the trail? I wouldn't care to be caught in a G-string."

Lil gave a shudder, and the motion had the effect of distract-ing Grievous. He enfolded her in a sudden clinch.

"Grievous, my love, you've got to think big," Lil panted.

"You're big enough for me," came his muffled reply.

"This is just a cop-out. You must convene a secret meeting of the crime bosses from all over Britain and tell them about Holmes."

He drew away from her. "I can't do that. They'll go berserk."

"And if you *don't* tell them . . . ?"

"They'll roast me," Grievous admitted. "You're right, Lil. I've got to face it."

"I'll help."

"I wouldn't let you within a mile of that lot."

"No," Lil explained. "I'll get to work on Holmes."

"You?" he sneered. "What do you know about computers?"

She puffed out her chest provocatively. "Why do you sup-pose I'm known as Silicon Lil?"

Grievous grinned. "It stands out, don't it?"

"Are you talking about my figure?"

"I'm talking about a silicone job."

She slapped his face. "Bloody cheek. There's nothing false about these. Silicon without an 'e,' get it? Ever heard of silicon chips?"

"Naturally, Lil."

"So?"

He stared at her open-mouthed. His face was giving him gyp. "You're a computer freak?"

"In my spare time," she admitted casually. "More to the point, I have some helpful contacts in the electronics world. Give me a week or two and I might be in a position to save your bacon, Grievous Harmer."

So a meeting was convened at a secret location in the capital. They were the top men in their respective fields: terrorism, drugs, armed robbery, protection and vice. Grievous ran the video and the air was thick with denunciations and obscenities. They denounced and swore for two days and well into a second night before deciding on the proper response of organized crime to this vile threat to its very foundations: They formed a sub-committee.

Within a week, one of the sub-committee was caught red-handed tunnelling into the Bank of England, and the word got round that Holmes was responsible.

"Already they're pointing the finger at *me*," Grievous told Silicon Lil. "They want action. What am I going to do?"

She gave him a serene smile. "Don't panic, sweetheart. If they want action, they can have it. I've found the only guy in the world who is capable of helping you."

"Thank God for that! Who is he?"

"Hold it a minute. What's in it for me?"

Grievous said cautiously, "What have you got in mind, Lil?"

"A trifling consideration. Six months' paid leave at the Palm Beach Hotel in the Bahamas."

"You sure this fellow can nobble Holmes?"

"Nothing is certain, darling, but you won't find a better hacker than this one. He's a professor."

"Fair enough. You've got your holiday. Now introduce me to this genius."

The safest place in the world for a secret rendezvous is a metropolitan railway terminus, so Grievous and Lil made an assignation the same day with the Professor under the station clock at Victoria.

To be truthful, the Professor, on first acquaintance, was a disappointment, if not an affront. He shuffles into our story in decrepit shoes, a shabby raincoat with the buttons missing, a battered violin case under his arm and an ancient bowler on his head. He is obviously very old indeed, desperately thin, tall, but round-shouldered, with deeply-sunken, puckered eyes. Around his neck on a piece of string hangs a notice with the words *Accident Victim*.

"He's a common busker!" said Grievous in disgust.

"Possessed of extraordinary mental powers," murmured Lil.

"He's as old as the hills!"

" '. . . from whence cometh my help,' " said Lil opportunely. She wasn't religious; some previous inmate had inscribed the psalm on the door of the cell she had occupied last time she was in Holloway.

And helpful the Professor proved. Over a couple of beers in the station bar, he enlightened them both as to how he could outwit Holmes. In a soft, precise fashion of speech that produced a conviction of sincerity, he said that he regarded the prospect as an intellectual treat. "I was endowed by Nature with an exceptional, not to say phenomenal, faculty for mathematics," he informed them. "At twenty-one, I wrote a treatise upon the Binomial Theorem which earned me a European reputation. I was offered, and accepted, the chair of Mathematics at one of the better provincial universities. Later, I was obliged to be attached to the military, but I retained my grasp of numerical analysis."

"What about computers?" put in Grievous anxiously. The old man was rabbiting on too much for his liking.

The Professor gave him a withering stare and continued to rabbit on. "In middle age, I had the singular misfortune to suffer a climbing accident in Switzerland. I might easily have perished, for the drop was sheer and I struck a rock in the descent, but I fell into water, which saved me. I was carried downstream by the force of the torrent and deposited in the shallows, where I was ultimately found by a Swiss youth. I spent some weeks in a coma. The Swiss doctors were beginning to despair of me when I opened my eyes one morning and asked where I was. Happily, none of my faculties were impaired. I recovered all my powers."

"Luckily for us," said Lil.

"If we ever get to the point," said Grievous.

The old man appeared to sense that some acceleration was necessary. He made a leap of many years. "With the advent of computers, I rediscovered all my old zest for numerical analysis. Are you familiar with the terminology? Have you heard of hacking?"

"Breaking into computers?" said Grievous with enthusiasm.

"Crudely expressed, yes. It is an activity peculiarly suited to my present capacities. Physically, I am not so active now. Mentally, I am as alert as ever. Hacking is my chief joy in life. No computer has yet been invented that is proof against my ingenuity. The Bank of England, the Stock Exchange—"

"But have you heard of Holmes?" asked Grievous.

"The name is not unknown to me," answered the Professor with a strange curl of the lip.

"The police computer—can you nobble it?"

"Give me a month," said the Professor, adding, with a fine grasp of modern vernacular, "So long as the money's up front."

In the next weeks there was astonishing activity. With Lil acting as the Professor's buyer, vast sums were invested in computer hardware. Such was the drain on resources that Grievous had to order a million-pound bank job to finance the operation.

"He must be knee-deep in chips by now," Grievous commented.

"It's a mammoth assignment, sweetheart," Lil told him, "but progress is spectacular."

They installed the machinery in a Surrey mansion owned by a

forger who was unavoidably detained elsewhere. In this secret location, the Professor worked undisturbed apart from occasional visits from Lil. After three weeks, word came through that he had succeeded in getting a line into Holmes.

Grievous lost no time in summoning the underworld bosses for a demonstration. One month to the day that the Professor had agreed to help, a stream of limousines with dark-tinted windows arrived at the Surrey mansion. The mobsters and villains hurried inside and stood uneasily in the ornate, pillared entrance hall muttering obscenities and dropping cigar-ash on the Persian carpet.

Grievous let them wait a full twenty minutes before making his entrance down the marble staircase. So that there should be no confusion as to who took the credit for outwitting Holmes, he was alone. Silicon Lil was already on her flight to the Bahamas, and the Professor had been given his fee and shown the door. This was the moment of triumph for Grievous, his confirmation as the Godfather of British crime.

"Today, gentlemen," he announced, "I will show you why Holmes is no longer a threat. Come this way."

He led them into a vast room as cluttered with computer hardware as the last reel of a James Bond movie. "Take your seats," he said in a voice resonant with authority. "There should be a VDU for each of you."

Porno Sullivan, the vice king, gave him a filthy look. "I didn't come here to be insulted."

"A visual display unit," Grievous explained. "A box with a glass front just like the telly, right? Now, comrades in crime, don't touch the keyboards yet. What you have at your fingertips is the underworld's answer to Holmes. Let's face it, a month ago we were in dead lumber. Holmes could have put us all away for the rest of our naturals. Holmes: Don't let the name worry you—that was just a public relations exercise. Sherlock Holmes was said to have been infallible, but we know he was just a work of fiction. Some nutters believe he really existed, and that he's still living in retirement somewhere on the Sussex Downs keeping bees. He'd be over 130 by now. I've heard of honey being good for your health, but that's ridiculous." He paused to let the audience appreciate his wit, but nobody laughed.

"Get on with it," Porno urged.

"All right. When I heard about Holmes, I didn't panic. I happen to know a little about computers, gentlemen. I've been working on the problem, and I'm glad to say I've cracked it.

What you see in front of you is our own computer, plugged into the private circuit out of Scotland Yard. I call it Moriarty.''

"Morrie who?"

"Moriarty, Sherlock Holmes's greatest enemy."

"Professor Moriarty, the Napoleon of Crime," said Porno, who had done some reading in his youth. "Not the happiest of choices, Grievous. He came to a nasty end, didn't he? Got pushed off a ledge by Holmes."

This came as a shock to Grievous. He was less familiar with the works of Sir Arthur Conan Doyle than he made out. He hadn't known, until Porno spoke up, that Moriarty had been a professor. Was it possible . . . ? For one distracting moment, he remembered the *Accident Victim* notice around his saviour, the Professor's neck. He pulled himself together. "Never mind about him. This computer is known as Moriarty, and you want to know why? Listen: Microcomputer Output Rendered Impotent And Rot The Yard."

A burst of spontaneous applause greeted this popular sentiment.

Grievous basked in their approval a moment and then went on, "To keep it simple, Moriarty gives us total access to Holmes. By using the password, we can call up our own police records and examine them. Better still, we can alter them, erase them—"

"Or give them to some other bleeder?" suggested Porno.

Grievous gave him a withering look. "That wouldn't be comradely, would it? Now I shall key in the password and you can type out your names on the keyboards and examine your form."

It worked like a dream. The coos and whistles that presently ensued were music to Grievous's ears. The delegates were like kids on Christmas morning. For a happy hour or more, Grievous went from one to another giving instruction and encouragement as they learned how to make their criminal records unintelligible.

It was "Hash" Brown, the drugs supremo, who had the gentlemanly idea of calling up Silicon Lil's record and erasing it for her. After all, she wasn't there to do it for herself.

He entered her name.

Instead of a criminal record, there flashed onto the screen a quaintly worded instruction:

PRAY BE PRECISE AS TO DETAILS.

With a frown, Hash cleared the screen. He called out to Grievous, "What's Lil's full name?"

"Lilian Norton." Grievous spelt it for him.

"This time, Hash got the following:

NORTON, LILIAN
A.K.A. SILICON LIL. BORN 1/4/54, KNIGHTSBRIDGE.
PARENTS: JAMES & MARY NORTON. NIGHT CLUB PER-
FORMER & ASSOCIATE OF GEORGE "GRIEVOUS" HAR-
MER (SEE FILE). PRISON RECORD: MAY, 1985, 1 MONTH,
DRUNK AND DISORDERLY; DEC, 1986, 3 MONTHS,
HARBOURING A KNOWN CRIMINAL. NOTE: GREAT-
GRANDFATHER RUMOURED TO HAVE BEEN CHILD OF
GODFREY NORTON & IRENE ADLER. SEE: A SCANDAL
IN BOHEMIA.

"What's this about a scandal in Bohemia?" said Hash.

"One of Sherlock Holmes stories," said Porno. " 'To Sherlock Holmes she is always *the* woman.' "

"Who?"

"Irene Adler."

"Let me look at that," said Grievous. "Move aside a minute."

He keyed in the name Irene Adler and got the following
response:

NOW, WATSON, THE FAIR SEX IS YOUR DEPARTMENT.

"Who the hell is Watson?" asked Hash.

Grievous was already tapping out another message:

AM I IN COMMUNICATION WITH MR. SHERLOCK
HOLMES?

Instantly came the response:

IT IS AN OLD MAXIM OF MINE THAT WHEN YOU
HAVE EXCLUDED THE IMPOSSIBLE, WHATEVER RE-
MAINS, HOWEVER IMPROBABLE, MUST BE THE TRUTH.

"Well, that beats everything," said Grievous.

All the others had left their VDUs to see what was happening. They watched in fascination as Grievous typed in:

ARE YOU REALLY WORKING FOR SCOTLAND YARD?

Holmes responded:

I SHALL BE MY OWN POLICE. WHEN I HAVE SPUN
THE WEB, THEY MAY TAKE THE FLIES, BUT NOT
BEFORE.

"I don't like this," said Porno. "I don't like it at all."

Precisely at that instant the screen went blank as if the power
supply had been cut. Every other machine in the room behaved
likewise.

Then a voice announced over an amplifier, "This is the

police. We are armed, and we have the building surrounded. Listen carefully to these instructions.''

Grievous rushed to the window. The drive was cluttered with police vans. He could see the marksmen and the dogs. Resistance would be pointless.

That, in short, was how the entire leadership of the underworld was taken into custody. While they were sitting in the van on their way to be questioned, Grievous blurted out the whole extraordinary story to Porno, and then asked, ''Where did I go wrong?''

''You trusted Lil. She was working for Holmes.''

''The computer?''

''No, the guy who fancied her great-grandmother.''

''Come off it, Porno. He isn't still around.''

Porno gave him an old-fashioned look. ''I've been thinking about this Professor of yours. Holmes was a master of disguise, and he played the violin. He retired to Sussex, which happens to connect with Victoria Station.''

Grievous was wide-eyed. ''Still alive? And into computers? Unbelievable!''

''Elementary,'' said Porno dismally.

THE ADVENTURE OF
THE PERSISTENT
MARKSMAN

Lillian de la Torre

Illustration by Sidney Paget of a scene from *The Hound of the Baskervilles* in "The Strand Magazine" 1901.

M r. Sherlock Holmes?" inquired the man in the door-way.

"At your service," replied Holmes courteously. "Come in, sir, sit down and catch your breath, for I perceive that you have come up in a hurry from Sussex, where you maintain a considerable stable of horses."

I surveyed the newcomer with the puzzlement I always felt when my friend displayed his powers of deduction. There stood a tall, handsome man, with the open, ruddy countenance and athletic bearing of a sportsman, dressed in country garb. So much I could see. But Sussex? And hurry? And horses?

Our caller stared.

"Remarkable, Mr. Holmes. How could you know all that? It is perfectly true."

"Elementary, my dear sir. In your haste you have thrust the return portion of your ticket on the Brighton line only halfway into your vest pocket; you have rushed up to town in your working clothes, which—forgive me for mentioning it—are redolent of horse."

Our visitor laughed shortly.

"I see. I apologize. I was in the paddock when it came to me, suddenly, that my situation is intolerable and requires expert advice. I rushed for the early train without stopping to change. You must excuse me."

"Willingly, when it attests to such eagerness to obtain my services. You may confide in Dr. Watson here, as in me. What is this pressing problem of yours?"

"Somebody is trying to kill me."

"Dear me, who?"

"I haven't the slightest idea, that is the problem."

"Pray tell us your story."

"I am Major Barrett Desmond. Perhaps you have heard of me?"

"Should I have?"

"If you were a betting man, you would have. I breed race-horses on my estate of Belting Park in the South Downs, and my gelding, Thunderbolt, is favoured to win the Sussex Cup."

"I felicitate you. What is the nature of these attempts on your life, Major Desmond?"

"Shots, Mr. Holmes. I cannot take out my gun to shoot rabbits of a morning, but someone shoots at *me* from ambush. I cannot sit quietly in my study of an evening, but somebody shoots at me, in through the window, and comes devilish close, too. Too close to be an accident."

"How alarming. But surely you have recognized the fellow?"

"I have never seen him. He is too sly."

"How long has this been going on?"

"A week now."

"What happened a week ago that caused it to begin?"

"Nothing, sir, nothing, I assure you."

"Who knows of these attacks besides yourself?"

"The gamekeepers, of course. And I suppose everybody in the house heard the shots—my wife, my sister, my stepson, and the household staff."

"Have you informed the local police?"

"No, sir, I have not. I consider myself quite able to deal with my own problems."

"Yet something changed your mind."

"Another shot, Mr. Holmes. A shot whistled past my ear as I stood in the paddock. I came to you at once."

"It seems you preserve."

"Yes, sir, there are pheasants and a thriving herd of red deer on the estate."

"Then you have poachers."

"Of course we have poachers. But Birkett, he's my game-keeper, he keeps down the poachers. And these are no random shots, Mr. Holmes, don't think it, they are aimed at me."

"Then who is so much your enemy, Major Desmond?"

"To my knowledge, Mr. Holmes, there is no one alive who owes me ill will."

"It's plain that somebody does," said Holmes drily. "The racetrack touts, perhaps? They can be dangerous enemies."

"No, sir, certainly not."

"Well then, whom do you irk? Whom do you balk? Whom do you stand in the way of?"

"Only Colonel Luttridge," said Desmond with a smile, "for my Thunderbolt is sure to balk his Comanche at the races."

"An American horse, Comanche?"

"That is so, Mr. Holmes, Kentucky bred, but how did you know?"

"Comanche is a red Indian name. But I think we may forget Comanche. Surely if the Colonel inclines to such desperate measures, he would shoot the horse, and not the owner? We must look elsewhere. Forgive me for my next question, Major Desmond, but we must examine all possibilities. You are clearly a man of substance. *Cui bono?* Who profits by your death? Who is your heir?"

"Oh, Mr. Holmes, there is nothing in that. My dear wife is my only heir, and she is herself independently wealthy and stands in no need of anything from me."

"Is Belting park your family estate?"

"It is now," said Major Desmond with pride. "It was purchased at the time when we married, that was eight years ago in Dublin, where I was stationed with the Carabineers. I sent in my papers at once; we bought Belting and set up to breed racehorses, with what success you know. But enough of questions, Mr. Holmes. Will you advise me? I will do whatever you say."

"Data, data, Major Desmond. It is a capital mistake to proceed without data. I must visit Belting Park. And," he added with a look at me, "Dr. Watson is my valued coadjutor; he shall accompany me."

Our client's blank look swiftly changed to one of pleasure.

"Splendid," he exclaimed. "I had supposed that a consulting detective stayed home to be consulted. All the better that I was wrong. You will both be most welcome. When will you come? Now?"

"By the first train in the morning."

The next morning we were on our way. A smart trap, with

uniformed groom, met us at the Belting halt and had us through the gates of Belting Park before noon.

As we approached the mansion down a long avenue of lime trees, we saw that it was a large, well-proportioned Georgian structure of rosy weathered brick. To the spacious center had recently been added long wings to left and right, which blended pleasantly with the original house.

Our client was at the door to greet us and show us around. From the wide hall with its Adam decoration and gracious curving staircase, he led us to the right down a long corridor.

"This wing," he said, "is my domain. Here is my snuggery."

We glanced into a handsome room, paneled in oak, with furniture in masculine style, and leather-bound sets of the best authors lining the walls. It all looked unused.

"This is the gun room."

Here, every wall bore cabinets full of weapons.

"Quite an armamentarium," remarked Holmes. "You must be a keen sportsman."

"Oh, I do my share," said Desmond carelessly, "but these are not my sporting guns. I collect weapons."

He dallied to display his treasures.

"Here, you observe a pair of duelling pistols that once belonged to the famous Fighting Fitzgerald. And here," he said, pointing to a long black gun of sinister aspect, "here is the very 'old foreign gun' with which the Appin murder was committed."

"Ah, the Red Fox," said Holmes, his encyclopedic memory for crime supplying the details at once. "But that was in the reign of George II. This gun is of later date. It is an Afghan jezail, such as Dr. Watson here met with at the battle of Maiwand, to his cost. I have made it my business to understand firearms, upon which I am writing a monograph. I fear, Major, that when you bought this gun as an historical weapon, you were bilked."

The major shrugged. "Bilking is the penalty of affluence," he remarked. "But I can afford it."

He turned to me, where I was viewing a placard posted on the adjacent wall. It was headed "Marksman of the Year," followed by names and dates.

"Yes, Dr. Watson," he said, following my gaze, "here at the Park we continue to honour the old local custom of shooting at the mark on Midsummer Day. All the men may compete, but it is mostly the gamekeepers who do so. Of course, I do not compete."

"Why not, Major?"

For answer, Desmond indicated the mantelpiece, which was crowded with trophies for marksmanship, all won by himself.

"I wonder," said Holmes, regarding the array of cups and plates, "that with your prowess as a sharpshooter, you have not drilled this wild marksman of yours before now."

"If I intended to kill him," said the Major grimly, "he would be dead by this time. But my only intent is to warn him off. While he blazes away in this reckless fashion, he is a threat to every living thing on the estate. But come, gentlemen, what we want to see lies next door."

Following our host, we left the long gun room. A door at the end of the corridor led outside, but our guide only indicated it, and took us into the last room in line. We found ourselves in another spacious chamber, again paneled in oak. A great fireplace with carven overmantel dominated the east wall. To the south, heavy crimson curtains were drawn back from a line of long, low sash-windows looking out on the sunny lawn. Against the opposite wall, the thick padded cushions of a Morris chair promised the ultimate in comfort. Equally comfortable armchairs flanked the hearth, and another stood ready in a sunny window.

"The snuggery was my wife's idea," remarked Major Desmond with a smile, "but this is my true sanctum. Here I keep my breeding records, and here are the books I read."

The great oak desk faced the fireplace, and the bookcases behind it presented well-thumbed volumes.

"And here are more guns," said I, surveying an open rack by the window.

"Ah, these are my real guns, my favourite sporting guns. This is the gun I snatched up to return fire the other night." He patted a well-kept deer rifle affectionately on its polished walnut stock.

"Yes indeed, the other night," said Holmes. "The scoundrel, as I understand it, fired at you through the open window. You were sitting where?"

"In the Morris chair, going through some papers. I had dropped one and bent to pick it up as the shot whizzed by."

"And it struck where?"

"I fear it has ruined my favourite chair." The major indicated a neat hole in the padded back-cushion, just about head height.

Instantly, Holmes had out his penknife and began probing, coaxing delicately with the slender blade.

"There." He displayed the small bit of lead on the palm of his hand. "A nasty little thing to get in your back some dark night." He stowed it in his vest pocket. "Well, Major Desmond, you had best keep your shutters closed after dark."

So saying, he suddenly snatched the deer rifle from the rack and brought it to his shoulder.

"Be careful, you fool, it's loaded," cried the major.

"Do you customarily keep your guns loaded?" demanded Holmes.

"I do now," said the major wryly.

"And you fired out the window?" queried Holmes, applying his eye to the sight. "Towards that clump of beeches?"

"The shot seemed to come from there."

"But you saw no one?"

"The fellow was off and away. Well, gentlemen, I hear the warning gong for luncheon. Shall we go in?"

We performed the ablutions necessitated by our journey, and started to descend. Loud voices emanated below as we came to the stair-head.

"You'll stay away from Sally Parker!" shouted the voice of our host.

A young voice answered rudely: "Do it yourself!"

"Don't speak to your father like that!" came the sweet tone of a woman.

"He's not my father!"

Tactfully noisy, we began to descend.

"That's enough, Denis," said the major peremptorily. "Come in, gentlemen. Agnes, my dear, here are our friends who have come to solve our little difficulty."

"They are very welcome," said she in her musical voice.

The major's wife was a dainty specimen of that womanly femininity that has always appealed to me, small-built but perfectly formed and straight as a wand. Her gown was of an elegant simplicity, cunningly fitted and draped in some light woolen stuff, adorned only with a broad pocket of black velvet, richly jet-beaded, that was pinned to her slender waist like an old-fashioned reticule. The muted green of her dress subtly set off the lustrous coils of her coppery red hair. She had a lovely face, one of those kitten faces, with large violet eyes, small nose, and tiny rosy mouth.

"Let me present my son, Denis Mullen."

Young Mullen resembled his mother, but without any of her beauty. He had quick green eyes in a closed pale face, a determined jaw, and a carroty thatch. He gave us scowl and mumbled something.

"Ah, there is the second gong," said Desmond with some relief. "This way, gentlemen."

In the spacious dining room a well-appointed table was laid for six. The five of us sat down and unfurled our double-damask table napkins. No comment was made on the empty chair.

We had disposed of the soup, and were discussing chops and beetroot, when I was startled by a rather husky contralto voice shouting, "What ho, what ho, what ho!" the newcomer displayed a rather broad, weather beaten face, a figure equally broad, and an astonishing garb. She was dressed like a groom, with chequered vest, breeches, and high gaiters. She set down her shotgun by the door and advanced.

"My sister, Penelope," said Major Desmond. "She's not the least of my trainers."

"I've had Starfire out." She sat down and began to help herself liberally from the silver platter proffered by the pretty serving-maid. "Starfire will equal Thunderbolt one of these days, Barry."

"I am glad you think so."

"Then you'll not sell her?"

"Don't be tedious, Penny. Starfire goes next week, and that's final."

"You'll be sorry!" With vicious stabs she attacked her chop.

"Our guests, Penny," the major created a diversion; "here are Mr. Sherlock Holmes and Dr. Watson."

An inimical eye raked us.

"The London sleuth-hounds, eh? Well, have you discovered our secret enemy?"

"I have no secret enemy, Penny," said the Major, annoyed.

"What, Barry, have you forgotten that dreadful little man in shepherd's plaid trousers who shouted so loud and scared you so, Monday was a week?"

"He did not scare me," said the major stiffly.

"He made awful threats," said Miss Penny with relish, "he said he'd break every bone in your body. He was so funny, Agnes, you should have heard him."

The kitten mouth compressed. "I did hear him, Penny."

Our host's face hardened. "Clegg is excitable," he said harshly, "but Clegg is no sniper."

Miss Penny gave a disagreeable snort, and Holmes quietly changed the subject.

"I observe, Miss Penny, that you go in for shooting."

"I have to do it," she replied darkly. "Crows, you know."

"My sister has a feud with the crows," said the major with a smile. "She thinks they mean no good to Starfire."

"You may laugh, Barry, but you'll see!"

Again Holmes changed the topic, turning to young Mullen and asking: "And you, Mr. Mullen, do you shoot?"

"No," said the youth flatly.

"Such a shame," said his mother. "As a shot, Denis is quite my equal, and almost as good as Barry, but he won't shoot."

"I don't like blood sports," said Denis between his teeth.

"Look here, Holmes," exclaimed Desmond with sudden resolution, "I am a man of action. I cannot any longer sit around waiting to be shot."

"What else can you do, Barry?" demanded Miss Penny.

"I'll tell you what I'll do. When darkness falls, with the assistance of Holmes and his friend here, I'll lay a trap and draw this fellow into the open. Are you with me, gentlemen?"

"Of course, Major."

"I'll come too," cried Miss Penny excitedly.

"No, you won't, Penny. This is dangerous work. You keep out of it."

"Why?" demanded she. "I hate you, Barry; you think women can't do anything. But you're wrong. I can protect myself. There's my gun."

Mrs. Desmond smiled at her.

"Quite right, Penny. We can protect ourselves."

Quietly she laid something on the table. It was an innocent-looking little bauble enough, a small pistol with a short bright barrel and gleaming mother-of-pearl grip. She handled it with cool competence.

"I have carried it since the trouble began. I am not afraid." She restored it to her pocket.

"I know you are not afraid, my dear," said Desmond, "but this thing tonight, this is men's work."

He turned to the pretty maid, who was again proffering beetroot. "Sally, please inform Maggie that we shall not dine tonight. She is to provide a sufficient high tea at seven o'clock precisely, on the terrace."

The girl gave him a look and a dimple, curtsied, and vanished.

"Very well, Barry," said the mistress. "But don't you all find this rather a dreary topic?"

At this the conversation changed direction, and soon, having done justice to the savoury, we all rose from table.

"Well, Major," said Holmes, "by your leave, we will now proceed to the servants' hall to learn what we can from them."

We found the servants' hall to be under the iron rule, not of the butler, a willing but rather green young chap named Tamms, but of the tight-faced housekeeper, Mrs. Sattler. She informed us flatly that the staff knew nothing, and that it was none of their business anyway. In spite of her, however, the staff agreed that they had heard the shots over the past week. Only a sharp Cockney pantry-boy had more to contribute. He had heard the shots last night, he said, looked out, and glimpsed the sniper as he vanished.

"Scarpered like a spook, sir, fair give me the mulligrubs, it did, sir."

Tall or short, fat or thin, dark or light, he could not be certain; but the mulligrubs he was sure of.

The cook was yet to be heard from. Holmes sent for her, and caught a Tartar.

"She says she's busy, let you come to her."

Accordingly, we waited on Maggie in her own domain. We found a wiry little woman with fierce eyes seated at a long deal table cutting bread-and-butter with an alarmingly long knife.

"High tea," she grumbled, "and me with a fine fat goose fresh-killed for your dinner! Well, what do you fellows want? Sit down if ye must." She waved her knife at a couple of wooden chairs.

"Now, Maggie—" began Holmes, seating himself.

"Me name's Mrs. Murphy."

"Now, Mrs. Murphy, I am sure you want to help your kind master—"

"Kind master, is it? O aye to be sure, 'tis always the master. He pays me well, don't he? And him swaggerin' about like a lord of the manor on the mistress's money, tomcattin' after every pretty face and bettin' on every race, which she can't abide. I told her no good would come of it, me bein' with her since Mr. Mullen's day. Kind master! Ha! I've got no use for men!"

She reached for her knife and began attacking cucumbers.

"Well, now, Mrs. Murphy, you know there's been someone about the place trying to shoot the major—"

"Do him good, too," muttered Mrs. Murphy to the cucumbers.

"And I should like to ask you—"

"Ask me, is it?" snapped Maggie. "Ask me, would I be shootin' at the major? Well, sir, I would surely, and glad to do it, if it would help me mistress. But it wouldn't, so I wouldn't. So you can put that into your pipe and smoke it. Good day to ye."

We retired in disorder.

"Dear me," said my friend in mock dismay, "I hope that this good woman is not a sample of the female of the future!"

Leaving the servants' wing, we paused on the back doorstep to survey the scene. To our right lay an inviting terrace, handsomely furnished in wicker-work. Beyond it stretched an expanse of green lawn, the meadow, and the wood. Before us the lawn sloped down to the paddock and the stables in the distance. On our left was the well-kept kitchen garden, and beyond that the shooting range from Midsummer Day. From that direction shots resounded.

"Come on!" said Holmes.

He led the way at a brisk pace. The shooting range proved to be merely an expanse of green turf with the target at one end and a sketchily marked firing line at the other. Squared away at the line, rifle in hand, stood young Denis Mullen.

"Well, Mr. Mullen," said Holmes, approaching him, "it seems that you do shoot, after all."

The youth surprised us with a courteous reply.

"At a target, yes, Mr. Holmes, that's different. I keep my hand in. That bullet in the gold, I just put it there. I can kill if I want to. But I don't want to."

"Tell me, Mr. Mullen, what do you know of these attacks on the major?"

The closed look came back to the young face.

"Nothing. Sorry I can't help you. Excuse me, I must hurry."

The sight of pretty Sally issuing from the back door explained his haste. As he hurried off, Holmes directed his attention to the target, which turned out to be no more than a large construction of hay, fronted by the concentric circles of the mark, much pocked by bullet holes. Sure enough, there was a bullet in the gold. Attacking the hay with his strong, nervous fingers, he soon had it out and tucked into his watch pocket; but he did not desist until he had a handful of the other bullets as well, safely stowed in his jacket.

"Good," he said. "There is no more to be learned here. Let us go on."

It was a perfect summer day. High in the cloudless sky the

larks were on the wing, and their unseen chittering came down to us from the deeps of the air.

"The South Downs are undoubtedly the Paradise of England," remarked my companion. "I sometimes think that it is here that I shall chose to end my days in peace."

"It is surely a heavenly day," I concurred. "On such a day it is hard to believe in such mischievous malice as we have come to quell."

"Yet it exists, Watson, and nowhere more than in the lonely reaches of the countryside."

We rounded the house, our objective now the clump of beeches on the south lawn, which we had observed from the major's window. Arrived there, Holmes started to scour the ground, eyes glittering and nostrils dilated like a hound on the scent. For want of anything else to do, I imitated him, but saw nothing on the thick green turf.

Nor did he. After a while he joined me under the beech trees, shaking his head.

"Too much good weather," he said. "Not a sign of the fellow. But here—" His questing eye had caught sight of something on the trunk of the tree. "What is this?"

It was a hole in the shaft of the tree. Again he went to work with his pocketknife, and quickly coaxed out another bit of lead, which he tucked into his breast pocket.

At this moment we were startled by a shot, and then another. As we hastily started for the house, we saw the major come into view at a run, gun in hand, heading for the wood. We altered our course and met him at the edge.

"Another attempt!" he cried as we approached. "Here, here's where he shot from, before he vanished into the wood. Why, what's this?"

It was a splash of blood on the forest floor.

"You winged the fellow!" I cried.

"Not effectually, I fear. He ran like a rabbit."

"Well, you have marked him," said Holmes.

Bending, he quickly dipped his handkerchief in the stain on the ground and put the reddened linen into an envelope he took from his pocket.

"You are certainly thorough," remarked the major, "but what good is that? We know it is blood."

"As you say, I am thorough."

Again he scoured the ground, but without success, the elusive gunman had vanished without leaving any further trace of his presence.

"Well, major, I can do no more here. Now, I propose to use the hours before our tea to call at the local public house."

"Of course," assented the major cordially. "I will gladly join you and introduce you round."

"Not so, sir. Your presence would surely close mouths I would rather have open."

It was two affable strangers in country corduroys that presented themselves at the Admiral's Head. We found a wainscoted public room already filled with locals in various stages of conviviality. The landlord was bright-eyed little fellow like a squirrel, who filled our tankards with a snap. My friend drank his ale in silence, his quick eye taking in the company, and his equally quick ear open to their talk. It was loud enough. In one corner a group was vociferously canvassing the merits of Home Rule. Close by, a voice rose up in anger.

"If Major meddles wi' my Sally," it said somewhat thickly, "I'll shoot him sure."

His companion, a thin, wiry young man in a groom's gaiters, grinned derisively.

"Happen you might miss, Jem."

"There's more than one shot to a gun," muttered the fellow, subsiding.

Holmes, over his ale, inquired casually: "Who is our friend who is so quick with his gun?"

The landlord laughed. "All talk. Sally Parker is a pretty thing, and her father is that suspicious of any man who smiles at her. But he's one of Major's gamekeepers, and he likes him fine when he's sober."

"And the lad with him?"

"Ned Bickford is no lad, but head groom at the stud."

"How does he like his employer?"

"Who knows? He keeps his tongue between his teeth. They do say he likes the mistress uncommon well, but he don't talk about that either."

"And who is the fellow who so strenuously defends Parnell?"

The garrulous landlord willingly provided further information about his patrons, but as it proved non-significant, it had best be omitted here.

Returning at seven sharp, we found the family gathered on the terrace for their tea. Mrs. Desmond, arrayed in a dainty gown of lime-green Irish linen, made us welcome. Denis, scowling, did not. Only Miss Penny was missing, but again nobody commented.

The redoubtable Mrs. Murphy had provided much more than cucumber sandwiches. I was able lavishly to indulge my secret passion for sweets, while Holmes applied himself sparingly to the cold roast beef. The major absently devoured scones, too absorbed in planning his trap to notice what he ate.

"But surely, Barry, he won't come back now?"

"We'll be ready when he does," said the major. "I've had enough of inaction. Finished, gentlemen? Come along."

I reluctantly abandoned a half-eaten gooseberry tart and followed. As we rounded the house, two newcomers silently added themselves to the party. I recognized the burly under-gamekeeper, Jem Parker. His tall, keen-eyed companion proved to be the head keeper, Wilt Birkett. On their heels, not so silently, arrived Miss Penny, accoutered for crow-shooting.

"Penny! Where have you been?"

"Guarding Starfire."

"Well, go back there. We're not shooting crows now. There's a desperate killer out there. *Go on!*"

Crestfallen, with dragging step and many a backward glance, she obeyed. The rest of us repaired to the major's sanctum. There, behind drawn curtains, we watched Sherlock Holmes as, with deft fingers, he quickly put together a scene to attract our quarry.

It was rather like making a Guy Fawkes effigy for the Fifth of November. With a sufficiency of cushions stuffed inside the major's smoking jacket, there sat the major in the deep chair by the window, but, rather disconcertingly, without a head. This lack was supplied when the major bethought himself and produced the tasseled smoking cap that went with the jacket. Then he assigned us our posts in a conspiratorial whisper:

"Mr. Holmes will cover the front lawn from the beech trees, assisted by Dr. Watson. Birkett, the west end, the rose arbor. Parker, the terrace. I'll shelter in the verge of the wood. Thus we may close in on him when he shows himself."

"And remember," said Holmes, "no shot is to be fired. Our aim is to take him by surprise."

He adjusted the smoking cap temptingly showing above the chair back. "There, that ought to fetch him." He positioned the lamp to silhouette the scene, opened the curtains on the deepening dusk and said softly, "Come, let us go."

In the shelter of the beech trees there was a comfortable lawn seat, and there we stationed ourselves. It was pleasant enough sitting at our ease, scenting the rose garden and watching the stars come out, if only we could have smoked. Suddenly a shot rang out.

Holmes was off like a deer. We all converged on the lighted window, Birkett, Parker, the major, Holmes and myself—and Miss Penny Desmond, wild-eyed, gun in hand.

"Who fired that shot?" demanded Holmes angrily.

"I did," said the major sheepishly. "I saw the fellow, and I'm afraid I lost my head."

"You saw him! Splendid! Who is he?"

"That I can't tell you. From the edge of the wood, I saw him approaching the window, but crouching. I could neither see his face nor judge his height. Then he straightened, a big burly man, as tall as I, and in the light from the window I saw his face. Mr. Holmes, the man is black!"

"Black! Are there blacks hereabouts?"

"Only Comanche's handlers."

"Well," said Holmes, "whoever he is, we have scared him off. He will hardly return when he knows we are thus on the alert. I shall leave you with my mind set at rest."

"Leave us!"

"I regret, Major Desmond, I must. I have an urgent appointment tomorrow with a distinguished personage whom I am not at liberty to name. When I have satisfied him, I will analyze the data I have collected here, and communicate with you further."

We accordingly proceeded to London by the early train, and Holmes had plenty of time to confer with his disguised client. He returned from the meeting smiling and shaking his head.

"It was his wife, of course, poor man. The matter is put a stop to, and will be decently hushed up. Now for my Sussex client."

He turned up his cuffs and at his acid-scarred deal side-table he applied himself to his test-tubes. Soon I recognized a rusty-red precipitate in one of them.

"Yes," said Holmes, catching my eye, "the Sherlock Holmes test for blood, which you saw me perfect when first we met."

"But we know it is blood."

"We know it with certainty now. Perhaps it will tell us more if we ask it the right questions."

I saw as he put away the test tubes and set up his high-powered microscope that he was about to ask a different kind of question of the poacher's blood.

Dinnertime came and went unnoticed. Immersed in Clark Russell's absorbing sea tale, "The Wreck of the Grosvenor," I barely looked up when he set aside his slides and produced his collection of bullets. At last he sat back, looking grave.

"These are deep waters, Watson. We must return to Belting Park at once."

In a trice I had opened the well-thumbed Bradshaw.

"We cannot do it, Holmes," I said. "The next train departs in the morning."

"I feared as much," said Holmes. "Well, we must hope for the best."

We caught the early train with time to spare, found a comfortable first-class compartment to ourselves, and settled down with the morning papers. I was first to open mine, and started in horror.

"Great heavens, Holmes," I cried, "the major's persistent marksman has fired one more shot—and hit his mark! Major Desmond is dead."

It seemed an age until we arrived at the Belting halt. As we were the only passengers to descend, it was no great feast of deduction when a fresh-faced young fellow approached us saying: "Mr. Sherlock Holmes?"

"My companion inclined his head. "You have the advantage of me, sir."

"Inspector Clempson, on the Belting Park affair, at your service. You have made good time, sir. I only sent my wire last night at midnight."

"Oh? I received no wire. I came down of my own motion."

"You expected this?"

"I feared some such mischief."

"We shall be glad of your assistance, Mr. Holmes. But come, I have a trap waiting to take us to Belting Park."

"Let us go, then. You may tell us the details of this tragic affair as we go."

As we proceeded at a brisk pace through the deep green country lanes in the fresh summer air, we listened to the inspector's story.

"It seems, gentlemen, that the appearance of a black man prowling about last night alarmed the family for the horses—"

"Why?" demanded Holmes. "Any man may black his face, and your smugglers hereabouts often did."

"Not being local, they did not think of that. They thought of Comanche's people, and protective measures were adopted.

Ned Bickford and his grooms stood guard over the horses. The gamekeepers took up posts ringing the stables.''

"Then, in effect, all protection had been drawn away from the house?''

"The major was personally quite fearless, and Mrs. Desmond equally so. They were coolly doing accounts when the shot came. Denis Mullen was strolling on the lawn and rushed in at once. He found his stepfather dead on the floor, shot through the heart, and his mother insensible in the Morris chair. He summoned the servants and sent for me. When I arrived a half-hour later, I found that he had matters well in hand; his mother conveyed to her bed, Dr. Ledyard summoned, and the solicitor sent for—Mr. Needleton from Brighton.''

"Be sure, Mr. Holmes,'' added the inspector earnestly, "that I did not fail to question everyone concerned. Denis Mullen, though in the grounds, saw nothing. Miss Penny was at the stables, guarding Starfire. All the people at the stables were greatly alarmed by the shot, but merely tightened their guard over the horses as a result. Parker and Birkett on the periphery saw nothing suspicious. But here we are at Belting Park.''

As we traversed the lime-tree avenue, a wild ululation filled the air.

"Good heavens, what is that?'' I cried. "A dog?''

"It is the pillaloo, or Irish howl,'' said Holmes. "Mrs. Murphy is lamenting a death in the family according to custom.''

The tight-faced housekeeper admitted us grudgingly.

"Mrs. Desmond is prostrated and can see nobody,'' she said coldly.

"We need not disturb Mrs. Desmond yet, ma'am,'' replied the inspector. "Mr. Holmes wishes to inspect the scene of the crime.''

At the sound of the door, a tall thin man in old-fashioned formal attire had appeared at the head of the stairs.

"Well, Mrs. Sattler?''

"The police, Mr. Needleton.''

"Humph. About time. A dreadful affair, sir. To think that when I was here little over a week ago, all was well, nothing had been heard of this dangerous assassin. Well, I have work to do. Good hunting to you.''

He vanished again before we could open our mouths. Holmes shrugged and led the way to the major's sanctum. There blood on the floor by the desk showed where Desmond had fallen. Beside it lay his rifle, cocked and ready, mute testimony that he had died defending himself, though in vain, against his assassin. Holmes looked about him keenly.

"The bullet, Inspector?"

"The bullet pierced his heart and lodged against a rib. It was recovered at the autopsy this morning. Here it is."

Taking it, Holmes scrutinized it carefully under his powerful pocket lens.

"And the gun?"

"Not found. The assailant no doubt carried it off in his flight."

"No doubt. And the major's clothes?"

"I have them here." The inspector produced them from a drawer. "No powder marks, you observe."

Holmes turned them over, the Harris tweed waistcoat, the shirt and undergarments of fine linen. He lined up the deadly little holes that had spelled death for the wearer.

"So small an aperture," he mused, "for death to enter." He laid the folded garments on the desk. "Well, now I think it is time to hear what Mrs. Desmond has to tell us. Come, Watson. No, Inspector, not you, I work better alone."

We found the lady reclining upon a Recamier couch of yellow chintz. She opened calm eyes upon us, but said nothing.

"Madam," said Holmes with the gentle gravity he was wont to use towards the fair sex on such occasions, "we come to offer our deepest sympathy to you on your double loss."

She came erect, eyes widening. "My *double* loss?"

"The tragic loss of your husband, Mrs. Desmond, and the still more tragic loss of your son, who will surely hang for his murder."

Mrs. Desmond gave my companion a long considering look and came to her feet.

"As to the first," she said quietly, "I thank you. As to the second, it is premature. Denis will never hang for killing Barry Desmond. It was I who shot him."

"I know that, Mrs. Desmond," said Holmes, "but I wanted to hear you say it."

"Well, I have said it. Now leave me alone."

"I also know, Madam," said Holmes, ignoring her dismissal, "that you shot him in self-defence."

She looked at him sharply. "How can you know that?"

"Let us sit down together and I will tell you."

Gently he seated her, unresisting, on the yellow couch, himself taking a chair at her side. I effaced myself in the background.

"Major Desmond," he said, "was a strange client from the first, showing no wish or expectation that I should investigate on the spot. Unusual, but it did not then occur to me that a client might have come to me expressly to deceive me. I proceeded as usual, coming down to Belting, collecting the data available, and returning to Baker Street.

"I am a scientific detective, Mrs. Desmond. With test-tube and high-powered microscope, I scrutinized my data—and discovered a very strange thing. My client was lying."

"Of course he was lying. Barry was a liar born," said Mrs. Desmond bitterly. "But how did you know?"

"The first indication was the blood we found at the edge of the wood. No sniper shed such blood—it was bird's blood—I suppose from that fresh-killed goose in the larder. And the bullets, Mrs. Desmond, the one the poacher shot into the Morris chair, and the one in the beech tree, shot by your husband in return—they had both been fired from the same gun."

"I could have told you that. I saw him. I was sitting at my casement, the night he came home from London. I saw him fire in at his own window, and then turn on his heel and fire across the lawn. I know his conniving mind. I saw in a flash that there was no sniper, that as usual he was up to something underhanded. What? Was he planning to shoot somebody and blame it on this sniper he had invented? Whom? Me?"

"You did not at once inform Inspector Clempson?"

"And have gossip and scandal spread all over the county? Certainly not. I took out my old pistol from Irish days, and pocketed it. You must have thought me very peculiar, Mr. Holmes, displaying a firearm at the luncheon table and bragging that I could defend myself. I was really telling Barry; but as it turned out, he would not be warned."

"When I perceived your husband's duplicity, Mrs. Desmond," said Holmes, "I saw your predicament and hastened back to Belting. But alas, having busied all his people elsewhere, he had already seized his opportunity to turn his gun on you."

"That is so, Mr. Holmes. But I was watching . . . and shot first. I am sorry I had to, but there was no help for it. But tell me, Mr. Holmes, how were you so sure that it was I who shot Barry?"

"You had the means, the motive, and the opportunity. The bullet, smaller than a deer slug, clearly came from a pistol like yours. True, the pistol was not found; but the first man on the scene was your son, who would certainly think best to burke it.

The major's missing jacket must have taken powder marks; I suppose Denis would burke that too.''

"As to that, I would not know," she said quietly. "After I fired, I knew no more until I found myself in my own bed. Well, Mr. Holmes, what happens now? Are you here to arrest me?''

"I am not officially of the police, Mrs. Desmond. What happens at the inquest will determine what follows. If you are indicted, you may depend upon it that I will testify that you fired in self-defence. Meanwhile, my advice to you is the old adage: Least said, soonest mended.''

Leaving her, we bade farewell to Belting Park and returned to Baker Street and other concerns. Left behind was that idyllic summer weather. The next mornings dawned cold and rainy. On the second day, as we sat by the fire after breakfast, Holmes laid down his paper.

"The inquest is over," he said, "and Mrs. Desmond is free. On the doctor's say-so, she was not called; and as all the talk, both indoors and out, was of the major's alleged assassin, the jury perforce brought in their verdict against a person or persons unknown. Well, in a way, it's justice. He was as nasty a piece of work as ever I had for a client. And he had the cold gall to make *me* a party to his murderous scheme. *I* was to swear that the whole thing was a plot against *his* life.''

"When all the while it was a plot against hers. But why, Holmes, why? What motive had he?''

"Who knows the mind of a murderer? But I will hazard a guess. Money. It was when the solicitor appeared that the pretended attacks started. Exasperated by his persistent gambling and wenching, had she turned against him? Was she planning to divorce him? Changing her will? Tying up her money for Denis? Whatever the threat, he knew her inflexible nature, saw her death as the only way out, and laid his plans to bring it about with impunity.''

"But how foolhardy, Holmes, to call in an eye like yours to oversee his proceedings! He must have been crazy.''

"Perhaps he was. *Quos Deus vult perdere, prius dementat.* But there was method in his madness. He was under the impression that a consulting detective stays home to be consulted. He said so. Under that impression he thought me his safest choice for a dupe. When he found he was mistaken, he put the best face on it and took the opportunity to provide me with some of the data I asked for—fabricated, of course.''

"But Holmes, how did you know it was fabricated? The blood, for instance? The Sherlock Holmes test?"

"The microscope, Watson. In a man, the red corpuscles are round; in a bird, elliptical. You may see the difference illustrated in Taylor."

I glanced across the room at the shelf where stood the two fat volumes of *Medical Jurisprudence*.

"I am acquainted with Taylor. But Taylor says nothing about identification of bullets."

Holmes smiled. "Why do you think I fired so many Boxer bullets into that wall?"

I viewed with disfavour the initials V R in bullet pocks, with which Holmes, in one of his queer humours, had adorned the inner wall.

"To express your loyalty to our gracious sovereign Victoria Regina, I suppose," said I sardonically.

Holmes regarded the neat initials complacently.

"Oh, that was to display my marksmanship. But the rest of the bullets, Watson, I took them out again and put them under the microscope. As I had postulated, they were identically marked! Subsequent observation confirms it—that every gun impresses its peculiarities on the bullet it fires. This finding will form the substance of my monograph. It is not yet an exact science, Watson, but fortunately the major's gun made a very particular mark, so gross that even my pocket lens could detect it, and I knew that the major and the sniper were one."

"What a cold-blooded would-be wife-murderer he was!"

"And how stupid, to think he could use *me* for a catspaw!"

Lighting a splinter at the hearth-fire, Sherlock Holmes applied it to his time-blackened old clay pipe and subsided, smiling, into a cloud of fragrant tobacco smoke.

THE HOUSE THAT
JACK BUILT

Edward Wellen

Illustration by Sidney Paget of a scene from *The Hound of the Baskervilles* in "The Strand Magazine" 1901.

By a clewe of twyn as he hath gon
The same weye he may return a-non
ffolwynge alwey the thred as he hath come.
  —Chaucer, *The Legend of Good Women*

1

"Yes, Watson, show it me. Let me judge for myself
what is fit for me to read."
  I looked up with a start as Holmes read my mind.
"How in the world did you guess?"
  Holmes sank into the chair across from me before the fire that
blazed gratefully this fourth of November. He frowned tiredly.
"When will you learn that I never guess? It's as plain as the
yesses on your face, Watson. You have hidden the paper while
weighing whether or not to let me see an item in today's
Times."
  "But how did you know?"
  "Were I to hold a mirror up to you, old fellow, you would
spy smudges on your chin."
  As of its own accord, my hand shot to my chin. "How does
that—"
  Holmes's hand rose with the force of Holmes's will behind it.
"Patience. I am in train of explaining. Something nearer black
than gray has got on your fingers and transferred to your chin as
you stroked it in thought. Yours is not the dyer's hand. What,
then, gave birth to the smudges? Though man is born unto
trouble as the sparks fly upward, you have not handled the coal
scuttle: I see by the thrifty distribution of the coals that our
landlady, not you, tackled that job. Nor, by the dryness of your

pen, have you taken it up to write. Add to which, you are kept
from the comfort and support of your chair back by the thick-
ness of a paper hurriedly doubled and stuffed behind you. Ergo,
you have been reading a fresh copy of the *Times*, smearing
printer's ink on your hands in the process, have come across
matter you wish to keep from me, and thus find yourself in this
chin-stroking dilemma.''

"Deucedly clever, Holmes.''

"Deducedly simple, Watson.'' He stretched forth a long lean
hand.

Reluctantly, I reached back for the sequestered paper and
handed it to Holmes. "It's the item on—''

He held up his free hand. "Kindly do me that much courtesy.
Allow me the small pleasure of ferreting out what you had
rather I not view.''

I felt myself flush and held my tongue while he ran his gaze
over the field of print. His eyes quickly view-hallooed but it
took him a long moment before he could speak, and when he
did so he spoke without looking up from the page.

"How did you know this meant *she* was in town?''

Speechless, I stared at him.

"You needn't equivocate, Watson. 'Adele Nerri' is an obvious anagram for Irene Adler.''

I glanced at the violin case in the corner, and in my mind's
eye I saw Irene Adler's biography sandwiched between that of a
Hebrew rabbi and that of Ahab, captain of an ill-fated whaling
ship, the *Pequod*. (In my account of the case that introduced
Irene Adler into our lives, I believe I referred to Captain Ahab
as "a staff-commander who had written a monograph upon the
deep-sea fishes.'' The rabbi, of course, was Chief Rabbi Nathan
Marcus Adler, religious leader of English Jewry during Queen
Victoria's reign.)

I blinked, recalling vaguely an item about one Mme. Adele
Nerri being found missing from her hotel suite. I warred with
myself a moment before owning up. "It was not that item,
Holmes, that had me of two minds. I was struck by the item
recounting the theft of the Zugruh jewels, thought that it would
seize your interest, and frankly doubted that you were up to it.''

His haunted face lifted to meet my concerned look. "Not up
to it? I noticed the item and dismissed the case as unworthy of
my while. Obviously a put-up job, a scheme to defraud the
assurance company. Not up to it?''

"Were I to hold the mirror up to you, Holmes,'' I said

defensively, "you would see why I felt—and still feel—fixing upon such a case is contraindicated at this time. You have come home late every night this past week, have not shaven in three days, and obviously verge on a breakdown."

"Nonsense. Fit as my Strad."

I looked into his burning eyes and my alarm for him grew apace. In time, errors erase the eraser. The crime-fighter had worn himself down eradicating crime. It could well mean his finish were he to involve himself in a case having to do with *the* woman. How to dissuade him? Sow doubt? Might the same letters in the two names not be owing to simple coincidence? "Come, come yourself, Holmes. I. A.?"

"*I* as in needle, *A* as in 'orses." He smiled a strained smile but spoke in a confident tone. "I seem foreordained to seek needles in haystacks." His eyes narrowed in sudden thought and he whipped feverishly to the agony columns.

This did not surprise me. I knew that he missed nothing there. They were his favorite covert for flushing game.

Still, I could not forbear to ask, "What do you hope to find in the agony columns?"

"Call them caryatids, Watson. Think of them supporting entablatures; for them, over time, it must indeed become agony." He seemed to be aware he spoke nonsense, for he fell silent and only facial twitches bespoke his overloaded mind as his encaustic gaze darted about the page.

Again without looking up, he made a long arm. "A pen, if you would be so good."

When I had dipped it and given it him he marked the corners of a number of boxes scattered over the page. At last, he handed me the pen and the paper listlessly.

I stared at him. "Why mark boxes only to toss the paper aside?"

"For your benefit, Watson." He touched a finger to his temple; I was not displeased to note he left a smudge there. "I have burned them in here."

I looked about the familiar sitting room and studied, with a fresh eye, its furnishings, determined that I would improve my mind so that I should not suffer such slurs on my mental capacity much longer. Indeed, I had already begun, but had not mentioned it to Holmes, fearing his smile of amusement—or worse, of kindliness. When I felt sure enough of my progress in stocking my mind with quintessential trivia, I would astound him with my accomplishment. Till then, and not one moment before, I would hold my peace.

"Out with it, Watson. To suffer in silence is to nurse a grudge."

I shook my head and dropped my gaze to the page. "I was but clearing my mind to study the boxes you have so thoughtfully marked."

And indeed as I scanned them I lost myself in the puzzle they presented. I say "puzzle" rather than "puzzles" advisedly, for they seemed somehow of a piece. A piece of nonsense. Not one of them appeared to demand ransom or even to hint at an abduction. Totally unrewarding.

Take the first one my eyes fell upon:

> Cold frog, dank hero on damp road,
> Feel bog hum gnat note, hear dawn tang.
> Lighten now your wearisome load,
> Shemlock quaff, let the world go hang.

" 'Shemlock'?" I murmured.

"Obviously a disingenuous misprint for 'hemlock'—and just as obviously intended to catch the attention of anyone named Sherlock."

"Then you think this is addressed to you?"

"I know they all are."

"But what does this one mean?"

Holmes shrugged. "If you study the juxtaposed words, a study in synesthesia, if you study the content, an invitation to euthanasia. I am to commit suicide."

I bristled. "How could the *Times* print such a clearly threatening message?"

Holmes smiled. "The answer is that it did not."

I shook the paper. If he did not see it he could still feel it. It was substantial enough to send a hair-ruffling breeze Holmes's way. "You deny the evidence?"

"I deny that the evidence is what it seems. I think if you went out and compared this copy of the *Times* with copies delivered to our neighbors, you would find this copy to be one of a kind, specially printed up for my eyes only."

"If that is so, someone has gone to a great deal of trouble."

Holmes's silence agreed.

I lowered the paper to my lap. "Why?"

"Why, indeed."

My mind reeled with the ramifications. "Then it is possible that Irene Adler is not missing?"

Holmes opened his eyes in a blazing stare. "No, that, I fear, is all too true." He drew a deep breath. "Moriarty is using her as bait." He seemed to brace himself for my explosion.

"Professor Moriarty?" I looked round as though to see the Napoleon of Crime's ghost reach out from the walls. With a shudder, I pulled myself together. "I see what you mean: The man left behind some master plan of crime, and either his old confederates are carrying on or some new band of criminals have come across the plan and are following in his nefarious footsteps."

Holmes's eyes blazed into mine. "I said what I mean and I meant what I said: This is the work of Moriarty himself."

"But the man's dead!"

Holmes's sinewy hands gripped the arms of the chair. "You and the world believed *I* had died. Yet I came back from the dead. Is it not within the bounds of the possible that Moriarty too may have survived? That is what I have suspected for some time lately, thanks to crimes that bear his unmistakable stamp, and that is why I have been abroad at night. I said nothing of this before, lest you and the world think me mad." He closed his eyes. "Now it seems from the paper that the prey is hunting the hunter. He means to get rid of me in connection with pulling off his greatest coup."

I had never seen Holmes this pale and tremulous, so consuming of his energy as to burn flesh from bone and sheath from nerve. A bit more, and I should offer to fix a needle for him myself. I felt numb. Either Holmes's mind had snapped or what he said was true. And either alternative was psychic needle enough to fill me with paralyzing dread.

Holmes, however, drew force from somewhere within and gestured fiercely for me to go on.

I did so, reading aloud in as controlled a voice as I could muster.

" 'I'm in the jam, I'm in the box,
Who'd ever look there for a fox?' "

Holmes sat brooding. He gave no sign that he even attended, but I knew not a sound, not a silence, escaped his notice, and I went ahead, self-consciously but doggedly.

" 'File on file, rank on rank,
Crocodiles on the bank.' "

And:

" 'Barking, I dog the upas tree;
     Dog afore his master, that's me.' "

And:

" 'I am Renard the Fox with tick tack toes.
     Follow my track by the sharp of your nose.' "

Still no sign from Holmes. I continued:

" 'Mark aright and ye shall have more;
     Seven times, and seven times four.' "

And:

" 'I'm flotsam, jetsam, lagan, the gift of surf;
     The back of my hand, a blaze but no kerf.' "

And:

" 'I'm the dog you let slip, the hound you incur,
     Whilst chain is to ingot as link is to spur.' "

And finally:

" 'I bark and embark at the port you see
     Midpoint a line NN to EEE.' "

Holmes stirred himself to light a contemplative pipe.

This comforted me while it lasted, but I was alarmed to see that when he finished it he knocked the plug into the fire instead of saving it on the mantel corner with the other slugs and dottles for the next day's breakfast pipe.

At the sizzle and flare-up he grew aware of his action and shot a look at me to see if I had noticed. He saw I had indeed.

He gave me a wry smile. "It might seem I had unconsciously concluded that I have no tomorrow. But I assure you, old fellow, such is not the case." Then, as though to assure himself, he repeated, "Such is not the case."

"Then what is the case?"

"I do not yet know whether these agony-column messages

form a chain of syllogisms or are merely linked non sequiturs, but I feel certain that they are all interconnected and that they somehow tie in with the disappearance of 'Mme. Adele Nerri.' ''

I nodded. ''A common thread.''

''I do know that when you follow two separate trains of thought far enough, Watson, you will find some crossing point.'' He pointed his pipestem at the page of agony-column boxes in my lap. ''That is a signal development. It takes us from the caviar to the general and from the general to the particular. Enquiry leads in that direction or it would be a world overrun by oysters—remarkable feat, for oysters have none.'' He put the stem in his mouth and sucked on the empty pipe absently.

I did not like the sound of this at all. I speak of the words, not the wheezing intake. But I had not long to fret about the sudden slide from seeming sense to seeming nonsense. With a rebound into energetic motion, Holmes put aside his pipe, sprang to his feet, and strode to his bedroom. He kept up a rapid-fire monologue while he changed to go outdoors.

''I make no bones about my ignorance of cosmogony—it is cosmogony and not cosmagony?—but I do know one salient fact about the universe: waste. The universe seems to predicate itself upon sheer wastefulness—or, more euphemistically, re-dundancy. It is my function, whether self-imposed or not, to bring order out of chaos. It is Moriarty's function to turn order into lawlessness.''

He came out buttoning the few buttons remaining to the most tattered and torn of his getups. His gaunt feverishness appalled me.

''Holmes, when did you last eat?''

He eyed me as though eating were a new concept.

I reached to the breakfast table, lifted the tea cosy and uncovered the dish, and in doing so made sure the aromas wafted toward him.

His mouth twitched more than his nose. He eyed the display unhungrily.

''You'll need strength,'' I said.

Holmes shrugged at my insistence, but as though to humour me he took a shelled hardboiled egg, sprinkled salt on it, wrapped the whole in a napkin and stuffed it in his pocket. I saw the pocket already held a box of matches and a candle.

He pocketed, too, his revolver, though (I thought) without pa-nache, as if arming for a battle already lost. I discerned fine lines of pain at the corners of his mouth. Cocaine-use produces euphoria followed by depression, anxiety, and paranoia.

With a leaden heart and a chill of foreboding, I made ready to company him.

He threw me a sharp look. "You do not need the heavy coat, Watson."

"The day is chill," I said reasonably.

Holmes gave a snort of exasperation. "You miss the point. Watson, you put me in mind of the absentminded professor who, invited by his host to stay overnight because of rain, went home to get his toothbrush."

I tried to smile but my face felt stiff. "It is not raining and I am home, and I have my toothbrush handy thank you very much." I expressed my own exasperation with a sigh. "Holmes, I sense you are being deliberately perverse for some reason. You do not credit me with ratiocination. You must know that once you set forth your line of thought I follow it quite well. Indeed, I may make so bold as to say that over the years we have come to think alike."

One Holmesian eyebrow lifted. *Supercilious* is the word that fits. The Romans knew the language of the body. "Have we now? Even did you not flatter yourself, Doctor, it happens often that one cannot abide a person who shares one's views."

His tone was overbearingly kind, yet—or perhaps because of that—his words chilled me to the bone. "One agrees," I said stiffly.

"Touché!" he said with a sudden twinkle, and as though despite himself. Then he gathered himself in a frown.

Suddenly, I thought I saw what he was at, and my heart surged. I spoke with mock severity to tone down the emotional color of my sincerity. "Holmes, enough of this havering. You are trying to put me off from accompanying you on a perilous quest. I insist— "

He was stopping out a canine tooth with black wax to make it invisible. He paused abruptly and shifted his gaze to me in his looking glass. There sprang to mind the famous mosaic, found in a Pompeian house, that represents a fierce dog with the warning words *Cave canem* beneath it.

"You insist? *I'm* the one who insists. If this be the only way to dissuade you, so be it: *Watson, I do not need you."*

I could not speak for the lump in my throat. Had I become that great an embarrassment? A millstone? For the first time in my memory I came near hating the man. I knew the man was not in full command of himself; that explained but did not excuse.

There is such a thing as Watsonian doggedness. I lay doggo while Holmes finished his seedy toilet. I watched him look through the curtain at the street below and pat himself to be sure he had his revolver and his keys. I returned his curt nod as he slipped out the door. I listened to his feet descend the scale of staircase treads. I waited till I heard the outer door close, then put on my overcoat, took up my stoutest walking stick, and followed.

He led me a long march at a brisk pace. I stayed a good hundred yards behind, but kept him always in view. He paused once, at the monument to the Great Fire that started at 2 A.M. on Sunday, 2 September 1666 in the house of William Farryner, the king's baker, on Pudding Lane. He eyed the base keenly, but when he moved on, and I stood where he had stood, I saw that he had not studied the historic inscription but a chalked graffito. MAE HEAR: RUM TERRA COIN. GO COD POE UP. MAX FERO.

The text seemed clear, perhaps too much so. Why would one Max Fero thus boldly order one Mae to trick one Poe, apparently with a queer earthenware piece of change? The name Fero must be as counterfeit as the coin, but I recalled the word from my school days. I could feel myself write it on the blackboard, see it white on black, even smell it in the floating chalk dust after I'd erased it. Latin verb, active, irregular, meaning to bear, to bring, to carry. Principle parts, *fero, ferre, tuli, latum.*

I trotted discreetly to keep from losing the seedy figure in the gap-toothed and vacant-faced navvies passing to and fro on their various errands. Beyond Guildhall, Cheapside becomes the Poultry. Holmes led me past Pudding Lane, Honey Lane, Milk Street, and Bread Street.

He did not stop again till Threadneedle Street. There, without a look round, he entered the building at 42 ½. I hurried now to close the gap, for I saw it was a building of offices, and I wished to know which office he went into. He was too quick or I was too slow.

When I reached the entrance and looked in, Holmes had vanished. I stepped inside. There was a commissionaire's desk but no one at that post. I studied the directory on the wall, but found no name that meant anything to me. No Mae, no Poe, certainly no Max Fero.

Any move seemed better than none. I stole along the corridor, listening discreetly at doors for Holmes's voice.

As I passed a door half-open on stairs leading down to the basement, I caught a blur of motion out of the tail of my eye. I tightened my grip on my stick and whirled, but too late. Blackness.

2

Holmes stopped in mid-stride and dropped the match just before it burned down to his flesh. It wisped out in thready smoke as it fell to the flagstones. In the darkness, Holmes touched his fingers to his temples as if to establish his balance, or to hold himself steady against faintness. He had come too far on Moriarty's trail, had come too close to Moriarty, to falter now. Will must bolster flesh, the fox's skin patch out the lion's.

The breathing technique he had learned in high Tibet stood him in good stead now in nether London. Foul, musty air obtained down here in this sub-basement of 42 ½ Threadneedle, but he felt quite himself again.

He took the candle and matchbox from his pocket. He lit the candle and looked keenly around at the basement's labyrinthine ways before venturing farther along the corridor.

The litter was not all litter, the clutter not all clutter. There, in that corner, what seemed waste awaiting disposal was a cunning concealment of acids, oxygen gas, and blow-pipes. One trash can even held, under an unsavory cover of filthy rags, quite new dark glasses and quite clean work gloves. Someone meant to cut and melt metals.

Tap.

He started at the sound.

It seemed to have come from behind a door farther along the corridor. The door had a pebbly glass pane. A shadow moved on the glass. As Holmes neared, the silhouette forelengthened into the figure of a man, extremely tall and thin, the forehead doming out in a curve, forward-thrusting face oscillating from side to side above rounded shoulders.

Moriarty.

Holmes quickly wet his fingers, pinched out the candle flame, and pocketed the candle. So small a sound as blowing out the candle might have reached his alert adversary. He found himself drawing his revolver and taking aim at the figure.

Hardly sporting. But one did not give a cobra a sporting chance.

The closer the range the surer the shot. He took one more soft step nearer. He felt a levering action underfoot as his weight came down on a brick set flush in the earthen floor. And he knew—even as he vainly willed his foot to undo its pressure—that he had triggered some action within the room. Hard upon the give he heard a thump and a mechanical whir behind the door.

Holmes was never to know whether or not he would actually have fired had he not started his game. But Moriarty now had that sporting chance.

Moriarty neither darted aside nor darkened the room. Flushed, the Napoleon of Crime scornfully faced his Waterloo.

Grinning tightly and holding steady, Holmes fired.

The silhouetted form spun round but did not fall. Instead it impossibly winked.

Through the jagged frame of shards that remained after the center of the pane blew away, Holmes saw that the silhouette was indeed a silhouette, a cardboard cutout twisting slowly from a string hooked to the ceiling; and that the wink was indeed a wink, light from a lantern hung on the far wall flickering through the bullet hole Holmes had put in the head.

"Now, now, Holmes, you knew it wouldn't be as easy as that."

Moriarty's mocking voice.

Holmes grimaced. He had been humanly foolish enough to shoot his glance toward the cardboard cutout, much as a ventriloquist's audience might swing toward the dummy. But where else could the voice have come from? A quick but complete scan showed him no one in the room and nowhere for anyone to hide. The room was bare of furnishings save for a rickety table bearing a cornucopia shape.

A gramophone.

There was your voice. But the record had stopped turning; the voice had fallen silent. The gramophone needed a closer look, and Holmes took a step toward the lantern hanging on the wall.

Not so fast. What triggering devices might Moriarty not have planted twixt doorway and wall?

Holmes relit his candle and painted his path, past the flashing bits of glass, into the room. A sash weight lay on the floor near the table. A stout thread passed through the weight's eye, taking several turns and a knot.

The thread was a clew in the original sense, going back to Theseus and Ireneadler—correction, Ariadne.

Holmes shook his head to deny a flash of migraine. Follow the clew.

One way, the thread led from the sash weight to a lever on the gramophone. The other way, the thread led from the sash weight, through screw eyes along the walls, to a lax end on the floor.

Moist specks of soil coated the last several feet of the thread. Holmes carefully picked away shards of glass to uncover loose specks of the same soil. These specks formed a faint dotted line on the floor leading to the threshold. Under the pull of the sash weight, the thread had whipped back into the room, but Holmes saw where it had tunneled under the doorsill to the brick.

He stepped back out and worked the brick free to find what he had expected: locked into a painstakingly-cut slit in the brick's underside, a sharp blade. In the earthen cavity, the short severed end of the thread was still fast, knotted to a tenpenny nail hammered deep. The blade cut the thread, releasing the weight; the weight moved the lever, activating the gramophone's mechanism.

Holmes replaced the flagstone, dusted his hands, and returned to the room. He inspected the gramophone. A label pictured a dog cocking an ear toward a gramophone horn and proclaimed the manufacturer to be The Gramophone and Typewriter Co. (His Master's Voice.)

The needle was at the end of the track near the center hole of the record.

I am Renard the Fox with tick tack toes.

Follow my track by the sharp of your nose.

Holmes moved the lever back into place, cranked the handle to wind the spring to power the machine, lifted the horn to place the point of the needle in the groove at the outer edge of the record, then released the lever to start.

Moriarty spoke. A manic happiness came through the mechanical harshness. "These modern gramophones are a remarkable invention. With your powers of observation and interpretation, my dear Holmes, to say nothing of your familiarity with needles, you should have no trouble operating this machine. Simply crank the handle to wind the spring to power the machine, lift the horn to place the point of the needle in the groove at the outer edge of the record, then release the lever to start."

Holmes looked sharply about. Would Moriarty needle him if Moriarty were not about in the flesh to enjoy Holmes's discomfiture?

"Oh, I'm here, my dear sir. It is for you to find me out." But that was the voice on the recording.

If Moriarty were here in the flesh he would be near at hand, perhaps watching through a peephole.

Time was wasting as the record turned voicelessly. The cornucopia was empty of all but needle scratch and mechanism whir.

Holmes fixed his gaze upon the still-oscillating cutout. It moved because of a draught. He tested the door in its frame; in the process a few more shards came loose. The door fitted tightly all round, so the draught—before the pane shattered—had not come from there. Holmes moved the candle flame along the base of the far wall. The flame flickered. He thumped the wall. It was not structurally solid. But he saw no cracks of an opening.

"You need more light on the matter, Holmes."

Holmes took the recorded cue. Ready to spring aside or back, he used the front sight of his revolver to lift the lantern from its hook.

He sensed a device in operation and leaped back. Free of the lantern's weight, the hook tilted up. The entire wall slid aside, doubling the space.

Holmes stared at what might have been a hospital ward.

Four beds in a row, two occupied.

"You will have noted that there are a woman and a man, under restraining sheets; that, though they lie still, they are breathing; and that their breathing indicates the drugged sleep of the heavily sedated. You cannot see their faces because of the cumbersome helmets covering the heads, so, to spare you the trouble—and them the irreparable damage—of removing said helmets before this little experiment is over, I will tell you that the woman is indeed Irene Adler, visiting London incognito."

Even though Holmes could make out little more than the

torso, the figure was unmistakably a familiar one. Holmes felt a mixture of anger and bewitchment. "How did you entice her here?"

"The cleverest of women," said the Napoleon of Crime, "is the woman who is clever enough to conceal her cleverness."

"How does that apply here?"

"To hide the extent of her brilliance, she allowed herself to walk into a trap." The recorded voice took on a tone of asperity. "May I continue?"

Holmes remained silent.

"Thank you. The man is an idiot savant. Do not be unduly alarmed; he is not mentally disturbed, merely mentally deficient. To compensate, he has an incredible memory for dates and facts. You will have noted, also, that wires, leading in series to the voltaic pile in the corner, connect their helmets to each other and to the two helmets on the as-yet-unoccupied beds. You will, by now, be ahead of me. Yes, those other helmets are for you and for myself. Once you have hooked yourself into the thought-network, I will join you."

"How can I be sure you will not simply butcher me while I lie helpless?"

"You're not fool enough to trust my word of honour, but you're shrewd enough to believe in my egotism. At Reichenbach Falls I failed when I tried to pit my physical strength against yours. But I do not—now or ever—hesitate to pit my brain against yours. Have I not anticipated all your queries?" A pause. "Well, do you fear to take up the gauntlet? If so, go, and henceforth till the end of your miserable days be a whipped cur with your tail between your legs."

"Words. Names. What's to stop me from freeing the woman and carrying her out?"

"You would rescue an empty shell of a human being. If you forcibly disconnect her, you trap her mind forever in the idiot savant's mind."

Holmes felt his face twitch. "Very well. I accept the challenge. But may I at least know what I may reasonably expect?"

"Good. Of course." The voice took on the tone of a professor addressing his class. "The device puts the linked minds into semantic phase—into a quasi-telepathic state. You will find yourself in a strange, distorted world, which is the mind of the idiot savant. In that world you will find surveying by chain of reasoning to be your most unreliable measure. The normal brain is a labyrinth. Imagine the idiot savant's! I am counting on your brain to lead you astray in the idiot savant's. Your goal is the chamber in the centre of the maze. There, if you reach it, you will find *the* woman. Finding the way out, for the heroine and yourself, is another and more difficult labour. And all the while, I will be watching and misdirecting.''

''And, if I know you, sabotaging.''

''You know me. Too well for your own good. And I don't mind telling you that I will be using the new system of analysing thought processes by means of word associations, as espoused by Freud—''

''Cobra.''

''And you are the mongoose? Words. Names. No matter. You asked what you may reasonably expect, and I am telling you that you may expect the unreasonable. Are you ready?''

Holmes's face twitched again. ''Ready.''

''Then we proceed. You will find a double-throw knife switch on the wall adjacent to the voltaic pile. Throw the switch to engage the other set of contacts.''

Holmes drew the candle from his pocket and used its end to move the handle.

Behind Holmes, the partition slid to, walling off the inner room from the outer, and the air crackled and writhed with a voltaic arc.

Holmes smiled grimly at a gouge in the candle end. A close look at the switch handle showed him the implanted needle, and a good sniff told him the needle was poison-tipped.

Moriarty's recorded voice strengthened to speak over the rumbling partition and the crackling air. ''Caution when called for. Excellent. I am that way myself.''

Holmes' cheek twitched. ''Let us proceed. Does it matter which bed I lie down on or which helmet I put on?''

''Not at all. I would merely suggest the ensemble on your right as being the nearer.''

Without hesitation, Holmes lay down on the bed Moriarty merely suggested.

''Abandon when called for. Excellent. I am that way myself.''

Holmes fitted the helmet over his head. The seal was doubtless deliberately imperfect, for he could still hear Moriarty's voice.

''Abandon all hope, ye who enter.'' It appeared that the thought quite convulsed him, and Moriarty chuckled insanely.

At the very last, Holmes gripped the helmet to remove it. There had to be a way other than total submission to the mad professor. But a soporific gas filled the helmet. Holmes's hands loosened and fell away.

Faintly, faintly, Holmes heard, "Now, now, Holmes, you knew it wouldn't be as easy as that." And the gramophone turntable drawled to a standstill.

3

Fog. Mental fog. Wooliness.

Slowly it swirled with him as he turned to see where he stood. He stood in grayness, under grayness.

Tap.

Holmes started at the sound but could not tell whence it came.

He found nothing to grasp but nothingness. A tract of open wasteland stretched all about, untracked. Such sky as presented itself offered no guidance. Had there been even faint stars, he could have taken bearings.

At the thought, there briefly flared up in the gray heaven *UNDER NEW MANAGEMENT* in hunter's pink star-matrix block letters.

Sans-seraph, someone's mind snickered.

The message constellation faded, leaving nothing but bleak mindscape.

Moriarty had said there would be a labyrinth. Moriarty lied.

The disembodied voice of Moriarty spoke live inside Holmes's skull. "I did not lie. That it is not a set maze but a living, shifting one makes it no less a maze. Realize that it is a maze you make yourself as you move along. The rules of the game are that your every decision forms a division, that you create your own walls, your own forkings, your own baffles. And of course you have here these others to help you confound yourself. Your mind is linked to theirs, their views will force new vectors. Used to your own singularity, your own uniqueness, your own *aloneness,* you will find yourself constrained to be at one with others, to share the thoughts of others, to *confuse* with these other minds. Your most significant other is of course yours truly: your Virgil, your cicerone.''

''To lead me astray.''

''Right. Never trust me, in especial when I speak the truth. But, above all, beware yourself: For I have set you upon yourself, and the one person you cannot shake or sidestep is yourself.''

''As though I should wish to be rid of myself,'' Holmes petulantly thought to himself.

''You may think you think to yourself, but your mind is open to me and to the woman and the idiot savant.''

''My blushes, Moriarty!'' Holmes felt the light of exposure, however, rather than the heat of embarrassment. Never before had his thinking processes lain open to view, his ruminations come under scrutiny, his trial and error been on trial. But, in the last analysis, he had to trust himself to function under these conditions, trust his own mind to the singleminded task of hunting clews to clews in this primordial chaos.

How to start? In the beginning was the word. What words made sense of here and now?

Had there been word-rocks he could have piled word-cairns. Had there been word-sticks he could have erected signposts. How did one blaze a trail through a treeless forest?

Unbidden to Holmes's mind came a vision of ashes in a familiar hearth, blazing up, accompanied by the hoarsely silent cry, ''Bishop Blaise aid me!''

Saint Blaise (or Blasius), martyred on 3 February 316, became the patron saint of woolcombers.

The idiot savant's bit of trivia? Moriarty's disinformative prompting? Surely not Irene Adler's thought; she was not one to sit knitting! Never mind; Holmes seized upon wool.

Blaze a trail with wool. Unwind a mental skein of logic enabling the venturer to find his way back out of the maze.

There came to him the first rhyme he remembered, the nursery rhyme his nanny had read him over and over because he loved it so, the rhyme that had taught him reason:

> This is the farmer's sowing his corn,
> That kept a cock that crowed in the morn,
> That waked the priest all shaven and shorn,
> That married the man all tattered and torn,
> That kissed the maiden all forlorn,
> That milked the cow with the crumpled horn,

That tossed the dog,
That worried the cat,
That killed the rat,
That ate the malt,
That lay in the house that Jack built.

"The House That Jack Built" had made him see that things linked together in a chain of cause and effect.

"The House That Jack Built" is an accumulative rhyme thought to have its original in the Hebrew chant "Had Gadya," One Only Kid, which relates the serial adventures of kid, cat, dog, staff, fire, water, ox, butcher, angel of death. "Then came the Most Holy, blessed be He, and slew the angel of death, who had slain the butcher, who had slaughtered the ox, which had drunk the water, which had put out the fire, which had burnt the staff, which had beaten the dog, which had bitten the cat, which had devoured the kid, which my father bought for two Zuzim; one only kid, one only kid." This verse is generally regarded as a parable, descriptive of incidents in the history of the Jewish people, with some reference to prophecies yet unfulfilled.

Holmes gazed around at the nothingness. Here was an empty attic, his to stock with such furniture as he chose.

This is the farmer sowing his corn. He summoned up, from his youth and the man's old age, George Adkins. Old George, in the faded blue smock, with the fresh flecks of blood and mud and specks of clinging straw that showed he had been in the byre for a calving; and with the painful sweep of the arm, bullet-stiffened in the Peninsular War, that showed rain in the offing. George gazed about in puzzlement, evidently seeing nothing, nothing at all, but did what he was born to do: unceasingly sow the same handful and stand his ground.

Done. Here was the entrance to the labyrinth.

Holmes visualized the entrance as a Greek temple, with caryatids holding up the entablature. Mentally, he climbed the steps and passed inside.

Moriarty's mind-voice reechoed in the pillared room. *"File on file, rank on rank, / Crocodiles on the bank."*

A monstrously large pickled cucumber with slavering jaws and slithering tail sprang into being on the tessellated marble floor to bar Holmes's way.

The idiot savant's mind spoke. *"Crocodile. A sophism framed as a dilemma, from the tale in Quintilian's Institutio Oratoria, of the crocodile who stole a boy and promised to return him if the boy's mother gave the right answer to a question, 'Am I going to return the boy or not?' If the mother says 'Yes,' the crocodile keeps the boy, and the mother has answered wrong. if the mother says 'No,' and the crocodile returns the boy, the mother has answered wrong."*

The crocodilemma pickle wept salt brine and vinegar tears.

Holmes smiled to himself, taking it with a grain of Doubter's salt. Moriarty meant for him to get bogged down in the verbal quandary. "A crocodile," he remembered, "is also something else."

Thus prompted, the idiot savant thus, *"Crocodile. A long file of girl students out for a walk."*

The great living pickle melted down into the floor till only the nostrils, eyes, and part of its back showed and it looked like a floating log, then it vanished entirely and a queue of schoolgirls in middy blouses stood in its stead.

Tap.

Holmes mentally frowned. Where did the sound come from? —No, Moriarty was seeking to distract him; he could worry about the sound later. At the moment, he had the dilemma of this new crocodile to deal with.

The little girls looked at first blush all alike. Then he felt himself drawn to one in the middle. As his gaze fixed on her, she stuck out her tongue at him. the large, pale, and flabby tongue showed toothmarks along its edges; flakes of dried tea leaves adhered to it. The plump face had clear skin, though with a greenish-yellow tinge. The months Holmes had spent at Guy's Teaching Hospital came back to him. He eyed the girl clinically. She was not all that young. She had tightened a band around her to flatten her breasts and make her seem childlike, one of the girls. But she was a woman. Tight corsets led to this condition. Greensickness.

"Greensickness. Chlorosis. Anemic disease of young women, characterized by greenish or grayish-yellow hue of the skin, weakness, palpitation, menstrual disorders, impaired digestion, etc."

"Don't forget the tea leaves on the tongue. Pica."

"Pica. Morbid appetite for unusual or unfit food, as clay, chalk, ashes, etc., especially during hysteria and pregnancy."

The girl-woman glared at Holmes. One finger of one hand sharpened one finger of the other hand at him.

What did the allegator allege? Naughty? Shame? You did it?

Before Holmes could adjust to this, the girls of the crocodile held hands in a line and then threaded their way through the selfsame line.

"Thread-needle," he murmured.

"Thread-needle. Children's game in which the players hold hands in a line and then—"

"Yes, yes," Holmes thought impatiently. "I've just thought all that. It's Threadneedle Street I'm thinking of now."

"Threadneedle Street. Commercial street in the City of London, bordering on the Bank of England."

Bank. Crocodiles on the bank. Bank of England. Holmes felt his brain hammer links. The coveralls with worn, wrinkled and stained knees. The soiled work gloves. The pickax.

Moriarty had been digging his way into the Bank of England's subterranean vaults.

Tap.

Holmes cocked his head. At last he had a fix on the sound. It came from a curtained alcove. Did Greek temples have confessionals? Sacristies?

He started toward the alcove.

Not so fast. Remember to unwind the mnemonic skein: mark this spot.

That kept a cock that crowed in the morn. Holmes summoned up a dark Cornish cockerel. Comb the color of flaming dawn, the young rooster stood atop a dunghill. Weathercock, too: Manure piles smelled stronger before a rain, and the cockerel had its head thrown back for a loud crow "Shem!" at the red cloudbank to the east.

That tableau firmly in place, Holmes strode to the alcove and whipped the curtain aside. A pitcher stood under a faucet. A bead of water formed at the lip of the spout, heavied, and started its fall.

No. Wrong image for the sound, which was *thud* rather than *plop*. The drop froze in midair.

Tap.

The right sound, and it came from behind one of two doors in the alcove's rear wall.

Moriarty's mind-voice threw itself from behind the door on the left. " 'Tap is to ale as Pat is to hod.' " Then Moriarty's mind-voice thought again. "Or is it 'Tap is to hod as Pat is to ale'? I never can get them straight."

Not that it mattered. Either phrasing directed— or misdirected— Holmes to a public house. Perhaps Moriarty felt safe; London had a power of pubs.

When hunting *the* Adler, what else but *the* Eagle?
Holmes thought at the idiot savant: "What's on tap?"

> " *'Half a pound of tuppenny rice,*
> *Half a pound of treacle.*
> *That's the way the money goes,*
> *Pop! goes the weasel.*
>
> *Up and down the City Road,*
> *In and out the Eagle.*
> *That's the way the money goes,*
> *Pop! goes the weasel.'*

The reference is to the Eagle Pub on Shepherd's Walk, City
Road, London. To pop is to pawn. The object pawned, the
weasel, may be a tailor's flatiron, a leatherworking tool, or—
from Cockney rhyming slang 'weasel and stoat'—a coat."

That was more than Holmes wanted to know. He did not let
the idiot savant's trivia distract him. He was not after weasel but
fox, and must remember to unwind his skein.

That waked the priest all shaven and shorn. Holmes summoned up a surpliced clergyman such as had stood at the altar
of the Church of St. Monica with his Bible open ready to
solemnize a psalm of Solomon.

A touch of shaving froth on the right earlobe and a nick on
the left cheek, freshly stopped (as shown by the colour of the
drying blood) with a spot of paper (rather than alum), witnessed
that the priest had toileted himself hurriedly. He may have
wakened at cockcrow, but an oily stain on the full sleeve of his
surplice told that he had been called away almost at once to give
someone extreme unction and had not had a chance to shave till
just before this ceremony.

"The surplice is surplus when you're unfrocked." Moriarty's
thought-speech staggered Holmes into chagrin and surprise.

Holmes looked hard at the visualization to make sure it was a
turned-about collar and not a turned-about head. "Do you mean
to say that Irene Adler's marriage to Godfrey Norton was not
legal?"

"A marriage is a marriage." *The* woman's throaty voice,
though heard in the mind's ear only.

"Thank you." Holmes found his own boxless voice. Though
they dashed his hitherto-unacknowledged hopes, the sincere
words put him back on the right path. Moriarty had meant

Holmes to wander off and wallow in what might have been if the wedding were a sham, a ruse to throw the King of Bohemia and his minions off, and Irene free to consort with her true match.

Holmes mastered himself. He checked that the shaven and shorn priest was in place, then opened the door on the left and found himself in the Eale.

And alone, but for the jolly man dispensing cheer. Holmes seemed the first customer of the day, and when he ordered and paid for a pint of malt liquor, the publican bit the coin, then spat on it for luck.

Holmes drew himself to the end of the counter and leaned against it, sipping slowly. The brew tasted like one hop to a pint of water.

" 'On Old Monadnock's Peaked Tops, A Finn And German Picked Some Hops.' A mnemonic used by physiology students to remember the cranial nerves: (1) Olfactory, (2) Optic, (3) Motor oculi, (4) Patheticus, (5) Trigeminal, (6) Abducent, (7) Facial, (8) Auditory, (9) Glosso-pharyngeal, (10) Pneumogastric, (11) Spinal accessory, (12) Hypoglossal. A monadnock (after the mountain in New Hampshire, U.S.A.) is a mass of rock or a hill which, as weathering or erosion removes less resistant material, rises above the peneplain. A peneplain—"

"That's quite enough of that!"

The publican, in the act of washing a glass and leaving a sizable heeltap of water in it, almost dropped the glass. But the idiot savant had been leading the way up a well-worn garden path.

As Holmes nursed the sickly drink, it struck him that because of the malt, the Jack of "The House That Jack Built" had to have been John Barleycorn. He sipped and waited. He awaited chance.

Chance had to come into any equation.

"The Greeks portrayed Chance (Tyche) as a goddess with luxuriant tresses in front but bald behind. If you let opportunity pass you by, you cannot snatch at it again."

True. And as Holmes accepted the idiot servant's truism, he thought he saw at the far end of the counter a box with a glowing window, or with what might have been a bright screen of dancing particles. The box hummed with a steady tone like the ciphering of an organ note, and there appeared on the screen in ghost letters: TYRE-TV.

"Otto von Bismarck dispatched an archaeological expedition

*to Tyre in hopes of unearthing the tomb of Frederick Barba-
rossa at the site of the twelfth century crusader cathedral,
where the Emperor's remains were supposed to have been laid
to rest, though legend has the Emperor in a cavern in the
Kyffhäuser, sitting asleep at a stone table through which his
red beard has grown, awaiting the time for him to awake and
restore the Empire.''*

Holmes smiled at the idiot savant's Bismarck citation. A
patent red herring. The Emperor had no clothes, though he may
have had moths. The box was an impossibility designed to
immobilize Holmes as Barbarossa was immobilized in the cavern
in the Kyffhauser.

"The impossible does exist," Moriarty thought at Holmes.
"It may exist as an illusion, but illusions have energy if not
matter. Take the globe of glass of Master Renard.''

Thus cued, the idiot savant thus: *"The globe of glass of
Master Renard in the medieval beast epic (in reality, a satire on
human behaviour of the time) would show what was taking
place—no matter how far off—and would display data on any
topic ever recorded. It was a wonder that existed only in the
trickster's mind.''*

"No." Then, grudgingly (because his dictum was: Never
give or take an unqualified no for an answer; it may be no for
now or no for here, but it is never no forever or for everywhere.)
Holmes thought back at Moriarty and the ambience: "No for
now and here.''

The lettering turned to snow, then the glass went black and
the box fell silent. Sans faith or hope, it became the charity box
he had been staring at.

Quickly he switched his gaze to the wall and a hunting print
of red-throated hounds in deep hue and full cry.

The place rapidly filled up with boisterous regulars, who soon
thickened the air with alcoholic sweat and yeasty breath.

Holmes withdrew to a wobbly chair in a corner and observed
them keenly without staring.

A weasel-faced man kept reaching to his vest pocket for a
watch that was no longer there. Popped. The man sat alone at a
table for two, saving the other chair by tilting it to the table and
curving an arm over its back.

A gap-toothed man across from Holmes sat with his face
fixed in a silent scream, as though shouting at inner voices to
shut up. Holmes pitied the poor wretch, then his chair squeaked

on the floor as he straightened sharply upon seeing, with double shock, that he looked in a mirror.

A buzz and a turning of heads directed him to the eyemasked woman who had come in. Her carriage and bone structure put Holmes in mind of Irene Adler. She held a lorgnette to her right eye. Though she had cheapened herself with rouge and kohl, she was clearly above the other clientele in station. Just as clearly, she stooped to an assignation, for she joined the weasel-faced man at his table. They quarreled at once in fierce whispers.

Holmes got up to freshen his drink and to eavesdrop in passing. The woman shoved to her feet just as Holmes passed. Her chair knocked into him and she threw him an absent-eyed glance of irritation.

Her partner had not risen. She indicated to him with a nod that she headed toward a room at the rear.

The man wiped a fleck of foam from his mustache. "Will you be long?"

"A kissing while. —Your pardon, your reverence, a pater-noster while."

Holmes's and the woman's paths uncrossed as she made for the back and he for the counter. It took more than a paternoster while for Holmes to draw the tapster's attention, and for the tapster to draw another malt. But the masked figure with the lorgnette was only now returning as Holmes elbowed back toward his chair.

He caught just a glimpse, but that was enough. Though the getup seemed the same, this was not Irene Adler. And the bulge of an Adam's apple under the neck scarf said this was no woman.

Mind your p's and q's, Holmes thought. The lorgnette was now at the left eye, forming a q. Cosmetics smears on the frame and handle from previous facial contact added evidence that the lorgnette was wrong side to.

A scruffy man had taken Holmes's chair, but Holmes was grateful to have reason for a loftier view. He leaned against the wall and sipped his drink—more bite to it now—as he watched the masked figure rejoin the weasel-faced man. The man's eyes followed some word of the masked figure and a gesture of the lorgnette. Mind your p's and q's, Holmes thought again, this time with grim amusement, as the masked figure's other hand slipped powder from a paper packet into the weasel-faced man's glass.

Holmes thrust his own half-empty glass at the scruffy man,

who took the half-full glass with a glazed smile. Then Holmes was at the table in a trice, his iron grip on the wiry wrist before the masked figure could dispose of the paper packet.

"Good for you, Holmes." Moriarty dropped the lorgnette and used the free hand to remove the mask and the wig. An evil smile spread over his face. "I planted the notion of poison in your mind with the bit of doggerel: *'Barking, I dog the upas tree; / Dog afore his master, that's me.'* "

"The so-called 'deadly upas tree.' Antiaris toxicaria, ord. Artocarpeae, *a tree allied to the fig, having a poisonous secretion. Legend situates it in a poisoned valley of Java, where carbonic acid gas fatal to all life is emitted."*

Moriarty overrode the idiot savant. "But you should have minded your own pints and quarts, Holmes, rather than the supernumerary's."

Holmes knew too well that Moriarty spoke truth. Holmes sought to hold on. He was losing vision fast. His strength ebbed. He gave a gasp of rage and a choke of despair; his knees gave way under him, and he fell in an inert heap upon the floor.

" *'Dog afore his master' means the swell of the sea before a storm."*

And the sea did lift the cockboat unpleasantly high alongside the brig. A bucket of sea water drowned Holmes back to life and to the realization that he was shanghaied; a heavy boot kicked him to his feet, and tarry hands shoved him at and up the swaying Jacob's ladder—though the hairy red rope made it rather an Esau's ladder.

"Tradition has it that Jacob used a reddish-gray sandstone as his pillow when he dreamed angels climbed up and down a ladder reaching to heaven (Gen. 28:11), and that the Tuatha De Danaan brought the stone to Ireland and set it up in Tara as the Lia Fáil, the Stone of Destiny. The ancient Irish kings were installed upon this stone; Fergus brought it with him to Argyll, in Scotland; then Kenneth MacAlpin, conqueror of the Picts, removed it to Scone in 843. In 1296, Edward I carried it to London, where, as the Stone of Scone, it supports the rude Chair of St. Edward on which our monarchs sit to be crowned."

Leave the emordinalapidary Lia Fail unturned. Concentrate on what's crucial, not trivial. Holmes looked round as he painfully climbed not to the gray sky but aboard the brig. It was essential that he fix his whereabouts.

That married the man all tattered and torn.

He summoned up a wax bust on a pedestal, figured out in an

old dressing gown. A soft revolver bullet fired from an airgun had torn through the head, but enough of the sharp features remained for a likeness to Holmes himself. There. Now for the scene.

Faded curlicues at the bow said this was the *Matilda*. Seaweed with small berrylike bladders dripped from the figurehead and the rigging as though she had been trapped in the Grassargo Sea—

"Sargasso Sea. Approximately 25° to 31° North by 40° to 70° west. It—"

"Grassargo." Holmes was not about to defer to the idiot savant.

The idiot savant salvaged an allusion. *"The* Argo, *in which Jason sailed in search of the Golden Fleece, had a talking prow carved of oak from the grove of Dodona, where priests and priestesses interpreted what the rustling leaves said."*

From the tidal-pool smell, Holmes inferred they were hove to at the Nore, the sandbank at the mouth of the Thames. A bully mate cuffed Holmes for standing about and set him to holystoning the deck.

"Drop the pilot," said the captain, who looked a man would pass fish eyes for pearls.

The pilot climbed down into the cockboat with a Moriarty smile. The wind had waited for the cockboat to pull away; now it filled the sails and the brig sped out to sea and into a stormy night.

Night brought Holmes no surcease. With a vile epithet for the holystoning job, the mate set Holmes another task.

"Given the length of the ship and the height of the mainmast, find the age of the captain's cat."

Without thinking, Holmes answered, "Tender years."

The pounding of breakers saved Holmes from a taste of the cat. All hands took in sail to keep the brig from blowing onto the unseen reef.

While they busied themselves, Holmes slipped below to the captain's cabin, lit the lamp, and by its swaying light, studied the Mercator chart on the table. *I bark and embark at the port you see / Midpoint a line NN to EEE.* Where to draw the line?

" *'In fourteen hundred and ninety-three, Pope Alex nailed the deep blue sea.'* Pope Alexander VI (Rodrigo Borgia) drew a line marking the span of the Spaniards and the portion of the Portuguese—to seize, despoil, and enslave the New World in the name of Christ."

Holmes took up compasses that turned in his hand to horns.
He felt Moriarty wrestle with him to swing the idiot savant's
mind from papal bull to Irish bull.

*"To milk an Irish bull, there's the Irishman aboard the ship
that was ablaze; he calmed himself by thinking, 'Sure, I'm only
a passenger.' "*

Undiverted, Holmes drew a line from Dublin to Tripoli. NN
to EEE. Roughly midpoint, the line passed through Marseille.

Holmes doused the glim and slipped back up on deck. He
crept near the wheel and crouched in shadows cast by the ship's
lantern. He held fast to a lifeline as the *Matilda* rolled, pitched,
and tossed. A faint gleam to port answered to wind and wave in
the *Matilda*'s manner. Another ship's lantern.

The captain howled into the helmsman's ear; wind whipped
the words to Holmes's. "Sea room to spare while the craft's to
leeward. Follow her lead."

The wheel creaked and the brig shuddered at the change of
course.

The captain squalled, "Tell us, prow, what the restless waves
say!"

Holmes's skin crawled at the captain's mad expectation, then
crawled even more at the figurehead's voice. It seemed, however, siren song or keening rather than speech. At least it was
no argot known to Holmes.

The captain roared a laugh and called to the lookout, who
shouted down hoarsely, "It's the *Fox*."

The idiot savant had the poop. *"The* Fox. *A vessel of 170
tons burden, fitted out by Lady Franklin, put under the command of Capt. McClintock, to sail toward the North Pole to
fathom the fate of Sir John Franklin and his two ships,* Erebus
and Terror. *On 6 May 1859, the* Fox's *crew found in a cairn a
document stating that Sir John had died 11 June 1847 after
discovering the long-sought-for Northwest Passage."*

The *Fox?* Holmes did not like the unseen cut of her jib. *I'm
flotsam, jetsam, lagan, the gift of surf; / The back of my hand, a
blaze but no kerf.* The eye of the storm opened and a constellation blazed calmly. Holmes knew nil of astronomy, but the idiot
savant recognized the pattern.

"That is Puppis, the poop of the Argo, *as seen from the
southern horse latitudes. The horse latitudes are anticyclonic
regions about 30° North and South, most likely so called because sailing ships transporting horses to America and the West*

Indies jettisoned the horses, for lack of water, when becalmed in those latitudes. Anticyclone—''

"Enough." The *Matilda* had headed not north in emulation of the *Fox* but south, and followed a false lure. "Jibber the kibber" leaped to mind.

"Jibber the kibber. A wrecker's trick of tying a lantern to a horse's neck and checking one of his legs, so that walking him moves the light like that of a ship and decoys vessels on shore."

The eye of the storm closed and the breakers thundered in Holmes's ears. Holmes leaped to the captain's side.

"The lantern's a wrecker's trick! Sheer off!"

With an oath, the captain flung Holmes aside and bawled for the mate to clap the lubber in irons.

So be it. Leave the mad captain and his whole vile crew to their fate. Holmes gave the mate a baritsu chop that felled the brute. Holmes took the mate's knife and marlinespike. The marlinespike held off the none-too-eager sailors egged on by the captain, while the knife cut loose a boat and dropped it into the sea. Knife in his teeth, Holmes dove overboard, splashed to the boat, and pulled himself in. As he fended himself off from the *Matilda* with an oar, shivering wet and wondering which way Marseille lay and how far, he thought he heard Moriarty laugh. Holmes froze. Something white and wet fell onto him.

"You have been gulled," he told himself. But even there he found himself wrong. The wet whiteness was a shred of cloth torn from the firehead.

He looked up, aghast. The figurehead was not a carven prow but a living woman bound to the stemhead.

Irene Adler.

Holmes caught hold of the anchor chain, tied the boat to the chain, and climbed the cathead. From there, he could just reach to cut the woman's bonds. Her eyes were closed and she felt dreadfully cold and still, but he thought she breathed. He lowered her into the boat, then followed and shoved them away from the brig. He chafed her hands feverishly, and called her name. Just as he gave up hope, she moaned, opened her eyes, recognized him, and smiled. Lightning flashes showed him the perfect teeth of a singer; forcing out air cleared the teeth of food particles better than a crocodile bird.

They held to one another through the night and wakened to find themselves alone on the sea and drifting toward the tropical isle. Once ashore, they found breadfruit trees and a stream of fresh water. She touched his bruises as he touched hers. Here they could heal one another. It would be easy to forget, not merely Marseille—which was, of course, only misdirection—but the world.

Holmes looked into Irene's eyes and saw this was her dream too.

No. He must be strong. Moriarty was using Circe's wiles. While Holmes dallied here in fantasy, the real world ticked inexorably on.

Holmes marked the spot with an image of itself, *That kissed the maiden all forlorn,* then wrenched himself from Irene and called up, *That waked the priest all shaven and shorn.*

And found himself walking lubberly on his sea legs past the surpliced clergyman and into the Eagle and across its swaying floor.

All the regulars had gone but the scruffy man snoring in Holmes's chair.

The publican drew a gold watch from under his apron. He opened it and snapped it shut. "Time, gentlemen."

Holmes felt a shiver of realization. *Time.* Time was behind all things. Time was before all things. Time was in all things.

That kept a cock that crowed in the morn. Holmes stood again before the alcove. He passed again through the curtain and faced the two doors.

Tap.

No mistaking it now. The sound came from behind the door not taken.

Holmes gave that door's knob a turn. Locked. Holmes heard a gasp, then a stirring within. He set himself to smash the door. But first to fix it.

That milked the cow with the crumpled horn.

Holmes summoned up an Ayrshire, with the distinctive horns that were long and curved outward, upward, and backward, and made her blind in one eye to explain why the horn on that side had struck a stone gatepost. She flicked her tail at a fly.

The idiot savant was forthcoming:

>   " 'Four stiff standers,
>   Four dilly danders,
>   Two lookers, two crookers,
>   And a wig-wag.' "

Holmes eyed the cow's busy tail. It was sending a message in Morse.

"In wigwag Morse, movements to right are dots, movements to left are dashes, movements forward are ends of words."
FLY AT ONCE. ALL IS DISCOVERED.

Moriarty's work. Holmes stood his ground. Rather, he took two steps backward, the better to hurl himself at the door.

As he burst in, he caught a glimpse of a woman's shapely ankle vanishing out a door in the far wall. That door slammed shut and the sound of a key turning in the lock quickly followed.

Holmes found himself in a study, with shelves on shelves of ribbon-tied file folders and a quivering mahogany desk. Correction, mahogany. The desk stopped quivering. On the desk stood a typewriter and a crocodile-hide handbag. Had the typist been Irene Adler? Even if not, she was the admirable type of modern woman gaining independence by going out into the business world with this new skill.

Because she *was* skilled, to go by the neat typing on the paper in the machine, she had not been slowly and laboriously hunting and pecking. She had deliberately spaced the strokes temporally so the sounds would not convey typing. Either that, or Holmes's perception of real time was out of whack.

Fast or slow, time had a *now*. Now he read the message on the sheet of foxed foolscap in the machine.

CHAIN:INGOT::LINK:SPUR

For the time being, the ratio defied ratiocination. He unrolled the sheet from the carriage. Three small, rusty spots tracked across the page like tiny pawprints: foxing. The game was truly afoot. On close inspection, the spots proved strikingly regular:

" 'I am Renard the Fox with tick tack toes . . .' The pigpen cipher, also known as the Freemasons' cipher, puts letters of the alphabet in compartments of a figure formed by two vertical lines crossing two horizontal lines. Like so:

Thus, *spells FOX."*

There might be more such foxed paper in the desk, with spots conveying other messages. —No. Moriarty sought to mire him in the sty of the cipher. Holmes must look to the light.

He held the paper to the light percolating dimly through the marble tiles of the roof. He made out the watermark: quite appropriately, a lighthouse.

Ma Я k aright and ye shall have more; Seven times, and seven times four.

Holmes mentally nudged the idiot savant. "Mind your *R*'s and Я's."

"R is the littera canina, *dog's letter, because of the growling sound. Mark 7:28 is 'And she answered and said unto him, Yes, Lord: yet the dogs under the table eat of the children's crumbs.'* Я *is a Russian letter that transliterates as* ya. Ma ЯK *is the Russian word for lighthouse.*"

Holmes saw the light.

File on file, rank on rank, / Crocodiles on the bank.

A vision intruded of the long file of girl students out for a walk. " '*Ray of young girls blessed in virginity.*' " The middy blouses took on rainbow hues as the idiot savant held forth. "*That is a mnemonic for the colors of the spectrum: red, orange, yellow, green, blue, indigo, violet.*"

No. Focus on the one with the greenish-yellow tinge. No virgin, she.

She wept. Holmes hardened his heart and the girls vanished.

Crocodile tiers. He turned the paper about and rolled it back into the machine. He tapped six *A*'s in a row, made a carriage return, tapped six *B*'s, made a carriage return, and so on to *Z*. He did not stop but appended another sixfold *A* to *Z*. Now the sheet had two alphabets down, six letters across. He rolled the sheet out of the machine. He rummaged in handbag and desk, found scissors, mucilage, and a cardboard stiffener in a ream of paper. He glued the typed sheet to the cardboard, cut the end-to-end alphabets into thin strips. Now, with more cardboard for backing and frame and for bridges over the sliding strips, he had a slide rule with a window one vertical alphabet high.

He arranged the first three columns to spell out a three-letter word in the topmost line showing in the window.

YES
ZFT
AGU
BHV
CIW

DJX
EKY
FLZ
GMA
HNB
IOC
JPD
KQE
LRF
MSG
NTH
OUI
PVJ
QWK
RXL
SYM
TZN
UAO
VBP
WOQ
XDR

The serendipitous OUI affirmed the rightness of his course. And when he set the key line to CHAIN and LINK and found INGOT and SPUR below, he knew there was no turning back.

" 'I'm in the jam, I'm in the box,
Who'd ever look there for a fox?' "

He arranged the strips to show JAMBOX across the top line in the window.

JAMBOX
KBNCPY
LCODQZ
MDPERA
NEQFSB
OFRGTC
PGSHUD
QHTIVE
RIUJWF
SJVKXG
TKWLYH
ULXMZI

VMYNAJ
WNZOBK
XOAPCL
YPBQDM
ZQCREN
ARDSFO
BSETGF
CTFUHQ
DUGVIR
EVHWJS
FWIXKT
GXJYLU
HYKZMV
IZLANW

DUGVIR?
" *'When Adam delved and Eve span,
Where was then the gentleman?'* "
Yearning for paradise lost. Irene and himself on the tropical isle. . . .
No. One more overlook. Huic holloa! Tantivy!

REN
ARD

At this, Moriarty mindspoke at his most professorial. "You were wise to limit the strips to six. The odds are quite against anything longer than six-letter strips being in what I call 'semantic phrase.' The optimum is the three-letter string. I could give you the formula—Log z rad—" He broke off. "But it involves the law of entropy, so I'll spare your brain cells the wear and tear."

For all his subtlety Moriarty was coarse-fibred, and for all his self-possession he was cross-grained.

Holmes's opinion did not faze the professor. "In this letter-universe of ours, what are the chances of generating viable 'bywords'? Take the word AND and its permutations:

NAD AND ADN DAN DNA NDA
ERH ORB HER KUH
RUE ROB

That is the most meaningful array I can extract from the noise—and at that I had to dip into Chinese and German, with an admixture of French. But as we move forward and thicken our language, more and more blanks will fill in. Not to belabor the point, in this slide-rule phenomenon we see the working of our universe—our fortuitous connections, our accidental constellations, and now our conscious splicings. Another world's thinking creatures would discover other meaningful strings, come upon other serendipities. In the beginning was the word (indeed, we may say it all began when the first word spoke itself), that is, the jamming of meaning out of noise, the coming into being of life out of not-life.''

Holmes lent only half a mind's ear. He must fix this moment, this locale. *That tossed the dog.* He summoned up a foxfirescent coalblack creature, half bloodhound, half mastiff, that sat mildly with an ear cocked curiously to a gramophone.

Mind-deaf to Moriarty, Holmes worked out with his slide the potpourri ingredients of the graffito on the base of the Monument to the Great Fire.

MAE HEAR: RUM TERRA COIN. GO COD POE UP. MAX FERO

In clear, the serendipitous-cipher message read:

GUY DAWN TO GREENWICH WE SET FEU TO THE BANK.

Holmes went mind-cold. In the real world it must be nearly two in the morning on Guy Fawkes day.

> '' *'Please to remember*
> *The Fifth of November*
> *Gunpowder treason and plot;*
> *I know no reason*
> *Why gunpowder treason*
> *Should ever be forgot.'*

At two A.M., *5 November 1605, popery, in the form of Guy Fawkes, stood ready with slow match to touch off the 36 barrels of gunpowder smuggled into the cellar and blow up James I and the House of Parliament, but was caught in time.''*

Moriarty planned to blow up the Bank of England on the anniversary's dot. How much currency could even his fore-warned confederates hope to extract from the smoking ruins and make away with in the confusion? It would be simpler and easier—and more profitable—to bring paper to the Bank than to carry away its notes or bullion. Moriarty's motive had to be not to take but to plant. Not to purloin letters of credit but to foist them. To intermingle singed fake records of accounts among the rank debris and charred files, so that they would be salvaged with the rest and honored when Moriarty and his accomplices came to collect.

Fix this solution. *That worried the cat.* Holmes sought to summon up a unique cat. With some alarm, he felt for the first time the full force of Moriarty's intellect at work against him. The image faded as quickly as Holmes formed it. The most Holmes could conjure up to stay in place was the grin of a Cheshire cat. He fought to bolster the grin with associations. *The Cheshire Grinedge of time. Gravity gives levity that cat-in-airy form. "Catenary" is portmanteau for "looking like the cat that swallowed the canary"* . . . The grin ended up as much Moriarty's as the cat's, but that would have to do.

Holmes backtracked to *That milked the cow with the crumpled horn.* he stood once more before the broken door of the study. He disregarded the warning wigwag flickering in the corner of his eye.

He re-entered the room and made for the locked door in the far wall. Before breaking down the door, he unwound his skein. *That killed the rat.* Holmes summoned up the Giant Rat of Sumatra. Even Moriarty shied away from tangling with Holmes over that dread image.

He burst into a corridor that offered him two more doors. A sign arrow pointing to the nearer door said: *THIS WAY TO THE EGRESS.* Holmes smiled shrewdly to himself. The American cousins knew there was no such animal. Robin Hood's Barnum, was what it was. He made for the farther door. Its knob gave; but before he committed himself to that choice, he unwound his skein again. *That ate the malt.*

The door opened onto an empty storeroom. But it had to be the right place. Malt had been there. The Giant Rat of Sumatra, or some rat, had gnawed a hole in the sack of barley malt. A thief had shouldered the bag, leaving a trail of spilled malt, much like Guy Fawkes's train of gunpowder. The trail led to an open window. Holmes leaned out and spotted the malt trail leading away.

He climbed out the window and followed the partly-germinated and kiln-dried grain cross a cobblestone street to a door flanked by rosebushes. A look through its glass pane showed him the inside of a pub.

This had to be his last marker.

That lay in the house that Jack built. Holmes summoned up a pub sign depicting a tipsy bottle of malt liquor with face and limbs. Sir John Barleycorn. Holmes lettered the sign.

JOLLY
CHEER.

The pub itself, no more than an imitation, a mere stage set, such as the tavern near Newgate in John Gay's *Beggar's Opera* (had not Irene sung the role of Polly Peachum?), looked dark and still. He knocked, but no one came to open the door. He hallooed, but no one answered. He was searching for the key in the eaves or in the dirt of the bushes when someone said:

"Hello, Mr. Sherlock Holmes."

He had heard that voice before.

DEJAVU

JED

UVA

Though he could not see her in the flesh, he saw her as she really was. Irene Adler. His mind touched hers. They were as one.

They knew they had not long. Holmes must find his way back out to stop the Bank from blowing up. They parted for now.

He began to rewind the skein.

This is the house that Jack built.

This is the malt that lay in the house that Jack built.

This is the rat that ate the malt that lay in the house that Jack built.

This is the cat that killed the rat that ate the malt that lay in the house that Jack built.

This is the dog that worried the cat that killed the rat that ate the malt that lay in the house that Jack built.

This is the cow with the crumpled horn that tossed the dog that worried the cat that killed the rat that ate the malt that lay in the house that Jack built.

This is the maiden all forlorn that milked the cow with the crumpled horn that tossed the dog that worried the cat that killed the rat that ate the malt that lay in the house that Jack built.

This is the man all tattered and torn that kissed the maiden all forlorn that milked the cow with the crumpled horn that tossed the dog that worried the cat that killed the rat that ate the malt that lay in the house that Jack built.

This is the priest all shaven and shorn that married the man all tattered and torn that kissed the maiden all forlorn that milked the cow with the crumpled horn that tossed the dog that worried the cat that killed the rat that ate the malt that lay in the house that Jack built.

This is the

The thread had snapped.

Of the cock that crowed in the morn, nothing. The world

stretched blank under a blank sky. Only one thing passed: a quick red fox with grease and dark feathers on his chin. Then he, too, with a Moriarty smile, vanished into blankness.

The blankness communicated itself to Holmes. He looked about blankly. There seemed nowhere to go and there seemed nowhere to stay.

Yet he had to act. If he did not do, he would cease to be.

Holmes reached as though into another dimension. His hand closed on something wrapped up and stuffed in someone's pocket. By touch alone he made out that it was a shelled and salted hardboiled egg.

He found himself calling out:

"Dr. Watson, come here. I need you."

4

I thought I heard a familiar voice summon me. I could not move to obey.

The voice called again, and this time I knew that it was Holmes's and that it spoke in my mind.

I tried to answer in the same mode.

"Holmes! What is happening?"

"No time to explain. Can you get us out of here?"

"Where is here?"

"42½ Threadneedle Street. A room in the sub-basement."

Now I remembered the blow to my head. My head throbbed with remembrance. Had I been on my feet and able to see, I should have looked round for my assailant, my knuckles set, not for lengths of months, but for battle. Marquis of Queensbury rules. Put up your dukes or go down for the count. *Do Men Ever Visit Boston?*

"Whatever on earth is that, Watson?"

"Mnemonic for the ranking of nobility. Duke, Marquis, Earl, Viscount, Baron."

"My Lord, Watson, don't tell me you're the idiot savant!"

"The what?"

"No time, no time. We are trapped together in a mental labyrinth. Do you know a way out?"

Of course I knew my way about my own mind. Hadn't I been studying that very skill? *The Greek poet Simonides (500 B.C.) invented topical mnemonics, or local association, based on a mental map of a house or a room.* I had picked the sitting room at 221B Baker Street. I located languages and word meanings in the unanswered correspondence transfixed by a jackknife in the very center of the wooden mantelpiece. I attached military matters to the portrait of General Gordon, religious matters to that of the Rev. Henry Ward Beecher, musical matters to the violin case, and so on.

Apparently Holmes caught the drift, for he said urgently, "Then bring yourself to full consciousness, old fellow, and free us all."

I made a full sweep of the sitting room, then opened the door to the landing. I found myself under a restraining sheet, but by sucking in my abdomen I gained slack, and by squirming and wriggling I winkled my arms out. I was then able to remove a monstrous helmet from my head, through that meant tearing loose some wires that had been attached to my scalp. I sat up and looked round.

There were four beds in a dank room. Holmes, though I could not see his head for his helmet, lay on one. A woman, also helmeted, lay on another. I had a third bed. The fourth bed was empty, save for an unused helmet. Wires connected the helmets to each other and to a voltaic pile.

"Hurry, Watson!" The voice was no longer the mental voice, but a dry croak, barely above a whisper, from Holmes's own lips.

I swung my feet to the floor, shoved myself erect, and walked, almost drunkenly, to Holmes's side. He was not bound, but evidently his helmet, or perceptions the helmet was responsible for, immobilized him. Gingerly, I loosened the helmet from his head, and it came away, trailing wires.

Holmes opened his eyes. I had never seen them so haunted. His eyes leaped to the fourth bed. "Moriarty's gone!" His gaze snapped to me. "The time, Watson, the time!"

I hurriedly fished out my watch. "Five of two—though I can't say whether that is A.M. or P.M."

"Five minutes! I have five minutes to find and snuff out the candle fuse!" He seemed utterly drained of energy, yet struggled to sit up.

I tried to keep him from rising too soon. He pushed me away and got to his feet unaided.

"Look after *the* woman," he threw over his shoulder as he staggered out of the room.

I saw to the woman. Still under sedation. It was better so. Poor Mrs. Hudson.

Poor Holmes as well. The bedclothing on the fourth bed was smooth, with no indentations of a human form, and felt of no human warmth. At Reichenbach Falls he had had it out with himself, had come to terms with himself, or at least shoved Moriarty deep down into the abyss of his mind. And there Moriarty had remained buried as under an avalanche, till just latterly, when the Moriarty in Holmes surfaced to do battle with him once more, for possession of his soul.

Holmes had no opponent worth of contending with him, no match for himself but himself. As Holmes had said in "A Case of Identity": "Then the fact that the two men were never together, but that the one always appeared when the other was away, was suggestive." And ever since "The Adventure of the Bruce-Partington Plans," when Holmes had said: "It is fortunate for this community that I am not a criminal," I had been unconsciously prepared for what had happened to happen.

THE DOCTOR'S CASE

Stephen King

Illustration by Sidney Paget of a scene from *The Adventure of the Noble Bachelor* in "The Strand Magazine" 1892.

I believe there was only one occasion upon which I actually solved a crime before my slightly fabulous friend, Mr. Sherlock Holmes. I say *believe* because my memory began to grow hazy about the edges round the time I attained my ninth decade; now, as I approach my centennial, the whole has become downright misty. There *may* have been another occasion, but I do not remember it, if so.

I doubt if I should ever forget this particular case no matter how murky my thoughts and memories might become, but I suspect I haven't much longer to write, and so I thought I would set it down. It cannot humiliate Holmes now, God knows; he is forty years in his grave. That, I think, is long enough to leave the tale untold. Even Lestrade, who used Holmes upon occasion but never had any great liking for him, never broke his silence in the matter of Lord Hull—he hardly could have done so, considering the circumstances. Even if the circumstances had been different, I somehow doubt if he would have. He and Holmes might bait each other, but Lestrade had a queer respect for my friend.

Why do I remember so clearly? Because the case I solved—to the best of my belief the only one I *ever* solved during my long association with Holmes was the very one Holmes wanted more than any other to solve himself.

It was a wet, dreary afternoon and the clock had just rung half past one. Holmes sat by the window, holding his violin but not playing it, looking silently out into the rain. There were times, especially after his cocaine days were behind him, when Holmes could grow moody to the point of surliness when the skies remained stubbornly gray for a week or more, and he had been doubly disappointed on this day, for the glass had been rising since late the night before and he had confidently predicted clearing skies by ten this morning at the latest. Instead, the mist which had been hanging in the air when I arose had thickened into a steady rain. And if there was anything which rendered Holmes moodier than long periods of rain, it was being wrong.

Suddenly he straightened up, tweaking a violin string with a fingernail, and smiled sardonically. "Watson! Here's a sight! The wettest bloodhound you ever saw!"

It was Lestrade, of course, seated in the back of an open waggon with water running into his close-set, fiercely inquisitive eyes. The waggon had no more than stopped before he was out, tossing the driver a coin, and striding toward 221B Baker Street. He moved so quickly that I thought he should run into our door.

I heard Mrs. Hudson remonstrating with him about his decidedly damp condition and the effect it might have on the rugs both downstairs and up, and then Holmes, who could make Lestrade look like a tortoise when the urge struck him, leaped across to the door and called down, "Let him up, Mrs. H.—I'll put a newspaper under his boots if he stays long, but I somehow think—"

Then Lestrade was bounding up the stairs, leaving Mrs. Hudson to expostulate below. His colour was high, his eyes burned, and his teeth—decidedly yellowed by tobacco—were bared in a wolfish grin.

"Inspector Lestrade!" Holmes cried jovially. "What brings you out on such a—"

No further did he get. Still panting from his climb, Lestrade said, "I've heard gypsies say the devil grants wishes. Now I believe it. Come at once if you'd have a try, Holmes; the corpse is still fresh and the suspects all in a row."

"What is it?"

"Why, what you in your pride have wished for a hundred times or more in my own hearing, my dear fellow. The perfect locked-room mystery!"

Now Holmes's eyes blazed. "You mean it? Are you serious?"

"Would I have risked wet lung riding here in an open wag-gon if I was not?" Lestrade countered.

Then, for the only time in my hearing (despite the countless times the phrase has been attributed to him), Holmes turned to me and cried: "Quick, Watson! The game's afoot!"

On our way to the home of Lord Hull, Lestrade commented sourly that Holmes also had the *luck* of the devil; although Lestrade had commanded the waggon-driver to wait, we had no more than emerged from our lodgings when that exquisite rarity clip-clopped down the street: an empty hansom cab in what had become a driving rain. We climbed in and were off in a trice. As always, Holmes sat on the left-hand side, his eyes darting restlessly about, cataloguing everything, although there was precious little to see on *that* day . . . or so it seemed, at least, to the likes of me. I've no doubt every empty street-corner and rain-washed shop window spoke volumes to Holmes.

Lestrade directed the driver to what sounded like an expen-sive address in Saville Row, and then asked Holmes if he knew Lord Hull.

"I know *of* him," Holmes said, "but have never had the good fortune of meeting him. Now it seems I never shall. Shipping, wasn't it?"

"Shipping it was," Lestrade returned, "but the good fortune was all yours. Lord Hull was, by all accounts (including those of his nearest and—ahem!—dearest), a thoroughly nasty fellow, and as dotty as a puzzle-picture in a child's novelty book. He's finished practicing both nastiness and dottiness for good, how-ever; around eleven o'clock this morning, just—" he pulled his turnip of a pocket-watch and looked at it "—two hours and forty minutes ago, someone put a knife in his back as he sat in his study with his will on the blotter before him."

"So," Holmes said thoughtfully, lighting his pipe, "you believe the study of this unpleasant Lord Hull is the perfect locked room I've been looking for all my life, do you?" His eyes gleamed skeptically through a rising rafter of blue smoke.

"I believe," Lestrade said quietly, "that it is."

"Watson and I have dug such holes before and never struck water yet," Holmes said, and he glanced at me before returning to his ceaseless catalogue of the streets through which we passed. "Do you recall the 'Speckled Band,' Watson?"

I hardly needed to answer him. There had been a locked room in that business, true enough, but there had also been a ventilator, a snake full of poison, and a killer evil enough to allow the one into the other. It had been devilish, but Holmes had seen to the bottom of the matter in almost no time at all.

"What are the facts, Inspector?" Holmes asked.

Lestrade began to lay them before us in the clipped tones of a trained policeman. Lord Albert Hull had been a tyrant in business and a despot at home. His wife was a mousy, terrified thing. The fact that she had borne him three sons seemed to have in no way sweetened his feelings toward her. She had been reluctant to speak of their social relations, but her sons had no such reservations; their papa, they said, had missed no opportunity to dig at her, to criticize her, or to jest at her expense . . . all of this when they were in company. When they were alone, he virtually ignored her. And, Lestrade, added, he sometimes beated her.

"William, the eldest, told me she always gave out the same story when she came to the breakfast table with a swollen eye or a mark on her cheek; that she had forgotten to put on her glasses and had run into a door. 'She ran into doors once and twice a week,' William said. 'I didn't know we had that many doors in the house.' "

"Hmmm!" Holmes said. "A cheery fellow! The sons never put a stop to it?"

"She wouldn't allow it," Lestrade said.

"Insanity," I returned. A man who would beat his wife is an abomination; a woman who would allow it an abomination and a perplexity.

"There was method in her madness, though," Lestrade said. "Although you'd not know it to look at her, she was twenty years younger than Hull. He had always been a heavy drinker and a champion diner. At age sixty, five years ago, he developed gout and angina."

"Wait for the storm to end and then enjoy the sunshine," Holmes remarked.

"Yes," Lestrade said. "He made sure they knew both his worth and the provisions of his will. They were little better than slaves—"

"—and the will was the document of indenture," Holmes murmured.

"Exactly so. At the time of his death, his worth was three hundred thousand pounds. He never asked them to take his word for this; he had his chief accountant to the house quarterly to detail the balance sheets of Hull Shipping . . . although he kept the purse-strings firmly in his own hands and tightly closed.''

"Devilish!" I exclaimed, thinking of the cruel boys one sometimes sees in Eastcheap or Piccadilly, boys who will hold out a sweet to a starving dog to see it dance . . . and then gobble it themselves. Within moments I discovered this comparison was even more apt than I thought.

"On his death, Lady Rebecca Hull was to receive one hundred and fifty thousand pounds. William, the eldest, was to receive fifty thousand; Jory, the middler, forty; and Stephen, the youngest, thirty."

"And the other thirty thousand?" I asked.

"Seven thousand, five hundred each to his brother in Wales and an aunt in Brittany (not a cent for *her* relatives), five thousand in assorted bequests to the servants at the town-house and the place in the country, and—you'll like this, Holmes—ten thousand pounds to Mrs. Hemphill's Home for Abandoned Pussies."

"You're *joking!*" I cried, although if Lestrade expected a similar reaction from Holmes, he was disappointed. Holmes merely re-lighted his pipe and nodded as if he had expected this, or something like it. "With babies dying of starvation in the East End and homeless orphans still losing all the teeth out of their jaws by the age of ten in the sulphur factories, this fellow left ten thousand pounds to a . . . a boarding-hotel for *cats?*"

"I mean exactly that," Lestrade said pleasantly. "Furthermore, he should have left *twenty-seven times* that amount to Mrs. Hemphill's Abandoned Pussies if not for whatever happened this morning—and whoever who did the business."

I could only gape at this, and try to multiply in my head. While I was coming to the conclusion that Lord Hull had intended to disinherit both wife and children in favor of an orphanage for felines, Holmes was looking sourly at Lestrade and saying something which sounded to me like a total *non sequitur*. "I am going to sneeze, am I not?"

Lestrade smiled. It was a smile of transcendent sweetness. "Oh yes, my dear Holmes. I fear you will sneeze often and profoundly."

Holmes removed his pipe, which he had just gotten drawing to his satisfaction (I could tell by the way he settled back slightly in his seat), looked at it for a moment, and then held it out into the rain. I watched him knock out the damp and smouldering tobacco, more dumbfounded than ever. If you had told me then that I was to be the one to solve this case, I believe

I should have been impolite enough to laugh in your face. At that point I didn't even know what the case was *about*, other than that someone (who more and more sounded the sort of person who deserved to stand in the courtyard of Buckingham Palace for a medal rather than in the Old Bailey for sentencing) had killed this wretched Lord Hull before he could leave his family's rightful due to a gaggle of street cats.

"How many?" Holmes asked.

"Ten," Lestrade said.

"I suspected it was more than this famous locked room of yours that brought you out in the back of an open waggon on such a wet day," Holmes said sourly.

"Suspect as you like," Lestrade said gaily. "I'm afraid I must go on, but if you'd like, I could let you and the good doctor out here."

"Never mind," Holmes said. "When did he become sure that he was going to die?"

"Die?" I said. "How can you know he—"

"It's obvious, Watson," Holmes said. "It amused him to keep them in bondage by the means of his will." He looked at Lestrade. "No trust arrangements, I take it?"

Lestrade shook his head.

"Nor entailments of any sort?"

"None."

"Extraordinary!" I said.

"He wanted them to understand all would be theirs when he did them the courtesy of dying, Watson," Holmes said, "but he never actually intended for them to have it. He realized he was dying. He waited . . . and then he called them together this morning . . . this morning, Inspector, yes?"

Lestrade nodded.

"Yes. He called them together this morning and told them that he had made a new will which disinherited them one and all . . . except for the servants and the distant relatives, I suppose."

I opened my mouth to speak, only to discover I was too outraged to say anything. The image which kept returning to my mind was that of those cruel boys, making the starving East End curs jump with a bit of pork or a crumb of crust from a meat pie. I must add it never occurred to me to ask if such a will could not be disputed before the bar. Today a man would have a deuce of a time slighting his closest relatives in favor of a hotel for pussies, but in 1899, a man's will was a man's will, and unless many examples of insanity—not eccentricity but outright *insanity*—could be proved, a man's will, like God's, was done.

"This new will was properly witnessed?" Holmes asked, immediately putting his finger on the one possible loophole in such a wretched scheme.

"Indeed it was," Lestrade replied. "Yesterday Lord Hull's solicitor and one of his assistants appeared at the house and were shown into his study. There they remained for about fifteen minutes. Stephen Hull says the solicitor once raised his voice in protest about something—he could not tell what—and was silenced by Hull. Jory, the third son, was upstairs, painting, and Lady Hull was calling on a friend. But both Stephen and William saw them enter and leave. William said that when the solicitor and his assistant left, they did so with their heads down, and although William spoke, asking Mr. Barnes—the solicitor—if he was well, and making some social remark about the persistence of the rain, Barnes did not reply and the assistant seemed to actually cringe. It was as if they were ashamed, William said."

Well, there it was: witnesses. So much for *that* loophole, I thought.

"Since we are on the subject, tell me about the boys," Holmes said, putting his slender fingers together.

"As you like. It goes pretty much without saying that their hatred for the pater was exceeded only by the pater's boundless contempt for them . . . although how he could hold Stephen in contempt is . . . well, never mind, I'll keep things in their proper order."

"How good of you, Inspector Lestrade," Holmes said dryly.

"William is thirty-six. If his father had given him any sort of allowance, I suppose he would be a bounder. As he had little or none, he took long walks during the days, went out to the coffee-houses at night, or, if he happened to have a bit more money in his pockets, to a card-house, where he would lose it quickly enough. Not a pleasant man, Holmes. A man who has no purpose, no skill, no hobby, and no ambition (save to outlive his father), could hardly be a pleasant man. I had the queerest idea while I was talking to him—that I was interrogating an empty vase on which the face of the Lord Hull had been lightly stamped."

"A vase waiting for the pater's money to fill him up," Holmes commented.

"Jory is another matter. Hull saved most of his contempt for Jory, calling him from his earliest childhood by such endearing pet-names as 'fish-face' and 'keg-legs' and 'stoat-belly.' It's not hard to understand such names, unfortunately; Jory Hull stands no more than five feet tall, if that, is bow-legged, slump-shouldered, and of a remarkably ugly countenence. He looks a bit like that poet fellow, the pouf.''

"Oscar Wilde?'' asked I.

Holmes turned a brief, amused glance upon me. "I believe Lestrade means Algernon Swinburne,'' he said. "Who, I believe, is no more a pouf than you are, Watson.''

"Jory Hull was born dead,'' Lestrade said. "After he remained blue and still for an entire minute, the doctor pronounced him so and put a napkin over his misshapen body. Lady Hull, in her one moment of heroism, sat up, removed the napkin, and dipped the baby's legs into the hot water which had been brought to attend the birth. The baby began to squirm and squall.''

Lestrade grinned and lit a cigarillo with a match undoubtedly dipped by one of the urchins of whom I had just been thinking.

"Hull himself, always munificent, blamed this immersion for his bow legs.''

Holmes's only comment on this extraordinary (and to my physician's mind rather suspect) story was to suggest that Lestrade had gotten a large body of information from his suspects in a short period of time.

"One of the aspects of the case which I thought would appeal to you, my dear Holmes,'' Lestrade said as we swept into Rotten Row in a splash and a swirl. "They need no coercion to speak; coercion's what it would take to shut 'em up. They've had to remain silent all too long. And then there's the fact that the new will is gone. Relief loosens tongues beyond measure, I find.''

"Gone!'' I exclaimed, but Holmes took no notice. He asked Lestrade about this misshapen middle child.

"Ugly as he is, I believe his father continually heaped vituperation on his head because—''

"Because Jory was the only son who had no need to depend upon his father's money to make his way in the world,'' Holmes said complaisently.

Lestrade started. "The devil! How did you know that?''

"Rating a man with faults which all can see is the act of a man who is afraid as well as vindictive,'' Holmes said. "What was his key to the cell door?''

"As I told you, he paints,'' Lestrade said.

"Ah!"

Jory Hull was, as the canvases in the lower halls of Hull House later proved, a very good painter indeed. Not great; I do not mean to suggest he was. But his renderings of his mother and brothers were faithful enough so that, years later, when I saw color photographs for the first time, my mind flashed back to that rainy November afternoon in 1899. And the one of his father, which he showed us later . . . perhaps it *was* Algernon Swinburne that Jory resembled, but his father's likeness—at least as seen through Jory's hand and eye—reminded me of an Oscar Wilde character: that nearly immortal *roué,* Dorian Gray.

His canvases were long, slow processes, but he was able to quick-sketch with such nimble rapidity that he might come home from Hyde Park on a Saturday afternoon with as much as twenty pounds in his pockets.

"I wager his father enjoyed *that,*" Holmes said. He reached automatically for his pipe and then put it back. "The son a Peer of the Realm quick-sketching well-off American tourists and their sweethearts like a French Bohemian."

"He raged over it," Lestrade said, "but Jory wouldn't give over his selling stall in Hyde Park . . . not, at least, until his father agreed to an allowance of thirty-five pounds a week. He called it low blackmail."

"My heart bleeds," I said.

"As does mine, Watson," Holmes said. "The third son, Lestrade—we've almost reached the house, I believe."

As Lestrade had said, surely Stephen Hull had the greatest cause to hate his father. As his gout grew worse and his head more befuddled, Lord Hull surrendered more and more of the company affairs to Stephen, who was only twenty-eight at the time of his father's death. The responsibilities devolved upon Stephen, and the blame devolved upon him if his least decision proved amiss . . . and yet no financial gain devolved upon him should he decide well.

As the only of his three children with an interest in the business he had founded, Lord Hull should have looked upon his son with approval. As a son who not only kept his father's shipping business prosperous when it might have foundered due to Lord Hull's own increasing physical and mental problems (and all of this as a young man) he should have been looked upon with love and gratitude as well. Instead, Stephen had been rewarded with suspicion, jealousy and his father's belief—spoken more and more often—that his son "would steal the pennies from a dead man's eyes."

"The b———d!" I cried, unable to contain myself.

"He saved the business and the fortune," Holmes said, steepling his fingers again, "and yet his reward was still to be the youngest son's share of the spoil. What, by the way, was to be the disposition of the company by the new will?"

"It was to be handed over to the Board of Directors, Hull Shipping, Ltd., with no provision for the son," Lestrade said, and pitched his cigarillo as the hackney swept up the curving drive of a house which looked extraordinarily ugly to me just then, as it stood amid its dead lawns in the rain. "Yet with the father dead and the new will nowhere to be found, Stephen Hull comes into thirty thousand. The lad will have no trouble. He has what the Americans call 'leverage.' The company will have him as managing director. They should have done anyway, but now it will be on Stephen Hull's terms."

"Yes," Holmes said. "Leverage. A good word." He leaned out into the rain. "Stop short, driver!" he cried. "We've not quite done!"

"As you say, guv'nor," the driver returned, "but it's devilish wet out here."

"And you'll go with enough in your pocket to make your innards as wet and devilish as you out'ards," Holmes said, which seemed to satisfy the driver, who stopped thirty yards from the door. I listened to the rain tip-tapping on the roof while Holmes cogitated and then said: "The old will—the one he teased them with—*that* document isn't missing, is it?"

"Absolutely not. It was on his desk, near his body."

"Four excellent suspects! Servants need not be considered . . . or so it seems now. Finish quickly, Lestrade—the final circumstances, and the locked room."

Lestrade complied in less than ten minutes, consulting his notes from time to time. A month previous, Lord Hull had observed a small black spot on his right leg, directly behind the knee. The family doctor was called. His diagnosis was gangrene, an unusual but far from rare result of gout and poor circulation. The doctor told him the leg would have to come off, and well above the site of the infection.

Lord Hull laughed at this until tears streamed down his cheeks. The doctor, who had expected any other reaction than this, was struck speechless. "When they stick me in my coffin, sawbones,'' Hull said, ''it will be with both legs still attached, thank you.''

The doctor told him that he sympathized with Lord Hull's wish to keep his leg, but that without amputation he would be dead in six months . . . and he would spend the last two in exquisite pain. Lord Hull asked the doctor what his chances of survival should be if he were to undergo the operation. He was still laughing, Lestrade said, as though it were the best joke he had ever heard. After some hemming and hawing, the doctor said the odds were even.

''Bunk,'' said I.

''Exactly what Lord Hull said,'' Lestrade replied. ''Except he used a term a bit more vulgar.''

Hull told the doctor that he himself reckoned his chances at no better than one in five. ''As to the pain, I don't think it will come to that,'' he went on, ''as long as there's laudanum and a spoon to stir it with in stumping distance.''

The next day, Hull finally sprang his nasty surprise—that he was thinking of changing his will. Just how he did not say.

''Oh?'' Holmes said, looking at Lestrade from those cool gray eyes that saw so much. ''And who, pray, was surprised?''

''None of them, I should think. But you know human nature, Holmes; how people hope against hope.''

''And how some plan against disaster,'' Holmes said dreamily.

This very morning Lord Hull had called his family into the parlor, and when all were settled, he performed an act few testators are granted, one which is usually performed by the wagging tongues of their solicitors after their own have been silenced forever. In short, he read them his new will, leaving the balance of his estate to Mrs. Hemphill's wayward pussies. In the silence which followed he rose, not without difficulty, and favored them all with a death's-head grin. And leaning over his cane, he made the following declaration, which I find as astoundingly vile now as I did when Lestrade recounted it to us in that hackney cab: ''So! All is fine, is it not? Yes, very fine! You have served me quite faithfully, woman and boys, for some forty years. Now I intend, with the clearest and most serene conscience imaginable, to cast you hence. But take heart! Things could be worse! If there was time, the pharaohs had their favorite pets—cats, for the most part—killed before they died, so the pets might be there to welcome them into the after-life, to be kicked or petted there, at their masters' whims, for-ever . . . and for-ever . . . and for-ever.'' Then he began to laugh at them. He leaned over his cane and laughed from his doughy livid dying face, the new will—signed and witnessed, as all of them had seen—clutched in one claw of a hand.

William rose and said, "Sir, you may be my father and the author of my existence, but you are also the lowest creature to crawl upon the face of the earth since the serpent tempted Eve in the Garden."

"Not at all!" the old monster returned, still laughing. "I know four lower. Now, if you will pardon me, I have some important papers to put away in my safe . . . and some worthless ones to burn in the stove."

"He still had the old will when he confronted them?" Holmes asked. He seemed more interested than startled.

"Yes."

"He could have burned it as soon as the new one was signed and witnessed," Holmes mused. "He had all the previous afternoon and evening to do so. But that wasn't enough, was it? What do you suppose, Lestrade?"

"That he was teasing them. Teasing them with a chance he believed all would refuse."

"There is another possibility," Holmes said. "He spoke of suicide. Isn't it possible that such a man might hold out such a temptation, knowing that if one of them—Stephen seems most likely from what you say—would do it for him, be caught . . . and swing for it?"

I stared at Holmes in silent horror.

"Never mind," Holmes said. "Go on."

The four of them had sat in paralyzed silence as the old man made his long slow way up the corridor to his study. There were no sounds but the thud of his cane, the laboured rattle of his breathing, the plaintive *miaow* of a cat in the kitchen, and the steady beat of the pendulum in the parlour clock. Then they heard the squeal of hinges as Hull opened his study door and stepped inside.

"Wait!" Holmes said sharply, sitting forward. "No one actually saw him go in, did they?"

"I'm afraid that's not so, old chap," Lestrade returned. "Mr. Oliver Stanley, Lord Hull's valet, had heard Lord Hull's progress down the hall. He came from Hull's dressing chamber, went to the gallery railing, and called down to ask if Hull was all right. Hull looked up—Stanley saw him as plainly as I see you right now, old fellow—and said he was feeling absolutely tip-top. Then he rubbed the back of his head, went in, and locked the study door behind him. By the time he reached the door (the corridor is quite long and it may have taken him as long as two minutes to make his way up it without help) Stephen had shaken off his stupor and had gone to the parlour door. He saw the exchange between his father and his father's man. Of course his father was back-to, but he heard his father's voice and described the same gesture: Hull rubbing the back of his head.''

"Could Stephen Hull and this Stanley fellow have spoken before the police arrived?" I asked—shrewdly, I thought.

"Of course they could, and probably did," Lestrade said wearily. "But there was no collusion."

"You feel sure of that?" Holmes asked, but he sounded uninterested.

"Yes. Stephen Hull would lie very well, I think, but Stanley would do so badly. Accept my professional opinion or not just as you like, Holmes."

"I accept it."

So Lord Hull passed into his study, the famous locked room, and all heard the click of the lock as he turned the key—the only key there was to that *sanctum sanctorum*. This was followed by a more unusual sound: the bolt being drawn across.

Then, silence.

The four of them—Lady Hull and her sons, so shortly to be blue-blooded paupers—looked at each other in silence. The cat *miaowed* again from the kitchen and Lady Hull said in a distracted voice that if the housekeeper wouldn't give that cat a bowl of milk, she supposed she must. She said the sound of it would drive her mad if she had to listen to it much longer. She left the parlour. Moments later, without a word among them, the three sons also left. William went to his room upstairs, Stephen wandered into the music room. And Jory went to sit upon a bench beneath the stairs where, he had told Lestrade, he had gone since earliest child when he was sad or had matters of deep difficulty to think over.

Less than five minutes later a terrible shriek arose from the study. Stephen bolted out of the music room, where he had been plinking out isolated notes on the piano. Jory met him at the door. William was already halfway downstairs and saw them breaking in when Stanley, the valet, came out of Lord Hull's dressing room and went to the gallery railing for the second time. He saw Stephen Hull burst the study door in; he saw William reach the foot of the stairs and almost fall on the marble; he saw Lady Hull come from the dining room doorway with a pitcher of milk still in one hand. Moments later the rest of the servants had gathered. Lord Hull was slumped over his writing desk with the three brothers standing by. His eyes were open. There was a snarl on his lips, a look of ineffable surprise in his eyes. Clutched in his hand was his will . . . the old one. Of the new one there was no sign. And there was a dagger in his back.''

With this Lestrade rapped for the driver to go on.

We entered between two constables as stone-faced as Buckingham Palace sentinels. Here was a very long hall, floored in black and white marble tiles like a chessboard. They led to an open door at the end, where two more constables were posted. The infamous study. To the left were the stairs, to the right two doors: the parlour and the music room, I guessed.

"The family is gathered in the parlour," Lestrade said.

"Good," Holmes said pleasantly. "But perhaps Watson and I might first have a look at this locked room."

"Shall I accompany you?"

"Perhaps not," Holmes said. "Has the body been removed?"

"It had not been when I left for your lodgings, but by now it should be gone."

"Very good."

Holmes started away. I followed. Lestrade called, "Holmes!"

Holmes turned, eyebrows upraised.

"No secret panels, no secret doors. Take my word or not, as you like."

"I believe I'll wait until . . ." Holmes began, and then his breath began to hitch. He scrambled in his pocket, found a napkin probably carried absently away from the eating-house where we had dined the previous evening, and sneezed mightily into it. I looked down and saw a large scarred tomcat, as out of place here in this grand hall as would have been one of those sulphur-factory urchins, twining about Holmes's legs, One of its ears was laid back against its scarred skull. The other was gone, lost in some long-ago alley battle, I supposed.

Holmes sneezed repeatedly and kicked out at the cat. It went with a reproachful backward look rather than with the angry hiss one would have expected from such an old campaigner. Holmes looked at Lestrade over the napkin with reproachful, watery eyes. Lestrade, not in the least put out of countenance, grinned. "Ten, Holmes," he said. *"Ten.* House is full of felines. Hull loved 'em." With that Lestrade walked off.

"How long, old fellow?" I asked.

"Since forever," he said, and sneezed again. I still believe, I am bound to add, that the solution to the locked room problem would have been as readily apparent to Holmes as it was to me if not for this unfortunate affliction. The word *allergy* was hardly known all those years ago, but that, of course, was his problem.

"Do you want to leave?" I was a bit alarmed. I had once seen a case of near asphyxiation as the result of such an aversion to sheep.

"He'd like that," Holmes said. I did not need him to tell me who he meant. Holmes sneezed once more (a large red welt was appearing on his normally pale forehead) and then we passed between the constables at the study door. Holmes closed it behind him.

The room was long and relatively narrow. It was at the end of something like a wing, the main house spreading to either side from an area roughly three-quarters of the way down the hall. Thus there were windows on both sides and the room was well-lit in spite of the gray, rainy day. There were framed shipping charts on most of the walls, but on one was a really handsome set of weather instruments in a brass-bound case: an anemometer (Hull had the little whirling cups mounted on one of the roof-peaks, I supposed), two thermometers (one registering the outdoor temperature and the other that of the study), and a barometer much like the one that had fooled Holmes into believing the bad weather would finally break. I noticed the glass was still rising, then looked outside. The rain was falling harder than ever, rising glass or no rising glass. We believe we know a great lot, with our instruments and things, but we don't know half as much as we think we do.

Holmes and I both turned to look at the door. The bolt was torn free, but leaning inward, as it should have been. The key was still in the lock, and still turned.

Holmes's eyes, watering as they were, were everywhere at once, noting, cataloging, storing.

"You are a little better," I said.

"Yes," he said, lowering the napkin and stuffing it indifferently back into his coat pocket. "He may have loved 'em, but he apparently didn't allow 'em in here. Not on a regular basis, anyway. What do you make of it, Watson?"

Although my eyes were slower than his, I was also looking around. The double windows were all locked with thumb-turns and small brass side-bolts. None of the panes had been broken. The framed charts and weather instruments were between these windows. The other two walls, before and behind the desk which dominated the room, were filled with books. There was a small coal-stove at the south end of the room but no fireplace . . . the murderer hadn't come down the chimney like St. Nicholas, not unless he was narrow enough to fit through a stove-pipe and clad in an asbestos suit, for the stove was still very warm. The north end of this room was a little library, with two high-backed upholstered chairs and a coffee-table between them. On this table was a random stack of books. The ceiling was plastered. The floor was covered with a large Turkish rug. If the murderer had come up through a trap-door, I hadn't the slightest idea how he could have gotten back under that rug without disarranging it, and it was not disarranged in the slightest: it was smooth, and the shadows of the coffee-table legs lay across it without a ripple.

"Did you believe it, Watson?" Holmes asked, snapping me out of something like a hypnotic trance. Something . . . something about that coffee-table . . .

"Believe what, Holmes?"

"That all four of them simply walked out of that parlour, in four different directions, four minutes before the murder?"

"I don't know," I said faintly.

"*I* don't believe it; not for a mo—" He broke off. "Watson! Are you all right?"

"No," I said in a voice I could hardly hear myself. I collapsed into one of the library chairs. My heart was beating too fast. I couldn't seem to catch my breath. My head was pounding; my eyes seemed to have suddenly grown too large for their sockets. I could not take them from the shadows of the coffee-table legs upon the rug. "I am most . . . most definitely not . . . not all right."

At that moment Lestrade appeared in the study doorway. "If you've looked your fill, H—" He broke off. "What the devil's the matter with Watson?"

"I believe," said Holmes in a calm, measured voice, "that Watson has solved the case. Have you, Watson?"

I nodded my head. Not all of it, perhaps, but most. I knew who; I knew how.

"Is it this way with you, Holmes?" I asked. "When you . . . see?"

"Yes," he said.

"*Watson's* solved the case?" Lestrade said impatiently. "Bah! Watson's offered a thousand solutions to a hundred cases before this, Holmes, as you very well know—all of them wrong. Why, I remember just this late summer—"

"I know more about Watson than you shall ever know," Holmes said, "and this time he has hit upon it. I know the look." He began to sneeze again; the cat with the missing ear had wandered into the room through the door, which Lestrade had left open. It headed directly for Holmes with an expression of what seemed to be affection on its ugly face.

"If this is how it is for you," I said, "I'll never envy you again, Holmes. My heart should burst."

"One becomes enured even to insight," Holmes said, with not the slightest trace of conceit in his voice. "Out with it, then . . . or shall we bring in the suspects, as in the last chapter of a detective novel?"

"No!" I cried in horror. I had seen none of them; I had no urge to. "Only I think I must *show* you how it was done. If you and Inspector Lestrade will only step out into the hall for a moment—"

The cat reached Holmes and jumped into his lap, purring like the most satisfied creature on earth.

Holmes exploded into a perfect fusillade of sneezes. The red patches on his face, which had begun to fade, burst out afresh. He pushed the cat away and stood up.

"Be quick, Watson, so we can be away from this damned place," he said in a muffled voice, and left his perfect locked room with his shoulders in an uncharacteristic hunch, his head down, and with not a single look back. Believe me when I say that a little of my heart went with him.

Lestrade stood leaning against the door, his wet coat steaming slightly, his leps parted in a detestable grin. "Shall I take Holmes's new admirer, Watson?"

"Leave it," I said, "but close the door."

"I'd lay a fiver you're wasting our time, old man," Lestrade said, but I saw something different in his eyes: if I'd offered to take him up on the wager, he would have found a way out of it.

"Close the door," I repeated. "I shan't be long."

He closed the door. I was alone in Hull's study . . . except for the cat, of course, which was now sitting in the middle of the rug, tail curled neatly about its paws, green eyes watching me.

I felt in my pockets and found my own souvenir from last night's dinner—bachelors are rather untidy people, I fear, but there was a reason for the bread other than general slovenliness. I almost always kept a crust in one pocket or the other, for it amused me to feed the pigeons that landed outside the very window where Holmes had been sitting when Lestrade drove up.

"Pussy," said I, and put the bread beneath the coffee-table— the coffee-table to which Lord Hull would have presented his back when he sat down with his two wills—the wretched old one and the even more wretched new one. "Pussy-pussy-pussy."

The cat rose and walked languidly beneath the table to investigate.

I went to the door and opened it. "Holmes! Lestrade! Quickly!" They came in.

"Step over here." I walked to the coffee-table. Lestrade looked about and began to frown, seeing nothing; Holmes, of course, began to sneeze again. "Can't we have that wretched thing out of here?" he managed from behind the table-napkin, which was now quite soggy.

"Of course," said I. *"But where is it, Holmes"*

A startled expression filled his eyes above the napkin. Lestrade whirled, walked toward Hull's writing desk, and behind it. Holmes knew his reaction should not have been so violent if the cat had been on the far side of the room. He bent and looked beneath the coffee-table, saw nothing but empty space and the bottom row of the two book-cases on the north wall of the room, and straightened up again. If his eyes had not spouting like fountains, he should have seen the illusion then; he was right on top of it. But all the same, it was devilishly good. The empty space under that coffee-table had been Jory Hull's masterpiece.

"I don't—" Holmes began, and then the cat, who found Holmes much more to its liking than the bread, strolled out from beneath the table and began once more to twine ecstatically about his ankles. Lestrade had returned, and his eyes grew so wide I thought they might actually fall out. Even having seen through it, I myself was awazed. The scarred tomcat seemed to be materializing out of thin air; head, body, white-tipped tail last.

It rubbed against Holmes leg, purring as Holmes sneezed.

"That's enough," I said. "You've done your job and may leave."

I picked it up, took it to the door (getting a good scratch for my pains), and tossed it unceremoniously into the hall. I shut the door behind it.

Holmes was sitting down. "My God," he said in a nasal, clogged voice. Lestrade was incapable of any speech at all. His eyes never left the table and the faded red Turkish rug beneath its legs: and empty space that had somehow given birth to a cat.

"I should have seen," Holmes was muttering. "Yes . . . but you . . . how did you understand so *quickly?*" I detected the faintest hurt and pique in that voice . . . and forgave it.

"It was *those,*" I said, and pointed at the shadows thrown by the table-legs.

"Of course!" Holmes nearly groaned. He slapped his welted forehead. "idiot! I'm a perfect *idiot!*"

"Nonsense," I said tartly. "With ten cats in the house and one who has apparently picked you out for a special friend, I suspect you were seeing ten of everything."

Lestrade finally found his voice. "What about the shadows?"

Show him, Watson," Holmes said wearily, lowering the napkin into his lap.

So I bent and picked one of the shadows off the floor.

Lestrade sat down in the other chair, hard, like a man who has been unexpectedly punched.

"I kept looking at them, you see," I said, speaking in a tone which could not help being apologetic. This seemed all wrong. It was Holmes's job to explain the whos and hows. Yet while I saw that he now understood everything, I knew he would refuse to speak in this case. And I suppose a part of me—the part that knew I would probably never have another chance to do something like this—*wanted* to be the one to explain. And the cat was rather a nice touch, I must say. A magician could have done no better with a rabbit and a top-hat.

"I knew something was wrong, but it took a moment for it to sink in. This room is extremely well lighted, but today it's pouring down rain. Look around and you'll see that not a single object in this room casts a shadow . . . *except for these table-legs.*"

Lestrade uttered an oath.

"It's rained for nearly a week," I said, "but both Holmes's barometer and the late Lord Hull's—" I pointed to it "—said that we could expect sun today. In fact, it seemed a sure thing. So he added the shadows as a final touch."

"Who did?"

"Jory Hull," Holmes said in that same weary tone. "Who else?"

I bent down and reached my hand beneath the right end of the coffee-table. It disappeared into thin air, just as the cat had appeared. Lestrade uttered another startled oath. I tapped the back of the canvas stretched tightly between the forward legs of the coffee-table. The books and the rug bulged and rippled, and the illusion, nearly perfect as it had been, was dispelled.

Jory Hull had painted the nothing under his father's coffee-table; had crouched behind the nothing as his father entered the room, locked the door, and sat at his desk with his two wills, the new and the old. And when he began to rise again from his seat, he rushed out from behind the nothing, dagger in hand.

"He was the only one who could execute such a piece of realism," I said, this time running my hand down the face of the canvas. We could all hear the low rasping sound it made, like the purr of a very old cat. "The only one who could execute it, and the only one who could hide behind it: Jory Hull, who was no more than five feet tall, bow-legged, slump-shouldered.

"As Holmes said, the surprise of the new will was no surprise. Even if the old man had been secretive about the possibility of cutting the relatives out of the will, which he wasn't, only simpletons could have mistaken the import of the visit from the solicitor and, more important, the assistant. It takes two witnesses to make a will a valid document at Chancery. What Holmes said about some people preparing for disaster was very true. A canvas as perfect as this was not made overnight, or in a month. You may find he had it ready—should it need to be used—for as long as a year—"

"Or five," Holmes interpolated.

"I suppose. At any rate, when Hull announced that he wanted to see his family in the parlour this morning, I suppose Jory knew the time had come. After his father had gone to bed last night, he would have come down here and mounted his canvas. I suppose he may have put down the false shadows at the same time, but if I had been him I should have tip-toed in here for another peek at the glass this morning, before the parlour gathering, just to make sure it was still rising. If the door was locked, I suppose he filched the key from his father's pocket and returned it later."

"Wasn't locked," Lestrade said shortly. "As a rule he kept it closed to keep the cats out, but rarely locked it."

"As for the shadows, they are just strips of felt, as you now see. His eye was good; they are about where they would have been at eleven this morning . . . if the glass had been right.''

"If he expected the sun to be shining, why did he put down shadows at all?'' Lestrade grumped. ''Sun puts 'em down as a matter of course, just in case you've never noticed your own, Watson.''

Here I was at a loss. I looked at Holmes, who seemed grateful to have *any* part in the answer.

"Don't you see? That is the greatest irony of all! If the sun had shone as the glass suggested it would, the canvas would have *blocked* the shadows. Painted shadow-legs don't cast them, you know. He was caught by shadows on a day when there were none because he was afraid he would be caught by none on a day when his father's barometer said they would almost certainly be everywhere else in the room.''

"I still don't understand how Jory got in here without Hull seeing him,'' Lestrade said.

"That puzzled me as well,'' Holmes said—dear old Holmes! I doubt if it puzzled him a bit, but that was what he said. ''Watson?''

"The parlor where the four of them sat has a door which communicates with the music room, does it not?''

"Yes,'' Lestrade said, ''and the music room has a door which communicates with Lady Hull's morning room, which is next in line as one goes toward the back of the house. But from the morning room one can only go back into the hall, Doctor Watson. If there had been *two* doors into Hull's study, I should hardly have come after Holmes on the run as I did.''

He said this last in tones of faint self-justification.

"Oh, he went back into the hall, all right,'' I said, ''but his father didn't see him.''

"Rot!''

"I'll demonstrate,'' I said, and went to the writing-desk, where the dead man's cane still leaned. I picked it up and turned toward them. ''The very instant Lord Hull left the parlour, Jory was up and on the run.''

Lestrade shot a startled glance at Holmes; Holmes gave the Inspector a cool, ironic look in return. And I must say I did not understand the wider implications of the picture I was drawing for yet awhile. I was too wrapped up in my own recreation, I suppose.

"He nipped through the first connecting door, ran across the music room, and entered Lady Hull's morning-room. He went to the hall door then and peeked out. If Lord Hull's gout had gotten so bad as to have brought on gangrene, he would have progressed no more than a quarter of the way down the hall, and that is optimistic. Now mark me, Inspector Lestrade, and I will show you how a man has spent a lifetime eating rich foods and imbibing the heavy waters ends up paying for it. If you doubt it, I shall bring you a dozen gout sufferers who will show you exactly what I'm going to show you now.''

With that I began to stump slowly across the room toward them, both hands clamped tightly on the ball of the cane. I would raise one foot quite high, bring it down, pause, and then draw the other leg along. Never did my eyes look up. Instead, they alternated between the cane and that forward foot.

"Yes," Holmes said quietly. "The good Doctor is exactly right, Inspector Lestrade, The gout comes first; then, (if the sufferer lives long enough, that is), there comes the characteristic stoop brought on by always looking down."

"He knew it, too," I said. "Lord Hull was afflicted with worsening gout for five years. Jory would have marked the way he had come to walk, always looking down at the cane and his own feet. Jory peeped out of the morning room, saw he was safe, and simply nipped into the study. Three seconds and no more, if he was nimble." I paused. "That hall floor is marble, isn't it? He must have kicked off his shoes."

"He was wearing slippers," Lestrade said curtly.

"Ah. I see. Jory gained the study and slipped behind his stage-flat. Then he withdrew the dagger and waited. His father reached the end of the hall. He heard Stanley call down to his father. That must have been a bad moment for him. Then his father called back that he was fine, came into the room and closed the door."

They were both looking at me intently, and I understood some of the Godlike power Holmes must have felt at moments like that, telling others what only you could know. And yet, I must repeat that it is a feeling I shouldn't have wanted to have too often. I believe the urge for such a feeling would have corrupted most men—men with less iron in their souls than was possessed by my friend Sherlock Holmes is what I mean.

"Jory—old Keg-Legs, old Stoat-Belly—would have made himself as small as possible before the locking-up went on, knowing that his father would have one good look round before turning the key and shooting the bolt. He may have been gouty and going a bit soft about the edges, but that doesn't mean he was going blind.''

"His valet says his eyes were quite good," Lestrade said. "One of the first things I asked."

"Bravo, Inspector," Holmes said softly, and Inspector Lestrade favored him with a jaundiced glance.

"So he looked round," I said, and suddenly I could *see* it, and I supposed this was also the way with Holmes; this reconstruction which, while based only upon facts and deduction, seemed to be half a vision, "and he saw nothing but the study as it always was, empty save for himself. It is a remarkably open room, I see no closet door, and with the windows on both sides, there are no dark nooks even on such a day as this.

"Satisfied, he closed the door, turned his key, and shot the bolt. Jory would have heard him stump his way across to the desk. He would have heard the heavy thump and wheeze of the chair-cushion as his father sat down—a man in whom gout is well-advanced does not sit so much as position himself over a soft spot and then drop into it, seat-first—And then Jory would at last have risked a look out."

I glanced at Holmes. "Go on, old man," he said warmly. "You are doing splendidly. Absolutely first rate." I saw he meant it. Thousands would have called him cold, and they would not have been wrong, precisely, but he also had a large heart. Holmes simply protected it better than some men do.

"Thank you. Jory would have seen his father put his cane aside, and place the papers—the two packets of papers—on the blotter. He did not kill his father immediately, although he could have done; that's what's so gruesomely pathetic about this business, and that's why I wouldn't go into that parlour where they are for a thousand pounds. I wouldn't go in unless you and your men dragged me."

"How do you know he didn't do it immediately?" Lestrade asked.

"The scream came at least two minutes after the key was turned and the bolt drawn; I assume you have enough testimony on that to believe it. Yet it can only be seven paces from door to desk. Even for a gouty man like Lord Hull, it would have taken half a minute, forty seconds at the outside, to cross to the chair and sit down. Add fifteen seconds for him to prop his cane where you found it, and put his wills on the blotter.

"What happened then? What happened during that last minute or two, which must have seemed—to Jory Hull, at least—all but endless? I believe Lord Hull simply sat there, looking from one will to the other. Jory would have been able to tell the difference between the two easily enough; the parchment of the older would have been darker.

"He knew his father intended to throw one of them into the stove.

"I believe he waited to see which one it would be.

"There was, after all, a chance that his father was only having a cruel practical joke at his family's expense. Perhaps he would burn the new will, and put the old one back in the safe. Then he could have left the room and told his family the new will was safely put away. Do you know where it is, Lestrade? The safe?"

"Five of the books in that case swing out," Lestrade said briefly, pointing to a shelf in the library area.

"Both family and old man would have been satisfied then; the family would have known their earned inheritances were safe, and the old man would have gone to his grave believing he had perpetrated one of the cruellest practical jokes of all time . . . but he would have gone as God's victim or his own, and not Jory Hull's."

Again, that look I did not understand passed between Holmes and Lestrade.

"Myself, I rather think the old man was only savoring the moment, as a man may savor the prospect of an after-dinner drink in the middle of the afternoon or a sweet after a long period of abstinence. At any rate, the minute passed, and Lord Hull began to rise . . . but with the darker parchment in his hand, and facing the stove rather than the safe. Whatever his hopes may have been, there was no hesitation on Jory's part when the moment came. He burst from hiding, crossed the distance between the coffee-table and the desk in an instant, and plunged the knife into his father's back before he was fully up.

"I suspect the autopsy will show the thrust clipped through the heart's upper ventricle and into the lung—that would explain the quantity of blood expelled from the mouth. It also explains why Lord Hull was able to scream before he died, and that's what did for Mr. Jory Hull."

"Explain," Lestrade said.

"A locked room mystery is a bad business unless you intend to pass murder off as a case of suicide," I said, looking at Holmes. He smiled and nodded at this maxim of his. "The last thing Jory would have wanted was for things to look as they did . . . the locked room, the locked windows, the man with a knife in him where the man himself never could have put it. I think he

had never forseen his father dying with such a squall. His plan
was to stab him, burn the new will, rifle the desk, unlock one of
the windows, and escape that way. He would have entered the
house by another door, resumed his seat under the stairs, and
then, when the body was finally discovered, it would have
looked like robbery.''

"Not to Hull's solicitor," Lestrade said.

"He might well have kept his silence," Holmes said, and
then added brightly "I'll bet Jory intended to open one of the
windows and add as few tracks, too. I think we all agree it
would have seemed a suspiciously convenient murder, under the
circumstances, but even if the solicitor spoke up, nothing could
have been *proved*.''

"By screaming, Lord Hull spoiled everything," I said, "as
he had been spoiling things all his life. The house was roused.
Jory, probably in a panic, probably only stood there like a nit.

"It was Stephen Hull who saved the day, of course—or at
least Jory's alibi, the one which had him sitting on the bench
under the stairs when his father was murdered. He rushed down
the hall from the music room, smashed the door open, and must
have hissed for Jory to get over to the desk with him, at once,
so it would look as if they had broken in toget—''

I broke off, thunderstruck. At last I understood the glances
between Holmes and Lestrade. I understood what they must
have seen from the moment I showed them the trick hiding
place: it could not have been done alone. The killing, yes, but
the rest . . .

"Stephen testified that he and Jory met at the study door," I
said slowly. "That he, Stephen, burst it in and they entered
together, discovered the body together. He lied. He might have
done it to protect his brother, but to lie so well when one
doesn't know what has happened seems . . . seems . . .''

"Impossible," Holmes said, "is the word for which you are
searching, Watson.''

"Then Jory and Stephen were in on it together," I said.
"They planned it together . . . and in the eyes of the law, both
are guilty of their father's murder! My God!''

"Not both of them, my dear Watson," Holmes said in a tone
of curious gentleness. "*All* of them.''

I could only gape.

He nodded. "You have shown remarkable insight this morning, Watson. For once in your life you have burned with a
deductive heat I'll wager you'll never generate again. My cap is

off to you, dear fellow, as it is to any man who is able to transcend his normal nature, no matter how briefly. But in one way you have remained the same dear chap as you've always been: while you understand how good people can be, you have no understanding of how black they *may* be.''

I looked at him silently, almost humbly.

"Not that there was much blackness here, if half of what we've heard of Lord Hull was true," Holmes said. He rose and began to pace irritably about the study. "Who testifies that Jory was with Stephen when the door was smashed in? Jory, naturally. Stephen, naturally. But there were two others. One was William—the third brother. Am I right, Lestrade"

"Yes. He said he was halfway down the stairs when he saw the two of them go in together, Jory a little ahead."

"How interesting!" Holmes said, eyes gleaming. "Stephen breaks in the door—as the younger and stronger of course he must—and so one would expect simple forward motion would have carried him into the room first. Yet William, halfway down the stairs, saw *Jory* enter first. Why was that, Watson?"

I could only shake my head numbly.

"Ask youself whose testimony, *and whose testimony alone,* we can trust here. The answer is the fourth witness, Lord Hull's man, Oliver Stanley. He approached the gallery railing in time to see Stephen enter the room, and that is perfectly correct, since *Stephen* was alone when he broke it in. It was *William,* with a better angle from his place on the stairs, who said he saw Jory precede Stephen into the study. William said so because he had seen Stanley and knew what he must say. It boils down to this, Watson: we know Jory was inside this room. Since both of his brothers testify he was *outside,* there was, at the very least, collusion. But as you say, the lack of confusion, the way they all pulled together so neatly, suggests something more.''

"Conspiracy," I said dully.

"Yes. But, unfortunately for the Hulls, that's not all. Do you recall me asking you, Watson, if you believe that all four of them simply walked wordlessly out of that parlour in four different directions at the very moment they heard the study door locked?"

"Yes. Now I do."

"The *four* of them." He looked at Lestrade. "All four testified they were four, yes?"

"Yes."

"That includes Lady Hull. And yet we know Jory had to

have been up and off the moment his father left the room; we know he was in the study when the door was locked, *yet all four—including Lady Hull*—claimed all four of them were still in the parlour when they heard the door locked. There might as well have been four hands on that dagger, Watson. The murder of Lord Hull was very much a family affair.''

I was too staggered to say anything. I looked at Lestrade and saw a look on his face I had never seen before or ever did again; a kind of tired sickened gravity.

"What may they expect?" Holmes said, almost genially.

"Jory will certainly swing," Lestrade said. "Stephen will go to gaol for life. William Hull may get life, but will more likely get twenty years in Broadmoor, and there such a weakling as he will almost certainly be tortured to death by his fellows. The only difference between what awaits Jory and what awaits William is that Jory's end will be quicker and more merciful.''

Holmes bent and stroked the canvas stretched between the legs of the coffee-table. It made that odd hoarse purring noise.

"Lady Hull," Lestrade went on, "would go to Beechwood Manor—more commonly know to the female inmates as Cut-Purse Palace—for five years . . . but, having met the lady, I rather suspect she will find another way out. Her husband's laudanum would be my guess.''

"All because Jory Hull missed a clean strike," Holmes remarked, and sighed. "If the old man had had the common decency to die silently, all would have been well. He would, as Watson says, have left by the window. Taking his canvas with him, of course . . . not to mention his trumpery shadows. Instead, he raised the house. All the servents were in, exclaiming over the dead master. The family was in confusion. How shabby their luck was, Lestrade! How close was the constable when Stanley summoned him? Less than fifty yards, I should guess.''

"He was actually on the walk," Lestrade said. "Their luck *was* shabby. He was passing, heard the scream, and turned in.''

"Holmes," I said, feeling much more comfortable in my old role, "how did you know a constable was so nearby?''

"Simplicity itself, Watson. If not, the family would have shooed the servants out long enough to hide the canvas and 'shadows.' ''

"Also to unlatch at least one window, I should think," Lestrade added in a voice uncustomarily quiet.

"They *could* have taken the canvas and the shadows," I said suddenly.

Holmes turned toward me. "Yes."

Lestrade raised his eyebrows.

"It came down to a choice," I said to him. "There was time enough to burn the new will or get rid of the hugger-mugger . . . this would have been just Stephen and Jory, of course, in the moments after Stephen burst in the door. They—or, if you've got the temperature of the characters right, and I suppose you do, *Stephen*—decided to burn the will and hope for the best. I suppose there was just time enough to chuck it into the stove."

Lestrade turned, looked at it, then looked back. "Only a man as black as Hull would have found strength enough to scream at the end," he said.

"Only a man as black as Hull would have required a son to kill him," Holmes returned.

He and Lestrade looked at each other, and again something passed between them, something perfectly communicated which I myself did not understand.

"Have you ever done it?" Holmes asked, as if picking up on an old conversation.

Lestrade shook his head. "Once came damned close," he said. "There was a girl involved, not her fault, not really. I came close. Yet . . . that was one."

"And these are four," Holmes returned. "Four people ill used by a foul man who should have died within six months anyway."

Now I understood.

Holmes turned his gray eyes on me. "What say you, Lestrade? Watson has solved this one, although he did not see all the ramifications. Shall we let Watson decide?"

"All right," Lestrade said gruffly. "Just be quick. I want to get out of this damned room."

Instead of answering, I bent down, picked up the felt shadows, rolled them into a ball, and put them in my coat pocket. I felt quite odd doing it: much as I had felt when in the grip of the fever which almost took my life in India.

"Capital fellow, Watson!" Holmes said. "You've solved your first case and became an accessory to murder all in the same day, and before tea-time! And here's a souvenir for myself—an original Jory Hull. I doubt it's signed, but one must be grateful for whatever the gods send us on rainy days." He used his pen-knife to loosen the glue holding the canvas to the legs of the coffee-table. He made quick work of it; less than a minute later he was slipping a narrow canvas tube into the inner pocket of his voluminous greatcoat.

"This is a dirty piece of work," Lestrade said, but he crossed to one of the windows and, after a moment's hesitation, released the locks which held it and raised it half an inch or so.

"Some is dirtier done than undone," Holmes observed. "Shall we"

We crossed to the door. Lestrade opened it. One of the constables asked Lestrade if there was any progress.

On another occasion Lestrade might show the man the rough side of his tongue. This time he said shortly, "Looks like attempted robbery gone to something worse. I saw it at once, of course; Holmes a moment later."

"Too bad!" the other constable ventured.

"Yes, too bad," Lestrade said. "But the old man's scream sent the thief packing before he could steal anything. Carry on."

We left. The parlour door was open, but I kept my head as we passed it. Holmes looked, of course; there was no way he could not have done. It was just the way he was made. As for me, I never saw any of the family. I never wanted to.

Holmes was sneezing again. His friend was twining around his legs and miaowing blissfully. "Let me out of here," he said, and bolted.

An hour later we were back at 221B Baker Street, in much the same positions we occupied when Lestrade came driving up: Holmes in the window-seat, myself on the sofa.

"Well, Watson," Holmes said presently, "how do you think you'll sleep tonight?"

"Like a top," I said. "And you?"

"Likewise," he said. "I'm glad to be away from those damned cats, I can tell you that."

"How will Lestrade sleep, d'you think?"

Holmes looked at me and smiled. "Poorly tonight. Poorly for a week, perhaps. But then he'll be all right. Among his other talents, Lestrade has a great one for creative forgetting."

That made me laugh, and laugh hard.

"Look, Watson!" Holmes said. "Here's a sight!" I got up and went to the window, sure I would see Lestrade riding up in the waggon once more. Instead I saw the sun breaking through the clouds, bathing London in a glorius late afternoon light.

"It came out after all," Holmes said. "Top-hole!" He picked

up his violin and began to play, the sun strong on his face. I looked at his barometer and saw it was falling. That made me laugh so hard had to sit down. When Holmes looked at me and asked what it was, I could only shake my head. Strange man, Holmes: I doubt if he would have understood, anyway.

AFTERWORD MORIARTY AND THE REAL UNDERWORLD

John Gardner

Illustration by Sidney Paget of a scene from *The Naval Treaty* in which
Holmes is attired in his famous dressing-gown.

Mention the name of Professor James Moriarty to anyone who has even a nodding acquaintance with Sir Arthur Conan Doyle's Sherlock Holmes, and a picture is immediately conjured—the tall, gaunt, scholarly figure threatening Holmes in his Baker Street rooms; the fight on the ledge at the Reichenbach Falls; a vast army of criminals ready to do his bidding; the clop of horses' hooves in the streets, and the rumble of hansoms; gaslight casting eerie shadows; the thick yellow fogs, "London particulars," creeping up from the river; sinister figures lurking in alleys and passageways; robbery, murder, extortion, violence; the sly tongue of the confidence man, the quick fingers of the pickpocket, the wheedling of the beggar, the wiles of the whore: the whole wretched, dingy, yet compulsive aura of the nineteenth-century underworld.

Holmes himself is reported to have said of the Professor (in "The Final Problem"), ". . . his agents are numerous and splendidly organized. Is there a crime to be done, a paper to be abstracted, we will say, a house to be rifled, a man to be removed—the word is passed on to the Professor, the matter is organized and carried out. The agent may be caught. In that case money is found for his bail or his defense. But the central power which uses the agent is never caught—never so much as suspected."

This description has a strangely modern ring to it. It certainly

indicates that Moriarty undoubtedly would have spent the bulk
of his time within the underworld of his era, rubbing shoulders
and passing the word of command throughout that society of
villains which proliferated during the century.

Here we have a definite link which joins that shadowy world
to the organized crime of our own time, for the sprawling
regiment of criminals in Moriarty's day referred to themselves,
collectively, as The Family.

In 1841 an article in *Tait's Magazine* speaks of " 'The
Family' . . . the generic name for thieves, pickpockets, gam-
blers, housebreakers *et hoc genus omne*." The term was certainly still in use at the end of the century, and villians spoke of
each other as family men and family women.

We all know that today The Family, in criminal terms, takes
on sinister connotations. So Doyle's Moriarty could well have
been the Victorian equivalent of the twentieth-century Godfather. His influence would certainly have its starting point in the
whirling vortex of the nineteenth-century underworld.

Briefly, then, one sees Moriarty as a ruthless criminal leader
of high intellect and advanced organizational talents—the scientific criminal—a man determined to rule his chosen universe.

What sort of empire would he have ruled? Over what kind of
subjects would he have held sway?

The picture we have of the London underworld during the first
half of the nineteenth century is one of a perpetual war waged
between the respectable middle and upper classes, and the great
horde of criminals, many of them specialist technicians, who
lived in the Rookeries—those swamped, fetid, and congested
areas on the outer perimeter of the metropolis. These parasites
would emerge from the Rookeries to prepetrate their villainy,
only to disappear again into the warrens of courts, alleys, and
cellars of the tightly packed, rogue-infested hives such as the
great St. Giles's Rookery around Holborn—known as the Holy
Land—or the Devil's Acre around Pye Street, Westminster; and
a dozen more, including the terrain of Whitechapel and
Spitalfields, which contained such unlovely byways as Flower
and Dean streets, and Dorset Street—at one time known as the
most evil thoroughfare in London.

It appears to us now, looking from the distance of a hundred
years or so, that there was a marked contrast, a frontier almost,
between the glittering West End of London and the improverished
areas. Yet the whole period was one of gradual and massive

progress. Great changes made themselves felt at all levels. Legal, penal and social reform, a more effective police force, the cutting of roads through the Rookeries—all played a part in bringing the crime rate down by the end of the century. But the criminal, while adept at altering his techniques, is basically conservative in outlook: so the underworld of the eighties and nineties still clung to past ways. Thus, while London's criminal society became more diffuse toward the end of the century, its business methods altered little.

Playing a major part in the life force of the underworld were the fences—the receivers of stolen property. Almost anything could be disposed of through the small back-street pawn brokers, the market traders, the hordes of middlemen and the few really big fences who often set up or instigated large robberies.

The most colorful of these to emerge during the first half of the century was the great and legendary Ikey Solomons, who lived, in a house full of secret trapdoors and hidden rooms, at the heart of Spitalfields.

Solomons was almost certainly Dickens's model for Fagin in *Oliver Twist,* and when he was finally arrested, two coachloads of stolen goods were removed from his home on the first visit, while the officers had to return at least twice before the place was cleared of loot.

Working hand in glove with the fences were, of course, the cracksmen, screwsmen, and sneak thieves. They still operate today with as much verve as they did in Victorian London, and in Moriarty's time they stood high in the criminal hierarchy. The sneak thief was a particularly cunning operator, an expert in picking his moment to nip through an open window, or indulging in the occupation of "area diving"—slipping down the area steps of terraced houses and into the basement, taking what came to hand before making a fast exit.

Into this same category one can place the snoozer, who would plan his job with considerable care, posing as a respectable businessman, staying at good hotels, mixing with his fellow guests in order to pick the best victims before stealing from them as they slept—snoozed.

Cracksmen and screwsmen were possibly the most sophisticated of thieves, developing a whole armory of tools and cutting devices ranging from skeleton keys to the Jack-in-a-box—or screw jack—for prizing off the doors of safes. Before the end of the century, these gentlemen were expert in the use of explosives and oxyacetylene cutting devices.

Thieves of this kind certainly took their profession very seriously, using ingenious methods and careful preparation. Nowhere is this more clearly illustrated than in the great train robbery of 1855. This was probably the most sensational theft of the century, having an obvious parallel in the Great Train Robbery of 1963. In all, over £12,000 in gold and coin—a most considerable sum at the time—was stolen from a shipment en route from London to Paris.

The conspirators, Pierce and Agar, both professional cracksmen, and Tester, a railway clerk, spent over a year preparing the crime, going to great lengths in order to get information, to bribe the guard of the London-Folkestone passenger train on which the bullion was carried, and to provide themselves with duplicate keys to the three Chubb safes used for transporting it.

The crime was carried out with great flair. Pierce and Agar boarded the train with bags containing lead shot sewn into special pockets. Through the corrupted guard, they gained access to the guard's van, unlocked the safe, removed the gold, and substituted the lead.

The culprits were eventually caught in a classic manner. Agar's mistress, suspecting that she was being done out of her fair share, informed on them.

If the Victorian was not safe from bulglary in his own home, the streets were also full of hazards. By far the largest number of criminals worked in the streets. Many were pickpockets, a problem still with us today, as warning signs in public places tell us. It is doubtful if the Victorian Londoner needed any warning, for the artful mobsmen, toolers, whizzers and dippers, together with their stickman accomplices, were everywhere in the crowds, in the underground, on railway trains and omnibuses. It is, perhaps, indicative of their proliferation that Havelock Ellis in his book *The Criminal,* published in 1890, illustrates his chapter on criminal slang with a passage describing events in a pickpocket's life, in the dipper's own words:

"I was jogging down a blooming slum in the Chapel," he says, "when I butted a reeler, who was sporting a red slang. I broke off his jerry, and boned the clock, which was a red one, but I was spotted by a copper, who claimed me. I was lugged before the beak, who gave me a six doss in the Steel. The week after I was chucked up I did a snatch near St. Paul's, was collared, lagged and got this bit of seven stretch."

The translation follows:

"As I was walking down a narrow alley in Whitechapel, I ran up against a drunk who had a gold watch guard. I stole his watch, which was gold, but was seen by a policeman, who caught me and took me before the magistrate, who gave me six months in the Bastille [the House of Correction, Coldbath Fields]. When I was released I attempted to steal a watch near St. Paul's, but was caught again, convicted, and sentenced to seven years' penal servitude."

The streets also had their fair share of confidence tricksters, often layabouts who practiced simple dodges like pretending to find a gold ring which they would sell for a mere five shillings (fawney dropping, as it was called), or even children crying over a smashed milk jug, to whom the tender-hearted were fine prey. Begging also became a complex and truly histrionic art.

Demanding with menaces, mug-hunting and general foot-padding were common enough crimes in the badly lit streets, and in mid-century, law-abiding Londoners went in real terror from garotters who would choke their victims insensible before fleecing them. Only strong penalties, including the barbarous cat, together with better policing and street lighting, brought this epidemic to an end.

Yet even in daylight one was not safe from the macers, magsmen and sharps—tricksters, frauds, swindlers and cheats, the forerunners of every cheapjack and con man on our own streets and doorsteps and in the police files.

There were other villains who practiced their arts behind closed doors: the forgers, the shofulmen (the coiners), and the screevers, the writers of false character references and testimonials. Their heyday was in Moriarty's time, when anything which could be faked, from documents to bank notes to coins and jewelry settings, was duplicated in small crude dens or elaborate workshops equipped with molds, presses, engraving tools and electroplating devices.

Whatever its cause, vice has always been a magnet to criminals, and Victoria's London reeked of it. In mid-century it was estimated that there were over 80,000 prostitutes working in the city—good money for the cash-carriers (nineteenth-century ponces), the minders and madams—words which, like racket, mob and pig, have not altered with time. Many of these women doubtless doubled as pickpockets' accomplices and skinners— who literally stripped the clothes from the backs of terrified children; certainly women predominated among the "palmers"

—adroit shoplifters, often working in pairs—while the "canary," who carried a cracksman's tools and loot from a robbery, was usually a woman.

These, then, were the rank and file with whom, and through whom, a man like James Moriarty would have worked.

With this raw material at his disposal, it is easy to imagine how a man with the intelligence and standing of a James Moriarty could skillfully mold a criminal community.

One can clearly see him, as Holmes suggested in "The Final Problem," sitting "motionless, like a spider in the center of its web, but that web has a thousand radiations, and he knows well every quiver of each of them."

About the contributors

Jon L. Breen, born in 1943, began in the mystery field as a reviewer. He is an admirer of the old-fashioned whodunit. Many of his mystery stories are distinctive for their humorous slant. In 1981 he won an Edgar for a non-fiction work, *Novel Verdicts*.

Lillian de la Torre, born in 1902, began her writing career by publishing stories in "Ellery Queen's Mystery Magazine." She likes to focus on historical detail and writes mysteries based on actual crimes. Her creation, Dr. Sam Johnson, is a sort of 18th century James Boswell-equivalent of Watson. Beyond entertaining the reader, she sees crime fiction as being one of many important ways to probe the human imagination. She is also an accomplished playwright.

Loren D. Estleman, born in 1952, became a journalist and reporter. He writes Sherlockian and classical hard-boiled mysteries as well as westerns. Many of his books focus on modern themes such as drug dealing, prostitution and racism. He won two Golden Spur Awards for his western fiction and, in the crime field, is known for his Amos Walker mysteries and the Macklin thrillers.

John Gardner is British and was born in 1926. Other than his recent and praiseworthy involvement in keeping the 007 myth alive and intact, he is known for his superbly researched series characters: Professor Moriarty, Boysie Oaks and Derek Torry. Torry became a vehicle for commenting on the unpleasant side-effects of violence.

Michael Gilbert was born in 1912 and is British. He became a solicitor and worked for a while in the Middle East as a legal adviser to the Government of Bahrein. His legal background clearly contributed to the intricacies of his plots. *The Crack in the Teacup* is perhaps his most highly-rated mystery. But he is also known for romantic thrillers, espionage and police procedural novels and plays (which have been performed on radio and television). In 1968 he won an Edgar and more recently was named Grand Master of the Mystery Writers of America.

Joyce Harrington was born in the 1930's in New Jersey. Many of her mystery stories appeared in "Ellery Queen's Mystery Magazine" and "Alfred Hitchcock's Mystery Magazine." *The Purple Shroud* won an Edgar largely for the accomplished way suspense was handled, building up to understated terror.

Michael Harrison is a prolific novelist famous for his pastiches of Poe's Dupin tales. They became greatly in demand because of the small number attributable to Poe himself. Harrison wrote two important works of non-fiction: *In the Footsteps of Sherlock Holmes,* which recreated the London of Victorian times, and *Clarence,* an investigation into the possible identity of Jack the Ripper.

Edward D. Hoch was born in New York in 1930. He is on the Board of Directors of the Mystery Writers of America. His later writing style has been compared to John Dickson Carr's impossible crime tales, especially *The Vanishing of Velma.* He won an Edgar in 1967 for *The Oblong Room* featuring the tough but sensitive investigator Captain Leopold.

Dorothy B. Hughes was born in 1904. In the 1920's she worked as a reporter and reviewed crime fiction. After the popularity of *The So Blue Marble,* Inspector Tobin became a popular series character. She is praised for her descriptions of locale, particularly the South West. *The Fallen Sparrow, Ride the Pink Horse* and *In a Lonely Place* were all made into major motion pictures. She won an Edgar Award for criticism in 1950 and a Grand Master Award in 1978.

Barry Jones is an Englishman and is here making his writing début to what promises to be a productive career.

Stephen King is the immensely popular thriller-horror-writer whose fast-selling and fast-paced novels focus on strong characters. He has co-written contemporary novels of fantasy and the supernatural with Peter Straub. *Salem's Lot* and *The Shining* are his earlier bestselling novels, and the more recent *It* and *Misery* reiterate the writer's popularity.

Peter Lovesey was born in England in 1936. He is noted for his Sergeant Cribb and Constable Thackeray characters who figure in all of his intricately plotted novels. Like Lillian de la Torre, he is also an avatar of historical detective fiction focusing specifically on the Victorian class system, institutions and customs. In 1979 he won the Crime Writers Association Silver Dagger Award.

Stuart M. Kaminsky was born in 1934. He served in the US Army and later became Director of the Office of Public Information at the University of Chicago. In addition to his revered Toby Peters hard-boiled detective mysteries, he is—unsurprisingly—knowledgeable about the media and has written books on, among other subjects, filmmaking, Clint Eastwood and John Huston.

John Lutz is American born and worked in various jobs before becoming a writer in 1975. He has written over 100 stories, mostly published in "Alfred Hitchbock's Mystery Magazine." *Mail Order* and *Understanding Electricity* are thought to be his finest stories. His style bears witness to a high degree of literary skill.

Gary Alan Ruse was born in 1946. As well as the mystery he also writes science fiction and fantasy. His books are *Houndstooth, A Game of Titans* and *The Gods of Cerus Major*.

Edward Wellen is a veteran mystery writer who expresses his satiric wit in both the mystery and science fiction genres.